The
Bookstore

The
Bookstore

❧ DEBORAH MEYLER ❧

G

GALLERY BOOKS

New York   London   Toronto   Sydney   New Delhi

Gallery Books
A Division of Simon & Schuster, Inc.
1230 Avenue of the Americas
New York, NY 10020

This book is a work of fiction. Any references to historical events, real people, or real places are used fictitiously. Other names, characters, places, and events are products of the author's imagination, and any resemblance to actual events or places or persons, living or dead, is entirely coincidental.

Copyright © 2013 by Deborah Meyler

All rights reserved, including the right to reproduce this book or portions thereof in any form whatsoever. For information address Gallery Books Subsidiary Rights Department, 1230 Avenue of the Americas, New York, NY 10020.

First Gallery Books trade paperback edition August 2013

GALLERY BOOKS and colophon are registered trademarks of Simon & Schuster, Inc.

For information about special discounts for bulk purchases, please contact Simon & Schuster Special Sales at 1-866-506-1949 or business@simonandschuster.com.

The Simon & Schuster Speakers Bureau can bring authors to your live event. For more information or to book an event contact the Simon & Schuster Speakers Bureau at 1-866-248-3049 or visit our website at www.simonspeakers.com.

Designed by Jaime Putorti

Manufactured in the United States of America

10 9 8 7 6 5 4 3

Library of Congress Cataloging-in-Publication Data is available.

ISBN 978-1-4767-1424-0
ISBN 978-1-4767-1425-7 (ebook)

IN MEMORY OF MY FATHER, GORDON McLAUCHLAN, WHO
TAUGHT ME HOW TO BE HAPPY

The
Bookstore

❧ CHAPTER ONE ❧

I, Esme Garland, do not approve of mess. This is unfortunate, because ever since I woke up this morning I've had a feeling that I might be in one. I sip my tea, and wonder if I have forgotten to submit a paper, pay the rent, feed Stella's cat. Nothing springs to mind. I reflect that as I can't even name it, the likelihood of a genuine mess is remote. I carry on sipping my tea and I look out on Broadway beneath my window.

The buildings cut the sunlight so abruptly in New York that the shadows look like a child has made them with scissors and black paper. The sun floods the cross streets in the mornings and the east sides of all the avenues are in deep shadow. The sharp light is one of the things I love here. The sharp light, the sharp people.

I like waking up to the sun streaming in. When I arrived here, I had schooled myself to expect a first-year's room—a freshman's room, they would say—one that had a tiny window with a view of a fire escape. I opened the door of this apartment, back in August, and there was the sun, streaming, streaming. It's a studio, which means it is one room with a bathroom. It's a good word, though— it works. Makes you think that you are part of the fraternity of starving artists who have struggled in garrets for centuries. It's right above a twenty-four-hour deli, so it's not *quiet,* but—a view

of Broadway, curving its way through the rigid grid of streets like
a stream. It's October now, and I still can't get over it.

Irv Franks, in 14D, is lowering a basket down past my window. It has the usual shopping list and twenty-dollar bill pegged
to the string. I check that one of the Koreans from the deli below
is waiting for the basket. He is. He is smiling. Everyone, wherever
they come from, knows that it is funny to replay village life in this
way; everyone is pleased that it works.

I didn't come to New York to escape the confines of my small
town in England. I didn't imagine that I could better express my
personality in New York, nor that the city could rejuvenate my
flagging spirits. My spirits rarely flag. I haven't made the mistake,
or achieved the hope, of thinking that New York might be my
sanctuary or my redemption. Columbia University offered me a
place to study art history, and threw in a scholarship for good measure. Nowhere else offered any money. Therefore I am in New
York.

Things didn't seem promising initially. I arrived like everyone
else did, after swearing that I wasn't a spy or guilty of moral tur-
pitude, and that I hadn't got any snails. In the first bewildering
minutes outside JFK, on a Friday night in the rain, I stared out at
veering yellow cabs, airport staff screaming abuse at cowboy oper-
ators, sleek limos nosing along the bedlam, the whole teetering on
the brink of chaos. I thought, as so many people do, *This is impossible. I won't be able to manage this.* But then, we do manage—we
manage to get into the city at night without being murdered, and
wake up the next day still alive, and shortly afterwards we are
striding down Broadway in the sun.

I don't have to go into college today. I am going to meet
Mitchell for lunch, but first I am going to go to the Edward
Hopper exhibition at the Whitney Museum. I am here to do
a PhD in art history on Wayne Thiebaud, and I think Hopper is an influence on him. Thiebaud paints pictures of cakes.
Or I should say, now that I am getting the hang of it, that he
illustrates the demotic nature of America at the same time as

achieving a fine poignancy and awakening a never-quite-fast-asleep nostalgia for the prelapsarian innocence of a younger America, whilst staying within a formal rigor in terms of composition. Anyway, the lollipops and the cakes and the gumball machines are great.

I step across the hall to Stella's apartment, to give Earl, the cat, fresh water and food. He slinks around my legs while I sort it all out.

I am early; I can walk down Broadway for a while.

Outside Brunori's market, there is watercress bedded in ice, great boxes of lush dark cherries, asparagus bound with violet bands. It is owned by Iranians, who have sounded out the mood of the Upper West Side, and given themselves an Italian history and flavor. I go inside. It smells at first of warm bread baked with raisins and cinnamon. If you move a couple of inches to the right, it smells of fresh coffee. If you go over to the produce aisle, it smells cold, of grass and earth. It is not a big store; it's just that a lot is crammed in. I buy six apricots, yellow into orange into a flush of red, all downy perfection, imported from somewhere where it's still summertime.

I consider breaking faith with my usual bagel shop for the new one that I reach first. There is a crush of people trying it out, which makes the decision easier. The staff will be new, the customers won't know what they want, and I am not very good at waiting. I don't know what to think about when I'm waiting.

I go past the dull underwear shop. How does it survive, even on this radiant street, when there are such delectable places to buy underwear all over New York? Perhaps not everybody wants delectable underwear.

I go into my usual bagel place. It is basic, with peeling linoleum. In the back, in a room without windows, the bakers are shirtless and sweating. Sometimes you can glimpse into the back, the bagels all in rows, all bathed in red light. I don't know if it is the red light of fire. There are often two lines at the bagel shop, and when you get near the front, you can step up to the Perspex boxes on the counter and feel which are the warmest, and so the freshest. I ask for two sesame bagels. Then I order a coffee.

"The coffee machine is broken," says the girl behind the counter. I nod understandingly, and hand her a ten-dollar note. As she is getting my change, the man who is looking after the other queue of people troops over to the machine and pours out a coffee for his customer. The girl serving me and I both watch this little operation, and then we look at each other for a second.

"I think it's working again," I say.

The girl says, "I *said,* the machine is broken."

We appear to be at an impasse. She is banking on my not making a fuss, being a foreigner, young, female.

I say, "Can I see the manager?"

She says, without turning her head to check, "The machine is fixed." She gets me a coffee and when I pay for it, she suddenly grins at me. "Have a nice day," she says. By the time I step back out onto Broadway, I feel I have undergone a rite of passage. Trial by bagel. Am I now a real New Yorker?

Across the street, squashed between a Staples and a Gap, is The Owl, the bookshop I love to visit. Copies of *National Geographic* spill out on the pavement in front of it like treasure, yellow spines gleaming, promising further riches within.

Perhaps because it seems so insignificant, The Owl manages to remain a ramshackle old bookshop. Staples and Gap, blinded by their own brightness, barely notice its existence, nor, it seems, does any other behemoth on the hunt for suitable premises. But it glitters away there, a dark jewel in a shining street. It is easily overlooked, but it is deep-rooted in the city, and I like to think it shares something of older and greater endeavors. One age might pass over what another prized, and the next age might then revere it. Museums and libraries are in place, of course, to keep past treasures safe through the neglect, but the museums and libraries have a flotilla of insignificant vessels that are just as vital. Secondhand bookshops are some of the tugs that can bring the bounty safely to harbor. The Owl is small, and it is definitely shabby, but it is tinged with lofty purpose.

Regularly inundated with more books than he knows what to do with, George, the laconic and gentle owner, often tips some out into the dollar-only shelves outside the shop, and occasionally, here can be found hidden wonders. I keep an eye out for old auction catalogs; sometimes it is the only chance you might get to see a painting you need to study before it passes beyond the doors of some moneyed collector. There was an exhibition catalog out here for Robert Motherwell's *Elegy to the Spanish Republic* paintings, bound in the blue that he loved from the packets of Gauloise cigarettes—that milky blue shade on the spine was how I found it. Other people find even better things; maybe they are willing to look for longer. I was at the bookstore once when George was telling the story to those gathered around of finding a signed Robert Frost out here, the signature in spidery green ink across the flyleaf, clearly written in the frailty of age, but genuine too. He kept it for a while, the collector's impulse vying with that of the salesman. In the end, the poetic sensibility won out over both; George was better off, in his measured opinion, reading the man's poetry than gloating over his signature. "Something there is," he said, slowly, but with his eyes alight, "that does not love a signed first."

The name attracted me in the first place; it is not a name that seems calculated to bring in a torrent of custom, which immediately sets it apart from almost everything else in New York. *The Owl.* It doesn't even have any sign to indicate that it is a bookshop; it could just as easily be a bar, or a pet store specializing in raptors.

I love to slip into the bookstore. It is my haven—I don't have to prove myself there, as I do, endlessly, at Columbia. I can go to browse or go to listen. It is open until late, sometimes past midnight, and I usually go in the evening when I am too tired to do any more work. They have the books you want to be there; what would a secondhand bookshop be if it didn't have the poets and the writers that you will one day (oh surely!) read—Milton and Tolstoy and Flaubert and Aquinas and Joyce—but also all sorts of off-the-wall catalogs and criticism?

There is the smell, too, of course—the reassuring smell of paper, new paper, soft old paper, recalling each person to the first time they really did press their nose into a book. But what I like best is the company—I like the people who work there, and the customers who come in at night to hang around and chat. George works there a lot, and less often, a guy about my age called David. On Sundays the person in charge is a woman called Mary; she brings her dog with her, Bridget, a huge German shepherd. I would have thought that the presence of a large Alsatian simply could not encourage custom, but the contrary seems to be true. People rush in to see Bridget, and sometimes buy a book by accident. In the evenings there is a night manager called Luke who often wears a bandana. He is broad of shoulder and taciturn in aspect—he looks to be around thirty. When Luke is at the front counter at night, without George there, he sometimes has a guitar with him, and sits playing bits of tunes to himself. He nods in acknowledgment whenever I come in, but I can never think of anything much to say to him. I like to crouch down on the cheap brown carpet and browse the art section when Luke is learning some tune or other. He can't see me because of the Southeast Asia section, but I can hear him.

Now, I push open the door. On an ordinary day, coming in from the glare of sunlit Broadway, you will be able to see nothing at all, and you will stand there blinking, trying to adjust to the gloom. And gradually, you will notice that two eyes are fixed on you, and that these eyes, though apparently penetrating, belong to a stuffed owl that is nailed to a tree branch that juts out from a wall of books.

The store is narrow, about ten feet across, with a central staircase leading to a mezzanine. There are books on both sides of the stairway, in ever more precarious piles, and it is a hardy customer who will pick her way carefully up the stairs to the dusty stacks beyond. Downstairs is a tumble of books that I sometimes surreptitiously straighten. There are sections labeled with old notices, but they flow into each other in an unstoppable tide, so that history is compromised by mythology leaking into it, mystery books get mixed up with religion, and the feminist section is continually outraged by the steady dribble of erotica from the shelves above. When books do manage to make it to shelves, instead of being in piles near their sections, they are shelved double deep, and the attempts at alphabetization are sometimes noticeable, with "A"s and "Z"s serving as bookends to the jumble in the center.

I would like to know how long the store has been here; it looks as if it predates most other stores on the Upper West Side. It always looks as if it has descended from its peak to a sort of comfortable scruffiness, as Venice does, and, as with Venice, it might be that there never was an immaculate peak, where gold was all burnished and wood did not rot, nor paint peel. The store has probably had this cockeyed, lovably crooked look since it first opened its little door onto Broadway.

This morning, George is already there, and so is Luke. George, tall and stooping, is wearing a homespun shirt and a knitted garment in olive green that might have started life as a cardigan. He has a green stone pendant on a black shoelace around his neck. I think he might have been at Woodstock in his youth. He has the abstracted air of an old-fashioned scholar—as if he's pondering the great questions of Kierkegaard or Hegel, and has perpetually to wrench himself back into the quotidian world. He smiles in recognition when I come in, though I think he would be hard put to remember my name. Luke is up one of the ladders that run round the shop on a rail; he nods at me and says, "Hey."

His ladder is blocking the art section, so I wait at the counter.

"I keep meaning to ask how old the shop is," I say.

George is leafing through a book with tipped-in plates, making sure they are all there. He attends to one carefully before answering.

"It's been open for the browsing pleasure of New Yorkers for a fair number of years now." His speech, as always, is unhurried, and every sentence has a falling cadence. It is a restful voice.

"I thought it had been here for a while. It has that *feel,* doesn't it?"

He considers. "Yes, I think it does. They say that Herman Melville bought *A History of the Leviathan* here—"

"Really?"

"And Poe lived just three blocks north—if he came in here on a dark night, we could have been his inspiration for 'The Pit and the Pendulum' . . ."

"This is incredible. I had no idea . . . I should have looked it up . . ."

"Uh-huh. Hemingway used to look in a lot. On his breaks back here from Paris. And Walt Whitman, when he got tired of Brooklyn. They even say that Henry Hudson looked in when he sailed his boat up the river. It wasn't the Hudson then, of course, but I don't recall the Indian name for it." He pauses, casting a glance around the book-filled walls, and then says, with a bland countenance, "I would imagine he would have found something to interest him here."

"Henry Hudson," I say, finally getting it. "Okay. When did the store open?"

"Nineteen seventy-three," says George. He glances at me with his fugitive smile. "We do get Pynchon in here from time to time."

I shake my head. "You're not getting me twice."

"Oh, sure," says George, "believe Melville writes *Moby-Dick* because of this place, but not that Pynchon, who lives a few blocks away, would ever cross our threshold."

"Yeah. That part is true," says Luke. He comes down from the ladder. "So you stop by in the mornings too?" He walks with a pile of books to the back of the shop.

"Yes, sometimes," I say, to his retreating form. As he seems to think it is fine to ask a question and then walk away, I say to George, "I'm on my way to see the Edward Hopper exhibition. He's a big influence on Thiebaud—I'm working on Wayne Thiebaud, for my PhD."

"Oh, that guy," says George, managing to dismiss the man, his art, and my doctorate in three syllables. I decide not to get into Thiebaud with George.

"Have you always been a bookseller?" I ask him instead.

He considers. "It sometimes feels like it," he says. "Certainly for most of my life. After college, I was a teacher. I taught English at a small but perfectly formed college called Truman State. It's in Missouri. You won't have heard of it."

I shake my head to show that he's right.

"Anyway, at a yard sale on a street in Kirksville, I came across a book by E. B. White. You've heard of E. B. White?"

"*Charlotte's Web.*"

"Yes indeed, and the less well-known but equally rewarding *Trumpet of the Swan*. The book I found was called *Here Is New York*. If you read that book in your early twenties and you don't want to move to New York, there's something wrong with you."

Leaning past me, he selects a slender little hardcover book from the New York section and flicks to the last page. "He's talking about a tree, listen to this. 'In a way it symbolizes the city: life under difficulties, growth against odds, sap-rise in the midst of concrete, and the steady reaching for the sun. Whenever I look at it nowadays, and feel the cold shadow of the planes, I think: "This must be saved, this particular thing, this very tree." If it were to go, all would go—this city, this mischievous and marvelous monument which not to look upon would be like death.'"

He twists a smile at me, half-wry, half-solemn.

"Your bookstore is like his tree."

He nods as he closes the book, and looks up as another customer comes in. She makes a little shocked noise, so I look up where she is looking; she is staring at the owl nailed to its perch, and is backing away. As the backing away is theatrical rather than discreet, George obligingly asks if anything is wrong.

"That owl," says the customer—a woman who looks like she subsists on a diet of wheatgrass and worry—"is it—was it ever alive?"

George considers the owl for just long enough to make me want to laugh.

"Yes, ma'am, it was. But I don't think you should worry—its nocturnal peregrinations are long since over. Could I perhaps cross the border of good manners and ask why you seem so concerned? Are you missing one?"

She takes no notice. "It is organic matter?"

"I believe it is."

"It *must* be carcinogenic. I mean, ohmigod, you're breathing dead owl dust. I have to get out of here. I'm gonna call city hall—this is crazy. You need to get rid of that thing."

"Ma'am, ma'am!" says George, in a voice that stops her as she is halfway out. "Please don't let this get any further, but I see I will have to let you into our secret."

It is too tempting, despite the cancerous owl dust. She stops.

"It isn't real, ma'am, we just like to pretend it is. We're called The Owl, we wanted an owl for the store. But you are very right, that would constitute an environmental hazard. This *looks* like a real one, ma'am, but it is in fact a man-made artifact—in plain words, it's plastic. And please don't touch it, it's a valuable piece."

She doesn't look remotely like she wants to touch it. She comes back in fully, approaches the bird warily. I'd love it to suddenly squawk.

"They look like *real* feathers to me," she says. "I think they're hazardous also."

George says he isn't qualified to say whether the feathers themselves offer a clear and present danger. Luke has come back to the front, and is standing on the first stair radiating contempt. George has lost interest in the game, and says, "Ma'am, if you are so troubled by the bookstore owl, then, reluctant as I am to discourage patrons of secondhand bookstores, could I suggest that you might be happier at Barnes and Noble across the way, which, I am pretty sure I am safe in promising, you will find to be entirely owl-free?"

When she has gone, George gets the next book in a pile and prices it. Then he stops, and looks up at Luke.

"City hall. These people."

"Tell me about it," Luke answers. "George, I'm taking these books to the post office for Mr. Sevinç. There's nothing else to mail?"

"Sadly, no," says George. "For Sevinç? Those are the cartography books?"

Luke glances down at the brown package. "Yeah. The Vatican one is cool."

"Isn't it though? I would love to see those for real," says George.

"He's in town November," says Luke, looking impassive.

"Ah," says George. They nod at each other very slightly. "Mr. Sevinç is a customer of ours who lives much of the time in Istanbul," says George, in explanation, to me. "When he visits The Owl, he brings gifts from the mystic East."

"What does he bring?" I ask. Maybe they just mean marijuana. But I am imagining silks, brocades, spices.

George must be able to see the pictures in my head. "Oh, treasures, treasures," he says. "He brings elixirs made by wizards when the world was young, cloth of gold woven in Byzantium, he brings cardamom and cloves and nutmegs, he brings parchments from the great Library of Constantinople, plucked from the flames by good men and true. Some things they managed to rescue from the barbarous hordes."

I nod.

"By which, of course, I mean the Christians," he says. "The Fourth Crusade?"

I nod again. George is looking expectant. My knowledge of Crusaders is a little hazy; mostly I think of them as embroidered little men in St. George tunics. I begin to speak, hoping that inspiration or the memory of a history lesson will return, but Luke cuts in.

"Halva, and Turkish Delight," says Luke. "That's what Sevinç brings. And it's outstanding. George doesn't eat refined sugars or saturated fats, but he makes an exception for Sevinç's candy."

George spreads out his hands. "Once a year, some halva—and halva has nutritional value—from the old souk in Istanbul. So sue me."

"Good seeing you," Luke says to me on his way out.

I say to George, "The owl *is* real, isn't it?"

"Oh, yeah," he says, and grins. He cranes forward to check that Luke has not paused to tidy the outside books, and says, in a low voice laden with mirth, "You seem to have made some sort of positive impression on Luke. He is rarely so loquacious."

I do not stay very long today; I am too restless to sink into that Zen state necessary for truly accomplished browsing. I still have this feeling that something is different, that there is something I have forgotten, that something is *wrong*. But it won't come. I head for the park, to go to see the Hopper paintings.

Central Park is another place I can't believe I see every day. I had thought that it would be as flat as a tabletop, and municipal, a large-scale version of an English park with swings and flower beds, neat and clipped and regulated and depressing. It is nothing like that at all. Today, there are cyclists and runners and tourists and inline skaters and skateboarders and people practicing ballet moves on a patch of grass, and police on horseback and a girl with a snake, and a woman with three cats on leads, and a motionless golden man on a plinth. It is the jubilant blazon of the city.

I feel better when I reach the gallery. The first gallery I went to in New York was the Met—like everyone else—and I saw a sign that said "No strollers on the weekend" so I zipped through all the rooms at breakneck speed, looking reprovingly at people if they seemed likely to loiter. When I reached the picture I most wanted to see—*Garden at Vaucresson* by Vuillard, whose exuberant joy you can feel even as you walk into the room—I barely stopped to look at it for fear of Met officials bearing down on me with a loudspeaker: "Miss! No strolling! Step along there, miss. Look lively. It's the weekend."

All of it is like that, at the beginning. Every conversation seems fraught with difficulty, every pronunciation produces a frown. I spend time learning how to use the transport system, learning how to speak so that people understand me, learning how to melt into the pot.

You can't be slow. You can't hesitate, you can't ask questions with the usual polite packing around them—"Excuse me, would it be all right if . . . ?" Those are courtesies for a place where English is everyone's first language. Here, it is the lingua franca, and it has to be boiled down to its simplest form. If you want to be understood, you can't use irregular past participles. "Has he left?" results in blank stares. You have to say, "Did he leave?" You can't ask for tuna in a deli and pronounce it "chuna"—because the men, with a big queue of people and no time, will hear the "ch" and make you a chicken sandwich. You can't sound the "t" in "quarter" or "butter," because "quarter" and "butter" don't have any "t" in them here. You can't even ask for a hot-water bottle—it is one of the first things I need, being a sovereign remedy for period pains, and nobody seems ever to have heard of them. A hot-water bottle? A what? No, we don't sell them, miss. No, I don't know where you could buy one. Eventually I corner a hapless assistant who has already denied the existence of hot-water bottles in America, and I explain exactly what I am looking for. It is flat, and made of rubber. You pour boiling water into it, and then fasten it with a stopper and slip it into your bed. It then warms up the bed.

"Oh, yeah. We sell *those*. You mean a water bottle."

"Yes, that's it! A hot-water bottle."

"Yeah. Miss? They're not hot."

Once I get to the Whitney, the aesthetics of which escape my grasp, I breathe more deeply and move more slowly. I spend a long time with the Hopper pictures. I like to look at how he paints light. Somehow he uses light to make everything still. I am glad I am going to focus on Thiebaud, though, and not Hopper. Mitchell has a Hopper on his bedroom wall—the one with the gas pumps that looks like it is an illustration for *Gatsby*. Everyone is lonely in Hopper, everyone is sad. Everyone is waiting.

Unless I leave now, I will be late for lunch. I hurry.

I am meeting Mitchell at a diner. He doesn't take me to fancy restaurants, apart from the first night we met, and that was just for a drink. He loves discovering great hole-in-the-wall places. I don't think he wants to be told where is good by *Time Out* or the *New York Post;* he wants to find it for himself. Or he wants to already know a great place, so that he can be irritated when *Time Out* finds it too.

I am still perplexed as to why Mitchell ever asked me out, ever even approached me. Mitchell is the kind of man you expect to see with someone who has that sort of easy sun-kissed I-just-stepped-out-of-my-Calvin-Klein-shoot look. I am not bad, but I am not in that league. Men don't vault over things to get to me, or get tongue-tied in my beautiful presence. Most of the time, sad to say, they can't shut up. He has a kind of confidence that I really like. I've never met anyone like him, with even a fraction of his easy assurance. I spend a lot of time trying to second-guess other people, and hoping that they like me; Mitchell doesn't move through the world like that. He is like a sun; people react to him as if they are being warmed by the first spring sunshine. It is exhilarating to be with him, to be a satellite to that radiance.

On a more practical level, he tips waiters to get the best table, and it works. How do you know how to do that? How do you know how to give an amount that isn't stingy or stupid, and won't cause the waiter to stare down broadly at the note and say, "I'm sorry, sir, is this a *bribe*?"

He lives in an apartment on Sutton Place for free. It belongs to his Uncle Beeky. He really has an Uncle Beeky. Mitchell's family also has a house on Long Island, at the seaside, but I think it's empty most of the time.

His apartment looks like Edith Wharton has just vacated it. There are curtains made of lush brocade, sofas you sink into, fringed lamps, walls painted in heritage colors, books that are bound in fat shiny leather with raised bands, gilt mirrors, space to walk around. When I stay over, I curl my toes into the deep pile of the carpet and forget about my flat Ikea rugs. Mitchell doesn't notice the apartment, doesn't connect to it. There should be a person there who wants to stop and slip his hand over the curved oak banister, with its dull gleam, or pause at the sudden presence of a ghost, a spirit from an older New York, at home in the soft shadows. Mitchell would be better fitted to somewhere designed by Mies van der Rohe, somewhere with clean lines and clarity. Somewhere that doesn't weigh down into the earth and into a thousand social precepts from long ago.

In a place he's borrowing from Beeky, perhaps he can't imprint his own personality too much. There are a few things that are his—the sheets, I would hope, are his rather than Beeky's. They are a dark sinful mulberry color, but are redeemed by being made of the most beautiful cotton that has a sort of downy pile on it.

Mitchell is definitely tidy; his apartment is the most controlled space since NASA. This is, of course, very important indeed. I can't imagine falling in love with a messy person. He is thirty-three, ten years older than I am, but it doesn't feel as if there is any age difference. He teaches economics at the New School, but the nearest thing to a book in that apartment, aside from the leather ones that Edith and Henry left, are this year's copies of the *New Yorker* in the bathroom. He says he has put them all in storage, that he has everything he needs on his laptop and his iPad, but I don't agree. Loving my little bookshop, I don't agree.

CHAPTER TWO

When I get to the diner, on 3rd and 28th, he is already there. It's one of the many things I like about him; he's never late. I see him through the window as I get there, and I stop for a second just to look at him. It is a curious thing, to feel so glad that someone else is in the world, to feel that it is almost a privilege to love them. *That I should love a bright particular star.* I would like to watch him for a few minutes without his knowing I am there, to take pleasure just in his being, rather than in his relation to me, but of course he looks up, and smiles at me. I come inside.

"How are you, English girl?" he says.

"I'm feeling very English today," I say. "It's such a beautiful day, and everything I have looked at today has seemed . . . strange and foreign. Not alien, but not English. Doesn't it seem to you that everything is on display in New York, everything is spilling out—from the shops, from the cafés, from the people—and the result is a kind of psychic overload, a kind of sensory bliss? There are no hidden layers here, it's all just out there. What you see is what you get."

Mitchell leans forward, intimating that I should as well.

"You are so wrong," he says, his lips just lighting on the soft flesh of my ear. "There are layers, upon layers, upon layers. What you're getting—is theater." He sits back, flaps his hand at me, mock-impatient. "You should order. I am ravenous."

It's a Jewish diner, so I order matzoh-ball soup. I knew nothing at all about Jewish food when I got here. I thought Jewish people ate hummus and falafels and things to do with herring. I was in the outer darkness.

The soup comes. It is in a white bowl with a blue floral rim round it. The ball of dough sits like an island in the bowl. In a practiced movement, the waiter pours the golden consommé around it, with all the noodles. It is lovely. I eat it too quickly.

I look at Mitchell's plate. "Can I have some of yours? I am so hungry. I can't stop eating."

He grimaces. He often makes a movement—a facial expression, a gesture—that illustrates what he is about to say before the words come. "No," he says now. "Europeans are overly comfortable with stealing from each other's plates. It's not hygienic. Order something else."

"You're dating me. You kiss me. That's not hygienic either," I point out, but Mitchell clearly isn't for sharing. I attract the attention of the waiter and order more soup, with bread. Mitchell raises his eyebrows.

"You order bread with matzoh? That's like ordering bread with a side order of bread. You should be careful. I might not be so *madly* in love with you if you get fat."

"*Are* you madly in love with me?" I ask, ignoring the fat comment because I am so thin people mistake me for a twig. He hasn't said anything like that before.

He pours some sparkling water into our glasses. He is not looking at me. He is smiling, and trying not to.

"Oops," he says.

His eyes crinkle at the edges, and he looks almost wistful as he says, "It is a word that's much too laden, don't you think? I do know that you're different from anyone I've ever met, Esme. I think I'm—enchanted. You've enchanted me."

I am flushed through with happiness. I want to say, "You've

enchanted me too!" but I can't—we'd be verging on Hallmark territory. And I think I am supposed to receive statements like this, rather than respond to them. So instead I start to gabble.

"I haven't been eating properly. That is, I have, but I am still hungry. I am just always hungry. Maybe I have been working so hard that my brain needs more foo—"

You know when a thought strikes you and at the selfsame time you know with dreadful certainty that it is true? Here is the thought that has just struck me. The restlessness I have felt all day, that feeling of something forgotten, or wrong, crystallizes into this. *I am pregnant.* This is the unnameable anxiety that has been troubling me all day, the reason I felt that something was different. I feel sure of it. If I go and buy one of those tests from the pharmacy it will come up positive. I don't know how they work, because I have never thought about buying one, never thought about being pregnant—except one day, in the hazy future, when I am married and living in North London, with my architect husband and my collection of antique patchwork quilts; then I will be pregnant. But not now, at the age of twenty-three, near the end of my first semester of a PhD at Columbia. Because that would not be smart. And it would not be tidy.

The thought is so massive, and so personal, that it is difficult to maintain any degree of normality. I can't tell Mitchell. We've been dating five minutes. There has not been so very much sex to get pregnant *from,* for all his dedication to the erotic. And only one time unprotected. One time. If I tell him, and say *I know I am,* like some sort of touchy-feely, at-one-with-Mother-Earth-type person who weaves things out of hessian, and then it turns out that instead I have a tapeworm, I will not look good.

I don't think I am even late with my period. It is due to begin around now. I am frightening myself with no basis in fact. What I have to do is go and get one of those tests. And then see.

As I sit there, resolutely not worrying, I realize that I am also in the grip of a sudden and intense sexual desire. Not only for Mitchell, but for the waiter and the fat man by the window eating two cheeseburgers with a napkin stuffed in the top of his greasy T-shirt. They all look great to me right now. Fleetingly, I imagine the fat man's penis, and then the waiter's. Do penises match body type? Will the fat man's be pudgy and short, the waiter's long and droopy? Despite the imagery, the desire increases.

Logically, perhaps this means I am not pregnant. Surely the female body works well enough that if I am suddenly and unaccountably lustful, it means that my body is trying to *get* pregnant? Once it has achieved its aim of reproducing, of a sperm meeting an egg, don't all those pheromones just shut down? Sorry, boys, we're closed for business.

I feel a little better. Perhaps I am just having some sort of hormonal upset.

Mitchell is cutting a steak. I like to watch Mitchell in all his actions, in all his particularity. The tiny ripple of his tendons on the backs of his hands as he holds the knife and fork, the light tan of his skin contrasting with the white cuffs of his shirtsleeves, then the charcoal wool of his jacket. It is a part of loving, this delight in all the aspects of a person.

Once he's cut the steak into little pieces, he lays down his steak knife on the table and picks up his fork, in order to use it as a spoon. All Americans do this. It means that swanky restaurants have to wash a lot of tablecloths.

"I went to see the exhibition of Hoppers at the Whitney," I say, banishing both the noticing and the lustful thoughts. "I am really lucky that they're having one."

Mitchell shakes his head while he chews. "No, you're not, they're always exhibiting Hoppers at the Whitney because that's where they all are. In fact, that's all they've got."

"Apart from a few things by Julian Schnabel that they hide in the basement?"

"Exactly. Now you're getting it. And a couple things by that woman who painted vaginas and penises and pretended she was just doing flowers. What *was* her name?"

I give him a dry look.

Mitchell continues. "Mostly, it's just the Hoppers. So they have an exhibition and call it *Hopper in Context*—*'See now to avoid disappointment!'*—and then they open up again with the same pictures and call it *Hopper in New York*, or *Hopper and the East Coast*."

"Hopper surprise," I say, "Hopper and chips," and that makes him laugh.

His laughter makes me brave. I take a breath. He becomes aware of me, of my smile, of the fact that I want something. He smiles too, a little warily.

"What is it?"

"I've just had an idea."

"Which is?"

I lean over to Mitchell, bunching my breasts a little with my arms to give myself a better cleavage. He looks. I bite my lip to make it look redder and I say: "Let's take a cab back to your apartment and—fuck." The use of the word gives me a frisson. I don't use it very often in its proper context.

Mitchell pauses. He reaches for the salt, and shakes a little on his dinner, and then replaces the saltcellar in exactly the same spot. These are all big clues that there will be no afternoon on the mulberry-colored sheets for me.

He leans back in his chair and looks regretful.

"Esme. I can't. I can't just drop everything. I'm teaching at three. I always teach at three on Thursdays."

"Of course," I say, color flooding my entire skin. "Of course. I am so sorry. I forgot about the teaching."

"And tonight I am staying in New Haven, remember? The lecture on Keynesian economics by Baring? You *know* how important it is for me to be there. We discussed this. You said you would respect that."

A few minutes ago I was basking on broad, sunlit uplands; now I'm looking into the abyss of a new dark age. I don't exactly know how a proposal to have sex has become a refusal to respect his attendance at an economics lecture, but I do know I am suddenly in the wrong.

"Oh, of course, please—it was just a thought. I don't know what got into me."

Mitchell smiles, but in the taxonomy of his smiles, which I am learning, I hope this is a rare one. I feel as if I have transgressed.

The embarrassment of rebuff does not, sadly, put an end to the horniness. On the contrary, it seems a bit more intense. I wonder if there was something in the soup.

Outside the restaurant he says good-bye without any move to touch me, and I have already moved towards him when I realize this. I try to stop the gesture and end up looking like I'm having some sort of spasm. I turn on my heel and as I do, Mitchell catches my arm and turns me around again.

"Hold that thought," he says, as he kisses me. "I'll be back tomorrow morning. I'll call you."

He goes downtown and I walk over to the New York Public Library, to research Thiebaud's immediate antecedents. I am hoping that such an activity will dampen my suddenly fiery libido. I've never been here before, but my professor, Dr. Henkel, has recommended this library for the paper I am doing right now. With its dark mahogany and scholarly quietness it reminds me of Cambridge, except it is public, open to anyone who wants to study; there are no hoops to jump through, no porters at the gates of learning. I find the humanities and social sciences library, look up the books and journals I need, and go to the ordering desk.

They have a messaging system that I would ordinarily find charming, but today it is not helping to cure my condition. The librarian inserts my order slip into a smooth brass cylinder that could appear quite phallic to an overheated imagination. Then he prods the cylinder into a tube and pulls a lever. There is a pleasing whoosh.

"How does that work?" I ask.

"It's a pneumatic thrusting system," he answers. I nod carefully.

"And where does the order end up?" I ask.

"It goes deep into the stacks," he says.

I nod again, and wait quietly for my books. When they come, I force myself to read, try to concentrate, but it is hopeless. At the end of about forty minutes, I look at the notes I have made and accept that I am wasting my time. I close the books, return them to the right table, and leave. I take the subway right back home. I wonder if this is what women who go voluntarily into the sex industry feel like all the time. If it doesn't go away, maybe I will take up performance porn as a sideline.

As I come up from the subway, a UPS van is parked on the street. The UPS man leaps out with a parcel and a clipboard. He is black, about six feet two, and wearing shorts. The muscles of his legs are glinting in the sun. I almost faint from sexual need. I wish I were the sort of girl who could just go up to the UPS guy and say something cheesy like, *Hi, Big Guy. Want to deliver a package to* my *apartment?* But I am not that sort of girl. This is going to have to be a solo trip.

I do not own a vibrator. As I say, this rampant sexual desire is a new thing for me, and I've never felt the particular need for one before. I cast around my apartment for some accessory that would do the job better than I would on my own. Presumably its phallic nature is more important than the vibration—women must have been doing this since long before they invented batteries. John Donne's wife made use of the bedpost, for instance. And penises don't vibrate.

My deodorant looks about the right shape. And smooth. It wouldn't hurt. I could buy a banana, but the Koreans are probably the last of many to touch them, and bananas are usually a bit scraggly round the end. Or do you peel it? Carrots would be a better bet, but the carrots they sell downstairs are organic, with the tops. They are a little slender. I wonder if they sell parsnips?

Should I google the history of female masturbation? Maybe the women out there can teach me something. Switching the computer on and getting online is just more than I can bear in terms of delay. I pull down the blind, grab the deodorant, get under the covers, and wriggle out of my jeans. I often walk around my apartment with barely anything on, so undressing under the duvet must be about guilt. I think that even if God, my grandfather, and my Auntie Elsie can see me as I walk around New York, there is still a chance they can't see through quilts. They might know what I am up to, but they're not getting a visual.

As soon as I begin the procedure I realize that I am a gynecological nitwit. Inspired by necessity, I go and get my electric toothbrush. Five hundred vibrations a minute. As long as I keep the bristles pointing the other way, I should be fine.

I have been missing out. It is very enjoyable, though rather brief. I look at my watch when it is over. It is only twenty past two. Mitchell could have squeezed me in.

When I am dressed and feeling almost respectable, I feel ravenously hungry again. I realize that this, indeed, may be something very close to a mess. I go downstairs to the nearest Duane Reade and buy a pregnancy test. I come back, and read the leaflet in the packet, which must be written on the assumption that the purchaser is in a wild panic and needs very big print and very simple instructions. You are supposed to pee on the stick, not forgetting to first unwrap it from its sealed packet. Would anyone be in such a tizzy that they would urinate on the packet instead?

I pee on the stick, and having two minutes to kill before it will tell me anything of note, I leave the bathroom and look up the history of female masturbation on Wikipedia. In Arizona, vibrators are outlawed. I'm guessing handguns are fine. Sometimes, in Victorian times, in England, a woman was told to stimulate herself in order to relieve stress. Sensible enough. But other times, the doctor obliged, if it was felt that the woman was in need of immediate relief. That's just the kind of doctor I needed this afternoon.

This is taking longer than two minutes, of course. I don't want to go back in there and read it. If I am not pregnant—all well and good. I will be more careful, and thank my stars. If I *am,* what then?

I go into the bathroom, read the instructions again. If there is a blue line in both windows then it is a positive result.

As Schrödinger and his cat were well aware, these things cannot be until you look. I pick up the white plastic stick, averting my eyes until the last minute, as if some magic, hovering in the unknowing minutes, could change what my looking will forever fix as true. The control window has a pale blue line, as thin as a spider's thread. The real window has a deep, wide blue stroke. There is no ambiguity, no wondering when things begin. Someone is shouting, "*I am here!*"

CHAPTER THREE

It is not a thing to panic about. It does not mean that my life as I planned it (with great care, I might say) is ruined in a single second. It was an accident, and we do not have to be ruled by accidents.

I am trying to be calm and rational, but it is not working very well. I call Stella, across the hall, but her phone goes to voice mail. She's not back from California yet and I am not up to leaving a message. Stella and I only met because our rooms are across the corridor from one another. When I first saw her, I didn't think she would want to be my friend. She is doing a master's in film theory at Columbia and she spends a lot of time grumbling about Fellini and telling me how marvelous Antonioni is, because he films the barriers between us all. She was recently offered a job as a receptionist in a lesbian sex dungeon, in part because of the way she dresses. She turned down the job—"Even as a reception-ist, you're crossing a line, right? Working in the sex industry?" She asked if she could take photographs there instead, and some of the ones she's already taken make me think of Toulouse-Lautrec and Degas. Not what I expected. I wish she would hurry up and come home. I feel aggrieved that Stella is not there, because feeling aggrieved about something so little is much better than thinking about this unthinkable thing.

I go downstairs and buy two Payday bars and a take-way coffee from the Koreans. The older Korean man is behind the counter. He looks piercingly at me.

"Yooo . . . ," he says, in a way that is not meant to be menacing but has that effect.

"Yes?"

"Yooo in trouble. I know! I know!"

I stretch a smile over my face and pretend he is teasing me. How *can* he know that? Does he have some strange Eastern sixth sense? When I first got here, he pressed the palm of my hand near my thumb and said, "Yooo . . . constipated. I know! I know!" And I snatched my hand away and laughed, and said, "Not at all, not at all!" But I was.

I shouldn't rely on the facts as offered by some half-price pregnancy test that is probably past its sell-by date. When I've eaten the Paydays, I make an appointment to see the doctor. They say I can see her tomorrow. I am not used to such promptness.

I read theoretical papers on art history for the rest of the day and go to bed at nine, tired to the bone. I am not going to believe it until I am told by a doctor. It cannot be true. I hardly know Mitchell; I met him just a few weeks ago. Late August, at a gallery launch on 57th Street. I had gone with my friend Beth, who works as a curator at a cheekily expensive gallery down in the Meatpacking District. She always wears black, of course, and high heels, and her hair is smoothed and in a tight ponytail, like a Clinique girl. She's got a degree in philosophy from NYU, and the combination of sex and brains means she can extract large sums of money from a high proportion of the men who cross her threshold. Come into my parlor.

That night, when I first met Mitchell, Beth was swooped on by people in the New York art world, all air kisses and black leather. I moved away from the black leather people to find myself near a little coterie of men and women where the air kisses were still abundant, but the fabrics had changed. The women were in shiny golden cocktail dresses with leopard-skin accessories, not a tummy between them, and in very high, pointy heels. I—well, I can't remember what I had on. It might have been knitted.

I pretended to look intelligently at the pictures so that nobody would notice I was on my own. You can't, though. You throb with self-consciousness instead of thinking about what you are looking at. Mitchell—although I didn't know who he was then—was leaning on the wall a few yards away, alone, a man in a black suit with a black shirt underneath, a glass in his hand. He was looking out at the street, at the trees or the people below, with a look of wistful desolation, as if he were a soldier, looking far off to where his wounds had bled. As I was moving from one huge and very bad canvas to another, he smiled at me. I smiled back. He came over, and I thought he was going to look at the same painting as I was—that practiced pickup trick favored by men in galleries—but he didn't. He leaned on the wall between two of the paintings and looked straight at me. I thought it was a little bold to lean on the wall between two ridiculously overpriced pictures at the very *opening* of a gallery; surely you aren't supposed to get that close to them? He just stared at me. His eyes are blue; when he laughs, they are as blue as the sky. When he stared at me that night, they were as cold as the sea. Perhaps because seduction is a serious business.

"Are you very interested in this painter, or is it just that you don't know anyone?"

"It's the painter," I said, "I know everyone here. All of them. I've just decided to snub them all."

He inclined his head to the picture on his left, which he hadn't even looked at, and asked me what I thought about it, and I told him.

He says that when he first saw me, he decided to indulge in a mild flirtation for a minute or two, but that it is because of what I said about that one painting that he asked me out. All I said about the picture was that it was painfully derivative of Ivan Albright without the skill, and did the world need another miserable painting about How We Are All Going to Die Eventually? That is scarcely code for I'm So Hot in Bed You Would Not Believe It, but perhaps Mitchell was hoping otherwise. While I was still talking he cut through my words to say, "I'm incredibly attracted to you right now."

I felt breathless and frightened and ready to do whatever he asked me to do next. I must have been gunpowder, dry and black and unknowing. He lit me, and I flared up.

He asked me to go out for a drink with him at the Algonquin. The Algonquin was another trick, a rabbit pulled out of a hat, and I knew it, but I didn't care. I wanted to go and have a drink at the Algonquin with Mitchell van Leuven.

We never got there. I went to the bathroom first at the gallery, to the ladies' restroom, and I was checking my face in the mirror when he burst in, pushed me back against the wall, and kissed me. While he was kissing me, he thrust his hand between my legs, his hand like a fin, slicing upward. If he had carried on then and there, I would have let him. I have never felt like that before. But he didn't carry on. He stepped back, and smiled again, as if there was a secret joke, and said: "So. That drink?"

When we crossed the street, he peered in at the window of the Algonquin and said, "Full of tourists." He took me to the Royalton instead.

That was late summer, and now it is autumn. He was a total stranger when I was getting ready to go to that gallery launch, and now I am looking at a blue line on a plastic stick, as thick as a Franz Kline brushstroke.

The test was cheap. I'm sure it was out of date. And the tiredness might be due to all the concentrating I have done, because of all the notes in the margins I have made about the hegemony of content in art. I can't be pregnant.

✦

"YES, YOU ARE definitely pregnant," says the doctor. She is pretty, young, and is now sitting waiting, ready to take her cue from me.

I say, "I can only be about two or three weeks pregnant. I think I know when it happened."

She nods, looking helpful.

"Do you have any questions?" she says.

"How big is it?" I ask.

She smiles. "It's just a bunch of cells right now."

I nod, relieved. I have spent many minutes of my life persuading wasps to find the open window, I am as unhappy as Uncle Toby about swatting flies, and I wouldn't think of killing a spider. I always assume they must want to live just as much as we do. Why would there be a difference? But I don't feel so squeamish about cells.

I ask a few more questions. The legal limit for abortion in the state of New York is twenty-four weeks. Why do they talk in weeks about abortions when they talk of pregnancies in months? I divide twenty-four by four, but that doesn't seem to make sense. Six fours are twenty four, but that would mean six months, and they are always showing triplets or octuplets on the news who are born at five months, red faces with white hats above the line of a blanket, with all their fingers and all their toes, healthy as apples. Those babies *look* like babies, too. So I haven't got very long before things start to take human shape; I need it to be "just cells" if I am going to be able to do it.

The doctor says that there can be a termination within days, if I go for that option—that she could get me in on Tuesday. This reassures me because it could all be over as soon as Tuesday, and it frightens me because it could all be over as soon as Tuesday. Macbeth was forced by pressure of circumstance to kill the king before he had fully thought things through. Well, no. He might have killed the king from a sort of erotic entrancement with his wife, or because he thought it was written in the stars. But look how different it might have been if he'd sat down on his own and had a good think.

That was a king and this is just a bunch of cells. But that was a story and this is real.

"In any case," she says, "I'll give you a quick examination, and weigh you, and take your blood pressure."

While she is doing all that, she says that if I like, I can talk to an obeegeewhyen. It takes me a second to realize she what she means. She says that if I decide to go ahead, I might want to interview several of them. And then she gives me the card of a counseling service I can call to talk all about it. "No judgments" is written on the card. I am grateful. I leave.

Outside, I walk fast, as if I have urgent business, but I am not heading anywhere. I just want to walk. I should be in classes right now. But instead I walk.

Mitchell is Old New York, old Dutch money. To him, the pilgrims on the *Mayflower* are Johnny-come-latelies. He was at Yale, did his PhD at the London School of Economics. And if I tell him, he might be enough of an economist to think that this accident isn't one, that my motive for keeping a baby fathered by a van Leuven might just be economic. Even without his speciality, he might think that.

Does he have a right to know? It is half his, so yes. It is my body, so no.

When people say "to father," they generally mean that one biological act—the act of begetting a child. It is different with the verb "to mother." "To mother" implies care. A man's act of fathering can easily be that one seed sown; a woman's act of mothering can take up all the rest of her life. I do not have to accept this arbitrary burden. I have nobody to help me, and I shouldn't bring an unwanted child into the world. I think of unwanted babies, the ones in the orphanages that never get cuddled, that don't know what love is, that just lie there, not even waiting, not even crying, because there is nothing to wait for, and crying will not bring anyone. Better to adopt one of those than bring another one into the world.

I can't have a baby now. I can't.

A PhD at Columbia isn't something you can squeeze into the nooks and crannies of your life. You have to devote yourself to it.

I've worked so hard all this time—I *want* a career after Columbia. I can't have a baby now.

I am careful not to walk by any parks. I don't want to see any adorable infants and have my heart melt. Right now, it's cells. It won't know. I will make an appointment at the clinic and arrange for a termination. It will be awful, but then it will be done, and I will reclaim my life. I won't think too hard. I won't tell my mother, and I won't tell Mitchell.

When I get back to my apartment, I call the clinic. The office is closed. It reopens on Monday morning. I sit on the sofa and for once I do not look out of the window, or try to work. I look into the air. People say it is killing. I hear that, but I don't feel it. What moral imperative makes me think, even for a second, that I should have a baby? I should do it when I can love it, when I won't feel as if it has killed me.

✦

MITCHELL CALLS ME a couple of hours later. He has made his presence felt at the Yale lecture, has come back to New York, and now he is interested in what I proposed when I was in the center of my hormonal maelstrom. His voice curls round his words.

"You looked great yesterday, Esme."

"Thank you."

"I want to see you," he says. "Now. I want to see you now."

Although the surge of desire that had me imagining a ravishing by the UPS man has subsided into a dull murmur, it flares up again at this. But how can I make love with Mitchell, knowing that there is a baby there in the dark of me, in the death row of my womb?

I can't.

When you first come to New York, it is striking how many Jewish people there are, and striking too how, if you develop a liking for matzoh-ball soup and the rest, you are often unable to have milk with your coffee afterwards. Unexamined, this can be dealt with impatiently—God would mind if I had milk in my coffee? But the root of that injunction, according to a waitress I met in a Kosher diner, is in the Old Testament somewhere—*Thou shalt not eat a kid seethed in the milk of its mother*. Did the rabbinic fathers see this happen, see some Patrick Bateman of the ancient world relishing this particular practice? It must have offended against their sense of right and wrong in the cosmos. They could all get their heads round sacrificing lambs just fine, but to boil one in the very milk that was meant for its nourishment and life, that streamed out of its mother like love, they couldn't manage that. It would not be an offense against God but a betrayal of our deepest selves, a crime against the universe. And that is what letting Mitchell into my bed would be tonight.

It crosses my mind to tell him, to tell him about the baby, to tell him that I am going to terminate, to tell him that I can't see him because of the rabbinic fathers and the book of Deuteronomy, but it is all too hard. I need time to consider.

"Oh," I say as breezily as I can. "It was one of those spur-of-the-moment ideas. Not a big deal."

There is a pause. He might be wondering how to engineer himself from "not a big deal" into my bed. He says, "Esme . . . listen to me. I want to come over and fuck you."

Despite myself, I thrill to this. But I say no. It is the first time I have said no to Mitchell for anything.

"It's just that I'm so tired, Mitchell . . . ," I say. "I really—"

"Are you having a period?"

Nobody has ever asked me that question in my life before. I say so.

"Are you?" he repeats. "Because if that is the problem, we can do something else . . ."

"Oh, you mean like a drink or something?"

There is a silence, while I realize he doesn't mean a drink or something.

"Look," he says. "I'll meet you in Trebizond on 95th and Broadway in a half hour. They do food as well. Say yes, or I'll have to start looking through my little black book. Say yes, or I'll call Clarissa."

"Call Clarissa," I say instantly. She is Mitchell's ex-girlfriend, apparently the sum of all human perfections, except that they "grew apart."

"Oh, you know very well I don't want to call Clarissa," he says. "My threats are disappointingly lacking in weight. I want you. Why don't you just come out with me?"

"I'll come out for one drink," I say. I can almost hear his smile.

I go to my bookcase (a trusty Billy) and put one finger on the Bible, to get it down and swear on it that I won't let myself be seduced by Mitchell tonight. But then it feels wrong. Let alone the fact that I am altogether unsure of the whole God business, what, exactly, am I doing swearing on Bibles when I am about to go to that clinic? I push it back into position. Is there anything I wholly believe in that I could swear on? Shakespeare? I pull out the *Riverside Shakespeare*. What does it mean to swear on Shakespeare? That you believe in the perfect alignment of content and form? I stick it back. This is superstitious nonsense. I can keep some sort of honor through this black time without swearing on anything.

When I get to Trebizond, he is surrounded by girls. There are two sitting very close to him on the banquette to his right, and one on his left. He is laughing up at me as I stand there.

"Did you rent them?" I ask.

"I was sitting here on my own waiting for you!" he says, choking with laughter. "Wasn't I, Caddie? It is Caddie, right? They just sat down around me. There was nothing I could do! Anyhow, I was telling them all about you."

"He was," affirms Caddie, shaking back her white-blond hair. "He was saying that you were, like, really really smart?"

"It's Tania's eighteenth birthday," says Mitchell, indicating Tania with his head.

The girls make small screaming noises to indicate that this is indeed the case.

"Happy birthday," I say.

"Thanks," says Tania. She snuggles closer to him, and stares up at me, measuring me. The whole scene looks like a painting of the Restoration Rake. "If one of you could dangle grapes in his mouth, and contrive to have a white breast accidentally showing, that would be perfect," I say.

The girls exchange glances to show that I am weird, and then they giggle.

"What does she mean?" says Caddie or Tania. The one on his right lets her hand drop onto his inner thigh. Mitchell looks down at the hand and then looks appreciatively up at me.

"She means that your table's ready," he says as a waitress heads towards their empty table. He picks the girl's hand up and deposits it back in her own lap. "Have a lovely evening, ladies."

"See you on Facebook!" says Caddie or Tania over her shoulder, with a seaside-postcard burlesque of a seductive glance.

I sit down. I know this role now.

"'See you on Facebook'?" I say to Mitchell. "You've been here two minutes and it's 'See you on Facebook'?"

Mitchell stretches contentedly. "Yep. That one was Tania, right?"

"I don't know."

"It doesn't matter. I got them both."

"So how many friends is that now?"

"One thousand four hundred and fifty-one. All of them very dear, close friends. But the one who was on my left—guess what she is called."

"No."

"Eden."

"Oh."

"Oh? It's funny, Esme. Don't you get it, scholarship girl?"

"I don't want to get it."

"I'd be in paradise . . ." My sour expression amuses him. "Come on, you know I don't mean it. It's just our shtick, it's what we do."

"Yes. I know. I am not sure that I like it that much."

"Those girls—they were just—nothing. They're just sexual objects."

"I want to be a sexual object."

Mitchell, laughing, raises his eyes to the heavens. "Your Cambridge professors would be very proud."

"You know something? First, they weren't *nothing,* they were *women.* To them, *you're* probably an object too."

Mitchell looks pleased. "I've got no problem with that."

"Second, I think it is really bad mannered to talk about being sexually attracted to other women in front of me."

Mitchell leans back again. Satisfaction seems to be flooding his whole body.

"Bad mannered?" he says. "Ouch."

I lean my chin in my hand and look the other way.

"But do you really? You don't think it adds an extra . . . *capacity* to our intensely erotically charged relationship?"

"No."

"I like it when you're mad at me. It means I get to look at your profile, which is stunning. And your neck, likewise. Stay mad for a couple minutes, Esme."

I don't say anything. Mitchell sighs.

"What can I say? I look at women who look like that. And I've been looking since I was twelve years old."

"Why are you going out with me?"

"For your mind, sweets."

"Do you divide women into Madonnas and whores, Mitchell?"

He cranes to look past me, over to the dining area. "Caddie? Where are you? Tania? Come back, come back . . ."

"Very funny," I say. The waitress comes over.

"I'll have another merlot," says Mitchell, "and the same for . . ." He does not call me anything, just indicates me.

"I'll have soda water with ice and lemon," I say to the waitress. The same obscure idea of honor is at work. As she turns away, Mitchell says, "Esme, you are no fun tonight."

Outside Trebizond, with Mitchell full of wine and me full of water, I turn to him and say good night. He says, "Good night?"

"I'm really tired," I say, "too tired even to walk home. I'm going to get a cab."

"You can't go home yet. I want to show you the Soldiers' and Sailors' Monument, and it's just near here."

"It's dark," I say.

"By moonlight is the point. Come on. You won't regret it."

He has hold of both my hands, he is pulling me around the corner towards West End Avenue, and I am letting him.

"I should go home," I say.

"Come down here," he says, and whirls me down a step into a doorway. He pushes my shoulders hard against the wall and kisses me.

"I told you I wanted you," he says into my ear.

"I can't . . . ," I say.

"I know, your period," he says. He puts his hand up my skirt and his fingers slide into my underwear. "But you can do this. Just—enjoy it. Just my fingers. Let go, Esme, let go."

I shut my eyes, and let go.

Afterwards, he says, "That was good?"

I nod, still with my eyes shut. I cannot open them, like a child who hides from itself by shutting its own eyes.

"Then why are you crying?"

I shake my head, shrug. He will probably put it down to an overabundance of ecstatic sexual pleasure.

"Esme?"

"Yes?"

"My turn."

❧ CHAPTER FOUR ❧

When I wake up, six hours later, I feel better, fresher. I have a grapefruit for breakfast, and as I drink my tea, I think that I mustn't have much faith in Mitchell if I don't even contemplate telling him. He said that thing in the diner about loving me—what if he does love me? If I have a termination now, and we stay together, if we got married—would I have to keep this a secret forever? If we were to have a baby in the future, he would think that child was our first, while I would always know it was our second. It would be starting off with a dishonesty. And what if he is *glad* that this one is here?

I should tell him.

His voice is hazy with sleep when I call. "It's seven thirty A.M. on a Saturday. I could trade you in, you know . . ."

I ask him to meet me in the Conservatory Garden in an hour.

"Let me check," he says. I wait while he pretends to be looking at all his Saturday-morning appointments. "Yeah, that should be fine. But I've got to go to the gym after that."

I think of that garden, at the very top of Central Park, because I went there once before, in high summer, when I first got to New York. Then, there were roses clambering up trellises and rambling over hedges, blue violets and pink-edged daisies tumbling from the flower borders onto the paths, a fountain where Pan played the pipes, and another where the three Graces danced, delphiniums and hollyhocks aiming too high, probably a bee with honeyed thigh . . . It was a pastoral idyll of a place; there was the sound of sap rising, there might even have been a shepherd or two. It is possible that I am remembering through rose-colored spectacles, of course, but roses there certainly were, scented and dazzling and abundant.

Although summer is long gone, every season is concentrated in New York—the firework profusion of the summer flowers will have given way to a golden autumn.

I walk along the sinuous path along the top of the park. It is a gnarled day, nearly November, dull with white skies, not the golden autumn you might imagine for New York. There are leaves, heaped in piles, but they are touched with a baser metal than gold. There is no wind to send them skipping, no energy, no anything.

I pass a playground, with a couple of children playing in it, adults in drear attendance. The play seems desultory, as if they would rather be inside, and have been brought out "for their own good."

Around Harlem Meer, a couple of people are sitting on the benches, clutching plastic bags and gazing out at the steely water. A little while later, I reach the Conservatory Garden. I am much too early.

The garden looks like a black and white photograph of that other time. The three Graces are still there, but in summer, the sun and water and flowers lent them life; you could almost hear their laughter as they danced. Now the fountains do not flow, and the dancing girls are leaden. The flower beds that not so many weeks ago were an insane acid trip of color are now bare, and the soil, invisible before in the explosion of petals, is now as gray as boiled mince, and raked smooth. It begins to rain, one or two drops, and then gives up even on that.

The Pan statue with the girl is similarly wintry. The fountain, which in summer fell sparkling from the girl's bowl into a jostle of air-blue water lilies, now dribbles into the drained pool, soaking the few leaves that are stuck to the concrete bottom.

It isn't of Pan with a maiden at all; there is a flagstone that says it is the characters in *The Secret Garden*. This feels like a setback. Pan was from Arcady, his song was of love and death and birth, so it seemed a good idea to tell Mitchell about a baby with Pan in the background.

It is only an hour and ten minutes since I called Mitchell. An hour on the weekend is more elastic than an appointed time in the week. He isn't really late yet.

A nanny appears with a little girl walking demurely at her side. It's a Saturday—do her parents work so hard they can't even play with her on a Saturday? The little girl is in a cream wool coat with big buttons, and suede boots. She looks very well-to-do, a little New York princess.

Children are not in my purview. I feel a stab of fear. If I did this, I would be in a world where I would have to buy children's coats and boots, and it isn't time for that yet. I am twenty-three. I want to buy fancy boots for myself.

When they have gone, there is only me. I am so still that when a raccoon comes, nosing around the trash bins, he doesn't notice me. He is enormous, as big as a dog. How does such a creature live wild in Manhattan?

Mitchell strides up, and the raccoon is gone in a streak of gray.

He sits down next to me on the bench. He has a cardboard tray with two coffees and a paper bag.

"I brought a selection. Just in case you were hungry again."

"I am." I open the bag. "Oh, *pain au chocolat*! Lovely. How come the bagels are still warm? How did you get here?"

"It's a chocolate croissant in these parts, and I took a cab."

"There was a raccoon! I think so, anyway."

"No, they're nocturnal. It was probably a rat. So what's the matter? Hurry up, because I have to call my mother at ten."

"What do you have to call your mother for?" I say, momentarily distracted. He has mentioned her once in all the time I have known him.

"I always call her at ten on Saturdays. And she always says, 'What occasions your telephone call?' as if I always have a different reason for calling at ten on a Saturday. Sometimes we've had conversations that have lasted—oh, minutes. Especially if one of the horses has thrown a shoe."

"Don't you like her?" I ask. Mitchell laughs into the autumn air. I sip the coffee.

"Mitchell," I say, and stare at the statue that isn't Pan. "Mitchell," I say again. "I've got something to tell you, and I don't really know how to say it." I turn to look at him.

Mitchell was all smiles a second ago and now is not. He looks back at me intently. Across his face comes a kind of withdrawal, as if a blind is coming down. A second later he is as closed as a wardrobe.

"If whatever you have to say is hard for you, I should maybe go first," he says. His words are cold.

"No," I say, alarmed at the new shut-down Mitchell I have in front of me. "I can say it—it isn't that bad—"

"Esme, we've been seeing each other for a little while now—a few weeks."

"Yes."

"And I think you're terrific. You're a joy to be around."

He seems entirely devoid of joy.

"But I think we both know that it isn't really working out. Sexually, it hasn't been all that wonderful, has it?"

I am silent. A tiny beam of merriment sparks in me, so that I want to say, *Really? Even the time with the goose quill and the blindfold?* But the beam dies, vanquished by the overwhelming message.

"Look—there has to be—there has to be—lust. Pure and simple. And for me, when I have sex with you—there is no lust. At all."

I say nothing. There is nothing to be said.

He looks earnestly at me. He says, "I am sorry, Esme. That must hurt."

I smile.

"But I feel as if I have to be honest."

I nod. Does the nodding imply forgiveness, understanding, agreement? Does it say, *Yes, how could there possibly be lust when you are sleeping with me?*

I think back—flip-book style—to the sex I have had with Mitchell. He isn't like a Borgia prince or anything, waking me up five times in the night, but there has been *some*. There was some last night, in the doorway. I think of the time when, the time when, the time when. My foot in a high-heeled shoe trying to get some grip against a bathroom basin; the time when he led me into a lecture theater in the dark at the New School. "You're going to learn something now." No lust?

I say, in a small, puzzled voice, "No lust—at all?" It is a question I will very much regret. Self-respect is hard to hold on to all the time. Especially when you are twenty-three and fail to incite lust in your boyfriend. Ex-boyfriend.

He shakes his head, sorrowful, regretful, his knife glinting.

"From that first time you kissed me—when you put your hand between my legs—it always seemed that there was lust . . ."

Mitchell shrugs. "I do that," he says.

The cruelty is almost funny. A wicked grin flashes up; he catches my eye, ready to make me complicit in my own abasement. I flicker a smile back at him. I will not let him see that this is a tragedy rather than a comedy.

"I'm sorry," he says. "For me, it has to be—I want *disgusting* sex. With Clarissa, it was always *disgusting*. With you—it's nice. You know?"

I nod again. I even infuse a little sympathy into the nod. Poor Mitchell. "Then why . . . ?"

"Then why did I hold on this long? I like you, Esme. You're fun to be around, you're smart, you—I enjoy your company."

"Oh," I say, dully. "Thank you." That's what I say, instead of a stream of abuse or vitriol, because how does the world benefit from that? *Thank you.*

"You don't need to *thank* me," he says, his eyes alight with amusement. "That's so *English*, Esme."

He takes my hand between both of his.

"I don't want to hurt you," he says. A new kind of smile comes.

"No," I say, "no, of course . . . Mitchell—it didn't seem as if you were going to break up with me when—when I last saw you, or spoke to you. Have I done something wrong?"

He grimaces. "As to 'breaking up,' Esme, I'm not sure that's exactly the right term. I mean, it's not as if we're exclusive . . ."

I think dimly of country clubs, fancy hotels, Bergdorf Goodman.

"Exclusive?" I say.

"I mean, we never made that commitment to each other."

"You've been seeing other people?" I say. My voice sounds level, conversational almost. Mitchell knows it's bad, though.

"Esme, you know how it works . . ."

The nanny, with the princess, is walking sedately past again.

"No," I say, carefully. "Ask me anything about the Italian Renaissance though. I know how that works."

He says nothing. I feel as if I am falling, falling through air and space. I can't hold on to all that is happening. I am pregnant, and I am not supposed to be, and my boyfriend isn't my boyfriend. I am one of the girls he dates. I am alone amid the alien corn.

"You'd better tell me how it does work," I say at last. "Are you dating a lot of women?"

"I've been on dates with a couple of other girls, just one-off things. One—a few dates with one. I am sorry if there was a mis-understan—"

"Do you sleep with them?"

"Esme."

"Do you?" My voice is on a rising wail, but I can't help it. "I think I should know *that*. I didn't realize that when I went to the—when I had a checkup, I should have been asking for tests for HIV and, and *herpes*!"

I look at him; his eyes are glassy, as pitiless as a bird's.

I wonder how horrible it is to have an abortion. If it hurts. If I will need an anesthetic. If the nurses will secretly hate me. If my insurance covers it. If it will break my heart.

"Before I go—what did you want to say to me?" Mitchell asks.

The pregnancy is nothing to do with him, after all. I must walk away from him, call the clinic, and terminate what should never have begun.

"Nothing that matters now," I say.

He nods. "I thought so."

I hold my hand out to him. "Good-bye, Mitchell."

"You're hurting, I know," he says. "But, Esme, this is only me—just the chemistry of it, I guess. I daresay there are going to be a lot of men out there who will find you very attractive. Very attractive indeed."

After he has swiftly kissed my cheek and turned on his heel to the Fifth Avenue entrance, I sit down again on the bench. I have very pressing issues to address, but I think that for a minute, I won't address any of them.

This bench was given as a memorial. A brass label says it is in memory of "Mamami and Papapa." The nearest bench to this one has a brass label as well, so I go over to it. It says, "Sleep serenely, my darling Alice." The next one says, "In memory of Priscilla, from A., who adored her." What was a distillation of a garden is suddenly a churchyard full of love and loss. I find myself going from inscription to inscription. It seems both intrusive and courteous. Some are celebrations of lives lived long and well, wishing the dead peace among the flowers. Some are still stark with grief.

⁎

THE PATH I wanted to travel down was with him; all the other paths, which before I met him blued into endless possibilities, now seem long gray routes to nothing in particular.

I sit in the corner of the room, huddled on my bed. I watch as the light changes across the room, as the weary day pulls its gray-ness through thickening time.

There is a baby. There is a baby. I cannot have this baby. Will it bow out under the force of its unwantedness, loose the hawsers, slip away through the watches of the night?

On impulse, I walk all the way to The Owl. The destination is just so that I have some sort of purpose—you can't just walk for no reason, unless you have a dog.

Every beautiful woman I see in the street might incite Mitchell to the lust he cannot find for me. I look with a kind of secondhand carnality, desiring that girl's breasts and that girl's poise . . . the way this girl tosses her shining hair, this one's soft dark eyes say *love me fuck me love me fuck me*—other women have appraised me this way once in a while, and I thought it was simple jealousy. Now I see it is fueled by desperate longing, and a conviction that we can never measure up. This is how we are divided, and how we are conquered.

It is very restful inside the warm folds of The Owl. It smells of all that paper quietly turning to dust, and of a small electric heater that is on at the back, in contravention, surely, of all New York fire regulations. What do you smell when you smell an electric heater? Are molecules of warmed-up metal going up your nose?

I find a book that I always meant to read—*Eminent Victorians* by Lytton Strachey. It is one of those old-style American paper-backs on soft aging paper with yellow edges. It has nothing to do with anything I am working on; I should have read it when I was actually doing a degree that involved Victorians and their eminence. But now it represents a gap in my knowledge that I should fill, or that's what I tell myself. Really, it represents a link to the comforting past for me, back to when I was young and easy under the apple trees. I open it and read about Cardinal Manning. I dawdle.

George is at the front, deep in conversation with a bald earnest person who is holding a small, rolled-up rug. Nobody else who works here seems to be around.

"It's a question of being attuned," George is saying. "Attuned to the rhythms of the earth, the rhythms of nature."

"You're right, and I want to do that. But it's pretty hard to do it in New York," says the bald man.

"No, it's not, not if you try. The earth is the earth. You don't have to be in Taos, you don't have to be looking for a healing vortex in Sedona. You just have to pay attention."

Attention. I believe in that. I would like the bald earnest person to evaporate; I would like to be the one deep in conversation with George, ask him what he thinks of my predicament. Or Luke, or any of the people who work here.

George smiles a hello at me, and holds his hand out for the book.

"Ah, Strachey," he says. "A classic. I've sold many copies of this in my time."

I mutter something about having always meant to read it, and pay him the money. While he is ringing the sale through the till, George goes back to his conversation with bald earnest man, who is trying to talk over him, taking him to task for having no yogic writings *at all* in the store except for the Bhagavad Gita. I take my book and bolt out of the shop. I am ridiculous. It is a bookshop. They are not priests to absolve me, or therapists to guide me; they sell books. George doesn't even know my name.

I walk all the way home again. It feels like a very long walk. I try to overexert myself on the walk, so that there will be an unfortunate gynecological mishap, but nothing happens.

I call my mother as I am crossing 96th Street. She is worried about the cost, so I pretend I have a new phone plan. I ask her how she is, and she says that she and my father have just been to the garden center, and got a hydrangea that promises to be blue, but Dad reckons that unless you plow as many rusty old tools as you can spare into the earth around hydrangeas on a weekly basis, they will turn pink in revenge. She sounds happy. The ordinary, heavenly happiness makes me catch my breath, and I feel tears sting.

"That blue," I say. "The blue of the hydrangeas we used to have when we lived in Sheepfoot. I always think that's what T. S. Eliot meant when he talked about Mary's color. You must take a photograph if this one is the same blue."

"We will," she says. "And we got some more wallflowers to plant for spring."

"Oh!" I say. "It was you who taught me about wallflowers—their smell—I love that smell."

"What's the matter, darling?" she says sharply, as if liking hydrangeas and wallflowers is a sure sign that all is not well in New York. "Is college all right, and Mitchell . . . ?"

Well, no, not really, I want to say. I should say, *I fell in love with him, and he doesn't love me; he's gone. And not only that, but he—did I mention this?—he got me pregnant. And not only* that, *but he got me pregnant without feeling any lust. Having sex with me was "nice." Nice, like cups of tea with digestives. And so here I am, grieving and pregnant with the baby of a man who wants nothing to do with me. And I can't seem to connect myself to the fact that I am pregnant; I can only see that Mitchell has gone. And how was the garden center?*

It is shocking that I don't know what they would say. *Don't have the baby, it would ruin your life,* or *Don't get rid of it, we'll help you every step of the way . . .* Shouldn't I know my parents better than that? I don't know what they would say, but I don't want to turn their blue-hydrangea Saturday into a whirling maelstrom of rights and wrongs, duties and desires.

I tell my mother I am fine. I talk a little about the paper I am doing, about missing Stella, about going to see the Hopper exhibition. I say that I am "not quite sure" about Mitchell any longer, that maybe that is what is the matter with me.

"Oh," she says, and I can sense her brow clearing. "Oh, I see. I'm sorry, darling . . . We thought Mitchell was very nice, but if he's not the right one . . . but don't do anything hasty. And you can always talk to us . . ."

My parents came for a week not long after I started seeing Mitchell, and they met him for coffee at the Hungarian Pastry

Shop. Because they were so worried about my living in New York, I gave them a carefully choreographed version of it, including lunch at the Pierpont Morgan library, a trip to a violin maker's studio in Chelsea, a concert at Juilliard, and a tour of Columbia. They went home comforted. If I really had been thinking of keeping it, I would have told her.

I do not want a baby. The baby would have a resentful mother, a father it would never even meet. The resentful mother would not have much money, and not much time to devote to the baby. And babies need the devotion of time. If I have one, I should do it properly. I can't do it properly now.

≈ CHAPTER FIVE ≈

On Monday morning, the deadly gloom of the weekend weather has been replaced by crisp New York sunshine. The decisions I have to make don't seem so terrible any longer. On the brief walk to Columbia for my lectures, I think, *I will just do it right now. I will just get it over with*. I fish the business card of the clinic out of my bag and dial the number, standing on Broadway outside the big Rite Aid. A woman answers. I explain my situation. It is the situation they must hear all day every day. There are no appointments for two weeks.

"Two weeks!" I say, in the tone universally adopted to indicate that this isn't very good service at all, regardless of the fact that two weeks gives me breathing and thinking space. Then she says that a cancellation for Wednesday has just come up.

"A cancellation?" I echo.

"Yes, ma'am," says the voice. "For Wednesday, November fifth, at eleven A.M."

"Does a cancellation mean—someone changed her mind?"

"Excuse me?"

"Nothing," I say. Phone conversations are especially difficult in America. If you don't say what they expect, you may as well be jabbering at them in Esperanto. I think about that cancellation. What if the cancellation becomes a Mozart, a Shakespeare, a savior?

"Miss Garland, do you want the appointment?"

I look at the bright blue sky and the yellow cabs and the dove-gray plane trees and the energy of all the people, and I think what I am denying to the child inside me, and I swallow and for a moment I can't speak.

"Miss Garland?"

"Yes, I do. I feel terrible about it, but—"

"Wednesday at eleven A.M., for Esme Garland," says the voice, and hangs up.

✳

WHEN I GET home, there is music thumping from Stella's apartment across the hall. At last, she is back. I ring her doorbell. When she answers, she throws her arms around me and pulls me into her apartment, which is strewn with bags and open suitcases.

"I have so much to tell you," she says. "Let me make some coffee first. It was so great. L.A. is amazing. I want to move there. But not yet."

"Like St. Augustine," I say.

"Yeah, I don't know, I want to split myself in two—be in New York, be in L.A. I have made *so* many connections, there are *so* many possibilities right now. You know that feeling? I met a guy, Jake, Jake DuPlessy—I love his work—who wants me to direct a short, and another who wants me to be *in* a short, and Adele introduced me to all sorts of influential people, and oh my god, I milked the opportunity."

"I bet you did," I say.

"I did, I'm totally psyched. And when I *wasn't* schmoozing the Patrik Ervell guys in Beverly Hills, I was in a hot tub with Adele and Michaela, drinking frozen raspberry daiquiris. I know how to make them. It's so cool—you don't use ice, you just freeze the raspberries. We'll make them."

"That sounds great!" I say. I say it with an exclamation mark, and she immediately stops heaping piles of clothes from one spot of the room to another. Perhaps I am not normally so enthusiastic about cocktails. She is looking intently at me.

"What's the matter?" she says.

"I won't be able to drink them," I say. And then, because I have annoyed myself with that arch observation, I say quickly, "I'm pregnant."

"Sweet holy Christ," she says. She casts around rapidly and grabs her camera. This, I am used to. Stella is studying film, but she isn't really, she is studying humans. She wants to catch the mind in the face.

"Tell me," she says, from behind the SLR. "Look straight into the lens."

"You could be hugging me and telling me that it will be okay," I say.

"Yeah, because that's what girls do. Come on, Esme, it's important. Tell me." She holds the camera underneath, the lens protruding. The thick webbing of the strap is swinging free; Nikon, Nikon, Nikon.

"I got pregnant. I knew there was something—I felt—different."

The shutter whirrs, that familiar noise from photo shoots in movies.

"What kind of different? Look into the lens. What kind of different?"

"As if something had changed. But that might be my imagination—no, I don't think it is. I *knew* I was. It just came to me. And so I bought a test, and—" I shrug. The shutter clicks.

"Go on. Go *on*. Esme, please."

"And it was positive. There was a thick line. Not a 'maybe' sort of line."

"Oh, God," says Stella.

"Is that compassion or artistic excitement?"

"I don't know. It's amazing," she says. She appears from behind the camera. "I mean, oh, fuck!"

"I know."

"What are you going to do?" she asks, and raises it up again at me. *Click click click.*

I want to tell her about the clinic, that I've got the appointment. I try to heave the words to my mouth, but they won't come.

"Everyone always says they 'take pictures' or 'get some shots' or 'capture images,'" I say (although to be fair I have never heard anyone in real life say they are going out to capture some images). "Have you noticed that? The verbs are all about acquisition. But cameras don't really work like that. Cameras are receptive—they are just holes that let in light. But because men use them more than women, we get different words, words that don't go with what happens. Imagine if men went about saying, 'Hey, I'm just going to grab my camera because I want to receive some photos.'"

"They'd hang up their cameras," says Stella. She has let hers fall to her side. Then she grins. "Or, they would think about hanging them up, but the words aren't as important as the action"—she puts her hand again at the base of the lens and lifts it up with a wicked smile—"and the action's not as important as the shape. If cameras were vagina shaped, it would be a different story."

This makes me laugh, but she is still looking at me. She knows what I am doing.

"You must need time," she says. "Give yourself some time."

"I think that's the thing I don't want," I say. "It isn't as if things don't happen when you take time. It doesn't all stop while you think."

"No," says Stella, raising her camera again. "But the important thing is that *you* stop while you think."

"I wouldn't stop. I would change. I would get attached."

"That's the risk. But the other risk is that if you run at it, you will do something that you'll regret."

"Gosh, really? I wonder what that feels like."

"I know, honey. I'm sorry."

I turn away from her, and from the camera, and fiddle with an odd little wire thing she's got on a table; it has four tiny cards hanging on it, the four suits. The red diamond is at the front.

"Do you know something?" Stella says suddenly. "You're actually *living*. I'm not. This is living, Esme."

"I've just called the clinic to make the appointment," I say.

There is a silence. Then a click. She has taken a picture of my back.

"I've thought about it," I say to the table, "and it's the only real choice."

I look round at her. "I want to take your picture," I say. "You should see your face."

"When are you going?" she asks.

"Wednesday. They had a cancellation."

She says nothing.

"The coffee is burning," I say.

She leaps to the stove, throwing the camera on a beanbag. "Okay," she says. "It's not burning. It's just done. Wednesday. What does Mitchell say? Is he the father?"

"Is he the *father*?"

She grins. "You never know—you might have met a decent guy in the last few weeks."

She does not have a high opinion of Mitchell. He first met her when he came with me to meet a bunch of Columbia people at a bar in August, and said to her—to rile her, to flirt with her?—that she was gay because she hadn't met the right man yet. She stared straight at him and said, "I don't like dicks," and that was the end of a wonderful relationship.

"I haven't," I say. "Mitchell—though—everything is over with Mitchell. I was going to tell him; I thought he had a right to know. But when I met him, I didn't have the chance to tell him before he dumped me. He said that he liked me, but that the sex wasn't all that great. So I didn't tell him. I couldn't see the point except to abase myself."

Stella opens her hands, to show that everything I am doing is obvious and obviously wrong. "You get pregnant, you are about to tell Mitchell—why are you about to tell him? Because he might be delighted? Because he might put you on his white charger and ride off up Madison Avenue with you? But what he actually does is dump you without knowing about it—and the next thing you do is call the clinic? Stay *still* for a second, and think about what you want, from this point. Not because of what has happened, but because of how you want the future to look. You have to have time to see it and feel it. You have to stop, and you have to look."

"I am stopping, and I am looking," I say.

"Okay. But really stop, really look. We all spend so much time reacting—"

I shrug again. "Of course. Things happen, and we react."

"Mitchell being an asshole and Mitchell being the father of your baby are two different things. And another different thing is that you are pregnant."

"I didn't mean for it to *happen*. It was one time. I don't want to change my whole life because of some guy's—*whim*."

"Yes, but that's what I mean, that's a reaction to Mitchell. You need to react to the *pregnancy*."

"Stella, are you a secret pro-lifer?"

"You are not listening; I am talking about choice. I am talking about choice in the most profound way. Be still. Be quiet. And then decide."

"I am not sure that there is a choice, or that there are ever choices. Everything that has happened leads up to the next thing. It can look like a choice, but the way we fall is always determined by what went before. So we can't choose."

Stella is shaking her head. "Someone says that about photographs—about how the circumstances that lead to the shutter clicking mean that the photograph is a sum of all the events before it. But I don't believe it—it sounds great, it's really top-notch philosophical bullshit. But you do have a choice."

"Yes," I say.

She nods, and stands for a moment, considering me. "If you want to know, I think the whole business of this, all the guilt that you're suddenly in the middle of, is, is . . ." She gives me a rueful smile, and then, with her head at a cutesy angle, says, in a singsong voice, "A bourgeois social construct, imposed on us by men and internalized by us in the *worst* way."

I am quiet. The thick blue line isn't a bourgeois social construct.

"Aristotle didn't have a problem with abortion," she says.

"Oh, well, good. That's a comfort," I say. There's no point asking how she knows this. Americans have all these classes that mean they just know odd things, so engineers know about William Blake and poets know about analytical geometry. She probably took one on Aristotle and the politics of gender.

"He thought it took time for the soul to get into the body."

"Well, if he's right, all the more reason to take the cancellation," I say. I say "cancellation" on purpose, to brutalize myself.

Stella's shoulders suddenly go down. She walks to me, and puts her hand on my arm. "I'll go with you," she says. "I will."

I feel hot quick tears come, and try to stop them. "Are you going to bring your camera?" I say.

She looks how I feel. "I'll restrain myself," she says.

She strides away back to the counter, and pours the strong black coffee into her round white mugs. As she brings one to me, she says, "This does not happen when you're a lesbian."

"It's definitely a plus in the lesbian column," I say.

"What does your mother say?" she asks.

The reluctance to tell them is visceral. To inflict such disappointment. One of the lures of traveling down this road is that that telephone call never needs to happen. I watch as the cat settles himself comfortably on a beanbag strewn with underwear. "Earl's glad you're back," I say.

Stella just regards me over her coffee cup.

✶

THE NEXT DAY, after I've had breakfast, I flip open my laptop and start to work on my paper. I can't concentrate. If I have the baby, I won't be able to concentrate for the next eighteen years.

I keep trying, and manage some workmanlike stuff that

doesn't require inspiration, and then I check my phone, check my e-mail, go on Facebook. I read other people's posts, make jaunty comments, flitter away the time, profane the time.

Bryan Gonzales, another art history student, calls me and invites me to a party at Columbia tonight. I say I can't at such short notice. "Ah, come on, Esme. Bradley Brinkman is coming, and you all go weak at the knees for him."

I refuse again, tell him I am tired, tell him I will come to the get-together at the Hungarian Pastry Shop on Sunday instead. If I am going to do this, then I can at least pay some sort of respect, treat this with all due seriousness.

I lie in the dark. The rain is falling; I can hear the ebb and flow of tires on the wet tarmac, swooshing up dark spray. Through the blinds, blue ambulance lights flash on my ceiling from time to time, and car headlights arc by, ceaselessly repeated. Somewhere near, someone is playing a solo on a trumpet, making it sound more wistful than I thought a trumpet could ever sound, and I hear the notes dying, each one, on the air, like sparks from a fire fading into the dark.

The tiredness is real, but I do not sleep, cannot sleep. For hour after hour I keep vigil with the bunch of cells, the mourner and the executioner.

Sometime in the darkest part of the night, I notice that the trumpet has long been silent. There is nothing to indicate the time, no church clock chiming the hour, no early birdsong as advent to the dawn. I have been lying here the whole night long and it has been different from any other time in my life when I have been still and quiet and alone. I know why. It is because I am not alone.

I have been thinking about a lot of things—about what matters, what seems to matter, what doesn't matter at all. About God, too. I don't know if he's a he, a being with eyes to see us, ears to hear us, tears to weep for us. Or, if he can hear us, whether he can help us. I don't know—we none of us know—if he is there, or if he was there once, and then got tired and walked away, so that we were left alone. But whether there is a God or not makes no difference to me. I have been doing my own creating, and I don't believe *I* have enough of a reason to get tired and walk away. There are many, many reasons, good reasons, to terminate a pregnancy. But that my PhD at Columbia might be a bit trickier now is not one of them. Nor is the intolerable hurt that for this baby's father there was no hot night for its making.

With the New York dawn chorus of clanking crates from delivery vans, I reach for my phone, call the clinic, and leave a message on their voice mail canceling the appointment. I finally turn my head on the pillow to sleep.

*

WHEN I TELL Stella, she flings her arms around me and says that keeping the baby is cool, cool, cool. Then she says, "Hey, I'll be your birth partner if you want. Like a doula or something?"

"What's that? What would you do?"

She shrugs. "I dunno. I guess I would yell 'Push' or 'Pull' or something. But really, it's great. And now, Esme?"

"What?"

"Call your *mother*."

I still have no desire at all to tell my parents about the baby. When I was first offered the scholarship to Columbia they were perturbed—in part because of 9/11, in part because it is in New York City and I am their only child. What nameless dangers might await me? They could think of a few with names, but I don't think pregnancy was one of them. I am too *sensible* for that to happen.

As New York hasn't been a target since 2001, I researched the statistics in order to convince them I could come here and not get into trouble. It's more dangerous to cross the road in London, you're more likely to choke on a mint than become a victim of al-Qaeda, and so on. My father makes mathematical instruments for a living; if you present the right data, it calms him down. My mother is still nervous, but not because of al-Qaeda. I know that despite their visit, she is still afraid of gangs loitering on the brownstone steps from *Sesame Street,* who might surround me and take my money or my virtue.

And so I don't want to tell them yet about the baby, about how soon they are going to be grandparents and how there was, after all, trouble waiting. I need to get used to it myself first. The thought of my mother swooping in, imploring me to come home on the next flight, ready to enclose me in her ordered world—I will phone tomorrow. Or the next day.

In the afternoon, I go to the student welfare center at Columbia. They are surprisingly helpful. They do not seem to judge me as an idiot who doesn't know how to use birth control. They say that sure, I can stay in that apartment for now, because I won't be having the baby until the next academic year. And I can put my name down for accommodation for families. A mother and a baby; we will count as a family. It will just cost more, is all. She pushes the accommodation list at me, with the prices.

It will cost a lot more.

I ask if there are any jobs going, provided by the university. No, there are none available right now. The teaching jobs are like stardust; they and all the little extra ones are snapped up by those in the know before the semester starts. I can sign up to be told when new ones come, but they are usually grabbed before they get to the e-mail stage.

I sign up anyway.

I am on a student visa, and I am not supposed to work—except in those little, well-regulated Columbia jobs. But I am going to need a lot of extra money for the baby. More in rent. Nappies, a pushchair, baby milk. Other things that cannot be dreamed of in my philosophy. I do some research online. Nappies—diapers— cost a thousand dollars a year. A pushchair is at least $200. A cot is another $100, minimum. Apparently I need a baby bath, a bouncy seat, a breast pump, a high chair, a changing station, a Diaper Genie, a sterilizer, breast pads, a sheepskin rug. I don't know what half these things are. A sheepskin rug? Is that for the photographs?

I call a few places about waitressing; it is all tips, no salary, and they want people with experience. And, presumably, people who don't panic when they have to divide twenty-four by four. I don't mention that I am pregnant, of course, but that too wouldn't go down so well. I go over to my window, look out on my beloved Broadway. I have a few friends who might be able to help a little, here and there. But not old friends, and not family. When you need help, extended, selfless help, you need your family, the family I don't want to call because I can't bear to ask for my mother's selfless extended help. I want to do it myself. It is going to be so difficult, financially and in terms of time. Am I being absurdly stubborn about having everything—New York, the PhD, the baby? If I am going to keep it, I might have to go home.

In the next couple of weeks, I realize that that "if" is entirely rhetorical. There is no question at all, anymore, about whether I am going to keep it. Day by day, hour by hour, it becomes more precious to me. If it carries on at this rate, when it is born I will be mad with love.

I am walking down Broadway again. To think about Mitchell is still painful—the image is always of him having particularly lustful sex with some voluptuous beauty—so I am not thinking about him. Much. Except that I look for his face in every face, and when I think that I see him amid the surge of people on the pavement, my blood electrifies with desire and misery, and turns to dishwater again when it is not him. But the hankering will wear off more quickly if I do not indulge it. It wears off for everyone in the end, after all. Except A. E. Housman.

As I walk, I see every color, every form, every fall of light. It is like a Fairfield Porter watercolor, such bright sun and such shadows, and such radiance. I think that it is too beautiful to leave if I can possibly help it.

If I have to leave, it will only be because I don't have enough money. So I should think of a way to get some. Waitressing is out, teaching via Columbia is out—but in New York, there must be a million ways to make money.

A dog walker with a pack of hounds surging around him walks past. How much per dog per hour? That guy could be on hundreds of dollars a day. But the drawbacks are obvious and manifold.

I try to think of other jobs; managing hedge funds pays well, according to the papers, but I don't know what a hedge fund is. I could think of a fantastic Facebook or phone app that would take the world by storm—except I can't think of any at all, and I don't even see why people ever liked Angry Birds. Then I remember that I am only allowed to work in Columbia-sanctioned jobs. I am stuck. I could borrow from my parents, but I hate that idea. I must be able to make something work myself.

On the thought, I reach The Owl. I stand still. It has a lop-sided "Help Wanted" sign in the window, a grimy one, written in marker pen. It was not there last time I came past. Signs and wonders.

I push the door open, and step inside. Luke is there, as he was last time, although it is ten A.M. There is music playing. He nods hello.

"You're here a lot in the mornings," I say. "I thought you were the night manager."

"Yeah, I just opened up for George this morning; he had a book call. He's back, he's just in the john."

"Right," I say. I am embarrassed by the word "john." Can't help it. It is a word that makes it into a male toilet.

George reappears, and smiles vaguely at me. He looks at Luke.

"You thinking of pricing those cookbooks?"

"Nope," says Luke. He is getting up. "I just came to open up for you, George. I'm not staying. If I do, I'll miss *Little House on the Prairie*."

Luke has a light stubble, is wearing a bandana, a red T-shirt, and a pair of Lucky jeans. He does not look at all like he's going home to watch *Little House on the Prairie*.

"You're joking," I say. He looks surprised.

"I don't know which episode it is. But I'm assuming Laura will do something wrong, see the error of her ways, and go on to help the whole town of Walnut Grove learn a valuable moral lesson just in time to sing in church on Sunday."

"Luke," says George, "this is a shock. Are you trying to tell us something?"

"Yeah. This is my way of outing myself. I'll see you."

When he has gone, George says to the ambient air, "Maybe it's me, but the older I get, the stranger everyone else seems to become." He notices that I haven't gone to browse the shelves, and says, "Can I help you with anything?"

I take a breath. "The sign in the window. The 'Help Wanted' sign?"

"Yes?"

"I wondered how strict your rules were."

I tell him I have no experience whatsoever of working in a shop. I tell him that although I am in the country legally, as a student, it would be illegal for me to work, and also that if he hired me, he would be breaking the law too. "And," I say, "I'm pregnant."

"You sound like our perfect employee," says George.

✧ CHAPTER SIX ✧

I have arranged with George that I will come in after my classes, for my first shift. George says that he won't be there, but Luke will. He then tells me to be sure and exercise regularly for the baby's sake, and to drink distilled water whenever possible. I nod, and wonder if it is *ever* possible. Don't you need a still?

My classes are over at four fifteen; I get to The Owl a little before five. I push open the door, a little hesitantly, expecting to see George or Luke. Another man is sitting there. He is about forty, with grizzled black hair. On his T-shirt, which is in sore need of a good wash, the words *REO* and *Speedwagon* are just about legible.

The man says, "Help you with anything?"

"I'm Esme," I say, "Esme Garland. George—"

The man springs up.

"Sit down," he says, indicating his vacated chair. "Please, sit down. It's a pleasure to meet you. I'm Bruce. You need to sit down. Can I get you anything?"

"She's fine, Bruce," says Luke, dumping down a big pile of books on the counter.

"Can I get you some tea?" says Bruce.

"Yes," I say, playing my part. "Tea would be lovely."

I expect him to head towards the back, to a kettle, perhaps, but he pings open the till, takes out a couple of dollars, and makes for the door. He's going to *buy* me some tea.

Luke says, "Okay, so, this is your first time . . . just take a look around the store, tidy things up if you think it's necessary . . ."

As I raise my eyebrows in confirmation that it is very necessary indeed, the door opens and a woman comes in. She is in her fifties, with flowing blond hair and a frosted pink lipsticked mouth. She is wearing pale blue trousers with white running shoes and a pink fleece jacket. She smiles widely at me, and then around the shop. She is followed by a beige husband in a pale anorak.

"Oh my. Oh my. This is such a cute bookstore. Isn't it, babe? We don't have anything like this back home."

"Can I help you?" says Luke.

"Why, yes you can—I hope! I was looking for a book called *The Power of Pendulums.* Have you heard of it? Do you have it?"

Luke looks at me. "What section, do you think?"

I make a face to indicate the blankness of my brain.

"Science?" I say. "Clock-making?" The woman laughs broadly, and nudges her husband. He snickers.

"Nope," says Luke. "Self-help."

He walks rapidly to a section, fishes out a book from an apparently random pile, and slaps it onto the countertop. The woman seizes it.

"You *have* it!" she says. "That's wonderful. That's wonderful. This is such a great book. Have you read it?" She flips through it fondly, smiling. Then she puts it on the counter. "Can I just leave it here while I take a look around?"

"Sure," says Luke. She moves off towards the true crime section, and her husband follows dolefully.

"Shall I put it beneath the counter, so nobody else will take it?" I say to Luke.

He shakes his head. "No. She's gonna find a reason not to buy it in a second."

I don't know why he says that—she seems keen enough to me. I have shelved perhaps five books when the woman comes back with a book called *Bloodbath in Boise*. It has an embossed blood spatter on its cover, and we are selling it for three dollars.

"You know, I'm gonna leave *The Power of Pendulums* for now. I'm gonna take this instead. For my sister. She loves this kind of stuff."

Luke nods, takes the money, and slips the book into a paper bag for her.

"Thank you, sir," she says. "And this really is the cutest store. Bye now."

"Bye now," repeats Luke.

I pick up *The Power of Pendulums* and open it. I read out, "'The pendulum is a dowsing tool that allows you to access and connect with your higher power so you can make the best decisions in all aspects of your life.'"

"We get asked for that book a gazillion times a week," says Luke. "I can't believe you haven't heard of it. It's been on the *New York Times* bestseller list forever."

I flick through it. Pendulums are apparently in use the entire time by the CIA, the U.S. Navy, and the United Nations. These respected bodies are all holding pendulums over maps to locate the Enemy. You too can find your enemies, and ask the pendulum questions that it will answer with "genuine truthfulness."

"People believe this stuff?" I ask, turning it over. The paperback copy is $18.99.

"No. They just want to," says Luke.

Bruce comes back with tea from the Columbian café next door. He grimaces at the pendulum book, and moves it off the counter, before he presents the tea to me in a way that is curiously reverent. I am not in the least bit used to being pregnant yet, but I am beginning to feel that my status has changed. Unmarried, unpartnered, not very old but old enough to have known better, I am nevertheless being treated by this man as special. And it can only be because of the baby.

I am grateful for the tea; I was tired after my walk here. Bruce's manner makes me think suddenly of the Virgin Mary; she is the only famous woman I can think of off the top of my head who gets to do things when she is pregnant—which says something, right there. What did she say when she had had her baby, and the wise men brought her myrrh and gold and frankincense? What do you do with myrrh? They used myrrh to mask the smell of corpses, in ancient Rome anyway. Not the most sensitive gift for a newborn baby, if that was a normal use when Jesus was born too. I bet Mary hated it. I bet she shoved it under a pile of straw in the stable before they left. I wonder what she really wanted. I think, nothing at all; no myrrh, no frankincense, certainly no gold. Nothing that would draw attention to the fact of her child's existence, nothing that would distinguish him from other children. I am very glad that there will be no wise men and no star for this one. You don't want notice to fall on your precious love; you want blessed, blessed obscurity. I am luckier than Mary—most women are.

I notice that Bruce is watching me drink the tea.

"Thank you," I say. "It's very kind of you."

"It's a pleasure," he says, and smiles shyly. I don't mind so much now about his REO Speedwagon T-shirt; he's nice. "When you've had a rest, I'll show you the store. Unless it will tire you?"

I am about to say that I am not quite that delicate when Luke appears again. He says, "Bruce, I said she's fine. This isn't a sixties love-in. And it isn't gonna work if we treat her like she's disabled."

Bruce ruffles himself up in his chair and glowers at Luke. He turns back to me.

"I think it takes a lot of guts to do what you're doing. You're not in a relationship, right? I am sorry if that's too personal."

"No, I'm not in a relationship . . ."

"But you still decided to have the baby. That's brave. I respect that. I really do. If there's any way I can help you . . ."

I thank him, glowing with a pleasant sense of nobility and selflessness. But I remember the abortion clinic and say, "But I am not that virtuous. I did consider—you know—a termination."

Bruce nods understandingly.

"But when I rang to make an appointment, there had been a cancellation, and it struck me that that cancellation could now become anything—that for every baby there is every possibility—it might become a Mozart or a Shakespeare . . ."

"Or an ordinary happy human being," says Luke.

✦

CUSTOMERS COME IN all the time. It's a good sign, I think, for the intellectual health of the city, at least from this small sampling. I say so, but Bruce shakes his head. He emphasizes each of his words as an old-fashioned Shakespearean actor would, with a kind of manic pungency:

"Believe me, that's a very optimistic viewpoint. The reality is that we live in daily fear of being turned into a nail salon or a Starbucks. There are hardly any real bookstores left in the city; they've all gone. Arcadia, Book Ark, Endicott, there used to be a great Shakespeare and Company just across the street, there was a wonderful bookstore on Madison, and that's just the start. Gotham closing was the end for me. It's all Barnes and Noble and the Internet now."

"There's still a great one on Madison," says Luke. "Crawford Doyle are world class. But yeah, of course, mostly it's the Internet now."

"But in a bookshop you find things you didn't know about," I reply. "It's much more exciting than Amazon's 'customers who bought that book also bought this one.'"

"Honey, you're preaching to the choir," says Luke.

"But you seem to me to get plenty of people in here. And they buy."

"Yeah," says Luke. "Some of them buy. A lot of them fall in here and tell us we have a really cute store, and that they love to read, and that they read *Catcher in the Rye* once, and then they leave again. We get a lot of regulars in too; you'll meet them. Some of them are—a little on the odd side."

As he speaks, an elderly man comes in and nods with old-fashioned courtesy at the three of us. He is wearing a camel-colored mackintosh. He takes plastic spectacles out of a case, and, perching them on his nose, begins to look through the little grammar section we have near the door.

"He's Romanian," says Bruce, in what is meant to be an undertone. "He comes in to look for dictionaries to send home to schools in Romania. If he wants to buy something when you're at the register, give me a shout. We give him a discount."

"Though why we do, when he lives on Riverside Drive, is a little bit of a mystery," says Luke.

"Because you're nice?" I offer.

"Oh yeah, we're nice. Nice and losing money subsidizing millionaires."

I look again at the man patiently perusing the columns in an old dictionary. His mac is a little greasy at the cuffs; his scarf is one of the cheap ones that you can get on any street corner. Nothing about him suggests affluence.

"There's a whole bunch of people you'll get to know," says Bruce. "There's the guy who's really into Nabokov; he comes in looking for new editions, editions in paperback, everything. He's kind of weird."

"*Kind* of weird?" says Luke. "He hyperventilates if you mention *Lolita*. And he wears incontinence pants."

"They're not, Luke, they're just green."

"They look waterproof and they have elastic cuffs, is all I'm saying. Anyhow, there is a street guy, Blue, who is in the whole damn time. He is always on the point of going to make it big in Vegas. He always needs a couple of dollars to tide him over before he goes. And there's DeeMo and Tee; they're homeless too. Tee cleans the windows. And Dennis helps with the outside books—he's another street guy. He's an alcoholic. And there's a guy—a customer—who comes in wearing a towel on his head."

"A towel on his head?"

"Yeah, a green bath towel, he wears it like a turban. Don't ask why. Nobody knows why. And there's the Oz crowd. They're gay, mostly a little older, they're into L. Frank Baum."

I look blank again.

"He wrote *The Wonderful Wizard of Oz*."

"So—are they into it because of Judy Garland?"

He considers. "You know, I never thought of that. Which gay icon came first, Frank or Judy?"

Bruce purses his lips. "The people who like L. Frank Baum are not *always* gay, Luke."

Luke flickers a glance at me, and there is a change around the muscles of his mouth, but he does not smile.

At six o'clock Bruce stops work. He looks anxiously at me.

"I'm leaving you alone with Luke," he says.

I am not sure what he means. Will Luke turn into a seducer when he's gone?

"You worried about her virtue, Bruce?" asks Luke.

Bruce slaps his clenched fist down on his knee.

"Where the hell were you lurking this time? I was saying that to Esme in confidence."

"I think she'll make it through the evening," Luke says.

With a sympathetic nod towards me and a scowl at Luke, Bruce is gone.

It is now dark outside. I shelve more books, try to learn the sections, have a go at being on the till. Luke, who is fairly talkative when Bruce is there, relapses into monosyllabic responses to my questions, and sits listening to a raspingly miserable song about a downtown train on the CD player. I want to ask him if this is all he does, or if, like most people in New York, his day job is just a way station on the road to glory. I don't ask, though, because he clearly does not want to be particularly friendly. He wants to listen to the music.

I do not know how to be with one other person and not be friendly; it is a severe trial to me not to say all the chatty things that pop into my head. I shouldn't really want to try, given how he's behaving. I wonder if that line about my virtue was another dig.

I go upstairs and tackle tidying up the transport section. Nobody has done that in a long time. It is really a section about how to have wars. This is a very male store. In among books such as *Jane's Historic Military Aircraft Recognition Guide* and *From the Dreadnought to Scapa Flow,* I find *Zen and the Art of Motorcycle Maintenance.* It seems shelving is an art, like everything else. I decide to do it exceptionally well.

"Esme?"

I stand up. "Yes? Do you need me? I was just straightening things up here—"

"No, I'm just gonna step out for a second—maybe get a couple beers. You want one?"

I do, of course, and I can't have one. "Nice thought, but no, thank you."

"Really? Just one?"

"No, I can't. They have that picture of me on the side, with a black line through it. I'm not allowed."

"Okay. I won't be long."

I look at my watch. It is ten o'clock.

"Is it all right for me to be—on my own?"

Luke shrugs. "I'll be gone two seconds. What do you think will happen?"

"A . . . a huge sale?" I don't tell Luke I am nervous. When I first took a cab in New York, I thought my chances of survival were around fifty-fifty. The cab driver was sure to drive me to a deserted parking lot, à la every American movie ever, and murder me after taking all my money. Then he would put my body in the trunk of the taxi, drive to the East River, and tip me in. As it happened, the actual driver of my first cab was a Chinese guy, wearing a sky-blue shirt and a pink tie. He drove me in polite silence across the park at 66th Street, charged me seven dollars, and told me to have a nice day.

Luke is half out of the door. "If you get a huge sale at ten o'clock on a Monday night in November in the rain, sweet-talk him for the three point two minutes it will take me to cross the street, buy a beer, and cross back again."

I subside back to the transport section. A minute or so later, I hear the door open, and a voice calls out, "Luke? George?"

My heart sinks. The voice is deep, rough. I stand up again, at the top of the stairs, and look to see who is speaking. It is one of the men that the bookshop men call street guys, and Mitchell called bums. I like "street guys" better. He is enormous, about six two and not thin. I don't really see how you can be homeless and so well endowed with flesh. As I come down the stairs, I realize that he isn't fat at all—he is just swathed in layer after layer, as if to protect him from a New York winter, although November is only just beginning. There is a powerful smell of sweat, and something sweeter. The sweeter smell is scary; it reminds me of something, but the context is wrong.

"Can I help you?" I say. My voice sounds frightened. I am angry at its treachery. But really, why would he not pull a gun on me and make me empty the till? I am not sure I can remember how to open the till. If it happens, maybe I can hand him the entire cash register.

"George around?"

"No, George isn't in tonight."

"Where's Luke?"

"He'll be back soon—he's just gone out for a minute."

"Who are you?"

"I'm Esme, Esme Garland. It's my first night."

"Hi, Esme. I'm Don't Matter."

He is holding out his hand to me. Instead of instantly grasping it, I look at it. It has bumps on it in odd places. They might be warts, or they might be buboes. And I am pregnant.

I grasp his hand and shake it firmly. His hand is big, and rough as a gardening glove. "Hello, Don't Matter."

"You can call me DeeMo."

"Right. So Don't Matter is your more formal name."

He grins. "Yeah. That's my Sunday name." I am surprised that he gets this and feel instantly ashamed.

He is holding a big black plastic bin liner with books in it, which he starts to unload onto the table. They are all smeared with tomato sauce. I watch as the pile gets bigger and tomato sauce dribbles onto the counter.

"Ah—DeeMo?"

"Uh-huh."

"These books—they're covered in—"

"Oh yeah, the ketchup. I know. But you can wipe that off."

It seems reasonable to me. We have paper towels.

Luke comes back into the shop with two beers. He takes in DeeMo, the ketchup books, and me in one quick glance, and says, "DeeMo. What the *fuck* do you think you're doing?"

"You don't like the ketchup. I get it. I get it. I like your new assistant, Luke."

"Yeah, she's swell."

I don't know if "swell" is yet another barb, but I do know that DeeMo is good-naturedly shoving his tomatoey books back in the bin liner. When he has gone, I sit back in the chair.

"This is a weird job," I say. I remember about shaking his hand, and reach for the hand sanitizer next to the till. While I am squirting it onto my palm, the door opens and DeeMo comes back in. He sees what I am doing, and looks straight into my eyes. I flush. He says nothing at all.

Luke looks from me to DeeMo. "What is it?"

"I'm pregnant," I say to DeeMo. "I'm paranoid. I don't want— to hurt it."

He nods his head. "It's okay, honey, don't worry about it," he says. "Luke. Can you spot me ten dollars?"

"Nope," says Luke.

He looks at me.

"She can't either," Luke says. "But come back at eleven

thirty and bring in the books for me, and you can earn ten dollars."

DeeMo appears to think this is a reasonable proposition, and disappears into the rainy night again.

Luke hands me a Coke in a bottle. I say something about paying for it, and he shakes his head.

"What does he smell of?" I ask Luke.

"Ketones," says Luke promptly. "His body needs calories, and it doesn't have enough, so it's breaking down his vital organs."

"And the smell?" It is like pear drops, I remember now, something nice from childhood. "The smell is . . . ?"

"It's the smell of acetone. It's the smell of a man who is starving."

✦

DEEMO DOES COME back, promptly, at eleven thirty, and begins to heave all the crates of books inside. Luke nods at me and says, "You can get the vacuum cleaner out of the back and do all the aisles and the stairs."

I have a feeling that Luke expects me to cavil about the task, that I will object along feminist lines to being assigned domestic tasks. The source of his irritation seems to be the idea that I've been taken on out of pity, and that I will expect an easy ride. So I get the vacuum cleaner out without a word.

It is an ancient vacuum cleaner. It is made of thick white and brown plastic that has yellowed with age to the color of tinned rice pudding, like wallpaper in a pub, and it has a fabric bag, and the cord is looped round two catches. When I work out how to turn it on, from a switch on the base, it sounds like a jet engine taking off. I glide it up and down the aisles, pretending to be a happy housewife from the fifties. *Just what is it that makes today's homes so different, so appealing?*

When I have finished, Luke walks around, his eyes on the floor. He picks up a tiny speck.

"You missed some."

"I'm surprised, because it's such a state-of-the-art machine."

"You like vacuuming?"

"I like things to be tidy," I say.

"Okay, you did fine. You can put it away."

When I come back to the front, Luke opens the till.

"What time did you get here?"

"Five."

"And what's your hourly rate?"

"I don't know."

He looks up at me. "You don't *know*? You and George didn't fix—no, why am I even asking? How about ten dollars an hour?"

"How about twelve?"

"How about ten?"

"Ten is fine."

DeeMo is lounging at the doorway while we are discussing this, and suddenly breaks into a wide grin.

"She's on half my salary, man. I get ten for a half hour."

Luke counts out some bills. "That's seventy dollars. Enjoy."

I take the money and stare at it.

"I don't deserve all this. I didn't do anything."

He shrugs. "Then give it back."

I stick it in my pocket.

"Right," he says. "We should close up. DeeMo? You ready?"

DeeMo nods and slouches out ahead of us. Luke turns out the lights and we go out onto the pavement. He locks the door, and then leaps up and pulls down a big metal grille, which he then padlocks to a metal loop on the ground. The grille has graffiti on it, in the style of the subway cars in old films. He straightens up.

"Nobody meeting you?"

"Sorry?"

"I just thought the father might show up to walk you home."

"Oh! No, the—the father is not in the picture. I said, earlier, with Bruce . . ."

"Oh, yeah, yeah, where he wanted to get you on *Oprah* for keeping your kid. Well, okay. See you next time."

He raises his hand in farewell and walks off across Broadway towards the downtown subway stop while I am still struggling to answer him.

DeeMo is still there. He says, "If you're walking uptown, I can walk you home."

I look at him. I don't know what to say. He leans his head back on the wall and laughs up into the night air. I am thinking that he is a black homeless crack addict, and if I need any protection on the way home, it is probably from black homeless crack addicts. And he is laughing because I am thinking it.

"I live near Columbia; it's too far for me to walk this late. I am going on the subway. You can walk me one whole block if you like."

He pushes himself off from the wall and walks beside me, and sees me right down to the turnstile.

"You be okay now?"

"Yes," I say. "Thanks, DeeMo."

"Don't talk to anyone," he says, and retreats back up to Broadway. When I get to the platform, I see Luke on the opposite side. He lifts his chin in faint acknowledgment, and I give him an equally faint smile back. I want to shout that he has no right to judge me, to pass an opinion on what I do with my body, but how ridiculous would that be? My voice would probably come out too high-pitched, or too reedy; he wouldn't be able to hear over all the train rails, and the stray commuters on my side would hear all too well. We stand in awkward self-consciousness, or at least I do, until his train comes. Next time I will bring a book.

CHAPTER SEVEN

Up the ladder at The Owl, shelving books, I am thinking about the lift in Lerner Hall at Columbia. I can't bring myself to take it. It takes you up to the sixth floor only, and the university's counseling service is on the sixth floor, so just getting into the lift is like a public announcement of your mental state. But taking the stairs might be worse. You would only take the stairs so that nobody would see you in the lift, so if you're seen ducking into the stairwell you must have even more to hide.

Luke says, from the front, "So, the guy? The father?"

"Oh, yes. The guy. He's—" I shrug. Sometimes I think I am doing fine without Mitchell, and that's when the sadness of it sucker-punches me, when I am suddenly all skin and tears. I don't think I can speak through it for a minute. It must be such small-time grief, compared to death, compared to real bereavement. But I don't know what they are like; this feels bad enough. And grief, I see now, is for the loss of the future as well as the past.

I cling on to the ladder and stare at the spine of *A Thousand Acres* by Jane Smiley very fiercely, waiting for it all to subside. I can feel Luke looking up at me. After a while he moves away. I hear him shelving books, and then a customer comes in, asking for poetry.

I bring the Jane Smiley back down with me to take home, hoping I will be able to lose myself in it when I get sad. I sit down on the second seat at the front. Luke is cashing up, reaching for the sales ledger to note down the takings for the day.

"Are we doing all right, financially?" I ask.

"Yeah," says Luke, and then says, "I like the 'we.' We're doing okay. When you take into account ebooks and Kindles and such, we're doing pretty good. As long as the rent doesn't go up. Then we'll become a nail salon, like Bruce says."

"Maybe the landlord likes that this is a bookshop, and he won't put the rent up."

"Yeah, landlords are like that, especially in New York."

I laugh, and Luke looks up. He says, "You know—about the guy. It will get easier."

"Yes. I just—you know. I loved him."

I am not looking at him, but I am not crying either. Progress.

"You're pretty open about it," he says.

"I don't see any reason not to be."

"That's how you get hurt."

"I'm already hurt."

"Then maybe that's how you got hurt."

*

I FINISH A short afternoon shift that I spent learning about book descriptions with George. It is an arcane system of codification that the Internet is putting paid to, where fair is foul and good is bad and perfect means you're a charlatan. Price-clipped is bad. Second impression is bad. Inscribed is bad, unless it is by the author, and then inscribed is good, but not nearly as good as signed. Unless the inscription is to someone patently important—*To my dear Laura, love from Petrarch*. At the end of it I feel very tired, despite only having been working for three hours.

"You okay?" George asks.

"Yes. I had lectures this morning; I have a paper to write—I am just a little tired."

"You have to remember to take it easy—the baby—"

"I know," I say, hastily. "I know. I do."

He looks piercingly at me and then asks me to wait for a second, and pads off to the back of the shop. He comes back with a paperback, and hands it to me. It is called *Shackleton's Boat Journey,* by Frank Worsley.

"It's one of the greatest survival stories of all time," he says. "Enjoy."

It is very like George to think that a book about Antarctic exploration will sort out the stresses of being single, impoverished, and pregnant, with a job and a PhD to do.

I go to Barnes and Noble to buy some books on how to be good at pregnancy. I can't really afford them, but I've been using the Web so far, and it is too nebulous. I feel as if I need to impose a pattern on the days and weeks.

It is symptomatic of the problems facing cute secondhand bookshops that I don't think of looking for any pregnancy books at The Owl until I have completed my expensive and bulky purchases. As if the past can tell us anything about having babies.

All baby books are enormous; why? It seems like a subtle infantilizing of the mother. We are going to be mothers instead of women, so we have to have everything presented in fourteen-point type. It is the same with maternity clothes; I looked at them one day with Stella, but have not bought any yet. They had card rosettes attached to them that read, "I am a nursing item," or "I am a dress."

"I am a nursing item," said Stella. "Subtext: 'You are a pregnant woman, so you need to have your clothes talk to you.' For fuck's sake."

As I am walking uptown with my new springing step, I walk smack into Mitchell. He puts his hands on my shoulders and says, "Why, Esme Garland! What a wonderful surprise!" in a Cary Grant voice.

I get kissed on both cheeks, and held back again, to be viewed. I do not know what is going on, but I suspect mischief and misrule. I submit to the kisses and the viewing, with my heart pounding and my mind racing. I can barely breathe. I must not abase myself with Mitchell van Leuven again. I must not.

I do not ask him why he is up here, though this is far from any neighborhood he needs to be in.

"I am never up here now," he says. "It must be fate. It must be fate, Esme."

It is not fate.

"You look great," he says. "Come and have a coffee. Do you know the ratio of coffee shops to people in Manhattan? Three to one. It's true. Come on, pick one. Not Starbucks."

There are some people who will realize and appreciate the tremendous accomplishment of my next words, and others for whom it will pass by unremarked.

"I'd like to, but I've got a deadline," I say.

"I never knew you to refuse a coffee before," he says. His eyes are smiley. They are crinkling at the edges.

I shrug and say, "I've gone off coffee."

"Then," says Mitchell gravely, "I'd better buy you a chai latte."

I shake my head, resolute.

"What are your books?"

I say, "Oh, they're nothing in particular," and I try to be casual, but I make a slight movement towards putting the bag behind my back, as if to conceal it from his gaze. He has seen that there are books, so the gesture is worse than useless. He makes a dive for the bag, as if he is a boy after a present. I grab for it back and say, "No, Mitchell, you have no right, don't—"

And he tugs the books out of the bag. There are two enormous matching ones: *The Pregnancy Book* and *The Baby Book*. Then I've got one called *Eating Well When You're Expecting* and *The Mayo Clinic Guide to a Healthy Pregnancy*. I've put the one George gave me in with them, so I've got *Shackleton's Boat Journey* with them all. Somehow it is like buying four ball gowns and a tin of Spam; it makes me look mentally disturbed.

Mitchell stares at the books.

"Are you pregnant?" he says.

"Yes," I say. "And I'm going to the South Pole."

I managed a comeback, and my voice sounds pretty level. But after all, I knew, and he didn't. He is pale.

"Is it mine?" he asks.

"No," I say, "it's mine."

I stand there, Mitchell stands there; the weight of all the baby books is in his hands. I am not thinking of anything.

"You—weren't going to tell me?" he says finally.

I say nothing. He looks around at the people passing by. He says, "Oh, oh, wait—was it the park? Was that what it was? You were going to tell me *that*?"

I lift my chin fractionally.

He starts nodding, as if I have confirmed what he always thought about me. He looks as if he wants to rope in the passersby now, as audience to the gross crime inflicted upon him, as witnesses to my unreasonableness.

"And you're going to have it," he says. "Just like that." He snaps his fingers. "I—could I—just tell me something here. Could I have gone through my whole life being a father and not knowing it? You weren't going to tell me?"

"Why would I tell you, if you didn't want to be with me?"

"It's my right? For instance?"

"Why is it your right? Why isn't it your burden, if I tell you?"

"Why can't a right be a burden? You're going to have my *baby*?"

I am silent. He screws his eyes up, and then says, "You don't think—it didn't cross your mind to think, that in this situation, you—it—someone—might *need* me? You, you . . . I . . . you don't see that this changes things?"

"I see that it changes things," I say, hotly. "It's because I see that it changes things that I didn't tell you—"

He is shaking his head. "You—are—unbelievable."

I am being subjected to this on the most public street on earth. I want to escape from him, to bolt. In most places, if I walked away, he would just be able to follow me, telling me how unbelievable and bad I am. But this is New York. I walk to the edge of the pavement and raise my hand. A yellow cab curves to my feet. I open the door.

He strides up to me and catches hold of the door so that I can't move it. I think for a second that he is going to shout at me, but when I lift my head to face him, he looks stricken.

"Why is this happening like this?" he says, and I think I can hear tears in his voice. "Surely we could manage it better than this? You are hurting me, Esme. This hurts."

A thousand petals of penitence unfurl in me—I have not considered him properly. I was too busy being hurt myself to think about him.

"I am sorry—" I say, "I didn't—I didn't think that you—"

"I miss you," he says, his voice as soft as a flower. My breath catches. Slowly, he raises his free hand and tucks a lock of hair behind my ear; it is something he used to do.

I am electric at the touch of his hand. He knows. He looks, unsmilingly now, into my eyes for a long time. His eyes are like the sea. The North Atlantic.

He leans forward, his breath brushing my ear. "I chose you, Esme," he says. "I singled you out from all the world."

✦

I STRETCH OUT on the mulberry sheets.

He walks back in from the kitchen with a cheese board and a dish of peaches. He is still naked.

"Where are they from?" I say, peering at the peaches. "Not Gristedes?"

"What have I wrought?" he says. "No, Miss New York, *not* Gristedes. They're from Apple Tree Market."

I bite into one. It tastes like a peach ought to taste.

"You should buy some melons there," I say, "they might taste like melons instead of cucumbers."

He grins as he looks away and then meets my eyes, the special, secret grin, that makes me feel I am loved

"I have made you in my own image," he says. "I'm very proud."

"I can be annoyed when fruit doesn't taste good all by myself."

"No, you can't. You were like all the English in England when I met you. 'This peach tastes like shit, and it cost five dollars. Oh well, at least we won the war . . . '"

"Yes, I do, I talk about winning the war all the time. But it's true that you've taught me to be a real New Yorker." I glance over at his closet. "Or a gay New Yorker . . ."

"Cheap, Esme, cheap. And I've only taught you how to be a gay *male* New Yorker. Lesbians don't care. Lesbians don't eat peaches. They're too busy eating—"

"Apples!" I say, and slap my hand over his mouth. He is laughing, tumbling sideways on the bed. He pulls me on top of him, and starts to kiss me, and forces the peach that is already in his mouth into mine.

I push him away and make a face. He laughs.

"You're revolting," I say.

"I'm adorable," he says. "And you're all tousled. A tousled girl in a tousled bed."

"I can't be tousled. Only my hair can be tousled. Mitchell, what you said—did you really break up with me because you thought I was going to break up with you?"

"Of course. I play by the old rules. Get in first."

"But—you made me so sad."

He shrugs lightly. "Self-defense. I'm a master. And you're not sad now."

"No. I'm not sad now."

"Neither am I. I'm happy, Esme."

He looks over at me—one look. But it is a smiling glance of such unadulterated happiness that I think he does love me, that in this one connecting glance I know he does, I know he does, as I know the sun will rise in the morning to flood the cross streets—and my bedroom—with radiant light.

I am lost in him, and I can't be lost in him. I have to present a semblance of detachment.

"How did you end up in economics?" I ask.

Mitchell looks quizzical. "I'm sorry, are we on our first date?"

"Really. I was just wondering what it was that made you choose it."

"Have you met my mother?"

"You know I haven't. So, why?"

"Because," he says, stroking the inside of my arm with one slow finger, from my elbow to my wrist, "because advertising would have been too obvious. Your arms are nice."

"You managed to cope with the lack of lust, this time?" I say.

He nods thoughtfully. "Yes. It was pretty tough, but I got through it somehow. If maybe next time you could wear a bag over your head?"

I try to hit him. He catches me again, tickles me again. I am laughing and so is he. He leans up on one arm.

"See, Esme? Oh, I have *missed* you. We have a good time. Listen, I've been thinking, since the initial shock—do you think that—maybe—I don't know—maybe we're too young for this? That it might destroy us?" He pauses, looks out of the window and then back to me. "I think, if you do go ahead, that it will destroy us."

I lie there like a rag doll. The energy in the room—or was it in me?—has been turned off like a switch. A trick. It was a trick.

"I would take such care of you, Esme. I would be there with you through all of it. I'll find out the name of a good clinic. The best. I can set it up now. And I'll come with you, of course. I'll be there every step of the way."

He touches my cheek with the backs of his fingers.

"I think it's important to do it quickly. Before you get attached to it."

As I get up, and get dressed in silence, he watches me. I do not speak, have not spoken. I wish I could just zap myself instantaneously back to my apartment; I cannot find my shoe and all I want to do is go.

"Don't be upset."

"I can't find my shoe."

"We'll talk about this some more later."

"I can't find my shoe."

He makes no move to help me look.

"If you have it, Esme, it will start us off on the wrong note. Don't you see that?" He sits up. "I want to be with you. I think you're amazing. But don't do this to us."

How can a shoe disappear from the universe without a trace? Mitchell's apartment is immaculate, but it is not under the bed, not entwined in the despised mulberry sheets, not in the bathroom. It has gone.

"Think of your scholarship," he is saying, as I get down on all fours again to look for it. "A Forster scholarship—you don't think you have a responsibility to the people who awarded you that?"

✦

I STAND BAREFOOT outside Mitchell's building. The pavement is cold beneath my feet. There are no cabs—Sutton Place is in its usual postapocalyptic state, devoid of humans. It would be all right to do this in summer; I could pass myself off as pleasantly whimsical. I walk down the street, and pretend that I have shoes on, and eventually a cab comes by. I take it, and go home.

⤗ CHAPTER EIGHT ⤗

When I go in to work the next morning, I am at odds with all creation. It was so easy to get me back—I was so easy. There wasn't a word of regret or remorse, and I was never going to speak to him again after being so demeaned. Ten words and one caress later I was spread across his bed. I cannot bear myself.

I am opening The Owl up for Bruce, who has been beguiled away from his shift by a symposium on cars from the fifties. Dennis, the white homeless man, is going to be my assistant for the morning setup. He is already there, sitting on the pavement outside Staples, tucking into what looks like chili in a white enamel dish.

He beams at me in welcome. I was intent on gloom, but I look at Dennis, and think of his minute-by-minute life, maybe rooting through trash cans and sleeping in doorways, and I think how paltry that resolve was.

"Is that good?" I ask him.

"No," he says.

He gets up as I unlock the shutter, gives me a hand scrolling it up. We can't get in until we have wheeled out all the outside books that are currently blocking the aisles, but he won't let me help him.

"I heard you was expecting," he said. "So don't take risks."

"It isn't a risk," I say. "They're not heavy. They're on wheels."

He fans out the copies of *National Geographic* in their yellow curves and minutely adjusts the sign that says all books are a dollar. Then he steps back to make sure all is in order.

I turn the lights on in the shop and straighten the bookmarks and postcards. As I do it, I notice a tiny sculpture of a tree, finely modeled out of some dark wood, and hung with even tinier wooden apples that are painted gold. It is exquisite. When Dennis comes back in, I hold it up and say, "Have you seen this? Isn't it beautiful?"

"Oh, yeah, I brought that in. I brought a whole bunch of other stuff too, but George just wanted that and a book. One book."

"I wonder if he would sell it to me."

"Bet he would. It's pretty, right? They were throwing it out, the house clearance guys. They got no souls."

"'This must be saved, this particular thing, this very tree.'"

I stand on the chair to put the precious little tree high above the normal line of sight of the customers. If we could stop it from being accidentally sold, it would be better if it could stay here.

"Dennis," I say, "I am going to get something to eat. Don't let anyone buy that tree. Do you want anything?"

He says he will have a plain bagel, and recommends a diner five blocks away.

"It's a good place. Tell them I sent you. You should try their breakfast—it's better if you stay there, because it don't taste so good from those aluminum cartons."

I go obediently to the diner, but just buy two sesame bagels and a cup of herbal tea to go. It is only when I am on my way back that I realize I left the whole shop in the charge of a homeless alcoholic. I run the rest of the way.

Inside the shop, Dennis is not immediately in evidence, but DeeMo is sitting in the main chair looking through the newest batch of CDs. He has a can of Fanta open by the register.

"Have you seen Dennis?"

DeeMo jerks his head back towards the right-hand aisle. I peer behind the Far East section. Dennis is shoveling one art book after another into a big mail sack.

"Dennis? What are you doing?"

He looks up in surprise, but finishes packing the book he is on.

"I'm a thief. You're not supposed to leave me here alone. Didn't they tell you?"

"No. You don't seem to be very good at it, if you don't mind my saying so."

"No. Guess that's why I'm in jail a lot."

DeeMo stands up. "Which jail you in last time, man?"

"Hudson," says Dennis briefly.

DeeMo looks respectful. "That's a good jail."

"I know. It was okay."

DeeMo says to me, "People commit crimes to get into Hudson," and then turns back to Dennis. "There's fucking *meadows* there, right?"

Dennis looks at DeeMo blandly, and after a couple of beats, he says, "Didn't see any meadows." They both start laughing.

I think of what it must be like in a state prison here; I only know from what I've seen on TV and from *The Shawshank Redemption,* which the BBC must have bought cheap at some point, because it is on every seven minutes in England.

"Meadows!" moans Dennis. "Fucking meadows!" They are both helpless now with laughter. When it subsides, I say, "DeeMo, have you been in prison?"

"Yeah. Last one, I was ninety days in Rikers."

"Rikers is okay," says Dennis, and DeeMo agrees.

"What makes it okay?" I ask.

"Nobody in there doing triple life," says DeeMo. "You get on the wrong side of someone doing double life, triple life . . . he just kills you. 'Cause what's gonna happen? You're dead, and he gets quadruple life. That's what."

This is making Dennis laugh again.

"So, Dennis—you'll put the art books back?"

He stops laughing and sighs.

"I guess."

I stand over him while he puts them back. As he does it, he says, "You got no ring. You're pregnant, though, right?"

"Yes."

"And there's no father?"

"No. No father. Well . . ." I amend that. "There is a father, he just . . ."

Dennis nods. "Yeah," he says. "Yeah." He stands up, dusting himself off as if he were pristine before the thievery, and says, "D'you get my bagel?"

I give it to him, and offer the other one to DeeMo, who lifts his can of Fanta to show he's fine. He says he's going to go.

"Don't go yet," I say. I have forgotten to check the till, and if all the money is gone, then the chances are that Dennis stole it. But would he be stupid enough to stay on to steal the art books? I have some ill-formed idea that if he has, then keeping DeeMo there for a minute might mean I can persuade him to give it all back. I open the register, and the money is all there. All of it.

I shut the drawer, flushed with guilt that I could suspect him.

"It's okay," I say to DeeMo. He is looking at me with raised eyebrows. So now I look as if I thought it was DeeMo.

"What's okay?" he says.

"I mean, it's okay, you can go."

"That's good, but I could go anyhow. Masser Lincoln sez I'm free."

"No, no, I wasn't . . . I'm not . . . I didn't—I just thought Dennis might have stolen the money, and you could help me get it back," I say. That lets me off the hook with DeeMo, but Dennis straightens up, looking aggrieved.

"You think I'd steal from George?"

"You were stealing the art books."

"They're just books. I wouldn't steal from George. I sold him a book last week; it was a first edition. He gave me a hundred bucks for it! You think I'd steal from George?" He looks disgusted.

"I'm sorry," I say. The niceties of thief etiquette are lost on me, but he is offended.

"I'm really sorry," I say again. "I just keep getting everything wrong."

Dennis says, with quick forgiveness, "Don't worry about it."

DeeMo lifts a hand in farewell, and says he will see us later.

I watch Dennis finishing his bagel. He eats it as if he has been brought up by wolves, tearing at it and swallowing. I do not think it is because he is terribly hungry; it is more that he eats as if nobody has ever looked at him.

"How do you manage about eating?" I ask.

"There's places. Soup kitchen on 72nd. When people give me money I buy food."

"Do you?"

"No," says Dennis. "No. If I get money, I buy liquor."

"Do you go through the bins, through the garbage?"

"No!"

"I'm sorry, that wasn't a polite question—"

He shrugs. "I do. Sometimes." Then he says, "I have a daughter."

I feel more guilt, because I am surprised. Why shouldn't home-less men have daughters?

"What's her name?"

"Josie. Josie Jones."

"Does she live in New York?"

"No."

"Right." I am nodding away, wondering what it must be like for Josie, to have her father living rough on the streets of New York. Unless he had hoped to set his rest on her kind nursery, and is rooting through his rubbish bins with a broken heart.

"She got me an apartment, wanted me to live nice. She's a good girl. But I couldn't do it. I like the street."

"Why?" I ask.

"Dunno," he says. It is the easiest answer, the one everyone gives to prevent the obligation to think. Or perhaps nobody ever really expects Dennis to think, or wants an answer.

"I mean it," I say. "Why do you prefer the street to an apartment? I would really like to know."

He sits down heavily in the second chair, staring ahead of him. I make a bustle of opening a book and starting to read. I've read three extraordinarily dull paragraphs when he says, "See—in the apartment, nobody was going to come, and nothing was going to happen. There was nobody there except me."

As he says that last thing, he lifts his eyes to mine. It is a confession of vast loneliness. He indicates a battered money belt fastened around his waist and says, "I'm gonna look after the outside money."

When he goes outside, I feel a vast loneliness too. The loneliness is much worse when you want someone you can't have than when you are just on your own. All of yesterday with Mitchell is crowding in on me, to show how singularly alone I am now. Should I have left? Was it really a trick? Did I overreact? Underreact? Have I lost him again? Should I care? I wish Dennis hadn't gone outside. There are no customers in the store, and I cannot stand my own company. There is nobody here except me.

That thing that Hamlet says—*there is nothing either good or bad, but thinking makes it so.* Not quite true if you are stuck under a grand piano, not quite true for genocide, but surely it must be true about love. If I could stop believing that I love him, I would be free. I don't even believe he makes me happy, it is just that now that I love him, I don't know how to go back. He is the apple I should never have bitten.

I look up to the ceiling, at all the hardcover fiction. So very few people want it. It is operating as insulation rather than stock. The argument rages on about whether it is better to have books or ebooks, but while everyone gets heated about the choices, the hardcover fiction molders quietly away. I will ask if I can put some outside for a dollar, free up some space. It is not going to help very much economically, and thinking about what to do with old books is not enough to obscure unrequited love, but it is a start.

As I am staring at old Tom Clancy spines, the door opens and Mitchell comes in. He looks all around, indulgent and rather bewildered, as a stockbroker might look at a children's birthday party.

"Cute," he says. "I brought you a present."

He puts my shoe on the counter. I swallow the impulse to ask where it was.

"Can I talk to you? We have to resolve this."

We don't. It's resolved. I'm resolved. Do not talk to me, do not touch me, do not persuade me.

"I can't really talk here," I say in a low voice, to give the impression that there are hidden depths to the shop, where browsers lurk unseen.

Mitchell looks down the aisle, up at the mezzanine, and steps forward to check the right aisle.

"Not in front of the cockroaches?"

"There are no cockroaches," I say. "There are customers. Not at this moment, but there were some, there will be some."

As Mitchell smirks, Providence very obligingly sends me a customer, a woman who asks if we have any Helmut Newton. I have to ask who he is, which makes Mitchell shoot a glance of amusement at the woman, but she does not notice. I send her to the ordinary photography section while I check the expensive ones upstairs, searching especially diligently, to give me time to calm down. No Helmut Newton, but she has found other things she likes, so she might stay for a bit.

"Isn't anyone else here, who can cover?"

"Only Dennis, outside, and he's a homeless alcoholic," I say. I think this sounds very funny, especially as I, his coworker, am illegal and pregnant, so I add, "We were both headhunted by the same company."

Mitchell doesn't laugh. He says slowly, "A homeless alcoholic?"

and looks around again, this time as if there is a bad smell. "I am not sure I like you working here."

"In that case I'll resign immediately."

"I'm serious."

I laugh up at him. "I know."

"Let's talk tonight. I'll meet you at your apartment. Let's figure this out."

"I can talk, Mitchell—"

"That's for sure."

"—but I can't do what you want me to do. I can't."

Mitchell makes a gesture of acquiescence to that. I agree to meet him later, after I've finished my studying for the night. He is clearly not pleased at taking third place to the bookshop and school, but I can't see a way around it. He leaves looking stony; two seconds later he sticks his head back in.

"Your homeless guy?"

"Yes?"

"He just took ten dollars for a pile of books from some guy and walked off downtown."

⁙

AFTER MY SHIFT at the bookshop, I go to the Avery Library and settle down for some real work. It is difficult to get to at the moment, but once I am in it, it is almost like being in a bower. Because the critics say that Thiebaud is in the grand tradition that Jean-Baptiste-Siméon Chardin exemplifies, I have a look at Chardin and for the first time, I wonder if I was right to settle so early on Thiebaud. I thought I was being directed towards some staid old pictures from three hundred years ago that it would be hard to find the merit of with modern eyes, but instead, I am moved to tears. To look at his water glass, or his strawberry basket, is like feeling the sun on your face; it is to be filled with rapture. I want to know if I can locate the rapture; why do these paintings make me happy, why do I want to cry?

Becoming enraptured makes me late, and when I finally get to my building it is quarter past nine, fifteen minutes after I said I would meet Mitchell. He is in the lobby, sitting in the only chair. There is that shock of pleasure, which all the rationalizing about how he is Bad for Me will not dispel. Then fear stirs and moves in me, like a cat woken from its sleep. Can he bewitch me into what he wants?

I start to apologize for being late. He holds up the palms of his hands. "I come in peace," he says.

We go up the stairs to my apartment, and he stands in the center of the room. "Esme," he says, "how did we get here?"

I can only think of flippant replies, so I keep quiet. He spreads his hands out.

"For me, it is about making the right decisions at the right time. This might be the right decision if we stay together, Esme, but now? If we go ahead with this now, we'll never know whether we would have been together without this."

I go over to the sink, reach for a glass, and fill it with water from the tap. He comes closer. I am not thirsty; I simply want to make something else happen in the room. I leave the water on and it surges, foaming, from the tap. As I watch it, I wonder if the fact that I have introduced a new thing into a closed room means all the other atoms are closer together now. Have I increased the pressure, when I wanted to release it? Only by the volume of a column of tap water. There is a Larkin poem: *If I were called in / To construct a religion / I should make use of water.* Cleanse me, wash away my sin, wash away my desire.

"Esme!"

I jump. I offer him the glass, the chalice; he shakes his head, impatient.

"Tap water. I want to have you in my life as a matter of choice, Esme. I don't like being constrained to it."

"You're not being constrained to it."

"You're forcing a connection between us."

"That connection is made whether we like it or not," I say.

He whirls away from me, as if we are in a movie.

"You slept with me yesterday so that I would be easier to persuade," I say.

"You're wrong," he says, looking out of the window.

"Then why?"

He shrugs. "I wanted to? I thought I wanted to? Why did you do it?"

"I wanted to."

"Okay. So no harm done."

Being pregnant tires you out as much as jet lag does. Sleep becomes a craving; if you could buy it, pregnant women would steal money to get it. I am desperate to lie down. I can see my bed through the doorway, and I want to lie on it. I want Mitchell to go away. I sit down on the sofa and then, because it is too tempting despite the big drama, I curl up on it, with a cushion under my head. If I am tired, then the baby might be tired. I must rest myself to rest it.

When he turns back to me, his chin is up and his eyes are closed, as if he is trying to work out the irrationality of the person he is dealing with.

"I had no idea that you were pro-life. Are you religious?"

"No," I say, "I am just sleepy." I don't feel like fighting my corner, explaining that pro-choice doesn't mean pro-abortion, pleading that I just can't do it, apologizing to him for keeping the baby.

"I know you're tired," he says. "But we need to get this figured out. I don't *want* a baby, Esme."

I say, to his trousers, because he is still standing, "You needn't worry about it, you don't have to have a baby. You needn't see it as anything to do with you. The connection doesn't have to be a big deal. You needn't worry about either of us—me or the baby. I am not planning to turn up on your doorstep wearing a shawl, with a babe in arms."

He crouches down, puts a hand on my shoulder. His hand is big and warm and heavy. I wish it were there to protect me and the baby, instead of to sever us. "My family," he says, "my family cares an awful lot about doing the right thing. Having an illegitimate child isn't doing the right thing. I would be letting them down. And when you let my family down—you're letting down generation upon generation who have striven, Esme, *striven* to do the right thing at every step."

"Your family? You definitely don't need to worry about them. How would they ever know?"

"How would they ever know? Are you insane?"

"No, why would they? We're not together . . ."

"Not together?" says Mitchell. He looks incredulous. Then he gives me a self-deprecating grin. His grin is very charming. "Aren't we?" he says. "I didn't get the memo."

I sit up. "Of course we're not. Of *course* we're not. We never ever were. I thought we were, and we weren't. We weren't. You had all those other ones . . ." I hate crying. I will not cry. What possible use can tears have been, in early cultures? They just show our weakness; that can't be good.

There is a silence. Then he says, "Oh, Esme. I see now. That's what this is. I see. This is Esme and her baby *contra mundum*."

"I don't speak Latin."

"You know that much Latin. You are pissed that I was dating other women, and so you've got some Harlequin-romance idea in your head that you are going to go off and bring up the baby alone—"

"Sleeping with other women," I say, correcting him. This is an arrow shot into the dark—he didn't actually say he had slept with anyone, the day that he dumped me in the park.

He stops. He is suddenly glittering.

"I didn't sleep with all of them," he says.

I turn away from him, so he cannot see that my own arrow has curved around and pierced me, but turning away makes no difference. The hurt isn't something seen but something known, communicated along the atoms that make up the quivering air.

"Esme, I'm joking. About sleeping with them all?"

As he hasn't succeeded yet, he is still talking. "This was just an accident!" he is saying. "It was just a mistake. We don't need to pay for that mistake for the rest of our lives! You are punishing me."

"I am doing nothing to you."

He looks at me as you would look at a recalcitrant child. He changes tack:

"Babies should be brought into a stable environment. They should be—planned. They should be wanted. They shouldn't be forced into the world come what may. This—it isn't even a baby yet, Esme."

"It is a baby."

"For God's *sake*!" He slaps both hands down on the table. His hands are pale; his face is pale too, and his eyes are once more like the eyes of a bird. He continues more quietly. "If you have a termination now, it wouldn't *know,* it wouldn't *suffer,* and it would be getting rid of something that is smaller than—a—a . . ."

"A what? A cockroach? A rat?" I say. No, I shout. I am shaking. I think he is right—it wouldn't know, it wouldn't suffer—and yet I can't do it. Regret that it has happened consumes me.

"Why are you doing this to me?"

I stare up at him. He is quivering with fury, with passion. It seems as if the sheer force of his will could annihilate the small thing inside me. He stands there like a pale white god in the center of the room. If I turned out the light, I have the uncomfortable feeling that he would shine.

"Choose," he says. The one word.

"Choose?"

"Choose."

"Between you and the baby?"

He assents with a tiniest motion of his head, a Bond villain. I stand up too. I am frightened of him, of his power, of his will, I am even frightened of him physically. And I am liquid with rage.

"I do choose," I say. "I had already chosen when you met me in the street. And so, if you remember, had you."

He does not move at all. He says, with the same repressed violence, "Then that's the end. I am sorry you have brought it to this. It could have been a wonderful relationship. We were special, Esme. I am sorry that you didn't realize that."

I walk over to the heavy brass bolt on the door and yank it open.

He gets his bag, and walks past me and out.

On the table is the untouched glass of water.

I am in a lecture hall in Columbia. I am going to devote myself all day to the PhD, without diversion. The first lecture is called "The Renaissance and the Pitfalls of Presentism." I sit at the front.

I replay the scene from last night with crucial, feel-good differences. I respond to Mitchell's arguments with a quiet wisdom beyond my years, and Mitchell sees that I am a noble and admirable person. He also realizes how desirable I am, and is overcome with lust.

"It is important," booms the professor's voice from the front of the lecture hall, "to challenge hegemonic assumptions about the Renaissance—we must remember that in large part, our ideas of it have been culturally normative."

He is pushing me backwards upon the sofa, his mouth hard on mine, his hand between my legs as on that first night.

"And we can better avoid the many pitfalls of presentism if we are thorough in our research into the history and context of the Renaissance. The word itself is politically freighted . . ."

But he didn't do that, and he didn't want to do that. I think again of how pale and cold he looked. Presentism. I never heard the word before I saw the title of this lecture. I remember googling it last night but I don't remember what came up. I must have had four hours' sleep, with all the thinking about Mitchell. What are hegemonic assumptions? I need some coffee. If they are going to ban coffee for pregnant women, they should give us some substitute, some sort of caffeine equivalent of methadone. Not herbal tea.

The lecture ends. I have taken no notes. Some people are still manically scribbling; the guy next to me is typing notes on his phone. Bryan Gonzales, who was friendly on the first day and still is, despite my uneven displays of friendship in return, comes over to say hello.

"Hey," he says. "You going to Fischer's lecture now?"

I am. I get up to walk with him.

I realize that the Esme Garland who got a first in art history at Cambridge is not the same as this Esme Garland. This one is the living cliché of a girl who throws everything up for love, or would, given half a chance. All I want is to be in the warm sunshine of Mitchell's approval once more, but to do that involves terminating the pregnancy, and the pregnancy is now something that stands beyond my own desire. So I have to stay in this drear world instead. And instead of fastening on to the difficulties and fascinations of an art history degree, I am going through the motions. Sitting in the lecture hall, staring at the lecturer, pencil poised, I dream of boys.

Maybe the daydreams of ravishings on the sofa are hormonally induced. After all, in my present state, even Thiebaud's paintings of hot dogs have an undesirable effect.

Bryan says, "Want to get a coffee after this one?"

I say that would be nice. My nefarious plan is to be friendlier to Bryan so that I can have his notes.

"Why didn't you take notes?" Bryan says, pleasingly on cue. "When I came over, you had a blank notebook."

"I forgot," I say. "Bryan, please can I borrow yours? I know it's a lot to ask . . ."

He shrugs. "It's okay," he says. "I'll type them up and e-mail them to you. But—you forgot?"

"Yes. I'm pregnant."

He says, "Oh, right. So you were thinking about that."

I stare at him. It has so shaken my world that I expect everyone to stand still in shock and say "ohmigod" several times.

"Yes," I say, nodding at him. "I was thinking about that."

✦

NEXT TIME I have a shift at The Owl, George is waiting for me or Luke to turn up, having been on his own in the shop for several hours. He is going out to get some sustenance in the shape of vegan soup and distilled water, at a new place that has opened up, to his high delight. It is called Fallen Fruit and caters to all the Georges on the Upper West Side. I ask him if I can buy the little tree hung with golden apples. He looks up at it and says I can have it in exchange for the night's work.

"But I want it to be here. It should be here. I am just worried, in case it gets sold. Imagine if there were price tags on things in museums, how stressful that would be."

"I like it too," says George, standing up to get a better look at it. "Yes—let's put a note underneath it, and keep it up here, and let the little tree take its chances."

"Under our curacy."

"Curatorship, I think. But yes."

Then, with promises to bring me back a green tea muffin, he leaves me alone.

I do not put music on. There is always music in the shop, whoever is taking the shift. When it is George, it could be Gregorian chant or violin concertos or Bob Dylan. When it is Bruce, it is often English stuff from the sixties. He is always disappointed when I haven't heard of it. David, who is nineteen and wants to be an actor, plays lots of things that apparently sound like Radiohead.

Luke comes in, and takes his guitar upstairs. He carries it in with him most nights, and carries it away at the end. I don't ask him why, probably because he is so taciturn. I so often feel this tension with Luke—I wish I could batter down whatever barrier is between us.

"No music?" he says when he comes down.

"I was between CDs," I say. I have discovered that saying you don't mind silence makes everyone who works in the store uneasy.

Luke does not reply, but sits down in the second chair. He does not speak. I decide I am not going to force him to speak with an opening gambit; I will just be quiet too. We go on sitting, silently. I wonder how a person can be so quiet, why he doesn't want to make friends. Why does he sit with me, if he doesn't want to talk to me?

He gets up, as if to end this line of questioning, and scans the CD shelves.

"What do you like?" he asks.

I can't think what to answer. I wish I had a smattering of knowledge of jazz or folk or hip-hop. To Luke, I am going to sound as if I've landed here from another century. He turns his head to make sure I heard. "What kind of music?"

"I like that aria from *Lakmé,* and Strauss's *Four Last Songs,* and I *love* the bit in *Dido and Aeneas* when she is laid in earth. A lot of Purcell, in fact. And Debussy and Satie."

Luke is staring at me.

"And absolutely *anything* by Mozart," I finish.

"I'm kind of relieved you mention him, because I was thinking that you weren't showing enough appreciation of the classics, there."

"Yes, well, be funny if you like, but Mozart is—"

"You like anything from the twentieth century, or beyond?"

"Yes," I say. It is not a good time to mention that Satie made it to the twentieth century. I know what must be the inevitable next question, and my mind is boiling with nothingness, as it used to chemistry lessons, when my teacher asked me to balance moles. The twentieth century. I try to think of obscure bands to impress Luke. But all I can think of are the Beatles and Abba.

"So? Who?" says Luke, turning to the CDs again.

"From the twentieth century?"

"Or the twenty-first."

"I like Radiohead," I say.

Luke laughs. "Which songs?"

"Lots of them. All of them."

"Who else?"

He is waiting patiently.

"Lady Gaga," I say.

"Really?"

"Yes," I say.

"Interesting. Any more?"

"Björk."

"Right. And what about Elbow? You're English. Do you like Elbow?"

"He's okay," I say.

"So, if I suggested that you have absolutely no idea what you are talking about, how would you feel about that?"

"I would feel that you were an insightful sort of a person."

Luke nods. He flicks the corner of a CD down from the ranks, and opens it.

"We're going to listen to this, from start to finish. You can go upstairs and listen if you like. Your musical education is going to start with this album."

"Is it Elbow? What is it?"

"Never mind. Just go upstairs, sit in the armchair at the back, and pay attention. I don't think you let yourself pay enough attention, Esme."

I look at him, but he is not looking at me; it wasn't as portentous a statement as I thought. Should I feel offended? I don't, at any rate, even though he is surely wrong. I go upstairs, obedient as a well-trained puppy, and sit in the leather chair in the back, reserved for people who are considering making a lavish L. Frank Baum purchase, and I wait for the music.

Now that the pressure is off me, I think I can guess what the music will be. I think that it will be *Kind of Blue,* by Miles Davis.

It's one of those iconic albums that is always on people's lists on Amazon and Facebook and everywhere. I hope it is that, because I have heard it before, and I think it's quite good.

The chair is that old-fashioned leather that is glossy from decades of bottoms, and it is plump and taut. It probably has horse-hair in it. Nothing comfortable, anyway. But it is nice to sit far away from the door, with a bookcase hiding me, under instruction to be still and listen.

A short silence, a crackle, and then the song begins. It is sung by an old man, with a voice that seems thin, and recorded in the bottom of a saucepan. It doesn't sound right. It sounds like he can't sing very well. There are no instruments with him. But as I listen, it is no longer a thin voice, but a rich one, with experience in it that I can't imagine. It is full of suffering, full of hope, with a plaintive-ness that is hard to listen to. It speaks across all the years.

Then I notice the words:

"Takin' away all of my sin, takin' away . . . all of my sin . . ."

Luke is making yet another jibe at me. Is he?

I stand up and go to the edge of the mezzanine. Luke looks up. "You like it?"

I am being narcissistic, oversensitive. There is no twinkle of mischief in Luke's eye.

"What is this?"

"It's the foundation of modern music. If you get this, the rest falls into place."

I come down the stairs, and reach over for the CD case.

I read out: *"Negro Folk Music of Alabama,* volume five."

"Yeah," says Luke.

"Negro Folk Music of Alabama, volume five, is the foundation of modern music?"

"No, sweetheart, not one CD, not ten CDs. But this music, from Alabama, from Mississippi, this is . . ." He stops. He must be thinking he is wasting his time. "It's beautiful, is all. Go back upstairs. I knew you had a problem with your attention span."

I go back, a little sulky now, and I sit down again, and listen.

The music rises and falls, and I listen to the man's voice, and sometimes a woman singing with him, and I know that he is expressing something that I can't express for myself, that I haven't been able even to acknowledge to myself, ever since I saw that blue line in the window in the test. He is being more honest than I can be. I have been pushing it all away; this man is letting it all come in. I don't quite know what he is singing about—something about God—but I do know it is about being in all the dust and the dirt and yet being given the grace to touch the eternal. Tears, of gratitude, or pain, or delight, are pouring down my face. I let it happen. I let the Negro folk music of Alabama, volume five work its strange magic of release and renewal upon me.

"Are you for real?"

I open my eyes, try to focus. I am in the chair, still, but I think I might have been here a long time. I think all of my limbs have been in the same places for a good while. Luke is standing over me, in an aspect that appears to be rather belligerent.

"You were *asleep*?"

"No. No. I just, er—closed my eyes. I liked it. Has it finished?"

"Unbelievable," says Luke, and goes back downstairs.

TODAY IS MY first appointment with the doctor. I made it for four thirty because at one there is a lecture from a postdoc on Richard Diebenkorn, and I love Diebenkorn.

Stella is in the waiting room when I get there; she said earlier that she would try to come, because I "could maybe use some company." She is sitting opposite a couple who are holding hands. The woman is looking at Stella, and now me, with sharp, judging eyes.

Stella is dressed in ripped black tights and high boots and denim shorts. She looks down at her outfit. "Don't say anything. I'm taking photographs at Sappho's," she says. "I have to integrate."

"You look great," I say. The woman's eyes widen.

I am summoned to the desk to fill out the insurance forms.

I ponder what kind of mess I will be in if my insurance doesn't cover it. According to the stunningly unfriendly girl at the desk, it will be a thirty-thousand-dollars kind of mess, unless I have a caesarean, "and then it will be expensive." Thirty thousand just to have a baby? Why? They are conceived, they grow, out they pop. People have them in cabs, on sofas, in fields. Where does the thirty thousand dollars come in?

"How was the lecture, honey?" Stella asks when I sit down again.

"Oh, it was great. I really like Diebenkorn, and he fits in with Thiebaud. I was thinking that if I found a third person that fitted in too, I could write the kind of thesis that you can turn into a popular book. Which wouldn't hurt with the whole career thing. If I could make money writing, I could be with the baby more."

Stella nods. "And you know, I'll still be around. I will help as *much* as I can."

There is a change in the way the couple are sitting, or in the atmosphere of the room. Disapproval hangs in the air. The woman purses up her mouth and glances at her partner, who does not see, but carries on reading his magazine. Stella, unfortunately, does see. She instantly covers my hand with hers.

"I just want you to know that what *you* are doing for *us* is *so* amazing," she says to me, and flashes a big smile at the couple. "She's made me *so* happy," she says to them. The woman starts to smile back automatically, but it dies on her lips. The man just stares.

"Are you here to see Dr. Sokolowski?" asks Stella.

"No. Dr. DeSales," answers the woman with a shade of relief, as if she could be contaminated by having the same doctor, and might wake up lesbian in the morning.

"Where are you guys from?" Stella says. "New York?"

She knows they aren't. Even I can tell that, and I've only been here since August. The woman has a little frizzed fringe and is wearing too many colors, a high stripy polo-neck and a down vest. And she's fat. And she's wearing trainers. Nor does she have any of the weapons that every New Yorker inevitably acquires for their defensive armory: the middle-distance stare, the iPod, the newspaper, the "don't talk to me" radiation field.

"No," says the man, and flexes his magazine to show that he doesn't want to talk.

"No, Esme isn't, either, are you, baby?" says Stella, leering fondly at me. "She's from Englandshire."

"Esme Garland," says the receptionist. Thank God. I get up and whisper in Stella's ear, "Stay here, you lunatic. I want to go in by myself."

I was expecting Dr. Sokolowski to be a woman. He isn't. He is a melancholy old man, and he is sitting behind a huge oak desk. He looks up, smiles bleakly, and says, "Miss Garland. I am Bartosz Sokolowski."

"Pleased to meet you," I say.

"So you got yourself in a little trouble?"

That makes me laugh. "Do you say that to all your pregnant patients?"

"No, no. I take sometimes a chance, and I see"—he taps his notes—"that you are European." He waves all that aside, indicates that I should sit down, runs through the obligatory questions. He sighs.

"Please get undressed behind the curtain. Put on the robe that you see there. It opens up the front."

I nod.

"Since I don't see you before, I will give you a whole examination," he says.

"Okay," I say. I don't expect him to be enthusiastic about this prospect, but he seems to be feeling lackluster about the whole encounter.

I come out in the green front-fastening gown. I am to lie down on the examining couch. He gets two paper towels and lays them assiduously in the stirrups.

"The metal is cold," he explains.

He checks my breasts and my tummy, and then does an internal exam, first with his fingers, then with the cold prongy thing that I have never seen but I imagine to look like an Alessi lemon squeezer. Then he washes his hands and goes over to the window. He sighs again. I am lying there practically naked, the gown open.

"Ah, Miss Garland from England," he says, looking out over the rooftops of the Upper West Side. The sky is azure blue, and the next rooftop that I can see has pots full of orange lantern flowers on it, and a table and chairs. It appears to afford him no pleasure.

"Is everything all right?" I ask. I am worried that he has found something awful.

"Of course," he says, and relapses into silence. Then he says, "You are young. You have everything ahead of you. When you have lived so long as I have, seen so much as I have seen, the savor goes out of your life. Perhaps it is best, so we do not cling on. You have chlamydia, but treatment is simple."

"I have chlamydia?" I say.

"Yes, but many people who are very sexually active have this. We can treat immediately with antibiotics."

He is still looking out of the window, and I still have my legs up in the air. My sadness flares up like a match lit in the dark. Very sexually active. I am one of many.

He turns back into the room, walks back over to me.

"And also you are a witch. You know this?"

I look up into his face. He looks back with wide-open blue eyes. "I am a witch?"

"Certainly." He indicates two moles on my torso. "Secondary nipples—they are to feed a familiar. The witch's mark."

I tug my gown edges together. This is so different from the National Health Service.

"It isn't to worry about, Miss Garland. It is special, but not to worry about. You can get dressed now."

When I come out dressed from behind the screen, he indicates a microscope on the desk. It is facing towards me.

"Look, please."

I look. There are hundreds of horrible cell things on the slide.

They look like bacteria, but I have no idea. They might be anything.

"This is what is in your vagina. It is chlamydia."

Etiquette books are a little hazy on the proper response to this sort of remark. I say, "How interesting."

"This example, it is not from your vagina, but if we sent a sample off to a lab, we would see something very similar."

"So I am looking at chlamydia from someone *else's* vagina?"

He clicks the light on the microscope off.

I say, "Can you tell how long I have had it?"

"No, impossible. It can be dormant for many years, or it can be a fresh infection. It is bacteria." He hands me a prescription. "It is important to take this. You do not want still to have this when the baby comes. It is possible that it causes blindness in the baby."

I must have a very readable face. His expression softens. "Do not worry. It is easy to be treated. We will treat it. Your baby will be all right."

"Right. Thank you."

"At this stage of your pregnancy, I would normally see you each four or five weeks, but make an appointment for three, because of the chlamydia. You will also have a dating scan very soon, yes? The twelve-week scan, I mean. Good luck, Miss Garland. It is a pleasure to meet you."

Stella is not there when I get out. She has left a note with the receptionist. It says, "Lesbian bondage waits for no woman."

I wish I were a witch. I would cast pentagrams against hurt.

✦

AT FIVE, I get a call from George, asking if I can possibly fill in for an hour, as he is on a book call and Bruce has an appointment downtown. I say I can, and when would he like me.

"Now," he says. "I've got Barney sitting there looking after the store. Take a cab and pay for it out of the register."

Barney is a regular customer.

"Okay," I say, "but Barney can manage."

"Barney's a lawyer," says George. "If he opens the cash register he'll bill me for five hundred dollars. But he's agreed to sit there until you arrive."

When I get there, Barney says, "Darling, I am so glad to see you. Once or twice in the last few minutes, I've been dangerously near to a sale. But I can stay for a while—my friend Philippe is picking me up from here." He tilts his chin up, appraising me.

He often comes in late in the evening, and talks to George or Luke. He rarely takes much notice of me, but today he is short of options.

"You should wear Ralph Lauren. You would really suit Ralph Lauren."

"Thank you. But Ralph Lauren is beyond my price range."

"George said you were on some fancy scholarship at Columbia. But even if money is an issue—is there a man in this scenario?" He nods at my stomach.

"No," I say. "No man."

"So, my darling, the Ralph Lauren would be an *investment*. It's going to be very tough to find a man now that Junior's coming along. You need to bait your hook."

"I'm going to straighten up the aisles. They're looking really untidy."

Barney doesn't seem to be influenced by the fact that I have gone. He carries on talking to me, just in a louder tone, calling out, "Oh, wait a second, does he even *do* maternity? I'll google it."

I pick up the books that have slid into the aisles from their precarious piles.

"No maternity wear from Ralph," he sings out. "Not that I can see, anyway. But . . . no man? You didn't play that so well."

I come back to the front. He is leafing through a big coffee table book. "Barney," I say quietly. "There are customers. I am sure they don't want to know all about my private life."

Barney lays his head to one side, considering me. In a more normal tone, he says, "Does he even know? That he's going to be a father? Do you know who it was? Was it a one-night stand?"

He has that New York conviction that if you want to know something, you just ask it. The other party is free to answer or not. Unless your upbringing gives you no choice.

"Yes, of course I know who it was. And he does know. Please can we not talk about this?"

His eyes open wide. "And he wants *nothing* to do with it?"

"I don't think he does. He . . . shall we just say he's not involved, now?"

"Is he married?"

"No, no."

"Then what's his problem? How old is he? What does he do? What is his background?"

"Barney . . ."

"Come on, tell me. Maybe we can figure him out."

"I don't know . . . there's nothing . . ."

"Did he ask you to have an abortion?"

I hesitate, and so of course he says, "He *did*! And you wouldn't! Does George know this?"

"No, why . . . Barney, nobody needs to know this stuff."

"It's all over, with this guy?"

I say it is completely and absolutely over. Barney is looking closely at me. I can see why he makes a good lawyer.

"And you're devastated. That it's all over."

I am not going to say, *Why yes, Barney, that's absolutely true*. I say instead, "I'm all right, as a matter of fact."

He begins to browse through his book again. "Sweetheart, let me give you a word of advice. Get the guy's name on the birth certificate. You don't know what's ahead; nobody does. Do yourself a favor and write his name in great big letters in indelible ink, right in the column marked 'father.'"

"What kind of lawyer are you, Barney?"

"Corporate," he says.

A woman comes to the front of the shop to buy a couple of paperbacks. She nods. "He's right, sugar."

I take the money for the books.

"I am totally right," says Barney. He stares down at the book on his knee. "Oh, my, where is *that*?" he says. "The Church of the Ascension in Priego de Córdoba. Esme, look at this—you're into art, right, and architecture? Look at this place."

The woman smiles at me and leaves just as a very thin and handsome man comes in.

"Wouldn't that be just like being in a wedding cake? I've got to see that for real. Oh, Philippe, hello, hello. Look at this! It's in Spain, in Andalusia. I was just telling Esme that I have to see it."

Philippe expresses suitable admiration. Barney makes a note of the name of the place and shuts the book with a clap. He catches sight of a man ambling by in a blue T-shirt, with a huge belly.

"Oh *dear*. Look, Esme, that guy passing now—he's completely given up on women. You can tell by the way he dresses. Get my point about Ralph Lauren? I guarantee that guy is sitting there each night, watching *America's Next Top Model* and getting the pages of *Truck and Track* very sticky. Philippe, shall we go to Cafe Lalo? I am dying to try their new peanut butter mousse cake."

I am still alone in the shop when a customer comes in wearing pale green trousers with elastic cuffs at the bottom. He asks for George and for Luke, thus establishing his credentials as a regular. I remember the mention of green trousers from my first day, but I can't quite recall his particular peculiarity. He has ginger hair, parted to one side, and it curls a little over his ears. He looks anxious, and rocks slightly on his heels and wets his lips with his tongue before he speaks again. It is to ask if I have read *Lolita*. Now I remember.

"Yes," I say.

"How old were you when you read it?"

"I don't remember."

"Prepubescent?"

"I don't remember."

"Nabokov is my favorite writer. A lot of people underestimate him."

"But not you."

"No. I think I am one of the few people who have a true sense of his stature. I collect Nabokov—first editions, juvenilia, ephemera . . . I won one of his cardigans on eBay two weeks ago. I like to think he wore it when he was writing the sofa episode."

He stands still, waiting for me to speak. I say, "How can you be sure it is authentic?"

"There is a certificate, and I traced the provenance very carefully. And there are photographs of him in it. Well, one photograph."

"Ah."

"If you ever come across anything to do with Nabokov, no matter how inconsequential it might seem to you, please e-mail me. I'll make it worth your while." He hands me a card with "Chester Mason" written on it, and an e-mail address. I thank him. He holds his hand out to me.

"And your name is?" he asks.

"Esme Garland."

"Esme Garland—oh, you're the one . . ." He drops my hand. I am glad, because it was not a pleasant experience. He is backing away from me, with the same kind of restrained revulsion you would have if you were backing away from a deadly snake or a spider.

"Is anything the matter?" I say, although I think I know. The man who is captivated by a fictional nymphet is not going to be enthusiastic when confronted with a real pregnant woman. I feel like advancing on him down the aisle, womb-first.

"No," says Chester, his face averted. "George mentioned that you were . . ." He bumps hard into a bookshelf. "I'll just be at the N's . . ."

As he disappears into the nether regions of the bookshop and his own psyche, he is overtaken with a spasm through his whole body.

George comes back a little while later, disappointed, from a book call that yielded just one bag of novels. I do not need to help; I am released to study at home.

CHAPTER TEN

I am upstairs one day involved in the ever-absorbing task of data entry when the door opens and a tall man comes in. He is wearing sunglasses and a greatcoat that Dickens would have been happy in. Now, it is the afternoon, and Americans wear sunglasses more readily than English people, owing to the fact that there is sometimes some sunshine here. Today, though, it is very dull, and even now that he finds himself in the warm gloom of The Owl, he hasn't taken them off. This means he's either a jerk, or he's famous. Either way, he's going to be stumbling about like Mr. Magoo in a minute.

He glances at Luke, but Luke is deep inside the *New York Times*, and doesn't look up. The man, who has the floppy kind of hair that makes me think of posh boys at Eton in the 1930s, starts to look at the grammar and dictionaries section. He appears to be staring at our nine copies of Strunk and White, next to our much neglected Liddell and Scott. He keeps his hands in his pockets.

"Can I help you?" I call from the mezzanine. To turn to speak to me, he has to make a quarter turn. Most people in the world would do this. This man spins round the other way, through 270 degrees, and points up at me.

"I hope you can," he says. Okay.

He comes up the stairs and when he is at the top he leans on the banister. He takes his sunglasses off and runs a careless hand through his hair. It is Lyle Moore—international star of stage and screen. Well, screen. He has just won an Oscar for *Sapphire Dark*. There are probably women who would faint right now.

"You're Lyle Moore!" I say.

"I know," he says. "The truth is," he continues, now putting his head to one side to stretch his neck, and shutting his eyes, "the truth is that I am feeling stressed. I need a little quiet, a little calm. I thought I would come in here and—you know—chill a little bit?" He opens his eyes again, looks straight into mine.

"Oh, yes, well, feel free . . . ," I say. "There's—you know—a—a chair at the back here, if you want to sit and read quietly . . ."

He smiles, with the whitest of teeth. Then he looks down, shakes his head, smiles, and then looks back up. In real life, he favors the acting style of the guys who play adorable vampires.

"So, do you work here?"

I so evidently work here. He must have good directors. I am thinking this, but it doesn't matter what I am saying. My heart is pounding, and I desperately want to create a good impression. I say, "Was there a particular book you were looking for?"

"Yes," he says, and smiles again. It's like a weapon. "I want a book that is a classic and is still a great book to read."

I have a mischievous impulse to offer him *Lyle, Lyle, Crocodile*.

"I think you would like Graham Greene," I say, as I have just glanced around the shelves in a panic and seen his name filling a thick spine. "*The Power and the Glory* is wonderful."

"Why?"

"There's a great scene where a priest fights a dog for a bone," I say. He gazes at me in silence. Maybe I should say something insightful about the overarching meaning of the book, but I can't think of anything. Anyway, a *priest* fights a *dog* for a *bone*? I'd read the book that that was in.

"Okay," he says. "So, do you have a copy of this . . . *The Power and the Glory*?"

I go to the mezzanine railing and reach for it.

"Here," I say. "Greene was fascinated by God and guilt and death. Or Catholicism, for short."

"Right," says Lyle, flirting the pages with his thumb. "You're saying Greene's kind of a big deal."

"Yes, I think so."

He traces his finger down the blurb on the inside flap, and says, "So he's English." I am worried that he will think I am just recommending writers from my own village pump. I try to think of some Americans. I am surrounded by them. Who, who? The one who wrote about the horses.

"A lot of people think that one of the best writers of the last hundred years was David Niven," I announce.

"David Niven? That name sounds familiar."

"Yes. I think he has won the Pulitzer, and he wrote *Bring on the Empty Horses*—it won lots of awards, and it got made into a movie. It is supposed to exemplify Southern Gothic." As he looks blank again I say, "Like *Midnight in the Garden of Good and Evil*," and his face clears.

"Kevin Spacey," he says.

"Yes," I say.

I glance down because downstairs Luke has moved, suddenly, as if in response to what I am saying. He vanishes down the side aisle for a moment, and then runs lightly up to us.

"Here's a copy of the Niven," he says, handing it to Lyle Moore. "Good to see you. *In the Wintertime* was a good movie."

Lyle holds the book up at him in thanks, and then says, "Right, I guess I will go and sit back there for a spell."

He heads to the back of the mezzanine—the chair is hidden by a high bookcase full of leather-bound books and what George calls "ancient treasures." He can chill there for as long as he likes without being disturbed.

I go downstairs to see Luke, to marvel that we have a Hollywood A-lister upstairs. George has arrived, and is sitting on the second seat, so I stand at the counter. The store is now speckled with customers.

"What shall we do with him?" I ask.

"Do with him? We haven't captured him, Esme—he's not a golden marmoset or anything. Unless you want to creep up on him with your phone, take pictures you can send to *People* magazine?"

"Who are we talking about?" asks George pleasantly.

"We're talking about Lyle Moore—the actor. Esme's got him all settled in upstairs, reading David Niven."

George looks mystified. "David Niven? Oh, because of the acting."

"No. Because he's under the impression that Niven is the greatest writer of the last century. Thanks to Esme."

I clap my hands to my face. "Oh, Lord."

"*All the Pretty Horses,*" says Luke. "The pretty ones. Not the empty ones."

"But you *brought* him a copy of the Niven!" I say to Luke.

George is grinning broadly. "Esme, you should go and set the poor boy straight," he says. "You don't want him on Jon Stewart or Jay Leno talking about David Niven in the same breath as Philip Roth and Faulkner."

"All right," I say, despondently. "I'm going to sound great. 'Hi, I was so nervous because you're famous that I got mixed up between David Niven and Cormac McCarthy. And I have a hole in my tights.'"

"I think you blew your big chance," says Luke. "Never mind that he's dating Palermo Crianza and just broke up with Tamsin Bell."

Lyle appears at the top of the stairs with the copy of *Bring on the Empty Horses.*

As he comes down, I say, "I'm sorry, I told you the wrong book."

"No, you didn't," he says. "This is perfect. I'll take it."

CHAPTER ELEVEN

I am organized now, and make every second count, so that when I do laundry I am reading Danto, and when I have to sit at the front in The Owl I read Panofsky. I have Adam Gopnik to read in bed, and aesthetics journals in the bathroom; there is hardly a moment wasted.

I also read about what to eat, drink, do, think, and listen to for the good of the baby. I read *American Baby,* because I am going to have one. There are many things to worry about, and just about every worry can be lessened by a purchase. Unless you thoughtlessly purchase something worrying. You can apparently give your baby "head cancer" by using sodium lauryl sulfate, which is in most shampoos. Alternative shampoo-makers have lovingly removed it from their recipes, but rascally ones keep it in there, because it's cheap and foamy. The dangers of sodium lauryl sulfate are entirely fictional, as far as I can see, part of Internet-spread mythology—like all the dire warnings that my mother used to forward to me, about having my liver stolen in underground car parks in Nottingham.

There seems no end to the efforts to which pregnant women are exhorted for the sake of the fetus—play Bach, read Keats, take up aquarobics, abjure sad thoughts, and one that I respond to with especial sourness: "Be sure to get Daddy to talk to the bump. This can be a very precious bonding experience for all three of you." There is a picture of a woman who surely only lives in the pages of American magazines, wearing linen and cotton in Maine shades. She is smiling up towards the ceiling as she lies on her white sofa, smiling with her white teeth, as the father bends his ear to the giant bump, and smiles with his white teeth too. I cannot stop staring at the picture. She is a deliriously happy incubator, proud to be perpetuating the American dream in shades of taupe and pale blue.

The baby magazines have advertisements for new ways to separate fools from their money, including a pregnancy belly-cast kit. You get to make a huge plaster mold of your huge giant fleshy belly for twenty dollars, optionally *including your breasts*. It comes with acrylic paints so that you can decorate it. Then what do you do with it? Put it above the fireplace?

You can also "join the momversation at Momversation.com," and so I do, because my critical faculties are in abeyance. The post that is blazoned across its homepage is "Did you pick the right mate to co-parent your child?" Er, no. I didn't.

There are lots of pictures of dads in the magazines, strong of jaw and loving in aspect, and even if they are model men posing as model dads, the effect of seeing a minuscule bundle in the arms of one of these guys makes me wistful.

I think I might be lonely. I met Mitchell so soon after I arrived here that I stupidly haven't forged proper friendships with other people, except for Stella. I always mean to see Beth, my friend from the art gallery, for instance, but Mitchell always seemed to be the next person I ought to see; he was always the person who had just texted me, who had just e-mailed me, who was covering me with attention apparently as light as Irish rain, which actually soaked me to the skin. And now I'm in a dry season. If I try to make friends now, they will assume I see them as second tier, so I can't do it. I wish that I could tell Mitchell about the funny belly-cast kits, I wish I could ask him to come with me to the scan. I wish that the phone would ring this minute. It would be Mitchell, and he would say, "Oh, Esme. I love you."

At first, after he walked out of my apartment, I checked my phone compulsively for messages. None came. I haven't heard anything from him since. I have been shoving Mitchell out of my head whenever he has come near it. Americans call it denial, but I call it Getting Over Someone. It is a slow process. I still miss him. But not enough to call him.

Before the semester ends, I have two papers due: one on the masculine gaze, and one on Thiebaud, which might stand, if it's good enough, for one of the chapters of my thesis. Professor Henkel says that I should really present a paper to the department in the spring, and the idea of it makes me go cold with fear. There are now twenty minutes ahead of me in the spring when everyone will find out I am an imposter. I can see it: some curled darling of a PhD student—Bradley Brinkman springs to mind—will stand there in his scruffy clothes that are themselves an implicit decla-ration of his personal beauty, and he will ask me questions with unseen brackets in the middle of words, with a nod to Derrida and a little side joke about Hegel, and I will stand there for a second, rooted with fear, and then bolt out of the room as my notes float gently to the ground.

Women are more scared of this. Other women seem as scared as I am, while the men seem generally to look forward to it. Why are we scared? Is it because we are *giving* a lecture, giving our thoughts, our words, ourselves, launching ourselves out there as if we were chicks leaving the nest? Is it because our gift might be rejected?

I want to have an impeccable CV—the one accomplishment that the baby magazines touch but lightly—so I will have to do it.

It is easy to write about the male gaze in this city, where Rem-brandts and Vermeers and Picassos and Sargents are sprinkled about like sweets.

The other paper is about Thiebaud's influences, and I have been having some fun with some of that, from the early paint-ers of still lifes with dead geese and beautiful lemons right up to

Thiebaud's pictures, of cakes with their impasto of icing, of serried soup bowls, of a live white rabbit. Edward Hopper is supposed to be his biggest influence, but Hopper's people stare out from their own souls, suspended in a kind of ether of misery. In Thiebaud, there is the sort of sadness inherent in nostalgia, but also a joie de vivre, a joie de gateau.

I am trying to sort out my thoughts about this when I get another call from The Owl, and there is a tiny pang of pleasure when I see the number on my phone. I think they are going to ask me to come in.

After expressing hopes that he isn't disturbing me, George then proceeds to disturb me very much by voicing his concerns about ultrasound scans. The concerns all sound very rational, but this is a man who thinks headache tablets are deadly.

"Wouldn't more people talk about this if it were such an issue?" I ask. I am looking forward to the scan.

"There are a lot of people invested in not talking about it," he says. "Just because it is not surgical, do not be misled into thinking it is not intrusive. When I see you, I can give you more information."

"Okay," I say, dolefully. "Are you busy there? Do you need any help? It isn't that long until Christmas—I could come in and tidy up, ready for—"

"We're fine. It's just me and Luke but it's not busy. And we've got Thanksgiving on Thursday, so we don't need to focus on Christmas just yet. Stay home and do some studying. We'll see you for your shift tomorrow night."

I had forgotten Thanksgiving. Mitchell described a van Leuven Thanksgiving to me once in meticulous and malicious detail. He said that in rebellion, we would have Thanksgiving alone in his apartment, with a table festooned with orange paper turkeys, and then sex on the sofa. And then we would feel very thankful.

The phone rings again. It is George again.

"We were assuming you had Thanksgiving plans, Esme, but Luke says that I should ask you. We always have a small Thanksgiving celebration at my apartment, up in Washington Heights. Everyone from the bookshop is always invited. David can't come— I think he's going home for Thanksgiving—but Bruce comes, and Luke is coming this year. And so is Barney, and so is Mary, with or without the dog. You would be welcome."

That tumbling mixture of gratitude and misery; I want to be with Mitchell and his silly paper turkeys. The disappointment is so tangible I could chew it, the kindness with its casual delivery so like George I feel hot tears rise up.

"Luke says to tell you it's going to be vegan."

"No turkey?"

"I'm afraid not. Nor even the vegetarian approximations of it; no Tofurkey, no igturkey. And although personally, I have some grave suspicions about the ontology of mushrooms, we will be having organic mushroom roast."

"Norman Rockwell wouldn't like it."

"The turkeys, by contrast, are overjoyed."

"Thank you, George. I would love to come."

"We'll see you Thursday."

✦

I TAKE CRANBERRY sauce and applesauce to the Thanksgiving, as instructed by George, to go with the turkey that won't be there.

George's apartment looks like a storehouse for Bergdorf Goodman windows that a giant has stirred with a spoon. There are books everywhere, of course, on shelves, in piles—that was pretty much in the cards. But there are also the most peculiar and off-the-wall things propped everywhere: In a small patch of wall between two shelves, the pottery face of a Green Man looks wickedly down. Against a bookshelf that contains about a dozen volumes of the letters of Erasmus, a huge pale blue cardboard compass with golden lines on it is propped, and in front of me, two welded metal turkey cocks whose tails are dozens of rolled-up pieces of tin stand next to a little naked manikin made of newspaper—I think he is made from the *New York Times,* as he has an upside-down picture of Paul Krugman on his tummy. There are evident pathways through all this to a small clearing in the middle of the sitting room. Luke and Mary are already holding glasses. I produce my two Ziplocs full of sauce.

"Plastic!" says George, in tones of horror.

"Food-safe! For thirty minutes!" I say.

He takes them gingerly, then buzzes Barney in. Barney is walking into the center of the room when his attention is caught by a lamp on the top of a bookshelf—it is an ordinary turned wooden lamp base, with a parchment shade.

He pauses midgreeting to say, "Oh my, George, is that shade made out of plainchant? On vellum? Is it real? I don't care, I love it, I love the whole ensemble. How much do you want for it?"

George passes a glass of fizzy elderflower to me. "Barney. This is my home. The things in it are not for sale. Would you like a glass of *prosecco*?"

"Oh, that's a shame," Barney says, completely unfazed. "I brought a pumpkin pie. It's from Dean and DeLuca. I needed a bank loan to buy it, seriously. Oh, and I brought champagne. Hi, honey. How's the baby coming along?" He sits down next to me and beams. "I totally fucked up on that lamp thing, didn't I? I'm usually a lot classier than that, believe me. Still no sign of the father? What's so funny?"

By the time we have finished the pumpkin pie and the peach cobbler that Mary brought, I am the only completely sober one, and I don't feel sober; the company and sugar combined are making me feel giddy. Mary has just had one glass. The others, though, are all well beyond counting.

Barney is eating slice after slice of vegan cheese, remarking on how revolting it is after each mouthful. He is saying, "Seriously, how does anyone get pregnant by accident in this day and age? Or no—more interesting question—why anyone gets pregnant on purpose in this day and age?"

"You think I got pregnant on purpose?"

"Is the pope gay?" replies Barney.

"I think 'Catholic' is the adjective you're looking for there, Barney," says George.

"I got pregnant by *accident*," I say.

Luke says, "They say there is no such thing as an accident."

"There is such a thing as an accident."

"Not according to Freud," says George.

"I'm serious," says Barney. "I'm really serious. Esme, look at you, you're a smart girl, with everything ahead of you—what would induce you to take the risk unless you wanted it to happen?"

"I didn't want it to happen."

"Not consciously, maybe . . ."

I sigh. There is no argument against "not consciously, maybe."

"Is he rich? The guy?"

"That isn't important. That wasn't what it was about."

They all, except Mary, look as if enlightenment has dawned, even George.

"How rich?" says Barney. "What does he do?"

"He teaches economics at the New School," I say.

"Oh. Then he's from money already," says Barney. "What's his name? Esme? What's his *name*?"

"Mitchell van Leuven," I say. "No, Barney, do *not* google him, we're in the middle of a Thanksgiving dinner . . ."

He takes no notice. "How are you spelling it?"

I say, "I don't suppose anyone will believe me, but it wasn't ever about his being rich."

Mary says, "I believe you."

Luke says, "What was it about?"

I say, "It was about love. I fell in love with him."

"Yeah, we get that part. But why?"

I hesitate. "His iconoclasm, I think."

Barney rolls his eyes. "Ask a graduate student a simple question . . ."

"He's teaching economics at the New School?" says George. "He doesn't sound like much of an iconoclast to me."

"Would everyone mind," says Barney, "if we get back to the whole 'how rich is he' thing? This is going down a track I won't be able to follow for long."

✳

ON THE MONDAY after Thanksgiving, there are so many good back-to-back lectures that I skip lunch. This is the error of an idiot, and as I am pregnant, I feel guilty as well as hungry. I think I will get something between the end of the last lecture and the beginning of my shift, but Professor Vincenzo Caspari, as august a figure as it is possible to be without being dead, is delivering it, and it even has a name—"The Fermor Lecture"—so he can take just as long as he likes. Professor Caspari has an intellect as fine as his suit, and he is lecturing on the multiple lives of paintings. It is fantastic, but it overruns by twenty-five minutes. I will be late for work.

I fly out onto the street to find it pouring with rain, and all the cabs speeding by. People are standing with newspapers over their heads, vainly trying to flag one. They try to upstage one another by walking a few yards north, in order to bag the first cab. I can't compete in this environment—I'll end up walking to the Bronx. It would be quicker taking the local.

I go down into the subway, and the train does not come. From the fretful aspect of most of the people already on the platform, I gather there hasn't been one for a while. I try to calm down. I hate to be late.

The rain falls through the grating onto the track, making it glisten. I like that about the New York subway, that it is so close to the surface. In London, you are plunged down into the bowels of the earth, but here, you can tell what the weather is like outside. I hope they reinforce the ground where the tunnels are. It would be scary to think we are all walking about on a pastry crust.

After ten more minutes, the train arrives. It takes me to 79th and I join the press of soggy people on the subway stairs, then run full tilt to work. I burst into the bookshop full of apologies and explanations and raindrops, and they all peter out as I look around. The two lamps on the walls that nobody ever remembers to turn on are lit. There are no customers. It is all tidy. George is not here. Luke is sitting on the chair with his eyes closed, his iPod earphones in his ears. He hasn't heard me. I can hear the scratchy banjo music blaring out of the earbuds. Anyone could reach the till and rob the place.

I lean over to the till and press the "subtotal" button to see. The drawer whooshes open. I look back at Luke, who is now regarding me with steady brown eyes. He tugs the earphones out so they are around his neck.

"I was just seeing if I could rob you without your noticing," I say.

Luke nods. "That's what most thieves say, right before I beat the crap out of them."

"I am sorry to be late. My lectures ran on."

"Don't worry about it," he says.

I sit down heavily. Luke is now fiddling with the iPod. Without looking up, he says, "Go take your coat off, dry off, then you can come back and do some work."

But now that I've made it to work, a new urgent need takes over. I am so hungry I can hardly function. I am hallucinating hamburgers.

"Do you mind if I just go quickly to Zabar's before they close? I—I haven't eaten all day. I had seminars and meetings and lectures all day and I didn't—"

"Yeah, go."

When I come back, I sort myself out properly, then sit down and arrange my dinner on the counter. I have bought a piece of poached salmon with dill, and a rocket salad, a bagel, a slice of chocolate cake, and some water. Luke looks impassively at all this. I tuck in.

"So, Columbia and Zabar's. You have expensive taste."

I have just tasted the poached salmon. It is outstanding. I smile in delight at him because it tastes so good. He looks discomfited.

"I don't shop at Zabar's normally," I say. "It's just that it was close and it was raining and I was hungry."

I don't bother explaining again about Columbia and the scholarship. When someone has decided to resent you for your privilege, it takes a lot of work to shift their perceptions, and I am tired.

I eat some more. I waggle a bit of salmon at him and ask him if he wants to try it. He shakes his head quickly, looking repelled.

When I have eaten everything and tidied it all away, I go upstairs. I am going to spend the night doing data entry, uploading books onto the Internet. It will keep me from arousing the ire of Luke.

I spend a soothing couple of hours on the mezzanine, typing in authors, titles, ISBNs, keywords, condition—condition is my special favorite. I am learning book lore from George, and now I can do basic condition quite well. The words are becoming familiar and beloved, in the way that the shipping forecast is for my father. Very good in fine. Fine in very good. A bright copy. A crisp copy. A fair copy. A small quarto in three-quarters calf. Rubbing to spine. Lightly sunned. Slightly foxed. Signed on front free endpaper. Top edge gilt. All edges gilt.

I work so hard and so silently through the rainy evening that my lateness or spoiledness, or whatever it is that bothers Luke about me, seems to lose its power. By ten thirty, he is a lot more mellow. He comes up the stairs with some books and puts them away at the back. When he comes past me again, he pauses and says, "Quiet night."

I agree. There is a sudden run of customers for about half an hour, and then one customer all the rest of the night, the man who comes to look for dictionaries. He comes in his mackintosh, stashes his umbrella in a plastic bag, looks damply at the dictionaries for a while, buys a biography of Jimmy Durante, and goes away again.

"I burned you a CD."

I am surprised. He shrugs, looks the other way, says it's no big deal, that someone ought to teach me something about music before it is too late, that this will make me see where the big stars got things from, that he is thinking of getting a beer, that he hopes the Yankees will win Saturday.

"Put it on!" I say.

He looks reluctant. I say it again. He goes downstairs and puts the CD on the player.

As the first caterwauls sound, he says, "I'm gonna get some beers. Can I get you anything?"

"Yes. Can I have dandelion and burdock, please, or ginger beer, or—something that looks a bit like a beer but isn't?"

"Dandelion and burdock? There's a drink made from dandelions?"

"Yes," I say innocently. "Mashed-up dandelions, that have to be picked on a full moon. No idea what a burdock is. But the drink is delicious."

"It might be, but the Koreans won't have it. I'll bring you a root beer if they have no ginger. I'll be back in a little bit."

I come down the stairs and sit in the main chair while he's gone. The second song is another plaintive one, like the ones he played me the other night. I am not sure how we're going to get to Lady Gaga from these sad old men on porches in the Deep South. But as it did the other night, the music resonates with me, and I am again close to tears by the time Luke comes back.

"That's my chair," he says. The tears recede. The next song is "You've Got a Friend."

"Oh, I know this one!" I say. I don't see that it has anything in common with the others. I say so. To be specific, I say, "This isn't like all those banjoey fiddley things you keep playing."

Luke raises his eyebrows fractionally, but says nothing.

We open the beers—mine is bitingly strong ginger—and we sit in silence and listen.

I can't help myself. I say, "But really. Isn't this just straightforward American stuff? Like Frank Sinatra and—and Perry Como?"

I am briefly proud of myself over Perry Como. I pull him out like a rabbit from a hat. But maybe I should have said Elvis or the Everly Brothers.

There is no reaction from Luke. He doesn't change his position, he doesn't look at me, he doesn't say anything. Then, after a minute or two, he stands up. He is bounded by the bookshelves and the counter; the only way out is by passing in front of my seat. I get up, and he goes past me and upstairs without a word.

I think he has gone up there to have a good sulk because I have hurt his feelings about the song. But he comes down again immediately, holding a guitar. I have to get up again. All in total silence.

He turns the CD music off, sits down with the guitar, and twiddles the knobs to get it tuned. Is it likely to have become untuned since he last played it?

He is wearing a red checked shirt, jeans, and a denim jacket. He has stubble on his face. His jaw is very American and angular, like the Prometheus statue at the Rockefeller Plaza ice rink. Not quite so golden, though. His hair is dark. It needs a bit of a cut. Sometimes he wears a bandana, but not today. I never really look at Luke, because I worry that he would see me looking. He is intent on tuning the guitar, so he doesn't know he is under scrutiny. He looks nice.

"It's really kind of you to make—"

He shakes his head, in a fine amalgam of "it was nothing" and "shut up."

Without taking his eyes from the neck of the guitar, he says, "It isn't a straightforward song. It just *sounds* like it is."

He is strumming a little now.

"You probably think James Taylor wrote this song," he says. He is still overestimating my musical capacities. "But it was Carole King. She used to work in the Brill Building—just down the road here. Broadway and 49th. Carole King played it on the piano. James Taylor put the twang into it by playing it on the guitar.

"Everybody thinks it's a modern American folk song, but it isn't, it's a New York song. It's taking elements from the things I played you already, from Mississippi, Tennessee . . . it's got bluegrass in it for sure . . . but it's like New York—it takes all those things and makes something new."

I feel like a nature photographer who has managed to get very close to a mountain gorilla. I am worried that if I say something encouraging or pretend I know what he means, he will notice I am a human and bolt. I have to crouch there, Attenborough-like, and be as inconspicuous and nonirritating as possible.

He is plucking the strings now, seemingly at random, and suddenly the plucking resolves itself into something that promises beauty. A little late, I realize it is the opening bars of "You've Got a Friend."

"See, that was all the minor stuff at the beginning—'nothing is going right'—all minor, everything mournful and miserable, and then it builds up—'even the darkest night'—and then you fall into the chorus with a major seventh—'You just call . . . '—and then you build, you build to the climax—'I'll be there'—and then the suspension, and the opening riff again—it's just beautiful—and just when you think it's going to end he introduces the bridge, 'I'll be there / Hey ain't it good to know that you've got a friend . . . ,' and see, he pedals with a G on the bottom, but he plays an F, then a C over it—it's great—you get chords just thrown in that hadn't been there before . . . and the chorus . . . Carole King did it straight, but James Taylor used Joni Mitchell and stacked up those fourths, just great harmony . . . it makes it lonesome even though you feel better when you're in it—"

"Will you play it?" I almost whisper. "The whole song?"

He does. He plays those opening bars again, and sings the song, and his voice has yearning in it like that old man's in the Deep South had the other night.

His hands are brown, so different from Mitchell's. His fingers press hard on the strings and go white where he presses, and his fingernails are as big as dimes. He's right about the lonesomeness in the chorus. Lonesome, not lonely, because it has a whiff of mouth organs and mint juleps about it. It has the same magic a violin sometimes has, of being lost, and longing, and then, even when you think there is a resolution, of there still being heartache in it.

When he finishes, my eyes are full of tears, and I get up and walk to the back of the shop so he won't see. I am sure Luke would interpret the tears as sentimentality. He is fiddling about with the strings, playing a chirpy little thing. I think he is playing it to get us back to somewhere ordinary. I am glad.

"Come back and finish your beer," he calls out after a minute or two. "There's nothing going on tonight. You've done enough work."

I come back.

"That was lovely," I say. "Thank you."

"Yeah, well, you need someone to teach you something," he says. He turns and looks out of the window. "It's one hell of a night."

The rain is still crashing down in the dark. It is nearly midnight.

I love it most in the rain, I think, in the night rain when it rains and rains and rains like this, and Broadway glistens, and the Zabar's sign glows, and the wet street reflects all the headlights and the traffic lights and there is the canary yellow of the cabs against the black, and people running by, a short burst of speed to get somewhere sparkling and warm again. On these winter nights we are still open until midnight, so a Monday night in the rain in January, like this, this is a good night. When it rains here it's torrential, drenching and incessant, and I want to dance outside in it and turn my face up into it.

But I don't, of course. We sit without speaking, and listen to the music, looking out from our glowing little jewel of a shop onto the rainy night of New York.

⚜ CHAPTER TWELVE ⚜

I get up very early. Five forty-five A.M. Today I have my twelve-week scan, the "dating scan." After this, I get an official due date, although I know it is going to be 266 days from the no-condom day. That would make the baby due on July 20.

The scan is not until ten thirty, but my paper on the male gaze needs finishing touches. So I work on that until it is time to go.

This scan is to check that everything is in the right place, that everything is as it should be. The letter says I am to drink a pint of water an hour before the scan. I imagine the water is to plump everything up so that they can see the baby more clearly, so I drink as much as I can, in order for it to be more visible. I don't know what it will be like—New York hospitals might have such sophisticated equipment that it could be like a photograph. But it couldn't be color, because there isn't any color in the dark. Our blood isn't red until we bleed.

I wonder if I have any choice about seeing the baby. It seems intrusive, probing into the dark before birth. And yet, it is important to check everything. They check the thickness of the skin in the neck, apparently, to check its brain is okay. And what if something is wrong? The sudden fear of it curls round my chest. Do I have a termination then? Where is my moral line?

I can't think about that and write a decent paper, so I turn my mind away from it, and open my books.

I print out my essay so far, to take with me to the hospital. When you're pregnant and you've drunk this much water, walking is difficult; it is painful even to move. I stalk from the subway stop to the hospital, a cartoon person.

The scanning department has a shiny cash register at the entrance, by way of welcome. If your insurance papers don't cover everything, they accept credit and cash. I hand my papers over and fill in the forms I am given. Then I turn to face the waiting room. It is, of course, full of couples, holding hands. The hospital could have a special "single mom" time each day, no couples allowed. We could all grin sympathetically at each other. I find a seat, fish my essay out of my bag, and disappear behind it. The overwhelming need to pee means I can't concentrate on my soon-to-be-lucid prose. It is a form of low-level torture.

When it is my turn, I go with fairy steps into the dark room and lie down. The scan lady rubs my tummy with gel and then puts her scan gun on top. Then she takes it off again, and fits it back in its holder. She says, "Miss Garland, you read the letter about drinking, right?"

"Yes!" I say. Surely I drank enough. "I drank so much! I drank gallons!"

"You sure did. Would you like to go to the bathroom so we can maybe see your baby as well as your bladder?"

Sweet words. She wipes the gel off, I go, I come back, we begin again. This time, there is something evident on the screen. A small Martian. There is a section of it that looks like the suction tube on a vacuum cleaner. She makes measurements between bits of the image, like you can with Google Earth.

"Can you see your baby?" she says.

"Yes!" I say, all eagerness. "Except—if you could maybe point out the head . . ."

"That's the head. We can see it in profile right now—so you can see the forehead, the nose, the lips—that is the left arm, the left hand. Can you see now?"

"Yes," I say, because I don't want to disappoint her.

"All the measurements are fine," she says, as she clicks and makes notes, clicks and make notes. I stare hard at the arc of light on the black. It makes no sense at all. I can see something flashing.

"What's that pulsing thing?" I say.

"That pulsing thing? That's your baby's heart."

A heart. A tiny, beating heart.

She looks round at me because I haven't said anything. I am crying. Why don't we have a valve of some sort to control crying? It's like having a little sign over your head that says, "I am not in command of myself."

In general, I find it difficult to take in the fact that I am going to have a baby, that there is another human being growing inside me. I know it, but I don't feel it. It insisted on its presence that one crucial night, in order to save itself, but after that I slipped into saying "I'm pregnant" without the words resonating with any grasped reality. But there it is, a heart—a heart belonging to a person, a heart that will race with fear or excitement or joy one day.

"I'm sorry," I say. "Sorry. You must see this all the time, but to me . . ."

"I do see it all the time," she says, turning back to her machine. "And mostly it still feels like a miracle."

I smile at her white-coated back. But then I say, "Mostly?"

"Yeah, mostly."

"You mean . . . that it's hard when you can see something is wrong? Down's, or something?"

She makes another measurement. "That is hard. Yeah, that's hard. But it's hard as well when they're thirteen, and didn't know it was gonna happen, and don't know who the daddy is, or even that there had to be a daddy for it to happen. And some folks still say ignorance is bliss."

She hands me paper towels, and switches tone. "You can clean the gel off with this and then get dressed. Everything looks normal, Miss Garland."

I get in the lift, clutching a little windshield-wipe printout of my baby. There is a couple inside already—a black man with chunky dreadlocks, and a white girl with red hair and freckly skin. She looks to be a few months pregnant. They are holding hands.

I never say anything when I see that someone is pregnant—I am not sure that English people do, in general. Apart from the Victorian squeamishness about pregnancy (Good Lord, something rather sexual might have taken place fairly recently), there is the fear that the woman might just be fat. Or she might be fat and desperate to conceive, in which case you've randomly hurt her twice. Here, it is different. Everyone congratulates a pregnant woman. So I congratulate the girl.

She smiles, but looks embarrassed. The man smiles too, and rubs his other hand on her rounded tummy.

"Thanks," he says, "but we had our baby two days ago."

"Oh—well, then—more congratulations!" I say. I hope there isn't another one in there that they've not noticed.

"It's incredible," he says suddenly, as the doors open onto the ground floor. "We're going back to her now. We've been away from her fifteen minutes for my wife's checkup, and it's—crazy, we miss her like crazy."

They hurry across the sunlit lobby, over to an older black woman who is holding a precious bundle. She hands the baby over to her son.

I walk back to my apartment.

At the deli downstairs, I stop and buy flowers.

"What are these pink berries called?" I ask.

"They are called Pink Berries," says the Korean guy.

I buy them, and a bunch of yellow tulips.

It is frivolous, to spend money on flowers, but I want to celebrate seeing my baby for the first time. When I am hunting about in the kitchen for suitable jars to put the flowers in, my phone rings.

It is Mitchell. I have heard nothing from him since he walked out of my apartment. It rings again and again—I wonder if I should let it go to voice mail. But I can't let that happen. I press "answer."

"How are you?" he says. He doesn't say he is Mitchell, he doesn't check I am Esme. The flame flares up in me anew.

"I'm fine." My first impulse is to tell him I have seen our baby. If the Koreans had spoken English well enough I would have told them. But Mitchell is the kind of person who assigns motive to speech, always. So I keep quiet.

He says he wants to take me to lunch and suggests the MOMA museum restaurant—the Modern. I have never been there and it is supposed to be lovely. I look over at my laptop; it is in hibernation mode. Would it be too strange to celebrate seeing the baby with the father, without telling him that I am celebrating?

I do not ask him why he wants to see me. He might be holding in fine balance whether he does or not; I don't want to tip him into a rethink.

I say yes, I will meet him at MOMA.

✦ CHAPTER THIRTEEN ✦

When I arrive he is waiting outside, and looks very handsome. He is wearing one of those expensive suits that have an effortless fluidity to them. Two women going into the museum give him long looks, and their hips start to sway as they walk past him.

As he kisses me he says, "I'd forgotten that you always smell like roses. Or do you just smell like England? Roses and summer lawns." He ushers me into the restaurant.

Ladies who lunch, in Chanel and pearls, are all around us. Everything has a high-modernist feel: white walls and beautiful angles, sunlight pouring through all the glass. I could almost believe, doing a doctorate on Thiebaud, that I belong amid all this excellence and elegance.

"It's a great setting for a restaurant," I say to Mitchell as the waiter brings us bread and water and we unfold the soft white napkins.

"I know," says Mitchell. "I love that it has such a high ceiling."

I look up. Air is all that is overhead, for a long way. The air has its own quality of piercing clarity, like Arctic air, with the moneyed voices of the women tinkling up into it. *In the room the women come and go, talking of Michelangelo.*

The waiter comes.

"The portobello mushroom salad with goat's cheese is good," says Mitchell. The waiter nods in corroboration.

"It sounds nice, but you have fresh pea soup," I say, "and I am very partial to pea soup."

This is not true; I have never had pea soup. But if I mention that I can't have soft cheese because of the risk to the baby, we might tumble into a fight again. There are still long weeks stretching ahead where it would be legal to terminate. I don't want another fight about it.

"Two pea soups," says Mitchell to the waiter.

When we have had the soup and are eating our main courses, Mitchell is very, very nice to me. He lets me talk. I tell him funny stories about the bookshop, and about Stella and the photographs of the lesbian sex dungeon.

He is charming, and constantly refills my glass with San Pellegrino as if it is the best champagne. I keep sipping it out of nervousness, because I know Mitchell has some sort of objective. But he wants me to agree to a termination, and I can't do that. So what is the point of this?

When the plates have been taken away, and he has ordered fresh figs and Manchego cheese with quince jelly, he takes my hand. It is a gesture that he sometimes makes, a gesture I adore.

"Please—" I say, pulling my hand a little. But this time he has chosen well; I am not going to make a scene here.

"Esme, I have something to say. I want you to think about it in terms of—of what's best for everybody concerned. Of our happiness. The happiness of *all of us,* Esme."

"I can't do it, Mitchell, I am not going to—"

"I know, I know. It isn't that." He is holding my hand and stroking the back of it, his gaze intent upon it.

"I fought against this, Esme, as you must know. I fought like a caged lion. But it's all been in vain—"

The waiter comes back, with a bowl of fresh figs and the other things. Mitchell waits, his fist knuckling his lips.

"Your figs, sir. And your quince jelly, and the Manchego."

"Thanks," says Mitchell. He looks up suddenly, into my eyes. There is a little gasp of delight from one of the women at the next table. I look at her to see what is the matter; she is looking pointedly at the basket of figs. There is a black velvety box nestled in among the fruit.

I stare at the box as if it is a tarantula. By now there is a little hubbub around us. I begin to shake my head, and a ripple of laughter goes around; maidenly modesty, they think, the bashful young girl. Mitchell holds up a presidential hand, to stop them from laughing or me from protesting. It works for both. He takes the box out of the figs and presents it to me. The waiter is still there. I do not look at him, but I feel as if he is smiling. I can feel smiles from all directions.

I open the box. The diamond glints at me. It is not in a normal setting—it is held in a kind of pincer grip in a gap on the ring. It elicits another gasp from my nearest neighbor and her friend.

Until this moment, I never understood why everyone makes so much fuss about diamonds. I used to make Jell-O with my mother, and hold the red cubes up to the light, and think that a chunk of that translucent red was always going to be prettier than the glassiness of a diamond. I still think it. But I wasn't taking into account all that a diamond means, all the meaning any diamond has already accumulated by the time it is presented like this. There is the shock of pride that somebody wants me this much, and a deeper shock, to think that I could rate myself that way, in pounds and pence, dollars and cents. *Because I'm worth it*. I am diminished by it. People are exclaiming about the diamond now, muttering, "Harry Winston." I bow my head over it. For a second or two, nobody can see my face.

Marrying Mitchell, by almost any measure, would be a Very Bad Idea. He is as beautiful and cold and hard as the diamond in his ring. If I were watching this scene play out in a movie or in a book, I would be willing the heroine to say no with all my heart. Yes, he is the father of her child, yes, he is looking earnestly into her eyes, yes, he is, after all, doing the decent thing in proposing to her. But. But. But. His motive. Run away. Run away.

I want to stop him. I want to ask him real questions, and hear real answers. But we are center-stage here. I can't. Or is it that this is my very dream, and hearing the real answers would wake me up?

"Esme Garland," says Mitchell, well aware of all the listening ears, "will you do me the signal honor of becoming my wife?"

Our audience emits a collective sigh of happiness and then turns to me, radiating an expectant goodwill.

This audience is a just-off-Fifth-Avenue audience, one that is, moreover, lunching at the MOMA restaurant on a Wednesday. Is the goodwill entirely without nuance? Is there nobody here who came to think about her feminist interpretation of Emil Nolde, nobody here who has just finished a paper on the New Balance of Power in Sexual Politics? Nobody here who can save me?

Obviously, I need to do the saving myself. But just as Mitchell has all those van Leuven ghosts behind him, prompting him to do the respectable thing now that all other avenues are closed, so I have a gathering of English ghosts behind me. The English kind are not quite so sure of themselves as the Dutch pilgrim kind. My English ghosts think it is terrible to make a fuss, terrible to derail such a set piece, terrible to disappoint the ladies who lunch, who will go home to their husbands and call their daughters and say, "Such a delightful thing happened today when I was having lunch with Sibyl in the Modern" . . . I don't seem to have any of the strain of backup that won Waterloo on the playing fields of Eton.

I am lying. I believe that, but it is not that.

There is fury that he can set me up like this, but I can't, I simply can't, bring that out in front of all these people. If I were French, I would perhaps hit him or throw the quince jelly at his head. If I were American I might be able to articulate my anger in a more reasoned way, oblivious to the audience—or say "fuck you" and storm out. That's tempting—leaving him with his figs and his diamond ring. But I am so dreadfully English. In times of stress I become highly agreeable.

I ought not to be thinking about myself, anyway. I ought to be thinking not about how much Mitchell might love me or not love me, but about the baby. A baby ought to have a stable environment. I am sick of the phrase; it's been dancing in my head and it was spoken out loud by Mitchell when he wanted me to terminate, and here it is again. Isn't a loving environment much more important than a stable one? There is virtue in saying yes. Of course there is. He is my baby's father. I have decided to have the baby; therefore I owe it to the baby to give it the best start in life. Doesn't that mean I ought to at least try the old route—the two parents who love it, the economic stability—better than stability—*prosperity*? Not, for the sake of pride, to consign the pair of us to a walk-up studio and babysitters and to the worry about where the next twenty dollars will come from? The things we ought to do are more important than the things we want to do.

I am lying again. I believe that too, but it is not that.

"Esme," says Mitchell, lifting my chin with his finger. "I want you to know—it isn't just because of the baby." (Our audience nearly faints. Not a single forkful of arugula has got any farther than it had two minutes ago.) "It's because—for the first time in my life, the very first time, I've—" He opens his hands like Jesus when he gives the Sermon on the Mount. "I've fallen in love."

The New York chorus responds as they have responded to the rest. Aren't New Yorkers supposed to be cynical? People are taking out phones to photograph us.

Mitchell takes my hand again. "I was afraid," he is saying. "I was afraid of loving you, of loving anyone. This is a big day for me.

"When I say I would be honored if you would be my wife, I mean it—from my heart. For you, for me, for the baby, for the sake of all that stuff you are forever babbling about—love and beauty and truth and all—please say yes. Please marry me."

My eyes are full of tears. One gets very emotional when one's hormones are swishing around one's body like slops in a bucket.

"Don't cry, honey! Just say yes!" An old lady in a black lamb's-wool coat is nodding earnestly at me from a couple of tables away. After her the deluge.

They say I ought to, because of the baby. That "he's trying to do the decent thing." That we're darling together. That I won't regret it. That the diamond is from Harry Winston. I stare down at the ring that I do not care about, that I wish were red gelatin. It serves as a prop—I am an actor in this whether I like it or not. I look from the ring up to Mitchell. I want him to love me so much that I can't work out where my desire ends and truth begins.

I have been so up, so down, so spun around by this mercurial man that I can't remember what I was like before. I dimly remember a person who liked poems and pictures, a person who danced along in the happiness of paying attention, almost convinced of her freedom. This loving is greater than freedom.

"They will say it's a shotgun wedding," I say.

"They will say it's a whirlwind romance," he says. Then he gives me an arrested look. "*Will say'?* The future tense? Is that a yes?"

I smile. Our observers let out what, on the Upper West Side, would be a whoop.

"Yes?" repeats Mitchell, incredulous, making sure. He starts to laugh.

"Yes," I say, laughing too, and nodding. "Yes."

❖

AS MITCHELL IS sliding the ring with erotic deliberation over my finger, the old lady in the black lamb's-wool coat comes over to us. She has a small diary and a pen with her.

"What are your names?" she says. "I'll keep a lookout for you in the Metro section."

Mitchell grins at me. There is a complicity in his eyes now that makes my heart soar. I know I will regret this, I know that worthy heroines in Regency romances never say yes when there is any doubt as to the state of the hero's heart, but I am made of flesh, not words. I want to be with Mitchell. If I am with him, I can make him see that I am worth loving. Perhaps it is the other way round, and he doesn't see yet that he is worth loving too. I can make him see that. And if it all goes wrong, I will suffer, but the suffering won't be for the strangled impulse, the unlit lamp. I will light the lamp and burn myself on the flame.

"This is Miss Esme Garland, and I am Mitchell van Leuven," he says.

There is a kind of aftershock to this statement, and another whisper ripples round. A van Leuven.

The woman nods, as if she expected as much, and her old bejeweled fingers write it down painstakingly. She shuts the diary with a snap. "Then I guess you really will be in the Metro section." She looks piercingly at Mitchell. "You did a good thing today."

"I think so," says Mitchell, with a well-timed glance of pride at his newly affianced bride, who is still reeling from the actual proposal, let alone the idea of announcements in the *New York Times*. Mitchell is good at playing to the crowd. When it is this sort of crowd, at any rate.

We accept the smiles and congratulations for a minute or two, and then, the nine-minute wonder over, people resume their own lunches and we are left alone.

"A fig?" says Mitchell, picking one up. Its plump body is the color of claret, with a flash of pale green at the top and that dusting of powder all over it. I don't know if that powder is a natural bloom, or if everyone dusts figs with icing sugar as a matter of course, to make them look prettier.

I say yes to the fig, since it does not seem polite in the circumstances to say no. As with figs, so with marriage proposals. Oh, but I want to, I want to. Why does *he* want to? Mitchell slices it, and adds some of the cheese and quince jelly. He hands me the plate.

"Mitchell," I say, urgently.

"Not here, Esme," he says quietly.

"It isn't that. It's—please will you order a glass of wine?"

He grimaces before he answers. This habit he has of first making gestures to illuminate what he is about to say ought perhaps to drive me insane, and indeed might, over a lifetime. But now it just increases the tenderness; it is a foible that I know and recognize, that somehow belongs to me.

"But you can't drink," he is saying.

"I can have a mouthful. Order a glass of wine—anything you like—and let me have a mouthful. Please please please."

"No. It will harm—"

"It's my body."

"The baby's ours. Are we really having this argument again? Really?"

"No. But one mouthful. In England, some people even say you can have one small glass a day. I am asking for one mouthful in nine months. Come on. I got engaged today."

Mitchell holds himself still, tense, and then he relaxes. He signals to the waiter.

"One glass of champagne, please. Your best."

The waiter smiles, but bends over Mitchell, and mutters to him. Mitchell holds up an understanding hand.

"Yes, of course. Just a second." He leans over to the ladies at the next table. "Excuse me. I am ordering one glass of champagne for my wife-to-be and me to drink. The waiter says I would have to buy the whole bottle. I'm fine with that, but I'm not fine with it going to waste. Would you oblige us by having the rest?"

The women laugh and say how romantic and yes, why not, they will have the bottle. I smile like a Barbie doll.

The fact that it is champagne means we have to go through the painful rigmarole of the silver bucket and the little table to hold the silver bucket, and the ice, and the white napkin, and the grand withdrawal of the cork. And then, when our glass is finally poured, Mitchell holds it up to me and toasts me, and sips. Then he hands it to me.

As I take the glass I have a powerful feeling that someone is looking at me. I glance to my left—near the exit, the old lady in the lamb's-wool coat is staring at me. She is probably waiting to be picked up, and probably not smiling because I am pregnant and about to have a mouthful of champagne, but she seems suddenly baleful, the thirteenth fairy at the christening.

I raise the glass to Mitchell. I am in tumult, fearful in the very temple of delight. If I rang out the bells to celebrate, would they sound dully, would they ring true? My mouth is full of champagne. I hold it there for a second or two. It is expensive and yeasty and tart. It is glorious. I won't be allowed any more for months on end. I think of swans singing before they die, and butterflies with cornflower-blue wings living for a day, and then I swallow. As I do, I look back at the old lady, and raise my glass to her as well, but she does not respond. And then it is over.

Mitchell looks comically at the glass I hand back.

"Mitchell. You are sure?"

"Yes. I am sure. I had aching gaps, Esme. You fill them up. You fill up all my gaps."

❧ CHAPTER FOURTEEN ❧

Outside the restaurant, he kisses me. "I have to go—I don't want to go, but I have to. I have to teach—I'll call you," and then he is backing away with his arm up, to hail a cab that he will turn around to take him back to work.

I watch the cab turn at the cross street, and carry on watching it until it blends in with the others. I do not wave. Mitchell will not be looking back. I walk up Fifth Avenue and then take the bus across the park at 86th. I try to think. It doesn't work—I am in a kind of muted delirium. I accepted a marriage proposal half an hour ago, and now I am sitting alone on a bus, with a diamond on my finger. I wish he didn't have to go back to work. I have that sense that you have when you come out of the cinema or the theater, the shock of transition from big drama to ordinary life. The performance is over.

I get off the bus on Amsterdam. Before I get to The Owl, I take the ring off my finger and put it inside my change purse.

Luke is at the front desk. The ring is pulsating in my bag. I need space and quiet to think about what has just happened. I am not going to tell anyone yet. I take my bag, with the purse right at the bottom of it, down to the basement, and hide it in one of the darkest corners of the dark basement. Then I stay down there, just for a second, curled up in a fetal position in the corner. I could not have dreamed of this. It is both my heart's desiring and my heart's breaking.

David and George are sitting up on the mezzanine, dabbing brown shoe polish on the spines of some old leather-bound Dickens volumes where the leather has rubbed.

About suffering they were never wrong, the old masters, but the same could be said of anything that happens to us. David and George have been dabbing shoe polish on old books and buffing them with soft cloths while I have been in the restaurant, being proposed to, while Icarus falls into the water. "You can take over from me," says George. "I have a book dealer coming to see me in a second or two. Sit down."

"Isn't this cheating?" I ask as I sit.

George looks pained. "Cheating? On the contrary, Esme, it is *treating*. When you polish your furniture, is it cheating?"

"I don't polish my furniture."

"You don't? Why not?"

"It's from Ikea."

"It's from *Ikea*? You didn't ship over the Hepplewhite cabinet, the Knoll sofa, the ormolu clock?" George does want me to come from some sort of English manor house, with a lovely black and white tiled hallway and a sweeping Queen Anne stair.

"What is ormolu?" asks David.

George's features take on the expression that I have come to recognize as his Dangerous Chemicals face, which covers everything from smallpox to chocolate. His face contracts towards a central point, so that his brows are down, and his lips and chin are scrunched up to his nose. He looks at me from under his eyebrows, although now I come to think of it, everyone looks at everyone from under their eyebrows. He glowers.

"Is it bad for you?" I ask.

"As usual, it isn't bad for the people who own it, so much as for the people who make it. It is illegal now, even in your country. They used mercury to make the powdered gold stay put, and so of course, the fumes were deadly. Most ormoluists didn't make it past forty."

"Oh, yes, mercury. That is bad. That's what made the hatters go mad, wasn't it?" David says.

George looks gratified that the chemical instruction has been taking effect. "Yes, and not only hatters. I hope *you* don't have mercury fillings, Esme. That would be very bad for the ba—"

"'Ormoluists'?" I say. "Come on, George. You just made up 'ormoluists.'"

Luke calls out from downstairs. "Hey, Esme, have you asked George to check out the shoe polish? He might be poisoning you."

George stands at the top of the stairs, holding the tin of polish aloft.

"It is a good question, Luke, and I appreciate your concern. I'm not poisoning her. Take a look. I bought it online from California. It's made with natural plant dyes and free-range beeswax." Free-range beeswax? Can you get battery bees?

Luke shakes his head. George regards the tin pensively as I rub in the polish.

"It cost more than we'll get for the Dickens," he says.

⁕

WHEN I LOOK at my phone, there are seven texts from Mitchell. I open them, and the first one says "Mrs. van Leuven!!!" The next is a long line of kisses. The next is, "I managed that well, don't you think? You had to say yes!" The next wonders where I am. So does the next. The one after that wonders if I have changed my mind. The last is an apology for not being able to see me tonight, because something has come up. I immediately wonder if something has come up because I did not answer all the others. I call him to ask this, and he says no. There is an important economist here unexpectedly from out of town. Mitchell has to talk to him.

The shop begins to fill with the regular Friday-nighters, and George, who often takes himself to the Angelika or Film Forum to see something searing in black and white, decides to stay too. Barney strolls in, and Mary turns up. At midnight, we lock up, turn the main lights off, and sit up in the mezzanine with just the upstairs lamps on, with their pools of amber light. The wood of the bookcases and the leather spines glow warm, and people find places to sit, and become as mellow as the light.

"I think I should introduce a little test at The Owl for prospective employees," says George, accepting an organic ginger beer with shredded orrisroot from Luke. "You know, ask them who wrote *Winesburg, Ohio,* who wrote *Hamlet,* who wrote Plato's *Republic . . .*"

"That one would be easy," says David.

"They used to have such a test at Strand," says George. "I believe it was very effective."

We wait, and he grins, holding up his palm as if it is a piece of paper.

"You have a list of five books—let me see if I remember. *Oliver Twist, Das Kapital, Ulysses, The Origin of Species*—and I forget the last one. And then, jumbled up on the other side, are the authors. You have to draw lines to unite the right book to its writer."

Luke shrugs. "Seems like a plan to me."

"But if you pass this arduous test," says George, "then you might get hired, but for the first six months, all you're allowed to do is shelve. That's your apprenticeship at Strand. Esme, you're very blessed in learning book lore here, not down in that devil's punch bowl."

"Oh, Strand's fine and you know it. You're just jealous," says Barney, waving him into silence. "But my *favorite* place to buy books before I came here, of course, was the New York Antiquarian Book Fair at the Park Avenue Armory." This makes people chuckle, and he holds up both his hands. "Because really? Used bookstores—I mean, really? I was a lot more particular in those days. I only tolerate The Owl because my apartment is ten feet away and I like to watch Luke play the guitar."

"Listen, you mean," says Bruce.

Barney looks at him with exquisite blandness. "But the armory fair," he says, "it is a *joy* to go in there. The prices. I used to bring my mother down from Westchester for it, every single year."

"The prices?" I ask. "Do you get bargains?"

Barney shudders. "No, darling, never ever. Did I mention that I take my *mother*? And of course, they're not really used books, right? They're antiquarian."

"Used" is such an odd word, so much stranger than "second-hand." A prefix for condoms, and there's a certain squalor attached to the idea of reusing those. "Used books," as if someone else has had the best of them and you get the sere husk, or the lees, as if a book isn't the one thing, the one product, that is forever new. There's no such thing as a used book. Or there's no such thing as a book if it's not being used.

I say some of this to the assembled company.

"What would you like instead?" says Luke. "'Pre-worn'? 'Pre-read'?"

George looks wry. "Oh, if only," he says, and reaches behind him for a first—it is upstairs so it must be a first—of *The Information* by Martin Amis. "The publishers missed a trick in not printing the last three quarters of this baby blank. I've not read it myself, though I rate Amis. Sometimes books don't take."

✦

WHEN I GET back, late, to my apartment, I get the ring out of my bag. I am not as attentive as I ought to be about the economic disparities in the world, but a piece of jewelry like this, an example of such conspicuous consumption, can do the trick. How many cataract operations would this pay for? How much clean water? Could it train a teacher, a midwife, a doctor in the third world? And what *is* its significance here, when it isn't translated into something beneficial? That I am owned, perhaps. Or that I am loved. The fact that I accepted it means, at any rate, that I love. I look into its glinting, ice-blue depths, the shifting angles of light, like sunlight in a swimming pool, that bounce together and apart.

I take the ring off, and put it in my teapot, and put the lid back on. Hiding it from view makes no difference to its power.

While I am sitting there contemplating my pulsating teapot, there is a knock on the door—Stella, it could only be Stella. I let her in, and she says that she heard me come in and wants to tell me something. She is lit up—she's been invited by the Richard Avedon Foundation to take part in an exhibition of new portraiture. I feel once more the tiny shock that we, vain we, feel when we remember that other people have lives, which are going on as we sit hiding diamond rings in teapots.

She sits on my sofa.

"I've got to submit an artist's statement for the exhibition," she says. "I am trying to think about why I love taking photographs. Why do I?"

I think. "The obvious answer is to capture the moment," I say. "To notice things. To signify paying attention."

Stella is nodding. "Yes, that's true, but it is all sorts of other things. The woman from Richard Avedon said that there was an elegiac quality to my work."

"There is," I say. I think of her photographs. "Yes, there definitely is. They are so sad!"

"But *all* photographs are sad, because they record something that's gone," says Stella. "They make us pay attention to the fact that time is passing, that nothing lasts. But who doesn't notice that? I mean, I notice it anyway, all the damn time, camera or no camera. I sometimes think I do nothing *except* notice. Everywhere I look. Every blink is an elegy."

"That will do for your statement," I say. "Quick, write it down or you won't remember it."

She is tapping it into her phone. "Cool. Great. So, what's up with you?"

"I've got an engagement ring in the teapot," I say.

After a pause, she gets up, goes over, and lifts the lid. She peers in.

"Oh, yeah," she says. "So you do." Predictably, she isn't show-ing signs of great joy. She replaces the lid without getting the ring out or attempting a photograph.

"Mitchell has asked me to marry him."

"And you said yes. The ring. And it's in the teapot because . . . ?"

"Because I am not sure how I feel about it."

"Why did you say yes?"

"Because I love him."

She hugs her knees up to her chin and says, "Then I guess you'd better get it out of there and wear it."

"But I don't know if he loves me."

My phone buzzes. It is a text from Mitchell. Stella nods at it. "He's doing a good impression of it. But then, attention isn't neces-sarily love."

I look at her. "But we just said it was, sort of," I say.

She shakes her head.

"He doesn't do it for attention," I say. "He's not like that."

"Okay," says Stella. "Anyway, what does your mom think, about the baby? She'll be pleased about Mitchell?" Stella took to my parents when they came over. She thought they were sweet. They are, I suppose. Other people always like one's parents.

"She doesn't know yet," I say.

Stella's jaw drops. "What is the matter with you? Why don't you want to tell them? Your parents would support your decision. They're cool."

They are not in the least cool. When they were in Manhat-tan for that week, they lamented missing a program about tea caddies, and part of a BBC documentary series on the his-tory of hedgerows. "Cool" must mean something different for Stella.

"You should call them," she repeats. "They will *support* you."

"I know, I know. But if don't tell them anything, then they don't have to support me, and they don't have to repress their dis-appointment, and they don't . . ." I trail off. "It was fine for the termination plan, wasn't it? And not fine when there's going to be a baby." I cringe away from the thought of it. If I were in England, I would have to. But I have run away.

"Promise," says Stella.

"Oh, I can't promise. I was in the Brownies. If I promise, I have to do it."

She waits. I promise. She gets up to leave.

"And one other thing, engaged girl. You got engaged today. Where's your fiancé?"

"He's seeing an economist. He couldn't get out of it."

✦

IN THE MORNING, after a cup of tea, I call my parents.

It isn't a long call. There is no recrimination; they must be burning to do it. But I am crying, crying as I tell them, for shame at an obscure sense of having thwarted whatever hopes they had of me. I wish I had siblings, that I wasn't all the daughters of my father's house, and all the brothers too.

Although they can't possibly be pleased, neither of them seems to mind so much about the baby, and my mother says she will come over now, next week, and certainly when the baby is born. I agree to the last; I want her to come then. I don't know nothing about birthing no babies, or how to look after them afterwards. I wonder how much grief about this they are hiding, in the first shock of it. To my surprise, though, they openly mind about Mitchell. My father says, quietly, at the end: "Don't rush into marrying him. You don't need to panic."

"It's not that, Dad," I say.

"They will change everything; the family will change your path. If there is a money issue, we can—"

"It isn't money," I say quickly. "I would take Mitchell if he were—barefoot in the park."

"The scholarship—all you've worked for—"

"Is all still there; I am still working for it. I won't slack up, this will make me work even harder."

They are silent. Disappointment and fear are buzzing over the Atlantic. I say, "I love him, Dad," and I blush into the empty apartment.

After the phone call, I stomp down to Columbia and stride into its precincts. What endless ripples of disappointment flow from that one unguarded moment. And I could have stopped them. No, I could have stopped these particular ripples, but there are always ripples.

Columbia itself feels different now that I am engaged. I feel uncomfortable. It is as if I have short-circuited the educational process somehow, and made the lights go out. As I merge into the flow of people heading towards their lectures, I don't feel as if I fit any longer.

"Is this all you wanted?" say the names carved on Butler. "Is this what it was all for? A wedding ring?"

I stop, and sit down on the library steps and face them.

"Getting married won't change anything," I say. "This isn't 1870."

Herodotus Sophocles Plato Aristotle Demosthenes Cicero and Vergil all look back at me and purse their stony lips.

"A girl that knew all Dante once / Lived to bear children to a dunce," they say.

"Mitchell isn't a dunce," I say, "and getting married and having children makes no difference now. I can still have a career. I don't know why you lot should be annoyed, anyway. You're the Dead White Males, remember?"

They take no notice. "A career?" they say. "If you marry Mitchell van Leuven? You're dreaming. You got a scholarship here, Esme Garland, to study the history of art, and this is what you do with it? What a waste. What a waste. The old story."

"I'm busy," I say, standing up and slinging my bag on my shoulder. "It's been a treat talking to you. Do you know my father at all?"

"In five years," they say, as a parting shot, "you will be running a cupcake business."

✦

MY SECOND LECTURE is on Impressionism, and the person who gives it, Dorothy Straicher, is only a few years older than I am. I like her very much. She mentions that there is a Sargent and impressionism exhibition on at the moment on the Upper East Side, in a hotel, and that even the die-hard modernists among us might well get something out of it. After I have eaten some dreadful lunch with Bryan from Columbia, I ask him if he would like to come with me, but he makes a face. I don't know if the face is for impressionism or Sargent, but at any rate, I set out across Central Park alone. I wish Mitchell could come, but if I text him, I will get one back saying he is teaching or about to teach, and then I will feel rejected. It is better not to ask. I do have to remember that he has a job.

There are, as usual, various runners and tourists and walkers and peculiar people with cats on leads dotted about, even up near the top, so it doesn't feel too scary. I go in at 108th Street and walk fast toward 77th on the East Side. I pause to send a text to Mitchell, just in case he has a break and can come with me.

I go down a little path between two great outcrops of silvery schist, and when I come out, I see a man alone, with his back to me, sitting under a tree with a guitar.

When I am in the park, I walk with my phone in my hand so that if I see anyone menacing I can pretend to be talking to someone who is both burly and only about thirty yards away. This is my only protection, as I can't run fast and can't fight. I am about to pretend to talk to Luke on the phone when I realize that this particular strange man in the park is, in fact, Luke.

I get closer and then stop. He doesn't sense my presence; he is busy plinking away at the guitar. He plinks the same bit over and over. It sounds a bit tedious.

"Hi," I say. He looks around.

"Hi!" he says. It is a bit cold to be sitting on the ground, and he might get piles, but I prudently do not mention this.

"What a good idea, to play in the park," I say. "I love how hard they worked to make it look so natural. I suppose picturesque works really well once people have forgotten that it was made up in the first place."

"Yeah, sure, I guess," says Luke, which is American for "no." He hesitates, and then says, "It's just a place that lets people breathe."

I look at him. "Oh, you don't like it when I say it isn't real?" I say.

"Like you say, I don't think it matters if it wasn't real at the start. It's real enough now. The schist is real, the trees are real, the way it changes in the seasons is real."

I don't say anything. As so often with Luke, I can't quite say the right thing. Perhaps I am trying too hard.

"The park might be like a picture to you," he says, "but to me, it's like music. It's about time. I think I like it because it changes. It changes like music does. It has rhythms, like music does."

"Pictures change over time as well," I say, stealing shamelessly from Professor Caspari. "We look at a painting over a period of time, so it is experienced sequentially. And we can go back to look at them. They change, we change."

Luke nods. He starts to speak and then stops, as if he is venturing onto territory he's not confident will take his weight. "Yes, but—but not just in that way—the park changes for people as well—it is different things for different people, at different times. You know, for lovers, for guys walking in the Rambles, for the softball players and the beer sellers and the children, the tourists, the runners . . . they all move through the park, like notes in music—they all sound different notes, it all seems like discord, but it isn't. It's a harmony."

There is a silence. I don't know what to do. There is such a flash of gladness at what he says that I feel as if, in the very gladness, I am wronging Mitchell.

"Do you play here a lot?" I ask.

He scans his surroundings, nodding. "Yeah, I do."

"And don't you feel self-conscious, playing in public?" I say.

I wonder if he can hear that my voice sounds brittle. I can. He is looking around again, this time very deliberately. There is nobody in sight.

"I play gigs all the time, you know. That—if you can imagine it—is even more public."

I can't think of anything else to say. I say, "Well, I'd better be—"

"You just out for an afternoon stroll?" he asks. "Or are you going to work?"

"No, neither—I am going to look at some paintings."

"You walking across the whole park on your own?"

"Yes, but I'll be fine."

Luke gets up, and reaches for his guitar case. It is more of a guitar bag.

"I'll keep you company."

I am about to launch into an automatic polite protest but his expression is that of a man anticipating this and not looking forward to it.

If I were out with Mitchell, or Stella, and we were in a quiet part of the park, I would unbutton my shirt, so that the bright sun might penetrate to the darkness of the womb. Instead of blackness, it might be like being inside a plum.

"Thank you," I say instead.

"You're welcome."

As we walk, he says that the impetus for the park in the first place was not really to make something pretty.

"If it looks nice, that's fine by me. But that's not what Olmsted was doing, first off, right? When he designed the park? The idea was to make a democratic space, where people could just be. In New York City, where everyone is scrambling to make it, everyone can come to Central Park and look at the leaves in the fall, the snow in winter . . . we all see the same patterns, we're all moving through the same time. See?"

I don't really see, but I like how his mind works in a different way from mine, in a way that could open mine up.

"I sort of see," I say, smiling at him.

He asks me which paintings I am going to see, and so I talk about Sargent, and since Luke always makes me feel a little uneasy, I find myself in a long and complicated story about Madame X in the Met, and how everyone was shocked because the strap of her gown was painted as having slipped, and how her purple skin wasn't artistic license but the lavender powder that she wore.

"What did she want to look purple for?"

"I don't know. She didn't look purple like a Ribena man, or anything." That will mean nothing to Luke, but we both let it pass. "It was more a lilac pallor. The painting is really famous, and it's about twenty blocks from here. You should see it."

"It's in the Met? Let's go see it."

"You mean me as well? I was going to see the Sargents in the Mark Hotel, on 77th . . ."

"Oh, I thought you were going to the Met—forget it. It's okay."

"But—you could go and see it."

"I will, sometime. I thought it would be more fun with a know-it-all English guide, that's all."

"We could pay a dollar each, and just go and see that painting, and then I could go on to the Mark."

"Sure. We love it when the tourists rip off the city."

"I'm not a tourist."

"Yeah. You are. Pay the damn money."

It is very different, walking with Luke. Mitchell strides everywhere as if compelled by his own energy, and that energy streams out towards other people. Perhaps it bounces back from them and reinvigorates him, because he walks as if he is going to turn over the tables in the temple, hack the faces off the wooden angels, cut through the mediocrity to a purity as clear as ice.

Luke strolls along with his guitar, by contrast, with a kind of easy amplitude, as if he is about to break into something from Simon and Garfunkel. He is chatting about George's love affair with wheatgrass.

As we reach the band shell, where Boticelli's Venus should

really be singing a number, I get a text from Mitchell saying that he can't come to see the Sargents, but he hopes I will enjoy them, and that he will see me tonight. I ought to be annoyed at this last assumption, but I am just pleased. I am no more sure of him now than I ever have been.

Luke pauses on the outskirts of an intent little gathering of people. "We've maybe come down too far," he says. I want to see what they are looking at. A dancer on the stage, in cherry Lycra and a turquoise scrap of a skirt, falls forward without moving her hands to save herself. Without intervention, she will smash her brains out on the concrete. She falls like a plank, and inches from the ground, her partner catches her. It is all performed, or practiced, with a silent solemnity. They do it again, and again. Every time, she could die, and every time, he catches her. I stand and watch, the same thing, over and over, the fall, the risk, the catch.

"What is it?" Luke asks. I realize he has said it more than once. I do not know what he means.

He says, "You're crying?"

"Oh," I say, shaking my head. "It's nothing. Hormones. Let's go."

We turn to walk uptown again, and Luke says, "I guess it's all a little tough for you right now."

I think guiltily of how I have just been proposed to by the man I am besotted by, who is also the father of my baby, and who also happens to be very rich.

I say, "Oh, it's not all that bad."

When we get to the Met, Luke asks for one adult ticket and one student. The ticket person says, "Thirty dollars."

He pays the money, and then turns to me to give me my little metal badge.

"Thirty bucks? Do we get to keep the picture?"

CHAPTER FIFTEEN

I am on an afternoon shift. I have left my ring at home as usual, in the teapot.

David has been called in as extra help, because George is out on a big book call. David is always friendly, but I get the feeling he regards me as an object lesson in what might happen to him if he is not careful with the girls he dates. His taste, judging from the ones who come into the bookshop, runs to plump and pretty—the one who comes in most, Lena, is apple-cheeked and wholesome. David usually takes her "to look at the mystery section" for a few minutes if there aren't many customers.

Luke is shelving. Bruce is hanging around until George gets back—apparently a book call of this magnitude requires all hands. Bruce still gallantly brings me tea whenever I come in, and so I sit and dunk the tea bag in and out, vainly hoping for flavor, as David and Bruce chat.

David is saying that it is about time we asked Towelhead Man why he wears a towel on his head. Bruce shakes his head. "Luke!" David says. "You should totally ask him!"

"I'm 'totally' not going to," replies Luke, ramming some unhappy cookbooks into an already bulging shelf. "If the guy wants to walk around the city with a towel on his head, that's his business. He's a good customer."

"Man, I'd love to ask him. I'll get you a double caramel macchiato latte with extra whipped cream if you ask him."

"Tempting," says Luke, with no enthusiasm at all.

"Oh come on. And it's always the same one, right?"

"He might have several in the same shade," I say.

"The guy's a freak. Does he take it off in the house?"

"What about the woman whose hair is sort of solid on her head?" Bruce asks. "Or Captain Jim, with his parrot?"

"Or the entire family who dress up as the Romanovs," says David. "Freaks, man, I'm telling you."

"Who cares?" says Luke, suddenly impatient. "Are we all so perfect? Give them a break."

David looks abashed. Then he perks up and says, "I guess we could all come into work with green towels on our heads, make him feel at home . . ."

George pokes his head in the door.

"Can I get some help out here?" he asks. We all go outside to the cab that George is unloading—every conceivable space in it is filled with bags full of books. The driver is barely visible.

We lug all the book bags back into the shop. There is no room for any customers.

George gets us all to price the easy ones—the paperback fiction, the cookbooks, and so on—and sets about pricing the art books himself. He takes up the first one, looks through it, raises his pencil to write the price on the first page, and then he pauses.

"You know, what I've always done is take a look through a book, look at the paper stock, the printing, the publisher, the actual content, and, taking everything into account, I price it."

We wait.

"And?" says David.

"And now I can't. The fact that I can check this book"—he is holding a book of photographs by Yousuf Karsh, and he weighs it in his hand as if he can value it that way—"the fact that I *can* check this book on the Internet means that I *have* to check this book on the Internet. This could be the Karsh that all the Karsh fanatics out there have been thirsting for—I might be pricing it hundreds below its market value. And, equally, I can't take the chance that for this book, Abrams didn't have some sort of mental breakdown and had a print run of fifty thousand, so we'd get five bucks for it if we were lucky. It's a sad truth, but it is a truth nevertheless, that I can't price it without doing my due diligence. I have become imprisoned by the freedom of the Web."

He hands me the book.

"Or to be more precise, *you* have become imprisoned, Esme. Go up there and make a start, and I'll bring you some more when I have sorted through them."

"How do you know what to pay for the books, then, if you're so uncertain about what to price them at?" I ask.

George smiles mystically.

We work hard until the books are absorbed into the tiny space, and then Bruce leaves. I have a small pile of art books that I want to keep—working here there are constant temptations. One of them is a Christie's catalog of medieval Islamic astrolabes, another is on the sketches of Lyonel Feininger (Stella would like that), another is on Jim Dine's flowers. It is a fantastic batch. But I am being paid so little, and the baby is going to be so expensive. I can't buy them, even with George's discount. I can't let them go, either. I put them in the reserve cupboard with my name on them, as I have with my wonderful career as an art historian, where my burning and single-minded passion for art makes me a byword for incisive critique.

David is settled comfortably downstairs with George and Luke. They have put on some Bob Dylan, and he and Luke are discussing his music, with an occasional interjection from George. The shop is often like this; they just hang out and talk. George is never out of patience when people want to learn; he must have made a great teacher before E. B. White lured him here. I think I will just have a quick look at prams and pushchairs on the Internet.

Stella saw a pram on Madison Avenue the other day, in the window of a chi-chi baby shop. She says it was in dove-gray fabric and had shiny chrome hubcaps, and it was eight hundred dollars. Now, in my mind's eye, this pram is the platonic ideal of all prams, and it is the one I want. I keep meaning to stroll down Madison so that I can look at it.

But obviously, eight hundred dollars of pram would be lunacy. I might feel obliged to have more babies to get the wear out of it. I need to be more pragmatic.

I type "best pushchair" into google. Instantly, a pop-up comes to the middle of the screen that does not seem to have much to do with pushchairs and prams. It is saying "CLICK HERE FOR LIVE PUSSY!" It is flashing. The words are red on black.

I look downstairs. They have opened a CD, unfurled the paper booklet, and are arguing about lyrics. It is the word "live" that catches me, as if "pussy" is something that produces a repellent fascination, writhing under the gaze of the camera. Perhaps it gives a clue to both the fascination and the repellence. I could use this when I am presenting my paper on the male gaze; would that silence Bradley Brinkman? I click. I look. I am immediately sorry. They deliver on their promise. All the pictures look more or less the same to me, but then I'm not a connoisseur.

My curiosity is more than sated. I click on the little X to get rid of it. It does not go.

George is of course starting his ascent up the stairs with a new pile of books for me to check. I click the cross more frantically. More things pop up. There are many improbably large breasts, and ever more explicit pages are proliferating all over my screen. George is nearly here. I try to click on more Xs; nothing happens.

"These might need looking up on a number of sites," says George. "And for *Principia Mathematica,* you might try the auction records—"

I duck under the table, get hold of the cord, and pull it, hard. American plugs are much easier to pull out than English ones. The computer dies with a gentle electronic sigh.

George is frowning at me.

"You did that because . . . ?" he says.

"It . . . it was making a really weird noise," I say.

"What sort of a noise?"

"A kind of ratchety beeping noise," I say. I am scarlet.

"Were you doing something of a nefarious nature?" asks George politely.

"A bit," I say. "I was looking at prams."

"Prams?"

"Pushchairs."

"Pushchairs?"

"Strollers."

"Ah. And I came up and caught you."

"Yes."

"Next time, just try the confession part without the breaking-the-computer part."

He puts down all the books.

"I have another book call next week, Esme, on West End Avenue. I thought it might be informative for you to come along, if you would like to?"

"I would," I say. "I'd like to see how it's done. Are we going to play good bookseller, bad bookseller?"

"Almost certainly. It's at four next Thursday."

I check my diary, and have no lectures or seminars. "I can come. Thank you. It's nice of you."

"As a matter of fact, it isn't. I have a feeling you'll be an advantage in my hard-nosed dealings. I take a pregnant English girl with me, I might get a break on the books. Now, do you think you can put the computer back on?"

While I am back under the table, sticking the plug back in, I hear a voice I recognize. An assured, East Coast voice. He is saying he doesn't need help with anything, that he is happy to browse.

I freeze under the table.

George is sitting opposite me, reading the start of the first volume of *Principia Mathematica*. He hasn't noticed Mitchell. Instead of getting up, I peep from under the desk, down the stairs. He is standing at the counter, and Luke is standing too, almost as if he is squaring up to him. They make an interesting contrast. Mitchell looks immaculate, full of poise. Luke doesn't.

Mitchell is looking above Luke's head, at the sets of books that are above the CDs.

"Is that a Yale Shakespeare set?" he asks. Luke says it is, without looking. He is still standing; why doesn't he sit?

"Is it complete?" Mitchell asks.

Luke takes the first volume down to look inside it. It clearly doesn't help him, because he calls up to George and asks him.

George, disturbed from his studies, sees me on my knees under the table, evidently hiding. His gaze flows over me without any apparent pause. He says it is complete except for the sonnets.

"We could probably source a volume of the sonnets, sir, if you are interested in the set." He meets my eyes before adding, "We have staff who are very adept on the Internet."

Why am I hiding under the table? Because I haven't got round to telling Luke and George about the proposal. The last thing they knew was that the father was "not in the picture." And I decided not to wear my ring here either—it seems in bad taste to flaunt it in front of the homeless guys. And it feels so heavy. And I am not used to it yet.

I peep around the stairwell. Mitchell is holding his hand out for the book. "Could I take a look?" asks Mitchell. Luke hands him the little blue book. Mitchell says, "Is Esme here?"

I slide back into my seat and look over the railing. Is the tension in me or in the whole shop?

"Hello, Mitchell," I say.

"Well, hello," he says. They both watch me as I get up and come down the stairs. I am blushing again by the time I reach the bottom. Mitchell hands the book back to Luke without a look or a glance.

"Thanks, Luke," I say.

Mitchell's eyes widen at the implied rebuke. He turns and says,

"Yes—Luke. Thank you so much."

"This is Mitchell," I say. "And, Mitchell, this is Luke, and up there, that's George."

Mitchell nods up at George, and then looks around airily. "I've heard a lot about this place but I have never been in here before." He has, when he brought my shoe.

"Well, now you've found us, we hope you'll be a frequent visitor," says George.

"Esme is besotted, obviously. She can't stop talking about you all for two minutes together. I think she sees you two, in particular, in a mentoring capacity? At any rate, she quite clearly looks up to you, Luke."

Luke responds with the slightest motion of his head. I can't remember talking at all to Mitchell about Luke.

"Do you own the store?" he asks.

"No," says Luke. He doesn't volunteer anything else.

"Luke's a musician," I say.

"I'm not sure I would say so," says Luke.

Mitchell has already transferred his attention to me as Luke speaks.

"Do you have a minute?" he asks.

I am at the bottom of the stairs. I don't feel like giving him a minute. Am I imagining him through their eyes, or is he simply behaving badly?

"Come here," he says. His face softens as he says it. "Come here."

I put a hand on each banister. I say, "Before I come there, I should explain to Luke and—"

"I'm sure they don't mind waiting, just for a moment?" says Mitchell. "I'd like to see you outside." It is said in that pleasant way that is still clearly an order. The very evenness, the very courtesy holds in it the iron of his will, and he puts his will into every exchange, so that each interaction with him becomes a thing to win or to lose.

"Mitchell . . ."

He stands there and waits. I have read Elaine Showalter, Simone de Beauvoir, Marilyn French, Hélène Cixous. And Mitchell is demanding that I demonstrate, what? My allegiance? My subservience? Hélène Cixous indeed. *Our lovely mouths gagged with pollen.*

He waits.

"I can't right now," I say.

He lifts his chin, and walks out of the store.

CHAPTER SIXTEEN

Luke turns to me, incredulity on his face, as Mitchell strides past the front of the shop. I cannot bear all this again. Despite Luke, despite Charlotte Perkins Gilman and all of them, I bolt out as well. I run after him down Broadway, call out his name, shame streaming in my wake.

He stops without turning.

I come and stand in front of him.

"I'm sorry," I say, "I just couldn't come like that, like a dog to heel . . ."

He nods again; he always nods when he means, *I thought as much.*

"You wanted to demonstrate my subjugation, my allegiance . . . ," I say. Pathetic to say so, when I have just run out howling into the patriarchal storm.

"Your allegiance? You demonstrated that, for sure. Your allegiance is to yourself."

"No, it is to *you,*" I say, entirely losing my fragile hold on self-respect, and glad that nobody else can hear. Allegiance? Allegiance is more than loyalty. I am sure it is all about liege lords and suzerains and obedience, a hierarchical word. I am sure I have just abased myself. I hate myself for this, for the panic born in me when I think I might lose him.

I take a deep breath. "Come back," I say. "Come back in, and talk to them properly. And put your club down."

"My club?"

"Yes. You can leave it outside the cave."

He looks downtown towards the Ansonia. He starts to smile.

"I want to ravish you in front of them," he says.

"How thrilling," I say, politely. "But I am supposed to be clearing a space to put our new four-volume set of *Principia Mathematica*."

"I came by for a reason," Mitchell says, abandoning the attempt to shock. "To invite you to my parents' Christmas party. It's at their place in the Hamptons. They're in Paris right now, but they are coming back to New York soon. I knew they were—I can feel that cold wind starting to blow in. We can fly there with my cousin Pete and take the Jitney back."

"Your cousin Pete?"

"He's a pilot."

I do not like the idea of flying anywhere with someone called my cousin Pete, in a tiny plane. Rich people often die doing the things that they can afford to do—the skiing accidents and the hunting accidents and the hurtling-to-a-watery-grave-in-your-personal-aeroplane accidents.

"I don't want to fly, Mitchell. I would rather go by train."

"By train?" says Mitchell, as if I've suggested going by dragon or by magic carpet. Apart from the subway, trains are not in his ambit. He thinks they are there especially for poor people, along with Greyhound buses and Taco Bell. "Don't be silly. Flying is fine."

"I think it is better not to, when you're pregnant. I would much prefer not to, Mitchell."

He shrugs. "Then we'll drive," he says.

"Have you got a car?"

"Of course I have a car."

"Your parents won't like me. I never made it to Swiss finishing school."

"I know. But you've got a Cambridge degree. They'll cling on to that."

"So will I."

"Then we should all be fine."

"Come back to the shop, Mitchell. Just for a minute."

He nods. We turn back uptown.

I don't quite see how Mitchell is going to manage his reentry since he just left in a petulant huff. My own, I am not looking forward to.

We go inside, with Mitchell guiding me in by placing his hand on the small of my back. Luke is now sitting in the chair behind the counter, clearly still in the middle of a bi-floor chat with George. Mitchell smiles up at George and encompasses Luke in the warm glow.

"Shall we start that again?" he says. "I'm Mitchell van Leuven, great to meet you." He holds out his hand to Luke, who rises to shake it.

"I meant to say this earlier, but Mitchell asked me to marry him a little while ago," I say.

"And Esme accepted," says Mitchell.

"Yes, yes—I meant that. We are going to get married."

"Congratulations," says Luke.

Upstairs, George has drawn his eyebrows together to give me his Special Look. "Yes, indeed," he says. "Congratulations."

Luke is now tidying up the postcard rack, a thing nobody except me has done in living memory.

"We sell used postcards," I say to Mitchell.

"Used?"

"A lot of them are already written on. 'Having a lovely time in Coney Island, hope Auntie Margie is okay now' . . ."

"Right. Interesting."

"Everyone else sells them new," says George. "We like to inject a little bit of history into proceedings."

Mitchell leans over to get one with a picture of a boring

landscape on it. He turns it over. "It's to Eileen Hastebury in Michigan," he says. "Dolores is having a lovely time in Normandy. She went out snail hunting with Herman in the early morning."

"You see?" I say. "You miss out if you buy them new."

"So this is The Owl," he says, yet again as if he has never set foot in here before. "It's a cute store. Want to show me around?"

"There's not much to show you," I say. "It's really tiny."

As I take him down the first aisle, to the paperback fiction, Luke calls up to George that he is just going out for a minute or two. The door bangs closed. George comes down the stairs to look after the front desk.

"The fiction is stacked double deep," I say to Mitchell, repeating The Owl's mantra, "and there's no order within the letter."

"So I see," he says. He reaches for a copy of Ayn Rand's *Atlas Shrugged*. "This is a cult book, a phenomenal book. Have you read it?"

"No," I say.

"You should. It's great. Her other one is as well."

"Okay," I say. "You could buy it for me."

He looks on the flyleaf. "It's eight dollars—eight dollars for a beat-up used book. I bet you can get this free online." He puts it back.

"That's the kind of thinking that will stop people writing them in future," I say.

"No, it won't. People write for ego gratification, not money."

"We've got a postcard over there—a used one, of course, that has the John Ruskin quote on it, that people would rather buy a turbot than a book."

"I would, certainly. I love turbot, and I don't need to buy books. I've got the whole of the library at the New School, as well as my iPad. Why do people still buy books? They just take up space."

"What is the space for if you don't fill it with books?"

He smiles at me. "Light? Freedom?"

George says, "I hate to interrupt. But I feel that I owe it to Ruskin to say that he really wasn't positing a world where everyone is wondering whether to buy turbot or books, and that turbot wins every time. He merely observes that people will spend a very long time looking at even the best book, before parting with the *price* of a large turbot for it."

"I've never talked about turbot for this long before," says Mitchell.

"Really?" asks George. "Turbot could fetch very high prices in the nineteenth century, or quite reasonable ones—it fluctuated a lot according to the yield of the fishermen. It has always been a highly prized fish, I believe. There is a story of a bishop sewing its fins back on with his very own episcopal fingers, when his housekeeper was seen to have dressed it badly."

Mitchell raises his eyebrows at me. So does George. "It's odd to see you in here," I say to Mitchell. It is. He doesn't fit.

"I don't see why. I came before."

"I'm glad to see you."

"You work with men—just men?"

"Yes, just at the moment, though Mary is here on Sundays. David is around as well, the one I told you about who works at Starbucks too and wants to be an actor. And you just missed Bruce."

"But I didn't miss Luke. I don't think you mentioned him."

"Didn't I? Oh, Luke—I think he disapproves of me."

"Why?"

I pick a pile of books up off the floor. "I don't know. Perhaps because he thinks everything comes too easy to me. Cambridge, Columbia, the scholarship, even this job."

"Maybe he's right."

The door of the shop opens, and Blue, one of our regulars, comes in. I've met Blue once or twice now. I nod towards him, and say quietly to Mitchell, "That's Blue. Remember? I told you about him—the one who is always just about to leave for Vegas."

He is a small man, of Hispanic stock. His hair is black and hangs in lank curls to his shoulders. He has a narrow face and a goatee that accentuates his general angularity; he puts me in mind of Rumpelstiltskin. He never smiles. All his movements are rapid and jerky—he darts everywhere, like a wren.

Blue is unloading books onto the counter. I go over to him.

"Hi, honey. This is the last time I'm coming in," he says, "'cause I'm going to Vegas the day after tomorrow. Got the ticket booked and off I go. So if you could give me a good price for these . . ."

His books are candidates for the outside dollar shelves at best. I wish he had some good ones among them. He sees my expression.

"There are some good books there," he says. "I'm happy about that, you know, because it takes some money to start you off in Vegas. That's an expensive city. Oh boy."

Mitchell comes over. He leans against the poetry section. "You're pretty keen on Vegas," he says.

"Keen?" says Blue. "Best city in the world. Best city in the world. Oh, man, I can't wait to get there. A man can go there with the shirt on his back and come out with his pockets full of diamonds."

"You'll need more than the shirt on your back to start you off in Vegas," says Mitchell. Blue looks quickly at him; the statement sounds as if a cash donation might follow. Mitchell has his hands in his pockets, but they are not fishing for money to give to Blue.

"Yeah," says Blue, "but I can work once I get out there. And if you give me something for these, miss, that'll help me out a real lot."

"I don't think these are the sort of thing we can take," I say, reluctantly. They are not. I know without asking him that these authors fall within the wide net of George's disdain. "I can't give you anything much for these. They'd be going outside so they'd be a quarter each. It's not very much to help you out, I know."

Blue uses every muscle in his body to illustrate his disappointment. "A quarter apiece? Ah, miss, can you help me out? These are good books. They are books people like."

He calls out to George, who is reaching for a book. I see it is *The Anatomy of Melancholy*. The chances of George being able to hand over that book to his customer without opening it are slim to none. "George, come on over. She's new, she might be missing something."

George does open the book, and says absently, "No, no, she knows what she's doing, Blue." I am quite pleased that George has said that in front of Mitchell.

"A quarter apiece," I say again. "It might buy you a couple of coffees on your way to Vegas. That's the best I can do."

Blue nods sadly, and I open the cash register and count out his money.

Mitchell is leaning against the bookshelves, still in the attitude of a disinterested observer.

"Why do you bother with the Vegas thing?" asks Mitchell. "We all know you're not going."

I look up at Mitchell fast. I can't believe what he just said. "Mitchell, don't—"

"Esme, it's okay. You don't understand this, but this is my field." He turns back to Blue. "Going to Vegas is your shtick—we get it. But honestly, you would do just as well without it."

Mitchell stops slouching against the bookshelves and comes forward to Blue. He takes his wallet out of his pocket and selects a ten-dollar bill. He hands it to Blue.

"I'll take the two Robert B. Parkers," he says, and picks them up.

Blue takes the bill wordlessly, and then slides the three dollars and change I have given him off the counter. As he puts it in his pocket, Mitchell says again, "You don't need the shtick; you have an absolutely valid economic operation without it."

Blue is turning and pushing the door open, just as Luke is coming back in.

"He didn't mean it—" I call out, but he is pushing past Luke and then is gone, skittering down Broadway, weaving rapidly through the people, his head always down.

I turn to Mitchell.

"How could you? How could you hurt him like that?"

"Esme," says George, "I thought you knew better than to put Michael Connelly outside for a dollar."

"And, Esme," says Mitchell, "where is your ring?"

❧ CHAPTER SEVENTEEN ❧

It is Thursday, three forty-five. I am at The Owl prior to going on my first book call with George. The shop is full to bursting with customers. It is as if they've all been released in here for some sort of browsing competition; they are up the ladders, balancing on the little stools, crouching down looking at the piles on the floor. I catch sight of George; he is opening up the best cupboard for someone. It is usually kept padlocked; George and Luke are the only ones with keys. George sees me, and raises his eyebrows to show his astonishment at all this unlooked-for bounty.

He takes two or three books out of the cupboard, places them on the desk, and then takes the top one up carefully. He treats good books with as much reverence when he is alone as when he is with a customer. His solicitude for the books is genuine; I think it imbues the purchasing process with some charm. He looks down at Luke from the mezzanine.

"Luke—can you get David?"

Luke yells for David at the top of his lungs, and David appears from the back, with a pretty girl in tow who isn't Lena.

"You getting a lot done back there?" asks Luke.

"Enough," replies David, with an irresistible grin.

George comes down the stairs. "I have to stay here. Luke, can you go with Esme to this book call on West End? David can take over from you at the front."

Luke glances around. "It's fine, George. I can handle it when it's like this. You go on the call."

"No, I would feel happier staying here at the moment." He makes big eyes at us to indicate that the customer upstairs might be a serious one.

"But—can Luke do this? Does he know anything about it?" I ask.

"Thank you," says Luke.

"Luke is great at it," says David. "You don't know anything about him."

George fishes in his pocket for the name and address, and goes back up the stairs. Luke and I go outside together. We wait at Broadway for the light, without speaking, and then, when we get to the other side, I say, "So—that was Mitchell. The other day."

"Yeah," says Luke. "That was Mitchell."

We walk down 81st Street and turn the corner without speaking.

We get to the apartment building. The lobby is black and white tiles; the rows of mailboxes are pale gold. In the time we stand there waiting for the lift, three elderly people converge at the boxes to check their post. They greet each absently and yet formally, the one because they have obviously done this every day for years, and the other because the acquaintances began in a different age and have never developed. Mrs. Eliot, Mr. Bedel, Mrs. Begoni.

"I hope this doesn't take long," says Luke, when we're in the lift.

"Didn't you like him?" I ask.

"Who? Mitchell? I saw him for two seconds. I don't have an opinion."

"Right. He was upset because I wasn't wearing my engagement ring. We've just got engaged. But I didn't think I ought to flash a diamond around at the homeless people. I thought it would be insensitive."

"That was very sensitive of you," Luke says.

"I didn't tell anyone at The Owl because I wasn't sure how—"

Luke holds up his hands. "Esme, your private life is your business."

"I should have told you. When we went to look at the Sargent. I didn't want to."

"Why not?"

"I don't know. Because I thought it would change things."

Luke almost smiles. He says, slowly, "Are you sure? You're what, like, twenty-three years old? And you're marrying this guy? This one? Where everything is about status, and class, and . . ." He stops.

"Mitchell doesn't care about things like that," I say, as Luke raises his eyes to the heavens. "*And* I love him."

He shrugs. "Yeah, but you love chocolate, you love . . . poached salmon—those things—they're gratifying, but they're not necessarily *good* for you. How do you know it's not just infatuation?"

"I think there is no difference between love and infatuation. If it works out, we call it love; if it doesn't, we shrug our shoulders and say it was infatuation. It's a hindsight word."

He gives me a brief, sad smile. "Maybe. Like I said, not my business."

In the corridor on the sixteenth floor, the walls are papered, and thick with many layers of coffee-colored paint. All the doors are dark brown. A dead Christmas garland hangs forlornly upon one. We get to a door, and Luke consults a scrap of paper.

"Sixteen B. Mrs. Kasperek. This is it. You're not at work this weekend, is that right? George says you're off to the Hamptons."

"Yes . . ." I look at him. He is looking straight ahead, waiting for the door to open. We hear the bolts being drawn.

"Be nice," he says, still without looking. "Be English."

A slight and energetic old lady opens the door. She looks to me to be pretty old, around eighty. Wisps of white hair wreathe her head like clouds.

"Mr. Goodman?"she asks.

"No, ma'am. Mr. Goodman couldn't come at the last minute— didn't he let you know? He sent us—"

"Oh, that's right, that's right. He did just call. Come on in."

Luke strides forwards and shakes her hand. "I'm Luke, and this is Esme Garland."

"You're dead on time," says Mrs. Kasperek, and then she turns to me. Luke explains that I am learning the trade, on my first ever book call.

"I'm Esme," I say. She shakes my hand, and then holds it still for a second.

"And expecting a child," she says. Her blue eyes gaze into mine; they are alight with pleasure for me. "Congratulations, my dear."

"You can already tell?" I ask. I don't think you can, yet. I am just a little rounder. And she hasn't even looked.

"Why yes, when I shook your hand," she says, and does not explain further. She turns to lead the way to the books. Luke and I follow.

The apartment is a spacious one-bedroom, with high windows looking out over West End. On both sides of the sitting room, the bookshelves reach the ceiling. From a quick look, I can see we're going to be taking a lot. There are lots of hardcovers from Routledge, a couple of shelves of Faber poetry; the bottom shelves look full of artists' monographs. There are also higgledy-piggledy piles of paperbacks everywhere. On the seat of a worn and disreputable armchair is a little orange soft-cover called *Bell-Ringing: The English Art of Change-Ringing*. Next to the chair is a table with a reading lamp and a pair of glasses. Luke regards it all.

"You are a reader, ma'am," he says.

"Yes I am. Always have been."

Luke moves forward to get a better look. Mrs. Kasperek says, "Can I get you anything to drink?"

"No," says Luke. It bothers me that he doesn't add a "thank you."

"But for you—Esme, is it? You would like some tea. Wouldn't you?"

I am particular about tea, and I have apprehensions that she is going to ferret out some Lipton's tea dust that is past its sell-by date, but I say yes because Luke said no.

Mrs. Kasperek hurries past me to her kitchen.

"Come and talk to me. I like to meet new people. Unless you have to help your friend?"

I look back at Luke. He is reaching high up for a slim volume and says, "Her boss, as a matter of fact. No, no, she can take it easy. We don't like to overwork the pregnant staff."

"My boss?" I say.

"Sure," he says. He nods towards the kitchen and says, in a quieter tone, "Go keep her company."

Mrs. K is opening a cupboard. There is an array of glass jars with handwritten labels.

"They're all small, I don't buy big," she says. "I don't want them to get stale."

"Where do you get them all from?" I say. "I thought you would give me Lipton's."

She pulls a face that would not make the Lipton's people happy.

"From McNulty's. I take the local to Christopher Street. I like those guys. You know McNulty's? They've got time. A lot of places don't have time anymore. I like their Russian blend. We could have that. And I like the Nilgiri one, too. From the Nilgiri hills, in South India. It's not so expensive, but it's a nice tea. Do you want to try that?"

I say yes, and I watch as she goes about the painstaking business of good tea, fresh water drawn to start with. All the blue veins are visible beneath the taut skin on her hand as she fills the kettle.

I like the fact that Americans all have kettles on the hobs of their ovens; nobody has an electric kettle. It seems connected to the frontier way of life; whether you're in a New York apartment building or you're keeping the coyotes away on the prairie—you need boiling water? Then you need a flame.

She warms the teapot and measures out some teaspoons of tea. When it is brewing, she turns her attention from the pot to me, and says, "It's hard for me, this day. Selling my books."

"Why are you?" I ask.

"I'm selling up. My son fixed me up in assisted living. It's a pretty nice place. I will be better off there. But there's no room for my books."

"You do have a lot," I say.

"I know. But I never really got into the library thing. I always liked that I could put my hand on a book when I wanted it. And to know I owned them; that was important too. It's *important* to have a copy of Shakespeare, it's important to . . . to have Churchill, on the war." She considers me. "Both Englishmen. You've got a pretty good country there."

I don't think I can quite take credit for Shakespeare and Churchill, but say, inanely, that I like England. We taste the tea. It's great.

"I'm definitely going to pay a visit to McNulty's," I say. "Mrs. Kasperek—how did you know I was pregnant? Did George—Mr. Goodman tell you over the phone?"

"No, no. I always have been able to tell. Sometimes I can sense the sex too, but I never tell. I think a baby should get to surprise you when it arrives."

"Could you sense the sex with me, with mine?"

She nods, her lips firmly closed.

I put my hand on my belly. I was looking forward to finding out the sex, at the five-month scan, but the idea that I am spoiling the surprise is a powerful one. I might let my baby surprise me.

We take our tea back into the sitting room and watch Luke, who is deforesting the shelves steadily.

Mrs. Kasperek stands in the middle of the room and watches in silence. Luke is not leaving many, just a few old travel guides, battered cookbooks, and some hardcover fiction that nobody reads now. The old lady's arms are by her sides. Sometimes she reads the title of the topmost book of a pile Luke is holding, before it is slipped into a bag.

"The Walter Cronkite is signed," Mrs. Kasperek says, as it joins the rest.

"Dedicated," says Luke. "To Winifred K from Walter C. Is that to you, Mrs. Kasperek?"

"Yes. 'Walter C.' I thought a lot of Cronkite." She stands pensively for a few seconds, and then walks off towards her bedroom.

Luke calls out to her; "Do you want to keep it—his book?"

There is no answer. Luke jerks his head at me to indicate I should go in the bedroom. I go towards it cautiously and peep through the doorway. Mrs. Kasperek is sitting on her bed, staring straight at the wall, and evidently not seeing it. Her blue eyes are focused on the past, on the book signing decades ago, maybe. It is a high old bed, the kind that you can keep things under, and she is small enough that her feet, sticking out on thin ankles from her trousers, do not touch the ground.

"Luke wants to know if you would like to keep the Cronkite," I say, trying to be gentle. "Since it is signed for you?"

"Do you know who he was?"

I do not really know. "Was he a historian?" I say.

She shakes her head. "He was a newsman. He was the man who told everyone that Kennedy had been shot. On CBS. He was upset."

Luke is in the doorway. "I've seen the footage," he says. "He took off his glasses when he had to say that Kennedy was dead."

Mrs. K nods, and looks long at Luke.

"These books . . . ," she begins, and stops. I am frightened; for her, for myself decades from now, struggling to retain dignity with two strangers as they take away my books. I can see the straight line to her grave, to mine.

"I know, ma'am," Luke is saying.

"They are all my life. These books are all my life."

She looks out of the window. I can see the muscles of her face that are clamping her jaw. I know the action so well that it makes tears well in me too. She doesn't speak. Luke stands still in the doorway; he doesn't speak either. The silence goes on, and it is unendurable. It is the silence of the empty shelves, of the shutting down of a mind's exploring.

"Don't get rid of them all!" I say. "Keep your favorites. Keep the Walter Cronkite and the Churchill set. And the poetry and the Shakespeare. And the one you were reading."

"You're a good girl. A good girl. No, I don't want to keep any. Let them all go."

I don't see why she has to let them all go.

Luke then offers her what seems to me a lot of money—hundreds of dollars. Mrs. K nods listlessly, and Luke pulls a great roll of dollars out of his pocket, counts them out, and gives them to the old lady.

We have dozens of bags of books to move out. We stack them all in the corridor to begin with. When we've finished we go back in. Mrs. Kasperek is still on the bed.

"The assisted-living place is still in New York?" I ask.

She focuses on me with a little difficulty. "Yes, it's right here on Tenth. He might be able to make me give away my books, but nobody can make me leave New York City."

"Then—buy some more. Buy new books. Buy better books. You'd be hard-pushed to buy better ones than these, I suppose, but you could try. You could enjoy yourself trying. And Barnes and Noble still isn't far away."

Mrs. Kasperek breaks into a chuckle. I look behind me. Luke is standing with his eyebrows up to his hairline.

"Barnes and Noble?" he says. "You don't think maybe The Owl?"

"Oh, I forgot about The Owl. But at The Owl, Luke, she would see the outrageous markup George will put on all the books you're buying from her."

"That's true," says Luke, reflectively. "Maybe you should stick with Barnes and Noble, Mrs. Kasperek . . ."

Mrs. K spreads her hands. "Business is business," she says. "I don't blame a man for that."

Luke shakes her hand again. "Good-bye, ma'am. It's been a pleasure. I hope we will see you at The Owl, as Esme says."

I turn to Mrs. Kasperek; this feels urgent to me. "Do you know what Caliban says when he wants to take away Prospero's magic? 'Remember, first to possess his books; for without them he's but a sot.'"

Luke shakes his head at me, wanting me to leave it. Mrs. Kasperek says, "There comes a point when you don't need the books, because they're up here." She taps her head. "Same with you. You don't need a copy of *The Tempest*. Prospero's in your head. Lucky girl."

"All right," I say. "Okay, I'll stop."

"You love the father?" Mrs. Kasperek says.

I stare.

"The baby's father?" she repeats. "You love him? Because that's all that matters in this world. At my age, I know some things, and I know *that*. So make sure you love him. Because nothing else is worth a red cent."

I glance at Luke. He is already looking at me.

"Yes," I say, "I do."

She is looking from me to Luke. A false light dawns:

"Oh! You are the father!" she says to Luke. She strikes her knee with her palm, in exasperation that she didn't see this before.

"No, ma'am, I am *not*," answers Luke. He injects profound thankfulness into his voice. The old lady shakes her head.

"I thought you two were kind of a good fit."

"But thank you, Luke," I say. "That was very courteous of you."

I hold my hand out to Mrs. Kasperek. "Good-bye," I say. "We'll see ourselves out."

I glance back as I am pulling the door shut. I can see Mrs. Kasperek on her bed, in the apartment denuded of the books that were all her life.

❧ CHAPTER EIGHTEEN ❧

We are in a restaurant on Columbus Circle for lunch, exquisite in every particular, high above the city. It is so exquisite that I am subject to the now-usual sense that I do not match up—that this is the kind of New York that demands finish, and I am not finished. Their menu says that they don't want to impress me (oh, come now) but they do want to cook for me and make me happy. I am about to say something about this, when Mitchell says, "We're here to celebrate. I've just been offered a job."

"A job? What do you mean? What's wrong with the one you've got?"

"Nothing. But this one is at Berkeley. How does that sound?"

As I look at him, it is borne in on me that I am now joined to another person's will and desire. That in loving him, and meaning it, I might have to forswear so much I also love.

I spread upon my lap the heavy linen napkin that was probably embroidered by Andalusian Carmelites, smoothing out its ironed lines. I am much sadder at the sudden possibility of giving up the bookshop than I am about Columbia.

"It sounds amazing," I say. "Honestly—that's impressive."

"Thanks. Don't look so stunned. These things happen when you're an up-and-coming young professor . . . I told my mother about it today. They're just back from Paris. She said that if I was pleased, then she was pleased for me, but perhaps I should find out if there were any positions at Oxford or Harvard that I could think about. Isn't she a peach?"

"Berkeley doesn't cut the mustard for her?" I ask.

"Oh, it's not that. If I'd been offered Oxford, she would have wondered why I couldn't manage to get a job at Cambridge."

"But what does it mean, to be offered this?"

He beams at me. "Shall we order a single glass of champagne? Not a bottle, this time."

I nod. Oh, I will get another mouthful.

He calls the waiter over and orders it.

"It's a great department," he says.

I am a person. I am not an adjunct. "Mitchell, I—"

"We could live in Marin County. I love Marin."

"But, Mitchell—"

"Wherever we live, though, Esme, you will be able to concentrate a lot more on fitness and diet than you do at present. Running each morning, of course, but I think beach volleyball would also be a good choice. I bet you can find a group of other pregnant women who play it too."

"Beach volleyball?" I don't so much say this as echo it faintly. "You know, it might be rats for Winston Smith, but I think that for me it would be beach volleyball."

"Esme. I am turning it down. I am just teasing you. I mean, yes, it is pretty fine to be offered this, but it isn't what I want. It's very much a sideways move, so it wouldn't look like I was such a smart player. I am playing the long game."

"But then, why did you apply?"

"I didn't. I was asked." He smiles. "And then, you're at Columbia. If you wouldn't come with me, that's a heck of a commute. You need to trust me more, Esme. You are not a trusting person. Now, you won't mind meeting all my people at this party? My family and everyone? Uncle Beeky will be there, so that's good."

"No, I don't mind at all," I say. "I *want* to meet them."

"I am worried about your meeting them. They can be quite sharp."

I give Mitchell a Paddington stare over the top of my menu. He might see it as the furious stare of a human being, not the inscrutable one of a fictional Peruvian bear. "Some people think I'm quite sharp myself."

Mitchell shakes his head.

"Not that kind of sharp. Not everything is about how smart you are. Some of it is—social."

"Is it?" I say, marveling.

"You know it is. Don't be silly. My family can be difficult, if they feel there is a challenge to the accepted order of things. I am just trying to prepare you."

"I appreciate your concern," I say brightly. "And now I had better concentrate on eating, or I'll be late for work."

"That's another thing," he says. "Your job. I don't think you need to work for extra money any longer. I will provide for everything you need because of the baby. You don't need to worry about any of that. And I know it isn't up to me—of course, you're very much your own person—but I really think you should resign."

I hope they don't find other ways to make the pressure work in New York; the water towers are so beautiful. And simple, and intelligible. Can you love something because you understand it? Why don't they advertise on the water towers? You could do such funny things with them. They could make them look like giant tins of Bird's Custard. Bournville Cocoa. Lyle's Golden Syrup. A kind of English retail nostalgia across the skyline of New York. I bet there is a city ordinance to stop it.

"In fact, I don't want to insist, but please give it some serious thought, Esme. I don't want you working in that drab little secondhand store when you meet my mother."

*

AFTER MY LUNCH of quails and hegemony I come back to The Owl and say to George, who is in the main chair, "Who cleans the shop?"

"Excuse me?" says George. It is not a good sign.

"Who cleans? Do you have a cleaner?"

"Tee cleans the windows," says Luke.

"And Luke does the nightly vacuuming," says George.

"Esme does the vacuuming," says Luke.

"I don't mean that so much as actual cleaning. Who cleans the toilet?"

The toilet down there is revolting; it has a spongy red mouth glued fast to the seat, voluptuous and red. It bothers me for symbolic reasons as well as hygienic.

George gazes at me. "It's a question that has never occurred to me. Somebody must, I assume."

He has had the shop since 1973.

"Where are the cleaning things?" I ask.

"They would be—at the drugstore. If you take some money out of the register, Esme, you can go buy them."

"Okay," I say, but before I can even open it, George says, "But be sure not to get anything with harmful chemicals in it. Especially in your condition."

I shouldn't have asked. I should have just got them.

"I think you would be better getting some lemon juice and some vinegar. And a scouring pad. Not an aluminum one."

"Can I get bleach?" I say, as I open the till.

"Bleach!" says George, as if the word is a terrible profanity. "No. No no. Put the money back."

"I won't get bleach," I say. "I'll get Ecover."

George shakes his head. "Put the money back. Put it back, Esme. I'll go."

I close the register. "Okay. And please can you get some rubber gloves?" He turns to stare at me again. "You know—a pair of Marigolds—do you have Marigolds here? Yellow rubber gloves?"

"You know that latex can be incredibly dangerous? Especially with the cornstarch they're dusted with. Latex molecules adhere to the cornstarch, and you can breathe them in. If you are allergic, you can get anaphylaxis from latex gloves."

"I don't mean the kind that surgeons wear, and I wasn't going to inhale them. I mean the kind that you wear to clean the toilet. Yellow ones. No cornstarch."

He trundles off down Broadway in search of cleaning agents that don't work.

"How can he be more worried about Marigolds than germs?" I say.

"What's with the sudden urge to clean?" asks Luke.

"My cleaning urge is not sudden. But Mitchell said—I mean— I think the store might be a bit drab. I don't know—"

Luke nods.

"What?" I say.

"Nothing." Luke walks rapidly to the back of the store with a pile of books, and then rapidly back again. He still has the pile of books in his hand.

"What?" I say again. "What's the matter?"

"Nothing. You're being very—wifely."

Luke doesn't talk to me like this. It stings.

"I think he has a point," I say.

"Evidently."

"Whatever," I say. I hate that word, but I am hoping Luke hates it more.

"Take charge of the front," Luke says. "I'm going to be dealing with the Internet orders."

"Fine," I say. I watch him stalk up the stairs.

There are two customers in the shop. They look very settled. I think of ways to get rid of them so that I can argue with Luke.

"Gosh," I say loudly, "I had no idea that it was so late. We're closing early, aren't we?" He stares at me over the banister in disdain and puzzlement, and then goes back to the computer screen. I wait for the power of suggestion or discomfiture to propel the people out of the shop, but it doesn't work. Scanning our little shelf of CDs, which still sell quite well, I pick out *The Best of Christian Rock* and take the disc from its pristine case. I press "play." After a minute, both customers shoot out of the shop.

Luke is looking in their wake. "Esme, take this crap off," he says.

I leave it playing. I think about what I want to say to him, and then I decide that I will forgo being nice, and be truthful.

"You're treating me badly," I say.

Luke makes a good job of looking bewildered. "I'm not treating you badly. I just don't want to hear that Jesus loves me with a lame guitar riff in the background and a drummer who sounds like he's playing a different song."

"Not the music. You were mean about Mitchell."

He shrugs. "Yeah."

He carries on working at the computer. I leave the music on, just to infuriate him, and start to put the new CDs in order. The uncompanionable minutes tick by.

"You're so wrong about Mitchell," I say.

"I told you before, I don't have an opinion on Mitchell," Luke says. He types. He picks up another book, opens it to the title page, types some more.

"You don't know *anything* about him."

"I know, that's what I said. I kind of have to work, here?"

"You just seem to be judging him. He has a perfect right to express an opinion on what the shop is like—anybody does."

Luke says nothing at all.

"Really. Free speech. You're supposed to be fond of that?"

"Esme. Leave it alone. Please."

"You just have no idea. He has had to work really hard to get where he is."

"Oh sure, it's nice to see someone from that kind of background struggle through. And when you say 'where he is,' where is that, exactly? I have no idea. Does he manage hedge funds? Sell arms?"

I feel a surge of unholy triumph that I've got him to respond. Perhaps I am deeply unpleasant.

"You want him to be a hedge fund man so that you can despise him more. He teaches economics at the New School, that's all. He's not a stockbroker. He's got a PhD from the LSE."

Luke is in full flow now. He is standing up, his fists clenched. "A PhD from the LSE? Does talking in acronyms that no one else will understand make you feel better? Seems to me you two are a good fit."

"And it seems to me that you're desperate to justify your lack of ambition by *sneering* at other people who have some. Mitchell's just been offered a faculty job at Berkeley. You don't get invited to a place like that just because of your background."

"Er, yeah, honey, that's exactly what you do."

I say nothing at all. I squeeze the pencil in my hand until it snaps.

"Berkeley," says Luke. "Wow. I guess you've made it. We'll sure miss you."

I go downstairs, get my bag, and come back to the front. "Tell George I feel sick," I say. "You won't be lying." I march out of the shop.

I hear the door burst open again behind me. Luke runs out and stands in front of me on the street.

"Let me past," I say. I try to push past him, but he just moves again. I say, "I want to hit you."

"Too bad," he says. "We've just covered for and tried to help you for days because of the baby—now we cover for you because you're pissed off? You're coming back inside, or you're fired."

"You can't fire me."

"Watch me."

He stops. So do I.

"You're going to Berkeley with him? Just like that? You're at the start of a PhD yourself, right? Is that just bullshit too? It means nothing to you now that you've got your man?"

I raise my hand to slap him. I want to slap him very, very hard. He catches my wrist. "Think," he says. He is almost gentle.

We both—I think we both—see George at the same time. He

is standing a little way off, his arms by his sides, holding two carrier bags from Whole Foods.

Luke lets go of my wrist. I am out of breath. George looks at us, and then pointedly back at The Owl.

"I hate to interrupt," he says, "but the store doesn't seem to be quite so well staffed as it was when I left."

"Come back inside," Luke says to me, in a quieter tone. "Come back inside. I'm yelling at a pregnant girl on the street."

"I think you should apologize," I say. He casts his eyes to the heavens.

"Yeah, I should. And so should you, for coming out with that—that misguided crap about ambition. So, shall we go back into the drab bookstore and apologize to each other?"

"If you both want to continue in your employment, it might be a good idea," says George.

"All right," I say. Luke takes my arm and propels me back round. We follow George inside. The very dreadful Christian-rock lyrics are still playing, and nobody has stolen the money from the register.

I turn the music off and sit down in the chair at the front. Luke stands on the bottom stair, a hand on each banister. George has put the carrier bags on the counter and is standing in front of them. We are all silent. Nobody apologizes to anybody.

I go to the basement, with its single, low-watt lightbulb illuminating the grime, and I set to work. I wear the rubber gloves, and I clean the toilet with its horrible red mouth seat cover, and the stained basin, and all around the revolting little bathroom. I am deeply ashamed that I didn't think of it before. I spend so much time making sure the shop is tidy, but I was assuming that somebody else did all the menial cleaning. Maybe I am going to fit right in with Mitchell's people after all.

When I come back up, Luke has finished his shift and is gone.

✦

THE FOLLOWING MORNING, Mitchell turns up outside my apartment in a black car. I knew he had a car, but I have never seen it before. I don't know where he keeps it, but when people have finished telling you how near you are to a rat in any part of Manhattan, moving on from the near certainty that you've just inhaled cockroach limbs, they start talking about how insane it is to have a car here, naming prices for parking that are on a par with my rent.

I come down with my bags; the tiny boot is full of Mitchell's stuff, so we have to put mine in the back. The back is tiny too, and yet the car seems long and sleek. It is all car and no space.

"Do you like it?" asks Mitchell, casting a loving glance at its insides, which probably cost the lives of several cows and a couple of tortoises. Or is it walnuts?

"Yes," I say politely. "What kind is it?"

He says that it is a twin-turbo double-jewel-powered Aston Martin with a wraparound lynx action, or something very like that. I say that that is very nice.

"But you won't be able to keep this when the baby comes," I say. "You'll have to get—I don't know—the kind that is the very safest."

Mitchell turns to me. He looks like a model for Munch's *The Scream*. When he speaks, even his voice is pale.

"The . . . baby . . . can go in the back," he says.

I glance over my shoulder, enjoying myself.

"Then I'd better not eat much between now and July," I say. "Are we going to go soon?"

Mitchell switches the car on and we swoosh off to the Hamptons.

As we are driving out along the flat American expanses of the Long Island Expressway, Mitchell says that there is nothing to worry about in the way I am dressed, and that I shouldn't be nervous.

I reply that I am not nervous.

"There's no reason to be."

"Good. And there is nothing wrong with the way you're dressed either," I say, in reassuring tones. He looks a little puzzled, but doesn't pursue it.

"Are *you* nervous?" I ask.

"I rarely introduce women to them," he says.

Mitchell can say things that scald me, as if I have inadvertently stuck my hands in boiling water.

"And this time you're introducing your pregnant fiancée."

"Yep."

"Will they think you are only marrying me for the sake of the baby?"

There is no answer. There is just the black sound of Mitchell's laughter.

"Are you?" I say. "Mitchell? Are you?"

He stops laughing. "No, as a matter of fact," he says. "No. I told you, Esme Garland. I have singled you out from all the world."

I am basking in this sentence when Mitchell, very uncharacteristically, lets out a long and sonorous fart.

He starts laughing again at my expression.

"My mother can't bear people farting," he says, "I mean, in a really OCD fucked-up way. So, I guess either I need to fart because I am getting near to her, or I let them out before I get there. But nobody farts in the Hamptons."

"Really? The air must be very clear."

"You can see for miles."

✦

WE EVENTUALLY ARRIVE in a seaside village: clapboard houses of pastel hue, a pretty little schoolhouse that ought to have Laura Ingalls on the steps, and a post office that is open alternate mornings in the winter.

We go first to the Winslow House, owned by a man called Carter Winslow, who has said we can use it for the whole visit. Outside the house is a whitewashed fence, and then the Naples yellow of the sand and the pale blue of the winter sea stretching out to the horizon. On one of the fence posts, someone has tied a red bow, for Christmas.

Carter Winslow is in Singapore, doing something with money.

Mitchell checks his phone for instructions. The house is unlocked, and we have been given the Blue Room. When we go in, we are greeted with an outpouring of light, of sea light, from the window. Even the shadiest corners of the room are lightened by the radiant turquoise light. Outside, a rickety wooden jetty juts into the sea.

The walls are papered with some soft blue floral pattern, and there are twin beds with a wool blanket on each, the old-fashioned kind that have a silk edge in the same color as the wool. The beds are iron; they have a flavor of wartime England, as if they were painted by Eric Ravilious.

"Like it?" Mitchell asks.

I beam at him.

"Not sure about the twin beds," he says. "That's probably Mother, allowing us a room together but making herself feel better by making sure they're twins. No, Esme, don't get comfortable. We should walk across and meet them."

Mitchell's parents live in the next house along the shoreline. Their house is grander than the Winslow House, which twenty minutes ago I would have been hard-pushed to believe.

Mitchell ushers me into a room with pale gray walls and gray woolen rugs on the wood floor. Translucent white blinds are pulled down; otherwise we would be able to see the sea. Over the fireplace is a painting that looks like a John Marin. It probably is a John Marin. Mitchell's mother—I assume it is Mitchell's mother—is sitting on the sofa. She is reading.

"Mother!" says Mitchell, and goes over to the sofa to kiss her. She submits to the kiss, and then finds her bookmark and lays her book carefully aside. She stands up, looking at me.

"Mother, this is Esme. Esme Garland, my mother, Olivia van Leuven."

Mitchell's mother moves forward, murmurs, "So pleased," holds out her hand, and places her cool cheek against mine for a scant moment. She is a scented person—she smells of violets. She withdraws from me and stands still, without saying anything. She is wearing an English Liberty print blouse and a pair of beautifully cut trousers. And pearls.

"And here is my father," says Mitchell, as a man comes quietly in. Mitchell performs the introductions again. Cornelius van Leuven is an older, more chiseled, more tanned version of Mitchell. He shakes my hand and says good afternoon.

"You have cut your hair quite charmingly," Olivia says. "Presumably you have done it yourself. I doubt that a salon would have managed it with so much—*brio*."

Her manner of speaking has some sort of affinity with dandelion clocks—her words float gently in the powdery air of her living room without any seeming intent. The manner is somewhat at odds with the message.

"My friend cuts it," I say.

"Yes," she says. "And is hairdressing his profession?"

It is tempting to say, of course, that Stella is working on an exhibition of lesbian sex-dungeon photographs, but no. Treat each blow with a kiss.

"She's at Columbia with me."

"Oh yes. Mitchell spoke of that," she says. "Drinks, Cornelius?"

Mitchell's father asks us what we would like, and then Mrs. van Leuven indicates a sofa for us to sit on. Mitchell holds my hand when we sit down on it together. I think this is very nice of him. Then I see him grinning at his mother, and the hand-holding suddenly feels like a performance. There is something in all this that is amusing Mitchell.

Mrs. van Leuven enfolds our hand-holding in her impassive gaze, and then accepts her glass gracefully from her husband.

"And your trip over?" When she speaks to someone, she looks somewhere else, anywhere else, as if with a wistful hope that there will be something elsewhere in the room to engage her interest.

When she gets an answer, her glance passes briefly over the speaker and then away.

"It was fine," says Mitchell. "Is everything all on track for your party?" He turns to me. "My mother's Christmas parties are famed throughout the land."

Olivia does not react to this. She says, "Julia seems to have everything under control. I brought Hervé with me from Paris, and he is proving invaluable. That, I rather think, has been my only contribution thus far."

"Hervé is Mother's hors d'oeuvres chef," explains Mitchell.

"Ah," I say.

"And the piano has been tuned," Olivia adds.

"Every year we sing carols around the piano," Mitchell says. "At the party, not tonight. Esme has a nice voice, Mother, she'll be an addition."

A ghost of an acknowledgment flits across Olivia's face. Her absolute want of interest stifles any impulse in me towards polite denial.

Cornelius sits down too, with his drink.

"You're staying at the Winslow House?" he says.

"Yes," says Mitchell. "It was decent of Winslow to give us the use of it."

"Carter Winslow is that kind of man," says Cornelius.

There is a silence. We all sip our drinks.

Mitchell says, "Although I think someone else might be staying there too tomorrow, just for the party—a friend of Portia's?"

"Oh?" says Cornelius, his brow furrowed, "I hadn't heard—"

"He might not come," says Olivia, "I believe it is a teacher. An old teacher of Portia's."

"Ah," says Mitchell. "Good."

I nod in affirmation that it is good.

"It is a beautiful house, the Winslow House," says Olivia tranquilly.

"Yes, it is," I say.

"When I came up here for my first summer, as a bride, and I

saw the Winslow House, I wished that the van Leuvens owned that house instead of this one," she says.

"The Winslow House is a lot smaller," says Cornelius.

"Yes," says Olivia. She does not go on to say that of course she prefers her own, larger house now. She merely sits.

"We are in a blue bedroom," I say, to fill up the silence. "It is lovely, all different shades of blue. It has long windows that look out to sea. And it has its own dressing room!"

Olivia's face, not particularly animated so far, now shuts down, in a manner that reminds me irresistibly of Mitchell. I look back rapidly over what I have just said and realize that, of course, I have referred to our bedroom. Where Mitchell and I might be thought to be having lots and lots of sex.

"Has anyone arrived here yet?" says Mitchell.

"Anastasia is here, Mitchell," says his father, with what I decide is far too much gravity.

"Ah, yes, I knew that." Mitchell nods. "How is she?"

Olivia looks sharply at him.

"She is very well," she says.

"Good," says Mitchell. He steeples his hands together. "It will be nice to see her. I'm very fond of Anastasia. I am glad you're going to meet her, Esme."

Cornelius gets up abruptly.

"If you'll excuse me, I have a great deal of work to do before dinner," he says. He nods formally to me. "Pleased to have met you, Miss Garland."

I stammer something about being pleased too, and I glance at Mitchell. He is looking at the top of his steepled fingers.

"Anastasia?" I say, and I don't like the sound of her name in my mouth.

"You won't have met her," says Olivia. "Her photograph is over there—she was in her late teens then." She indicates a white bookshelf, on which are ranged a few silver-framed pictures, before she adds, with deadly timing, "We've always kept her with the family."

Mitchell gets up to go and have a look. It is a black and white photograph, a good one. She looks very fair, a kind of Swedish or Icelandic fairness, and the photographer has caught her in a moment of pure happiness. Her head is back, her glance is slanted towards someone; she is laughing, hard. The wind is whipping her hair around her face.

"She looks lovely," I say.

"Oh, she's by no means at her best there," answers Olivia. "She was busy getting ready for—Milan, I think it was, Mitchell; the Milan show? Who is she wearing, there, darling? Is it Alexander McQueen?"

"I don't know," says Mitchell, shortly. Then, "In fact, I do remember that dress. It's Hermès."

Olivia's graceful nod corroborates this. "Yes, that's it. The McQueen I'm thinking of had a completely different neckline."

"Milan?" I say. "I didn't realize she was a model."

"Anastasia?" says Mitchell, and his grin is perplexed. "She's not a model *now,* she just did a little a few years ago, for fun. She's working on Wittgenstein."

An ex-model who is working on Wittgenstein. God made her to make me humble.

"He ate powdered eggs," I say. I know two things about Wittgenstein: that he was partial to powdered eggs, and that he said the limits of our language are the limits of our thought. In this scenario, I'm going for the eggs. They both stare at me.

"Well, there you are," says Mitchell. "You'll be able to have a conversation with Anastasia when you meet her." He turns back to the array of photographs. "Do you have one of Clarissa, too, Mother?"

Mother winces. "We did have one, of Clarissa and Devereaux on their wedding day. It was taken down."

Is the implication that Mitchell had some agency in this? Anastasia, Clarissa. Once, they must each have believed they were all in all to him, as I now do. It is impossible that they would not still love him. Once you have been bathed in that radiant charm, it is surely impossible not to want its light forever.

"Was that you?" I ask him, in an undertone. He looks astonished, then widely amused. He bends over with laughter. It takes a while. He straightens up again and looks at Olivia. "Esme wants to know if I am responsible for Clarissa and Dev!"

Olivia smiles. I wait for one of them to explain. Neither does. Mitchell sighs at the end of his laughter, and says, "And so is Patrick still persona non grata around here? Is he still—what was it—an apprentice DJ?"

A wisp of genuine amusement crosses Olivia's face. "He's in law school now," she says. Mitchell yelps with joy, and then begins to hum the opening bars of "Another One Bites the Dust."

"But Margot says that Clarissa is seeing someone else, someone at McKinsey," says Olivia, pursuing the topic. "So perhaps all's well that ends well."

My cranberry juice is finished. I fix my attention on the empty glass while they carry on talking about all these people that I don't know. I might gossip about them one day too, but I do believe I wouldn't be bad-mannered enough to do it in front of a stranger.

I wonder who will bring this to an end. If it doesn't happen soon I might fake an early contraction.

"I have certain things to see to this afternoon," says Olivia. "We are all going to gather for drinks in the drawing room at seven, if you would like to join us there before dinner. Just the family tonight—and Anastasia." She rises from the sofa and I try to get up with equal elegance, but don't manage it. Mitchell goes to open the drawing room door for her. She pauses at the door, and they look at each other. I can't see her face. Mitchell smiles at her. It is a complicated smile. He is acknowledging whatever pain she has just presented to him, and asking her to be both staunch and sanguine.

It is hard to take, the fact that I am the cause of all this stiff-upper-lip business. That I and the baby are disappointment made flesh.

Mitchell and I are coming down the steps at the front of the house when we hear the sound of hooves.

I say, "People keep *horses* here?"

"Yes, of course," says Mitchell, surprised.

"Surely it's even more trouble to have a horse here than it is to import a Parisian hors d'oeuvres chef," I say.

"Don't be a bitch, Esme. It doesn't suit you," says Mitchell.

I stand still. It is as if he has slapped me.

The sound of hooves gets louder, and a horse and rider trot round the corner.

The rider is female. She is wearing jodhpurs, a warm jacket, and a black velvet riding hat. She looks startled when she sees Mitchell, and she pulls the horse up. Mitchell is standing still on the step, gazing at her. His eyes are soft, his aspect wistful. "Ana," he says. Like a conclusion. He stands still for another second, and then comes down the steps, and she bends to have her cheek kissed. She closes her eyes when it happens. Her lashes against her skin, her eyebrows raised and drawn together in what looks like yearning. I am like a camera, intruding, taking. I see what I should not see. "Every blink is an elegy," but I wonder for whom the elegy is written.

"They told me you had arrived," she said. Her voice has a foreign lilt to it—I didn't expect that. She holds her hand out to me.

Mitchell half turns to me. "This is Anastasia Stael von Halmstad," he says.

"Ana is fine," she says. "And you are Esme. Congratulations. When are you due?"

She is the first person in the Hamptons to mention the inescapable fact that I am pregnant. I could kiss her. I could kiss her except that I think Mitchell wants to. I tell her it is due in July.

"Do you know the sex?" she asks.

"No. I didn't want to know," I say, thinking of Mrs. Kasperek and her empty shelves. I say "I" and "me" on purpose, instead of "us." I think "we" would be less than generous, if there has been something between them.

"That's nice. So often now it is 'Baby Joshua will be born at three P.M. on Wednesday,'" she says. The horse is becoming restive, and she pats his shining brown neck. "I would get down, but Foldar needs a run," she says. "We're going to gallop at the Cove. It is lovely to meet you."

"We will see you at Mother's drinks before dinner," Mitchell says.

"Oh yes, for sure," she says. She wheels round the other way and lifts her hand in farewell. The horse picks its way down the coastal path. Mitchell stands and watches, then turns to me, businesslike.

"Let's walk over to Beeky's," he says. He strides towards the icy woods.

Stepping on a woodland floor instead of a New York sidewalk feels lovely—spongy and full of possibility, even at this time of year. Dark greens and russets and browns and sudden flashes of limes and white. I wonder what American toadstools look like. I can't see any.

"This is such a nice wood. Do you have mushrooms here?" I ask him. He doesn't say anything. "It's so beautiful," I continue, in his wake. "All the blue peeping through the trees, and the sparkle on the sea, and all of it is clean and fresh. You're lucky, Mitchell."

"My mother decided to be embarrassed when you were impressed with the dressing room. Did you notice? She is a piece—of—work."

"She's very close to Anastasia," I say.

"Yes."

"Is that why it didn't go anywhere?" I feel quite breathless when I ask this, both with my bravery and my phenomenal insight.

"Don't do that, Esme."

"What?"

"Don't give me your—your handy-pack Freud, your pocket Piaget, your Melanie Klein lite. I did all that stuff, for years, and that's not it. There isn't an 'it,' there isn't a mystery. It just didn't work out."

He carries on walking, then he stops and turns to say, "Do you mind if I just walk by myself a little while? I'll see you later? Is that okay?"

I still haven't worked out whether Mitchell says things to wound, or because he is caught up in an idea of himself that he projects willy-nilly, wounds or no.

"Of course," I say. There is no point in arguing with him, in following him doggedly through the undergrowth. I turn around and head back towards the Winslow House. I wonder if this is part of being grown-up, acquiescing to someone else's needs. It doesn't feel like it. It feels something like erosion.

I do not see him again for a couple of hours, when he comes back to dress for dinner. I don't say anything when he comes into the room. He puts a hand on my shoulder and turns me round, and then kisses me hard, his hand on my breast. It is not an apology, it is what Mitchell does instead of saying sorry.

"Is there time?" he says.

"For what?"

"For this."

Afterwards, we walk together over to his parents' house.

Tonight, for the family dinner, he is in a black shirt and a jacket that feels liquid to the touch, as if it is made of thickly woven silk. Tomorrow, for the Christmas party, it will be black tie, and I have never seen him in black tie. It is quite cold; Mitchell slings his jacket over my shoulders. Just before we get to the door, Mitchell says, "I didn't love Anastasia. I don't want to talk about it, but that's the truth. I know how I feel about you, and I know the difference."

Anastasia is the first person to greet us, seconds later. That Mitchell has just declared this, moments before she comes forward smiling, makes me feel guilty, complicit in some sort of unspoken mockery—I wanted him to say it and now that he has I feel defiled by my own want, a kind of common or garden Salomé.

We have scarcely exchanged pleasantries when Olivia floats over to join us.

"My dear, have you heard any more from Harvard?"

Anastasia nods regretfully at her. "Yes, sadly I have. They appointed someone else. I was the second choice." She pauses, then says, "And nobody likes to be that."

"I'm so sorry. Still, perhaps the first choice will find it not to their liking, or something else will happen. One simply cannot say what fate has in store for us all," Olivia replies.

When she has passed on to another group, Anastasia says, to me, "I was so destroyed by not getting the Harvard job. It looked *so* likely, at one point. I even started looking at rentals in Cambridge. Counting chickens." She shrugs, smiles.

Mitchell is looking at her without speaking, and she doesn't speak either.

"Second place!" I say, because my nature abhors a vacuum. "That's not bad! Mitchell was offered one at Berkeley, but he didn't take it." Anastasia is hesitating; I realize too late the indelicacy of seeming to crow over Mitchell's success. He looks appalled.

I try to say I am sorry. She shakes her head. "It's fine. Congratulations, Mitchell."

"It's nothing," he says. He takes my arm. "Come with me. We'll see you later, Ana." He steers me across the room. "Ana didn't need to know about Berkeley. It wasn't very sensitive. But never mind that now." He stops before his mother and father, who are both standing next to a chair where an old woman is sitting. The matriarch.

"Esme, I'd like you to meet my grandmother, Marguerite van Leuven. Ninin, this is Esme Garland."

The old lady grasps my hand. There is a robust, eighteenth-century quality about her that makes me wonder how she gets along with Olivia.

"Isn't her hair lovely, Ninin?" says Olivia. "Esme was telling me that her friend cuts it, rather than a stylist—that tousled look is so charmingly kooky."

"She does cut it, it's one of her many talents," I say. "She's been asked to exhibit her portraits by the Richard Avedon Foundation—she's a really good photographer."

"What a coincidence," smiles Olivia. "Richard is the person

who took that photograph you were admiring, of Anastasia. We all miss him very much."

"Is it a boy?" old Mrs. van Leuven asks, cutting through Olivia's malice without regard.

"I don't know. I didn't find out the sex."

"They don't have the technology, in England?"

"Oh, no, they do—I was in New York—but I didn't *want* to find out."

"Why not? You need to make plans. If it's a boy, you'll have to make sure you get a good surgeon."

"A good surgeon?" I ask.

"For the circumcision. And get his name down for the right schools."

"Ninin," says Mitchell, "don't worry about that kind of thing."

"Don't worry? If it is anything like it used to be, you'll have to get his name down for Browning before he's born. You're leaving it a little late. We put you down for Browning when your father *married* Olivia."

"We didn't, Mother," says Cornelius. "They don't accept names on their waiting list until the name belongs to a human being."

"They do if you know the right people. Don't be naïve, Corny."

Cornelius must be used to his unsuitable nickname, and to his mother's manner, as he just looks resigned.

Then she says, "And then St. Paul's, of course. And that's coed now, I believe."

"For about forty years, Ninin," says Mitchell. "As you very well know. Stop playing the grande dame."

"If it is a girl, we can put her name down for Nightingale," says Olivia. "That's a pretty school. Isn't that near the Y, Mitchell?"

"Further east, but still on 92nd," says Mitchell.

"Nightingale-Bamford?" pipes up old Mrs. van Leuven. "No, no, not so good as Hewitt. Put it down for Hewitt."

They all carry on squabbling about the schools. My heart is racing away. Then I cry out, in a contorted squeak, "I am not going to circumcise my baby."

It is loud enough to be heard over the high-society bickering. For a second, nobody speaks. Mitchell looks at the ceiling. Then Olivia turns her head to me and says, "Why not? Boys are always circumcised."

"No, they're not," I say. "Not in England, not in most places. It is so . . ." I want to say it is barbaric, but I am not brave enough or bad-mannered enough. My heart is beating even more madly. I peter out.

Mitchell leans towards me and says, in a low voice that he knows his grandmother will still be able to hear: "I didn't hear you complain about the finished result."

Old Mrs. van Leuven bursts out laughing.

"He'll be an American. You must circumcise him," says Olivia, taking no notice of whatever crudity has amused her mother-in-law.

"But why?" I ask her.

She shrugs her elegant shoulders and quivers slightly, as if she has just inhaled some sherbet. Mitchell is leaning back now, his face averted from his mother.

Olivia says, "Isn't it—Cornelius—isn't it hygiene?"

"I believe so," says Cornelius shortly.

"And tradition also. The boy—if it were a boy—would feel himself to be very much an odd one out if he were not circumcised. You wouldn't want him to feel alienated from other boys, from the very beginning of his life."

"I don't care. I don't care at all. I would rather alienate him than—than *maim* him."

There is a general recoil at this word.

"My dear," says Olivia, her voice a scalpel, "it isn't *maiming*. I did not maim my son. It is an absolutely normal surgical procedure. You use such emotive words."

"It *is* maiming," I say. The fear that they will somehow get their way over this has me in its thrall. I can't retreat into silence. They all look so sure that circumcision is the best way to go. I say, with an earnestness I know Mitchell despises, "It is *genital mutilation*." Olivia turns her head away, in sharp distaste.

"Please," she says, "this is a sensitive issue. The Steins live just next door."

She accompanies this with a concerned glance at the wall, as if we are in a little terraced house, and the Steins are all crowded round a glass on the other side. In reality, I don't think she is in the least bit concerned about what they might think, and you probably need a golf buggy to get to the Steins' house within a reasonable amount of time.

"When it's religious, it's different," I say, assuming that the Steins are Jewish, rather than that they are particular advocates of random circumcision.

"I don't follow your logic," says Cornelius. "This is a cultural issue for us. Are cultural issues so very far from religious ones, in your opinion? Where does the divide lie?"

"Esme, shall we talk about this if and when we do have a boy?" says Mitchell. He smiles fixedly at me. "It seems pointless to have that argument now, when it might just as easily be a girl."

"You *want* it to be circumcised?" I say.

"Circumcision hasn't done Mitchell any harm," states Olivia.

I turn to her, astonishment trumping decorum. "But you're his mother, you can't—" But of course, I can't go down that route. "And anyway," I say, "it *has done him some harm*—the sensitivity is seriously—"

Mitchell stands up. I feel as if the walls are about to burst apart.

"Excuse me," he says. He nods to his mother as he walks out of the room. She receives his nod and turns back to me, her face a placid mask.

"I would really," says Olivia, "so much rather talk about something else."

*

THE NEXT DAY I wake up in the blue room, with sea light flooding through the edges of the curtains. I glance over at Mitchell, who is asleep and facing away from me. He hasn't said anything about yesterday's unfortunate conversation. I tried to apologize afterwards, but he wouldn't let me. I have alternated ever since between feeling self-righteous and shamefaced. I am right but I was rude.

I slip out of bed to the window, to look out at the sea beyond the fence and sand. Yesterday was gray; today is cloudless and the sun is shining. I stand and look out at that pale mystic blue, bathed in the fresh light of morning.

I suppose you need a lot of money for everything to look this simple. The iron beds were probably shipped from an antique shop in Chipping Norton; the fence is probably from Bloomingdale's or flown in from Antigua. But if they can afford it, why not make things beautiful?

Mitchell is still sleeping. I would like him to wake up and make love to me; on the thought, my nipples harden under my T-shirt. I take it off, and slip with nothing on into the little bed behind Mitchell, curving my body round to fit his. I like the feel of my skin, cool from being out of bed, next to the warmth of his. I put my hand round to the front of him, to stroke him into being hard, and as I do he jerks awake, pushes me away, and sits up. I am nearly thrown out of the bed.

He says nothing. He sits and rubs his face. I lie still.

"You can't just do that, Esme, I wasn't ready."

"I'm sorry. I just wanted to, I thought it would be okay. I even thought of sucking—"

"No!" He clutches his hair. "No, not like that. It can't be like that."

"I'm sorry."

He stalks away to the bathroom. I lie there on my own for a minute, but I don't want to look as if I am waiting for him.

I go down to the huge and icy kitchen; sunlight stripes the great oak table. The cold of the stone floor seeps into my feet. I wander around—it is as lovely as everything else; if I could paint, I would paint an ink wash of it. There's a sketch by Diebenkorn that looks just like it. The sink is one of those heavy square ones; there are pans hung up all around, and bunches of lavender. I have never seen anywhere as unrelentingly beautiful as this place; everywhere the eye falls is a delight. Why didn't Mitchell want to make love to me? Because he wants Anastasia. I look in the fridge—there is a huge bowl of blueberries in there, and a jug of cream. It wasn't there last time I opened the fridge, and yet I have never seen anyone here. It is like living in *The Elves and the Shoemaker*. I help myself to a smaller bowl of blueberries, and pour the cream on. The cream delineates those little stars that blueberries have where the flowers were.

There is a newspaper too, on the table. I didn't see it before. The *Green Light*. I look through it while I eat the blueberries. There are articles about mooring rights, and about someone who is retiring from the post office after forty years of dedicated service. In the classifieds, there are lobster boats for sale—some are scallopers too. I try to be interested in what kind of extra machinery you might need for your lobster boat to qualify as a scalloper.

Mitchell walks into the kitchen. He goes over to the stove without looking at me, gets out the hexagonal coffeepot, asks me if I would like some. I say I would.

His eyes are on the coffeepot when he says, "Esme—I know that maybe I should be more modern, not so stuck in my ideas of how women—but really, I think of you as pure. When I think of you, I think of you in your cotton nightdress, or your pajamas, or, or in calico. You don't have to change for me. You don't have to do that."

"It isn't really like that," I say. "I do find you very—"

He kneels down next to my chair.

"Purity means a lot to me," he says. "I don't mean virginity. I mean something more abstract; something clean, white, clear. You are purity to me, Esme."

I look at him.

"Shall we go for a walk?" I say. "After the coffee?"

"No," he says. "After the coffee, we're going back upstairs."

CHAPTER NINETEEN

We are at Olivia's Christmas party. Apparently the necessity to fill your house with poinsettias at Christmas stretches across the Atlantic. The regulated bustle that was happening right up until the first guest appeared has been replaced by a cool urbanity. Olivia is in a green dress threaded with gold. There are waiters.

As Mitchell goes to get a soft drink for me, I see Anastasia with a group of other women; she is telling a story and the others are laughing. She catches sight of me at the end and comes up.

"Hi," she says. "That's a beautiful dress. I was thinking—do you think it would be a good idea to talk?"

I am not sure I want to. I don't want to know about her past with Mitchell. And I am fearful that she has a present.

"Making friends?" says Mitchell, coming up with a glass.

"Is that a problem?" says Anastasia, with a speaking look at him.

"Not at all. But don't go giving away all my childhood secrets, Ana."

"We give those away all on our own, I think," she says in swift return.

He nods towards a man who is just collecting a glass of wine from a waiter and is standing alone. He looks like a hawk.

"That is Tony van Ghent."

"You mean Anthony van Ghent? The literary critic?"

"Yes!" Mitchell looks at me approvingly. "Have you read him?"

"Yes—his essays helped me a lot."

"Go and tell him."

I think how great those essays were—there was a whole book on rhetoric, too, that I started but didn't finish, and I hang back. Besides, that leaves Anastasia and Mitchell by themselves. Mitchell gives me a little push.

"Go on."

I go over to Anthony van Ghent and introduce myself. I say that his essays on modernism helped me through my final exams.

"Which were at . . . ?"

"Cambridge."

He gives a little nod. The right answer.

"And the college?"

"Corpus."

"Ah. Yes, I know Mariella quite well . . . ," he says. "You must give her my regards when you next see her."

Mariella is the first name of the master's wife, a woman whose taste in dresses and shoes I spent three years admiring from afar. We're not quite on the terms he is imagining; I was just one of the many.

"I'm not there anymore," I say. "I'm at Columbia." He looks blankly at me. "Are you working on anything at the moment?" I say.

"Woolf," he says. He glances around, plainly looking to see if there is someone more interesting to talk to. Last night's dinner conversation with Mitchell's family was mostly about mooring rights, so I doubt it.

I plow on, because I don't want to fail under Mitchell's eye. "I read somewhere that Virginia Woolf didn't understand 'Hills Like White Elephants.' She didn't get it." I am rewarded with a bit more of a spark.

"Do you think his phallocentrism got in the way of Woolf's appreciation of his finesse?" he asks.

"You mean she couldn't see the mind for the penis?"

Van Ghent smiles slightly, and I begin to feel the cringe-back on that one instantaneously. He looks around as Mitchell's father puts a light hand on his shoulder. He says, "Tony," by way of greeting, and then says, "Esme, could you spare me a few moments? Tony, could you excuse us?"

He leads the way through the crowd to his study. It is wood-paneled; wood paneling seems to be a feature around here. The *London Review of Books* and the *New York Review of Books* are on the little coffee table next to where I sit down. Cornelius is standing by the white mantelpiece.

"The *London Review of Books* is terrifying," I say. "The articles don't end, you know, but nobody has ever got far enough into one to notice." I pick it up.

"Very amusing," he says. Then, "Miss Garland." Not Esme. "Miss Garland, I overheard your remark to Tony van Ghent, and it corroborated what I feared might be the case before I met you."

I put down the *LRB*. My heart is racing again.

"I am afraid this might sting a little bit. There is no easy way to say it. You—simply—do not fit—would never, I think, fit or find yourself happy, amongst us."

Adrenaline, or something, is surging through me, so that I feel my blood hot in my veins.

"I am not usually a plainspoken man," he says. "It's always more pleasing to me to attempt nuance." He is resting a tapered hand on the mantelpiece.

I am in full agreement with him that he is not plainspoken; everything I have heard him say up to now has shown him to be a man of the most intricate circumlocutions.

"But in this case," he continues, tracing the line of the plasterwork with one finger, "I feel that there is one cliché that sums up my position so admirably that it would be pure egotism to attempt a more interesting periphrasis. Plain speaking, therefore, there is to be.

"There is undoubtedly a strong possibility, notwithstanding the vagaries of contingency and misfortune, that my son might have fallen—or might, we could say, have voluntarily jumped, in accordance with the ethical codes with which he has been brought up—for a play you have made with some success, although, as I am persuaded you would concede, very little originality."

Plain speaking if you're Henry James, perhaps.

"The cliché, of course, concerns the book, and the oldest tricks therein. I am very sure that you know what I am talking about. Has my son been the victim of a play that has been used by women throughout history?"

"I didn't—" I say, but I stop. I cannot speak. If I speak, I will certainly cry, and I will not let this man make me cry. I want to say that as well as being the oldest trick, it is also the oldest accident in the book.

I have to turn my mind off from what is happening. I look at a brocaded cushion on a brocaded chair, and I think of a poem I learned at school and try to recite it in my head. *Our brains ache, in the merciless iced east winds that knive us . . . Wearied we keep awake because the night is silent . . . Worried by silence . . . what are we doing here?*

"Miss Garland!" He is standing there still. He has the same glinting invincibility as his son.

Then a fatal feeling of obstinacy and petulance comes over me. It is probably time for an explanation of what happened, however little it is his business, however unpleasant such an explanation would be to give. But I decide not to. If he thinks that's what I am, then that's what I'll give him.

I look straight at Mr. van Leuven, and I smile. My smile is meant to convey my Machiavellian soul.

A flicker of surprise passes over his face, and then it settles back into the hard lines that Mitchell will inherit.

He says softly, "Please do not think that I am someone who is unable to deal—summarily, let me assure you—with persons of your stamp."

I laugh, equally softly, a susurration of the breath. "A person of my stamp?"

"Oh, yes, it is very evident what sort of person you are."

The feeling that I am going to cry is replaced by a hysterical urge to giggle.

I do giggle. It reinforces my Machiavellian persona. He frowns. "Shall we get down to it?" he says.

My smile is one of acknowledgment this time, except I don't know what he means.

He looks above my head. "What sort of amount were you looking for?"

I should have expected that, but instead it is a shock. This really is how people in these circles behave.

I lean back in my chair and look directly at him.

"Oh, surely, Mr. van Leuven," I say, smiling, "you don't expect me to name the first figure?"

I am practically gleeful that I manage that. It represents the entire extent of my bargaining knowledge.

Mr. van Leuven is nodding—because he expected as much, or because it looks like we might be able to strike a bargain.

"Let us be clear. It is not too late to terminate," he says.

I say that it is not, and decide that I hate him.

"But as I understand it, there is not much time left?"

I shake my head.

"The money, were we to agree on a sum, would be paid only when the pregnancy had been terminated."

Do not cry do not cry do not cry be angry be angry be angry.

"Isn't this at all painful for you?" he says, a note of incredulity in his voice.

"Does Mitchell know?" I ask. My voice is a whisper, so that it won't break.

"Mitchell told me that he had asked you to terminate."

"Yes. He did." I forget to whisper, and my voice does break. "Does he know you're asking me this? Does he know? Does he *know*?"

He looks at me, measuring me. He doesn't believe in Wicked Esme any longer. He says, "Oh, my dear girl."

The tears spill out. I ignore them. If the light is right, he won't see them. If I wipe them away, he will.

Now his words seem to come from his chest instead of his head. "No. He doesn't know. But, my dear, you cannot possibly want to be in an impetuous marriage, saddled with a baby at your age and with your prospects—believe me, it changes everything. My wife—" He stops. Then he says, "And it is irrevocable. Mitchell told me that he was desperate for you to have a termination, and that you refused point-blank. That you are not religious, that you hold no particular ethical stand against . . . against terminating an unwanted pregnancy . . . I made a mistake, in my somewhat unfortunate phraseology about the money, but I am very happy to help you financially—"

I say, in a voice so small, so small, "It isn't unwanted, and the marriage—just because it might seem impetuous—"

"*Might* seem impetuous? You think that Mitchell—" He stops again. I remember how he got up abruptly at the mention of Anastasia. They all know something else.

He looks down at his green leather blotter. He does not raise his head for a long time. When he does, he says, with a slight shrug of his shoulders, "Your route is going to be the route of heartache."

What other way is there? I want to say. *What other way is there that matters at all?* To love is to be vulnerable; to love is to experience the heartache even in the very center of love.

"I have to go now," I say. I stand up, turn, and walk across the room to the door. I can't turn the doorknob. All the pent-up tension releases itself in a frantic conviction that Cornelius has locked me in.

"Let me out!" I cry out. "Let me out!" I rattle the handle manically, beat my palm against the panel of the door. Maybe there is a special dungeon, a Sag Harbor oubliette, where people who don't comply with the code are kept.

Mr. van Leuven walks over to the door as I carry on tugging it.

"Allow me," he says, and pushes the door slightly before turning the handle. It opens easily.

"Thank you," I say. Thank you. Politeness above all.

I run out of the house into the freezing air, without any clear idea of where to go except away from Cornelius van Leuven, away from his bribes, and most of all, away from the last thing that seemed to be in his eyes. I thought I saw pity.

The early dark is coming, flooding everywhere. Two lamps along the drive are already lit, throwing clear pools of light on the ground. I can hear the party, the famous van Leuven Christmas party, and I turn away from it. I will go back to the little blue room in the other house, and collect myself.

There is frost over everything; everything is still. The stasis of everything is discordant with my inner turbulence, and gradually it calms me down. I walk down Cornelius's boxwood drive to the public lane. It takes a long time. As I turn into the lane, I walk into the faintest cloud of boxwood scent, hanging as if left over from the summertime. It reminds me so much of long summer days in England that I can hardly bear that I am so far from home. I know that England is much more often about waiting for buses that don't turn up, under a sky as dismally white today as it was yesterday and will be tomorrow, but with that fragrance surrounding me, I am caught up in a strawberries-and-cream, leather-on-willow, Pimm's-in-the-garden-with-mint-and-cucumber sort of England that it now seems insanity to have left.

I fish my phone out of my bag, and try to call my mother. There is no signal.

I finally reach the Winslow House. It is not locked, of course, because nobody is worried about thieves. I peep into the sitting room—the French windows that face the sea are closed but there must be gaps in the frames, because the gauzy curtains move gently. The piano keys are glimmering softly in the twilight. There are Hopper pictures that have this juxtaposition of house and ocean, an open door with open sea beyond. When I saw them in England, I thought they were Magritte-like fantasies, but now I think he probably drew from life. How privileged they are, the van Leuvens and all the rest of them, that this is here whenever they want it. How privileged I should feel, to be here at all. But I do not fit.

I move into the center of the room, catch a wisp of a reflection of myself in the mirror that startles me. I turn to look fully. In the pale dress that I chose for the party, with my hair pinned up and some of it now falling down from the running, I could be the ghost of a sad girl who lived here a century ago or more. Sadness permeates the room—I don't know if it is mine or if it belongs to some forlorn spirit. Anyway, we suit each other.

I go over to the grand piano, sit down, stroke the keys. I can play to about grade one, the first foothill rather than the last pinnacle. I've never played on a grand. I start to play a very simple version of the *Moonlight Sonata* that I learned when I was a child.

I don't turn on the light. It's the *Moonlight Sonata,* after all, and it goes with the mood of the room. I get it wrong at first; it's a long time since I played. But I get the hang of it, and my absolute solitude is conducive to playing it well.

Music is like poetry. It can stop you thinking. But it can also open you up. I put my loneliness and my sadness and my happiness into the music; I play my simplified *Moonlight Sonata* for children as if I am Alfred Brendel. I play like a musical genius, except for all the wrong notes.

When I finish, I sit quietly for a moment. I wish that Luke could have heard *that,* so at least he would know I have some sort of soul.

There is a noise, and I jump. Cornelius van Leuven is standing in the doorway like a revenant. He has his hands in his pockets.

"You play exceptionally badly," he says.

"I know."

"Can you play the rest? Can you play the third movement?"

I look at him with my eyebrows up. We both know that I can't.

"I can," he says. He is leaning now against the doorway.

"From memory?" I say. I should say, *How could you say those appalling things to me, and haven't you ever heard of knocking, and are we really going to talk about Beethoven rather than the facts that face us?,* but I don't.

"No. But Carter will have the music." He pushes himself from the doorpost, rifles through a pile of sheet music on a table, and switches on the lamp near the piano. I get off the stool and he sits down on it, opens the music.

"Like you, I feel more like the first movement," he says. "Do you know enough to turn for me?"

"Just about," I say. He rests his fingers lightly on the keys while he studies the music for a few seconds, and then he starts to play.

He plays with the absolute assurance that I expected, but also with an emotion that I would never have imagined, not from the man who stroked the plasterwork in his study with such gentle menace. He plays what I played, without going wrong, and under his slower, more deliberate fingers, the sonata becomes a lamentation. Is it because I am not doing what he wanted me to do? A lamentation for his son? It seems deeper. It seems, because he is not a young man, to be sorrowing for all that should not have been, for all that might have been. It is sadness outpoured.

He sits in silence at the end, as I did, without moving. I walk over to the window, and then about the room, as if I will find a place where I am comfortable. It was perhaps clever of him to play the piano with me. Maybe in *The Art of War* it is offered as a tip for disarming your opponent.

I think of the music Luke played for me in The Owl, the music from the old men in Alabama, the music they play on the music system at The Owl. There is so much sad music that my baby is listening to in the womb: Emmylou Harris and Dock Reed and Leonard Cohen and now Beethoven. I wonder if it is influential— I don't want to set my baby's temperamental thermostat to "low" by accident. I have to hurry out and buy some jolly stuff.

"In my study just now," Cornelius says, looking straight ahead of him, "I put you through a test. It was important to me, to Olivia, to all of us, to know what sort of person you were."

I do not say anything. When plans go awry, and then someone

protests that they were just testing you, it seems so clichéd as to be almost comical. Almost.

"We are from a very old family. I know Mitchell saw it as his duty to offer marriage to you, and I respect him for that. But before allowing such a thing—'allowing'; Mitchell is an adult—before *acceding* to such a thing, we had to ascertain, beyond doubt, that you were not—that there were not ulterior motives involved.

"I know I was hard on you. It was hard to do it. But I am pleased to say, Esme, that you passed my test."

I stand in the middle of the room, on a faded blue carpet that is probably an Aubusson or something. I trace the arabesque pattern with my toe before I look up.

"But, Mr. van Leuven," I say, as softly as he spoke to me earlier, "I am afraid that you did not pass mine."

His skin whitens, and he moves out to the hallway without a word. He opens the heavy front door, and then pauses. Over his shoulder, he says: "You might think to be a little anxious about where my son is, Miss Garland. There was a time when he seemed incapable of straying from the side of the woman he loved. The explanation *might* be that he has outgrown that." He lifts his shoulders gently. "Good night," he says.

I go upstairs. I take off my party clothes, and brush my teeth. My doleful intent is to lie down and go sadly to sleep. Perhaps I can contract consumption in the next few hours and waste away poignantly, as I listen to the sea outside the window and the clinking of the chains on the boats. I imagine the stricken faces of the guilty around my deathbed. "Can we at least save the child?" Cornelius will ask, shadows in his cheeks from his secret understanding of the part he has played. And the priest, or the doctor, the authority in a black coat, will say, "In such cases, the outcome is doubtful. We can but pray."

This gives way to a more prosaic rehearsing of the interview with Cornelius and the rest. I decide that this passive-aggressive dream of death, and soaking my pillow with bitter tears, is all craven. I get dressed again, this time with a thick cardigan over the top of my dress. I splash my face with cold water and stride back to the party. The striding helps. The party is now an energetic and drunken buzz of noise. I can't see anyone I recognize. I go from one room to a second, but I falter at the third. I have come, sober, pregnant, wrapped in a cardigan, to find my fiancée, to tear him away from the party, and possibly from his love. I may as well be in slippers with my hair in rollers. Why did I even *pack* a cardigan?

There is no Mitchell, no Anastasia.

"Hi!"

A woman comes up to me; she is one who was speaking to Anastasia earlier. She looks glittery and brittle. She takes a long, practiced gulp of champagne.

"Esme, right? Such a pretty name. Where did you get it?"

"My name? I am named after my great-grandmother."

"That's so sweet."

"Thanks."

"Mitchell was looking for you a little while back. He's gone down to the beach," she says.

"Oh, right. Right. Thanks." I suspect her motives. Why would he be down at the beach? It's freezing.

I turn away, not to chase Mitchell anywhere, but to go back. The cardigan, the hurt; I can't hide either of them.

When the path forks, I know I should take the left fork back to the house. I stand still for a minute. The moon is up, and I can see my way easily. I will just see if he is there.

I reach the fence and take a few steps on the soft white sand. Then I see them. There, at the water's edge, is Mitchell, looking out to sea. And about two yards to his right, looking likewise out to sea, is Anastasia.

They are not in a passionate embrace. They are not touching, they are not speaking, they are hardly even moving.

I feel almost as if I am turned to stone myself. Their intimacy couldn't be more clear if I were catching them in bed together. People get drunk at parties and they have sex with each other and that is that, but this is something else.

I make myself stay, make myself face the truth.

The night is very bright. There is moonlight on her hair.

He turns slightly to her and speaks. I can't hear at all, they are too far away, but I can see very clearly, and their bodies and gestures are saying all there is to be said. Anastasia, when she has listened, turns her head away from him. Her neck is so elegant—all her movements are so elegant, like a dancer's. He speaks again, explaining, requesting—whatever it is, he wants her to understand.

She is wrapped in something against the cold, some blanket or other, and her arms are folded—not in the adamant way that people normally fold their arms, but as if to protect herself, shield herself. He is talking to her, and she is nodding. She looks down at her feet, moves the sand with her shoe. Mitchell moves to her, and raises his hand as if to stroke her hair, but then takes it down again without touching her. He moves away. Her head leans fractionally to his, as though she is yearning towards him. They stand and stand. After long minutes, his hand goes to her arm, and he just holds her upper arm through the blanket. It is a movement full of restraint, as if he can't permit himself more than this, the comfort you would offer a stranger.

He walks away, rapidly, to the left, towards the Winslow House.

Anastasia stays where she is for a minute, and so do I. I should go weeping away.

It isn't very pleasant, being the object of duty rather than desire. Their love turns me instantly into a pitiable object. No matter what I am like, I am the pitiful third, outside the charmed world that is its own justification.

Anastasia is unknowingly walking straight towards me. I do not move. When she sees me, she pauses for a fraction of a second and then comes, stopping before me. There is silence for a while. I say, "You love him."

She shakes her head. "No. I don't. I don't."

Tears are in my eyes, but I hope I can stop them from being in my voice. "It is all right," I say. "You don't need to—"

"No!" she says. "It isn't like that." I realize she sounds truthful rather than alarmed.

"I just saw—"

"What you saw," she says, wearily, "is Mitchell having his little drama. I knew he would have to find a way. He did; it's done." She pauses, and then says, "We didn't get to talk earlier. But here's what I think. I know he's the father. But my advice is to run."

I don't say anything.

"You love him, I know," she says.

I assent.

"Love someone else," she says, and then, after looking at me for a long time, she says, "I know. Well then. Come on, it's cold."

She parts from me at the path, and I go back to the house.

I go upstairs, and get ready for bed, again, and slip between the sheets. I stare up at the ceiling. Is life when you are going to get married supposed to be like this? What will it be like afterwards, if it is this difficult now? Mitchell is lying in the other bed.

Into the darkness his voice comes.

"Esme, I have to tell you something. I took Anastasia to the beach tonight. I was very worried, because according to my parents, she was still—she still had some feelings for me. I want to be completely honest. I took her to the beach to tell her there could never be anything between us again. She was upset—very—but I think, eventually, she will be all right."

I do not speak. He comes out of his bed with a bound, and crouches by me.

"I love you absolutely, Esme Garland. Body and soul. In the morning, I am going to wake you up, early, and give you hours of unimaginable pleasure. Now go to sleep." He pads back over to his own bed and lies down. In seconds, I can hear the sound of snoring.

⚘ CHAPTER TWENTY ⚘

When we come back from the Hamptons, I have an immediate shift at the drab little store that Olivia really would be pained by. It is sunny and cold. Tee, the guy from the South Bronx who sometimes cleans the windows, and sometimes sets up at midnight outside Barnes and Noble with a sheet full of books ("When Barnes and Noble closes, I open"), is at this moment fast asleep in the middle of Broadway, outside the shop. His hood is up, he has his bag under his head, his fingers are interlocked on his stomach, he is having a noonday snooze in the sun.

I watch from behind the counter. People stride or saunter around him, and he just sleeps. He doesn't care that people can see his face while he's sleeping, while he's not in control of it. Someone nudges someone else to look at him and his restful unconcern; a girl on her own, covert and uncertain, takes a picture of him with her phone. Someone else says that phrase that someone was bound to say, the prideful announcement of belonging and singularity: "Only in New York."

A thin man in jeans and a faded yellow sweatshirt looks intently at him as he passes, then glances quickly around. He has an undirected twitchiness about him that looks like guilt, but might be need. He has some mark of affinity with the ones I know are homeless, but I don't know what it is. He comes back, crouches down next to Tee with his back to me. When he gets up again, Tee is still asleep, but his bag is gone.

I put my hand on the counter as if I can vault over it, but my body stays disappointingly grounded. Instead I skirt around the counter, out into the street, and run as fast as I can downtown, after the guy. He has not even dodged down a side street; he is just walking along. I run past him and turn around to face him.

"Give it back," I say furiously at him. "Give it *back*. How *could* you?" I manage not to say, *And at Christmas too!*, but only just.

The guy stares right at me, and he is just as furious back. He rips the strap off his shoulder and slaps the bag into my arms.

"Who the *fuck* are you to tell me who I am?" he spits out, and pushes me out of his way.

I don't understand. "I didn't!" I say. And then, to his back, I yell, "But he's a street guy, he's homeless! You don't *do* that."

"*Fuck you,*" he shouts out, without turning around.

I run back again to the shop, running because I am still angry. Tee is still fast asleep.

I sling the bag underneath the counter and cover it with the *New York Times*. Luke is putting dust jackets in acetate on the upstairs table. I take the key out of the till and go up the stairs.

I recount to Luke everything that has just happened. He runs his thumb along the top of the acetate to make a crease, and turns the jacket to make sure it looks right.

"Dennis found this," he says. It's a first edition of *The Old Man and the Sea*.

I don't know why he is saying that instead of responding to my story. I stand still at the top of the stair and wait. Nothing happens. I go downstairs again and sit down. Customers come in and ask things, and I answer and look for books for them, and chat, and help them. The man with the towel on his head comes in and takes himself up to the mezzanine to look at the first editions, and I hear Luke chatting to him. Tee eventually stumbles in, rubbing his face.

"You seen my bag?" he says.

I give it to him.

"Thanks," he says, half out of the door again. "I'll see you later."

Towelhead Man comes down to buy a signed copy of *The Story of Edgar Sawtelle,* and Luke comes with him.

"You'll like it," says Luke to him. "I did."

Luke goes out, and comes back with a takeaway cup that he puts on the counter.

"Chamomile," says Luke. "I thought it might calm you down."

"I'm calm," I say. "You have a rapport with Towelhead Man."

"Or John, as he likes to call himself. Esme, you shouldn't have chased that guy for Tee's bag, it was really dumb. You know, he could have had a knife, yadda yadda yadda."

"How could he steal from Tee?" I say. I'm repeating what I said before. "I mean, they're both homeless. I don't get it."

"Oh, you really don't," says Luke. He is smiling at me. I find it disconcerting. "You want them all to be in a union? A merry band of thieves, like Robin Hood? The only people they'll steal from are Bill Gates and Donald Trump?"

"No," I say, injecting scorn into it, but I think, *Yes. That's exactly what should happen.*

He is cradling his brow in his hands now.

"Esme, honey," he says, and raises his face. "Neither one of us has any idea how rough, how raw, it is out there. No *idea*. But I like how you want the world to work."

"It *can* work that way," I say. "If we *imagine* it that way, it will be closer to happening."

He smiles again. "Drink your tea," he says.

I feel a flaring up inside me. "No," I say. "You're wrong."

"Am I?"

"Yes. You're—" I cannot think of the right word to express the enormity of his error. He waits.

"You're *acquiescent*."

He stares at me. I stare at him. He has the most beautiful eyes.

"I don't know if I mention this very often," I say, "but I do like you, Luke."

He gives me a wintry smile. "No, you don't mention that too often," he says.

✦

I HAVE FINISHED my shift and am waiting for Mitchell to pick me up. It is just past six o'clock. George is sifting through the contents of a new pink cardboard folder. He fishes out a letter and a postcard.

"Hmm. Is this a treasure, I wonder? It's a signed picture postcard from Percy Lubbock to—someone indecipherable." He hands the card to me.

"Who is Percy Lubbock?" I ask.

"Oh. That makes me think we're maybe not going to make our fortune on this one," says George, plucking it back. "We might do better on our inscribed first of *Three Guineas*. Unfortunately, Virginia Woolf is a woman."

"This just in," I say. "What do you mean?"

"It's a nebulous thing, but it is my belief—my experience, also—that women do not have that need to collect that men have. The number of women who have come in here over the years, thirsting for first editions, or things that are signed, or—speak of angels"—he nods a greeting to our resident Nabokov expert, Chester Mason, as he slides into the store—"or for the possessions of famous novelists, can be counted on the fingers of one hand."

"Hello," says Chester.

"Men seem to believe that there is some spirit imbued in these things, some extra sanctity from the fact that the writer touched them, as if there is a magic that will rub off on them, as if they can share the greatness." He smiles crookedly. "I hold fast to the belief that you can share the greatness, but only through the words themselves. The material texts are important, of course, but in a historical sense, a cultural sense. I have never been too sure about the people who want signed books. Still, an inscribed first. It won't do badly."

I cast an anxious glance at Chester, worried that his world is about to fall apart. It is not. He isn't listening.

I wonder whether to mention that in Cambridge I once held a small, hard leather-bound copy of *Tristram Shandy*, signed neatly by the author, and felt a shiver down my spine at the idea that this very book, this very object, had once been held and opened by Laurence Sterne, and that I am a woman, but I decide not to say anything. I didn't buy it, it is true, but it wasn't for sale.

"George, did you ever take peyote?" Chester says. "You did, right? In the old days?"

George says, "Violet ink," and nods absently.

"Once you've had it," he says, his eyes fixed on George, "you understand music differently, you understand color differently, you understand these things in relation to each other once you've had it. Don't you think? I mean, you and I, George, we remember those days, those hazy crazy days, and we know, don't we? With peyote, you become synesthetic. I wonder if Nabokov took it. He was synesthetic. I think he did, I think he took it."

"I doubt it. You don't get much peyote on the Russian steppes," says George. This is both dampening and provocative—George must know well enough that Nabokov didn't have anything to do with the Russian steppes. I think George finds Chester difficult. We all do. Luke asked him to stop telling a couple of girls about Balthus the other day, and he pleaded the First Amendment.

He begins to explain to George that Nabokov's Russia was the Russia of St. Petersburg, but George holds his hand up to him and says he was just teasing. Chester looks delighted at being teased.

"Anyway, in my eclectic batch this morning, aside from Percy Lubbock and Virginia Woolf, and two books on Maimonides, I got this thing." He pats a large, dirty, creased paperback Bible.

"Is it valuable?" I ask, with some misgivings. It is not a thing of beauty. He hands it to me as Mitchell comes in.

"Valuable?" says George. "Oh, hi there, Mitchell. Well, Esme— what is value? I am sure Mitchell could tell us."

"Value? I could try," says Mitchell.

"Shakespeare could tell us also," George adds. "'What is aught, but as 'tis valued?'"

"What *is* your most valuable book," says Mitchell, casually, "just as a matter of interest?"

"There is a copy of *Pale Fire* upstairs," says Chester, with the air of someone who can't help but disclose his precious secret and is taking a terrifying gamble on the chance that this man will walk away with it. "They have it priced at three thousand dollars."

"*Pale Fire* by . . . ?" asks Mitchell pleasantly. The book is safe. Chester looks pained. "Nabokov."

"What would you give me for this?" asks George of Mitchell. Mitchell looks dispassionately at the Bible. "I don't want it," he says, "but I would price it at three or four dollars."

"No, you don't want it, and we are all used now to being told what we do want by Amazon, which is busy protecting us from accident, precluding the serendipitous discovery. It belonged to Gregory Corso, who was one of the Beat poets—writers, I should say. Along with Jack Kerouac and Allen Ginsberg and such."

"*Howl,*" says Mitchell, like Lear. "Oh, and *On the Road.*"

George nods. "Yessir, *On the Road.* Although in my opinion, *On the Road* can't hold a candle to some of the other material produced by the Beats, particularly Ginsberg, as you say. Corso's poems outshine it too, at times—'Marriage,' and 'Bomb.' Esme, have you read 'Marriage'?"

I shake my head.

"You maybe should, both of you. It casts a cold eye, et cetera." George turns back to Mitchell, like the Ancient Mariner to the Wedding Guest, and says to him earnestly, "Corso was a New York street urchin. He showed up every day for school, he was even an altar boy on Sundays, and nobody knew he was sleeping in tunnels and such at night. And when he becomes a Beat he still manages, in the face of that showy, idealistic craziness, to hold on in some very real sense to his Catholic faith—I think that such a thing is oddly impressive; certainly it is moving."

Mitchell is stopped in his tracks. He gets impatient when he has to keep still and listen to anyone, but George seems to be exerting some strange Coleridgean power.

"In my opinion, there are moments in Corso's poetry that approach a kind of momentous lyricism that contains a kind of understanding of something both of the world and beyond it. There are moments, anyhow, when something divine happens in Corso's work."

"I'll have to look him up," says Mitchell.

"But to your question. You're an economist, and you ask what the most valuable book in here is? Well, the truth is, I don't know. Is it *Hamlet,* where every sentence is a mine, every word a gem, every thought a treasure house? What about the Old Testament, or the New, or the Qu'ran, or *Nicomachean Ethics,* or Plato's *Symposium* . . . we have no shortage of magnificent books. But for all that value, I think we have a copy of *Hamlet* for three dollars, and there are many places in the city where you can get a Bible or a copy of the Qu'ran for nothing."

"Sure." Mitchell smiles. "I was thinking more of a few pages of the Gutenberg. Or something quintessentially New York."

"We haven't so much as a molecule of the Gutenberg Bible. But perhaps we should consider this unprepossessing thing." He holds up the Bible. "It is, after all, linked even by our conversation right to New York City, right to where we are right now, and to the modernist poetry of the twentieth century, to the tension between existentialism, where everything is held absurd, and faith, where everything is invested with meaning. So might it not be the case"—here, he leans forward towards Mitchell, his eyes and being intent upon him—"might it not be the case that this ragged Bible, with coffee cup stains on the front, is the summation of New York? This Bible—is it Corso's? It's likely not to be, it's likely to be the line that some sharp New York dealer has spun—it hardly matters, Corso took a Bible *like* this through the streets of New York, from the church. When the city rejected him he stayed anyway, with a book *like* this in his pocket, and this book, with all its stains and all its creases, who knows how many subways and streets it has gone through, who knows how many times Solomon has built his temple, who knows how many times Jonah has been spewed forth from the whale, who knows what pyrotechnics of imagination it has wrought, whether it was in Corso or in some mute, inglorious Milton. I think, I really think, that this book is a symbol of the city, not because it is rare and strange but because it *isn't*."

All three of us stare at the floppy Bible in George's hands. Mitchell raises his eyes slowly and George does the same. Their gazes lock, and Mitchell grins.

"I'll take that copy of Hamlet."

George, sphinxlike, goes to get one. He comes back with it.

"Three dollars, please."

✦

THE WHOLE OF New York is becoming immersed in Christmas, although Thanksgiving kept it at bay for longer than at home. It is an all-out riot of commercialism, instead of the highbred results of it displayed in cool understatement out at the coast. The windows of the big stores on Fifth Avenue are glittering fairy tales draped with diamonds, and the Rockefeller tree is lit, and the Cartier building is wrapped in a huge red bow, and a vast crystal star sparkles over Fifth Avenue and 57th Street, and Salvation Army Santas ring bells on every corner, and every tree is wrapped from its trunk to its smallest twig in tiny white lights, and entry into any shop means being forced to listen to "A Holly Jolly Christmas" and "Jingle Bell Rock." The Owl is giving away little paper cups of mulled wine, heated up on a hot plate on the mezzanine. The wine is costing George a fortune, because he is insisting on organic ingredients. Organic wine is not so difficult, but organic nutmegs are a different story.

At the height of all this, when every New Yorker of any race or creed seems saturated in the yuletide spirit of bringing light and warmth to the darkest part of the year, I sell a book to a customer and wish her a merry Christmas. She stares back at me as if I have said, "Blessed be Odin."

When she has gone, Luke says, "We don't say 'Christmas.'"

"We do say 'Christmas,'" says George, "but we wish each other happy holidays."

"It's like saying 'Oriental,'" says Bruce. "You can't say 'Oriental.'"

"But I don't get that either," I say. "You can say 'Occidental.'"

"Only if you say it occidentally," says David.

"Is this real?"

"It's real," says George, in a considering tone. "It's just a courtesy that's arisen from so many different faiths and nationalities living cheek by jowl. It's more or less axiomatic that nobody should impose a belief system on anybody else, don't you think?"

"I suppose so," I say, although that doesn't count for George and his evangelism for goji berries and maca roots. "When I've finished work, I'm going to buy a holiday tree."

"You see, you pick things up real fast," says Luke. "You're gonna be fine."

The Christmas trees are brought from Vermont by monosyllabic men in warm clothes; they seem alien, closer to the earth, silently contemptuous, like gypsies. They bring in their trees and stand them up on the pavements, so that swaths of Broadway are suddenly transformed into dark, pine-scented avenues.

The Koreans beneath my apartment import their own trees, and then trim them all into uniformity with a chain saw—all the buds, all the branches that stick out beyond a supposed Platonic ideal are shaved off without compunction. In December, I go to sleep at night lulled not by the swoosh of passing traffic, but by the buzz of Korean chain saws, sharpening each Christmas tree to a fine point.

That evening, I buy a little tree from the Vermont men, since they troubled to come all the way down here and this might be their only income for the year. They shoot it through a netting machine and at first I carry it, but it is too heavy, so I drag it the last two blocks down Broadway.

I put it up in the corner of my apartment and drape it with lights from Duane Reade. Mitchell has work to do and can't come round, but he is amused that I have bought a tree, and says I should make it into a New York one, and that he will bring me baubles in the shapes of hamburgers, yellow taxis, New York pickles. It is a peculiar experience, to put a tree up by myself. It lends itself to loneliness, of course, but also to reverence. However little I involve myself with religion, I am still decorating a Christmas tree, unprompted, alone. It is not entirely empty of meaning.

Stella comes round, and tells me I need cranberries. She goes downstairs and comes back with a bag of them, and we spend a peaceful evening threading garlands of dark red berries. We wouldn't do such a thing at home; we feel as if everything has to be bought, made of plastic or glass, to be all right on the tree. Is it because England is damper, and they will go moldy, or because we have lost that connection with the earth that Americans still have?

When she has gone, I sit in the dark contemplating my bright tree for a long time before I click the switch and take myself off to bed.

IT IS FRIDAY morning, sparklingly icy and cold, and I am working at The Owl with Bruce and George. Luke isn't here yet. I am tidying up and taking down the Christmas decorations. They are discussing a film about a woodcutter who is a ski-jumper in his spare time. New Yorkers talk about films all the time, in the same way that the British are supposed to talk about the weather. They talk about old ones, new ones, big ones, obscure ones, the peculiar Polish one they just saw at the Angelika from 1937, the Matt Damon one they just saw at the big Sony on 64th, the English one they just saw at the Paris, and *The Godfather, The Godfather, The Godfather*. Reviewers come into the store, talking about movies, and then street guys come into the store and talk about movies with the reviewers. The street guys get to see all the new ones at the huge Sonys, because they pay admission for one, and then they just go from screen to screen all day long. DeeMo can keep up with any film reviewer who crosses his path, as long as the film has been shown at the Sony.

Sometimes people come into the store in midsentence, and the sentence can be about the sustained brilliance of Jacques Audiard, or that *How Starbucks Saved My Life* is *still* in development, or about how in the end you can't beat George Cukor, and didn't that lame remake of *The Women* a few years back prove it (that one was Bruce), about how an actor can go to either one of the Coen brothers and ask a question about the movie they're shooting, and the brothers are so in sync with each other that you will get the same answer no matter what, and isn't that something?

It could be a way of not talking about politics, religion, or sex, but I suspect they all care more about movies than any of those other three. I can't join in very well, and they don't like it when I do, so for a while, I just listen.

I am up a ladder when Luke comes in—I'm trying to dust the edges of the shelves with a feather duster. All I am really doing is rearranging the dust. They've moved on from the woodcutter movie. Now they're talking about the exceptional acting ability of someone called Petula Maybelle. I don't know who that is, but the name makes me think she isn't about to give Judi Dench a run for her money. I'm getting primmer by the minute. Luke is immediately in it with them, and now they're on to a discussion of Natalie Portman.

"Her looks, I can take or leave, you know? I just like her because she's so smart," says Bruce. I dust more vigorously.

"You okay up there, Esme?" asks George.

"I'm fine."

"I don't like you going up that ladder in your condition," says Bruce.

"I'm *fine*."

"What do you think of Natalie Portman, Esme?" asks Luke.

"I've heard her interviewed, and she's very, very smart," I say.

"And beautiful," says Luke.

"Very beautiful," I say. I look down at the three of them. "You must have a high bar, Bruce."

Bruce looks pained. "It isn't that . . ."

"Why aren't there any female directors?" I say.

"Any?" says George, his eyebrows raised. "Esme, I'm shocked. There's Jane Campion and many others."

"Amy Heckerling, Sofia Coppola, Nora Ephron . . . ," says Bruce, and saddens suddenly. "I'll sure miss her."

"You see?" says Luke. "You're trying to suggest these women don't matter? Are you an antifeminist, Esme? Is that a new movement?"

I don't answer. I feel very upset—in proportion, out of proportion? I stay up on the ladder so that nobody can see my face. They disperse to various occupations. Luke stays behind the counter.

"We were just teasing, you know," he says quietly. "You seem kind of prickly today."

I manage a tiny smile of acknowledgment, but the upset won't die down.

When a customer comes to the counter and claims Luke's attention, I go down to the bathroom in the basement. I decide, in the wake of the conversation upstairs, that I am not going to put up with the lipstick-mouth toilet seat any longer. I am going to speak to George.

Then I notice that there is blood on my underwear.

Dizzy with fear, I check. I am bleeding.

I make a bit of a pad out of toilet paper, and go back up. They are all still chatting.

I go upstairs to the dark green chair at the back and call Dr. Sokolowski's secretary. She puts me through immediately when I explain.

"Miss Esme Garland? You are bleeding?"

"Yes."

"It is spotting, or heavy?"

"Heavier than spotting, but not—not *very* heavy." It is difficult to judge, to separate reality from fear.

"Ah. Hold please."

I hold, and look at the bookshelves, and do not think.

"My secretary is calling the hospital now, and arranges you to have a sonogram. My secretary will call you back when this is arranged. You understand?"

"Yes."

"Do not worry too much, Miss Garland. Bleeding is in the first trimester very normal. There are many reasons, and often it means nothing to have bleeding."

"Thank you," I say.

"But—when you have had the sonogram, please call me again, Miss Garland, and we will proceed from where we are."

I stay in the chair. The Wizard of Oz books are all opposite, in a locked glass case. I wait.

My phone rings—it is the secretary, I can go immediately to the hospital for the sonogram.

I call Mitchell. His phone goes to voice mail, so I leave him a message and send a text. And then another so he will see I am in a panic. I get my stuff and come back up to the front of the shop.

"We're on Anita Ekberg," says Luke.

"We went a bit wild when you left," says Bruce, grinning as if they've all been naughty.

I turn to George. "I have to go," I say, "I—I have an appointment at the hospital."

George's frown comes quickly. "Is it anything serious?"

"No, they just want to check up on me. It's all right. I'm fine. I am sorry to be just walking out of my shift, though."

George waves that aside. "Do you want company? You shouldn't go on your own—"

I pretend to be impatient. "No, no, really, it's just a straightforward thing. I—"

It occurs to me that I should say that I forgot about the appointment, or they've changed the date of it, but I am not up for any of that. I just want to be allowed to go without fuss. Perhaps George can see that, perhaps he can't, but at any rate, he nods, says, "I'll get you a cab," and strides outside.

I pick up my bag and follow him out. The men are quiet. DeeMo strolls up as I wait on the pavement.

"What's happening?" he asks.

I tell him where I am going, and he asks me if anything is wrong. I say nothing is wrong. George gets me a cab, and as I get in it and tell the driver where I'm going, DeeMo gets in the other side.

"I'll come for the ride," he says. The cab driver looks round at me fast, his eyebrows raised, and I say it is fine.

"Did I ever tell you what first got me in trouble?" DeeMo says. I shake my head. "I was sixteen and I owed these guys some money. So a brother gave me a gun."

"That wasn't very responsible of your brother."

"And I went into the bank, to a teller, and pointed it at her, and I robbed the bank."

I look over at him. He's looking out of the other window. "How could you do that to someone, DeeMo? She must have been scared out of her wits."

"I wasn't going to hurt her."

"She didn't know that."

"No, and the judge didn't know either."

"Were you wearing a stocking over your head?" I cannot imagine the terror that woman must have felt.

"No, a ski mask." DeeMo starts chuckling. "That's where I went wrong, man. She gave me this money, but no bag. She said she didn't have a big bag, just those little bags for nickels and dimes and shit. So I get a shopping bag from this woman in the line, and fill it with the money, and run out, and ten yards outside the bank it fucking breaks, and the money's all over the sidewalk, so I take off the ski mask and stuff the money in there. And there's hundreds of dollars falling out of the face part, and I'm trying to run away, and I'm leaving a paper trail of bills . . . you laughing? This ain't a funny story, no, ma'am."

"So how did you get caught?"

"I stopped to pick up some of the money, and a cop shot me in the leg. Oh, yeah, that's funny too. A white man shoots a black man and the white girl laughs. You racist?"

"Yes, that's why I'm laughing. And so you got put in prison?"

DeeMo nods. "Yep," he says. "That was the first time."

"What did people do on the street, do you remember? Were they scared, screaming?"

"This was the South Bronx twenty years ago, girl. Mostly the other folks on the street, they was bank robbers too."

The driver pulls over and announces that we are there, and my fear floods back. I pay the cab fare, and DeeMo hops out of his side and opens my door.

"You'll be okay," he says, as I get out. "I say a prayer for you."

"Thank you, DeeMo," I say. I give him five dollars, so he can get a bus back to The Owl. "And thanks for the story."

He shrugs. "Don't matter," he says, and saunters away downtown.

✦

IN THE VAST reception hall of the hospital, I can feel more blood leaking out. It might feel like more than it is. I never wanted to read anything about it all going wrong—that's why I don't go near any sites or blogs about pregnancy. There's no news in someone being delivered of a bouncing baby boy, so the stories are the ones that grip your heart, about the seventh miscarriage, the maternal grief, the stillborn.

The blood might mean nothing, or everything. I can't think of this, or I will not be able to function. I must keep calm. If there is a chance of that tiny heart still beating, I must keep my own heart stable. I must be the eternal measure, like a grandfather clock in an old house.

First, they take blood tests. Then they direct me to the sonogram suite, where I am told to sit and wait. The girl at the desk reads my notes and gives me a sweet, sad smile.

There are about ten couples waiting already. I sit down. I am worried in case I bleed on the chair, because it is upholstered, so I get up again.

As I stand there, someone shouts out, "Miss! Miss! You're bleeding! There's blood on the carpet!"

I look. There is one red spot.

The red spot means I get to jump the queue.

I lie on an examining couch in the darkened room. The sonographer says we are waiting for a doctor and a trainee doctor, and is that all right. Yes, it is. We wait for a few minutes, and I look at the sonographer, who is making adjustments to her screen. I do not believe they are real adjustments. The doctor and trainee arrive in a bustle of white coats and officialdom.

"Sorry about the slight wait there—you're Esme Garland? Barratt James, and this is Colene Smith, she's training. You're having some first-trimester bleeding?"

I say that I am.

"Okay. We'll have a look at you. Your bloods are in, and they are normal. What would we be looking at in the blood test, Colene?"

"Progesterone levels?"

"Exactly, and they're fine."

Then he examines me, and frowns. "It is quite heavy."

"I know."

"Any pain?"

"No!" I say, seizing on this with extravagant hope. "No pain at all. Wouldn't there be pain, if—if . . ."

"Not necessarily." He nods at the sonographer, and she gets out a little stethoscope thing attached to her computer, sticks it on my tummy, and turns a switch. The sound of a baby's heart, fast and insistent, fills the room.

I dig my nails into my palms as hard as I can.

I can see shapes flickering on the screen now. It is again that mass of alien tubes and movements. Movements must be good. Movements and heartbeats must be good.

The sonographer makes her measurements in silence, then leans back and looks straight at me. "It all looks fine to me."

"It is looking fairly positive, but I am afraid the bleeding is more than just spotting. Miss Garland, I am sure," says the doctor mistakenly, "that you want me to tell you what is on my mind. There are times early in a pregnancy where a kind of genetic mismatch means that a miscarriage may occur. That's one of the main causes of heavy first-trimester bleeding."

"Is there?" I whisper. "Is there a genetic mismatch?"

"No, I don't know—I mean that if the bleeding continues, and you experience fetal demise, that will probably be why. If it does happen, there is no reason why you shouldn't have perfectly normal pregnancies in the future."

"That's true," chimes in the other one, the trainee. "You should look on the bright side. Many people never get this far."

I nod, because I can't speak. I wish I had someone here, to answer for me when I feel too sad to be polite. I turn my face to the wall.

Outside the hospital, I raise my hand slowly and carefully, and a cab slides over to me. I ask him if he can drive slowly and carefully back to my apartment. He can, he does.

At home, I call Dr. Sokolowski. He comes to the phone again immediately.

"Miss Garland, I have e-mail that the tests were all good. Thank you for calling me. I think that you ought to go to bed."

"I am in bed."

"Excellent. Is there still bleeding?"

"Yes."

A little silence again. I imagine that he has walked over to his window, to dolefully regard the rooftops once more. "There is a chance that you will miscarry, my dear. You must be ready."

He waits. I say nothing. He comes back, brisker.

"There is also a chance that you will not. My advice, if it is possible to take, is to spend two, three days in bed, monitor the bleeding, and people should be there to look after you. You have people who can be there, someone who can always be there? That is important."

I don't want Dr. Sokolowski to be any sadder than he already is, so I say, "Yes. Yes, I have people. Thank you, doctor."

Mitchell calls me back and asks what happened. I tell him about the bleeding and the hospital. He asks what the bleeding means.

"The doctors say I might—I might—that it might—"

Why can't we say what we fear? As if saying the word catches the specter of something and makes it solid. As if we all believe in magic.

"Where are you?" I say. "I need you." The words are out before I can think.

"I'm in a meeting in five minutes, and after that I am teaching again. I'll come as soon as I can."

I lie back on the pillows, feeling diminished. That will teach me.

I should think about organizing people to help me, if I am going to retreat to bed for days, like John and Yoko.

Almost as soon as I go to bed, I feel a dissociation from New York. Before, I've always felt that I fitted in—running to catch the subway train, hurrying to get a coffee that I drink as I walk, striding down Broadway to reach work on the hour, hurtling through Columbia corridors to get to lectures on time, meeting people for breakfast or at two A.M. in a diner because that's the only time they can see you between classes and waitressing, flinging up a hand to call a cab, praying that it doesn't get stuck in traffic, promising you will be at this gallery opening at eight, that bar for drinks at nine—needing, like everyone else, to get there now, ten minutes ago, yesterday. And the hurrying isn't necessary—it's just that you can hear the soundtrack to the startling new movie of your life, and this is New York, and so you run and run and run.

But now there is the blood, and so I draw down the blinds and I am still.

I will try to sleep, that balm of hurt minds.

I wake up again after two hours—it is three in the afternoon. Even with the blinds down, the room is light—the winter sunlight is shining through the pink petals of the carnations I bought the other day, the very cheapest the Koreans had. I can't see the flowers, just their pink shadows on the blind.

I am not in pain. I lie as still as I can. I try to make myself into a cup, a cradle. I try to be gentle and strong and make space inside myself for it to be, to live. I try to hold my baby in life by flooding love at it. A long time passes, and that is all that happens.

☙ CHAPTER TWENTY-ONE ❧

The buzzer goes. Mitchell. I get up, still trying to keep this calm fluidity. With the movement, I feel more blood spill. I press the button to let him in, but after a few seconds, it goes again. This time I press the intercom.

"Mitchell?"

"Er, no. It's Luke."

"Oh," I say, brightly. "Well, I'll buzz you in."

I look around the apartment. It is reasonably tidy. There is no underwear, no unwashed teacup. I am not dressed, but there is no way that the sight of a miserable pregnant girl in Marks and Spencer pajamas will inflame the dormant passions of Luke, so I stay as I am. How very odd, that Luke should ever be in my apartment.

When he gets here, he stops on the threshold. He says, "George sent me. He was worried about you. He thought everything you said back there was 'British restraint.'"

"Come in," I say.

He hangs back. "Yeah—no. I'd better get back to work. You seem fine to me."

It is three o'clock in the afternoon, and I am wearing pajamas printed with large cupcakes.

"I just called in because of George—we—he couldn't get you on the phone. I don't want to bother you—"

"Luke, there was some bleeding."

He looks absolutely petrified. If I wasn't so frightened myself it would make me laugh. He looks very scared indeed that I might mention tampons, or placentas. Thinking so reminds me that I don't have any sanitary napkins left—I am making my own out of toilet paper. I consider. Asking *Luke* to get them is clearly a very bad idea. Aside from how embarrassed he would be, it is just too intimate a request. But on the other hand, half the population bleeds; we shouldn't be so squeamish. And I need them. I ask him.

His expression is similar to the British at the end of Zulu. "Sure," he says. "I'll go now. Any—any particular kind?"

I shake my head. "No, any will be fine. Except—try not to get scented ones. They make me sneeze."

He comes back about ten minutes later, looking, if it is possible, even more deadpan. He hands me a Duane Reade bag.

"Did it go smoothly?" I ask, politely.

"No," he says. "I wanted to be sure not to get the scented kind, so I did what any sensible person would do."

"You read the label?"

"I sniffed the packets." He holds his nose to do an impression of a loudspeaker: "'Security in aisle three, security in aisle three!' That is definitely a store I can't go back to." The deadpan look cracks into a grin, just for a second. "I'm real glad you think it's funny."

I do.

"That looks healthy," I say, nodding at the brown McDonald's bag in his hand. There is another paper bag too; that's probably a bottle of beer.

"Yeah. If some researcher ever finds out that beer and McDonald's food are bad for a person, I'm screwed." He is looking at me with a concerned air. "What is going on? What did they tell you at the hospital?"

I explain that everything might be all right, that I have heard the heartbeat, but also what the doctors say about the chance of miscarriage.

"It's good about the heartbeat. So you should be in bed."

"Yes—I was, they say that, that I should stay in bed."

He is backing away. "Get back in bed. I'll see myself out. Go."

I do get back in bed. I feel self-conscious, but it doesn't matter. What matters is holding on to the one strand of hope that Dr. Sokolowski gave to me.

I hear him open the door, and he calls out for me to take care. I call back, "Thank you." The apartment door does not shut. He says, "Esme?" and then appears at the door of the bedroom. I am lying with the quilt up to my chin. "Have you had anything to eat? Since you noticed the—the problem?"

"No. I'm not hungry."

He spreads his hands. "I'm not a doctor, but I would have said trying to keep everything normal would be good—eating right's gotta be important. Can I go get you something?"

"I'm fine."

He sits down on the little chair just inside the door.

"Honey, you're not so very fine. I'm gonna go out and buy you some food, so you can either tell me what you would like, or I'll get you something I'd like." He waggles his McDonald's bag at me. It smells wonderful. It is tempting to ask him just to give me that, but it might be true that they are made of cows' eyelashes.

"I have some things in the fridge. You don't have to go out. Could you—if you don't mind—would you make me a sandwich? I've got bagels, and mozzarella, and rocket."

"Sure." He's getting up to go to the kitchen.

"And I have some cans of V8, can I have one of those? Would you like one too?"

"No, I'm okay with Sam Adams."

"And will you eat your lunch with me?"

"I guess—if you want me to . . ."

I smile at him to show him I do. Perhaps he can see from the smile how scared I am, because he stops looking awkward and embarrassed to be there, and just looks at me from the doorway. I want to say to him that I don't want to lose my baby. It is obvious, of course, but I want to tell him, I want to say something honest to him. I have not been honest to Luke, hiding things about Mitchell. If I can say this, it will be nakedly honest. But I can't say it. I can't say "lose" and "my baby" in the same sentence. The mystic power of words is too strong, I can't risk it.

"Oh, Luke," I say, instead.

"I know," he says, softly, like he said to Mrs. Kasperek, grieving for her books. "I know. There's a good heartbeat. It will be okay."

I nod, and smile, because he wants me to.

He comes back in with the lunch on my floral Laura Ashley tray. He does not look like he belongs in my apartment. I sit up. I am hungry. He has his beer but no burger.

"Where's yours?

"I ate it while I was fixing your bagel. They lose some of their culinary delicacy when they get cold."

"You've been working with George too long."

"I know it."

I drink some of the V8. It was nice of Luke, to realize that I needed some food. I had forgotten all the rest, in my fixation on keeping still.

"When I was with the doctor at Columbia, he said that it was possible that I would experience fetal demise."

Luke says nothing.

"Don't you think that's shocking? That he uses words like that?"

"I guess he's trying to save your feelings."

"Yes, but if he is, it's not working, because it turns round on itself, so that you think they are not according the tragedy of it enough dignity. It's—it's warding off the moral imagination. You know they say 'miscarriage'—I've been thinking about that too. 'Miscarriage'? Like 'miscarriage of justice'? Or like you are not carrying it right, like it's the woman's *fault* that she hasn't carried the child right. But, Luke, fetal demise—it's horrible, it's shocking—shocking, because it isn't honest, it's so cruel and clinical, '*you may experience fetal demise*'—if they say 'demise,' then you are not meant to think of a baby who will—never be born, a child that has died; you are meant to think of some process that you can't quite understand—that isn't to do with you. Why can't they say, 'Miss Garland, your baby might die'? That's plain and honest. There's a goodness in saying it like that, a kindness. The other way doesn't allow you to feel; there's a kind of command in it to see it as something that doesn't touch you—oh, but if it dies, Luke, if it dies, it won't ever be held by its mother and I won't ever see it, and it won't ever smell what wood smells like burning, or ever see the sky, or a flower, and I won't ever see it, Luke—I won't—see—"

He has his arm around me. I am crying into my hands, like a ridiculous nineteenth-century heroine. I've still got a bit of bagel in my mouth that I can't swallow. And I was trying to keep calm.

Luke says, "We'll all help you the best we can, Esme. If we can save your baby by keeping you still, we'll all keep you very, very still."

✦

WHEN HE HAS gone, I lie still again and focus on flowing love at the baby. I wonder if this is a kind of prayer. It feels a bit like praying. I haven't done any of that for a long time, though, ever since the evangelical Christians tried to ambush me when I was at college at home. And if you don't believe particularly in God when you aren't in trouble, it seems a bit fair-weather to me to decide to believe in him when you need some help. So I don't pray, I do this. I lie in the quiet, while the Broadway traffic outside murmurs on.

With nobody here, it is easier to think that something powerful is sustaining the baby, something I can't begin to understand, as if this focus is a real force, one that you could measure with machines. I don't want any music, or the laptop, or the radio, obtruding into our silence. If I stay quiet, I will be able to reach it, and it will know, and stay alive.

Stella comes after her classes and offers to get me some dinner, but I want to wait for Mitchell. She has even offered to cook for me, which I hope we don't have time for, because she would have to learn first. When she goes out to get my key copied so that I don't need to get in and out of bed for her, she comes back carrying two bright green smoothies from Whole Foods. I sip one. It's like drinking someone's garden.

She perches on the end of the bed, texting people and talking to me between texts or tweets or whatever she's doing. She does it all with a kind of blithe grace that wards away my attempting to express gratitude.

"I thought Mitchell would be here by now," I say to her. "Do you think anything has happened to him?"

"When people are late, it's never because they're dead."

"It must be sometimes," I say.

She says, "Mitchell's not dead, and he's not lying unconscious somewhere either. He will definitely come. He just won't come quickly."

As she says it, the buzzer goes. Stella smiles blandly and goes to answer it.

Mitchell appears holding a huge bunch of flowers. I don't recognize them as being part of the Koreans' repertoire, or from any of the other delis around here. He might have bought them from a real florist.

"Are you okay, Miss Esme Garland?" he says. He holds the flowers aloft and says, "I thought you might prefer these to grapes." There is the predictable sound of a shutter clicking, and Stella lowers her camera. "Thanks," she says.

He bends to kiss me. Stella takes the flowers with the air of a disapproving servant. She says, "I'll do these in my apartment. Text me when you need me."

"Oh, yes, Stella—thanks so much for helping out here," says Mitchell. "Esme will be all right now." He turns to me. "So, okay, let's sort you out. What do you need?"

Stella turns, and says to Mitchell's back, "She doesn't need anything, because other people have helped her out all day. The store knows, her professors know, I've been shopping for her, and she's fine."

"Great. That's great," says Mitchell. He rolls his eyes at me comically.

"Esme, I'll bring the flowers back in the morning. You shouldn't have them at night because they give out more carbon dioxide then." She slides her eyes towards Mitchell. "Grapes would have been better."

"Thank you," I say, "and thanks for all you've done today." She waves a careless hand. When she has gone, Mitchell says, "Grapes? That lesbian friend of yours takes photographs of me *all the time*. I'm just saying."

"She takes photographs of everyone."

"No, she doesn't. She's irresistibly drawn to my animal magnetism."

"I think she's immune to your animal magnetism."

He shakes his head. "There's not a woman born. Hey, I'm starving. You can eat regular food, I take it? I don't have to get you broth or something like that?"

"You don't have to get me broth. I can eat."

"That is excellent news. I am famished. Should I order Mexican?"

"Yes," I say, feeling exasperated and fond at the same time.

He gets the menus out, sits down at the table, and says, "You look hot in those pajamas. I haven't seen them before."

I look down at the pajamas. The brushed cotton, the pale blue shade, the cupcakes. I am ashamed of them.

"You're kidding," I say.

"No, you look innocent. Deflowerable." He taps the number into the phone and says in an aside as he's waiting for them to answer, "Don't let any men in here."

When he's ordered, he says, "What's the matter?"

"Nothing," I say.

"How are you feeling?" As he asks me, he doesn't look at me, but he fishes out his iPad instead and frowns at it. I don't say anything, because it doesn't seem to me to be a real question. He produces a handkerchief and rubs the glass with it, painstakingly.

"Ah," he says, sitting back and regarding the screen. "That's better. I feel like a new man."

"So do I," I say. I grin at him, because I think that's funny.

He looks speculatively at me over the top of his iPad. After a moment, he comes over, sits down on the bed, stretches one arm to the other side of my body.

"You do *see*," he says, "that I am trying to keep things as normal as possible? You see that, right? It is important not to panic. You will be fine. We will all be fine."

He leaves me after the food, so that I can rest. I pass the night in an anticipation of the sudden and desperate pain that will herald loss, but it does not come. The morning comes instead, and I decide that after all bed rest does not mean the blinds have to be kept down, but when I pull them up a blanket of dull white cloud is revealed, which makes me think of home. I pull them down again.

I think that the bed rest is working. I am *sure* the baby is still alive. And perhaps the longer it stays alive, the more likely it is to keep on going. I can't feel any bleeding either.

I will be all the sadder, thinking like this, if it doesn't work. I have such a conviction that my own will, my own love, my own body, can save it. As if love is the only fortress strong enough to trust to. As if that ever works. Where would the tragedy be if love could save us? Love can't save all those soldiers killed in battles. It didn't save them at Agincourt, it doesn't save them in Afghanistan; instead the immense love of the mothers for their sons flows on, with no recipient, like light flowing into space, never ending and never coming back. "The family has been informed," they say on the news, when you hear of another twenty-year-old pointlessly dead. "Relatives," they often say instead, because "family" hurts more. There is a solemn face from a government person, as permanent as a leaf, and a photograph of a grinning guy my age or younger, with short hair, in an army shirt. Sometimes they're not smiling, but look grave, as if to show they have undertaken a serious business. First battalion, second battalion. Royal Fusiliers. Wootton Bassett. He was nineteen, he was eighteen, he was twenty-one. His commander described him as. It is with deep sadness. He will be greatly missed. *Dulce et decorum est. When I died, they washed me out of the turret with a hose.*

Love doesn't work, love doesn't save anyone, love can't save anyone.

And yet do I get up, go to the library, abandon the chance? I do not.

I go, with extreme care, to the bathroom. There is still bleeding. Perhaps quite not as much, but I don't know if hope is skewing my judgment.

As I am prudently getting back into bed, Stella comes in with a box of herbal tea called Bedtime.

"You know I swear by pharmaceuticals normally, rather than granola-head stuff, but this tea is great. It helps me sleep. It doesn't have any health warnings on it, even for Californians, so I figured it was safe. It will help you to rest."

"What's in it?" I ask.

She reads. "Valerian root. And it's got St. John's wort in it. I think that cures the blues."

"It doesn't cure the blues, it cures insurrections," I say. I was trying to say "impotence" and something about erections at the same time. I start laughing. For some reason everything is funny. "What's the word I want?"

She says, "'Erectile dysfunction,' though it's not a phrase I have to worry about too often. I'll put the kettle on."

Once she has made me the drink that will cheer me up/make me sleep/cure my erectile dysfunction, she has to go out to a lecture. I am left to silence again, and so I do the same as I did yesterday, because there is nothing else to do except be still and hope.

It is late afternoon when Luke phones up to see if I am all right. I say I am, and he says in that case he will not come up. I ask him where he is, and he says he is on 116th and Broadway. About three minutes from me.

"Then come up," I say.

"Oh, no, not if you don't need anything . . ."

"I need . . . I need . . ."

I want to say apples, but I think it is bad to say apples. I think of different fruit.

". . . some sliced watermelon," I say. "They sell it, ready sliced, at all the corner delis."

"You don't need any watermelon. And it will be frozen. It's freezing out here."

"I do need it! It has special vitamins in it. And I like the juxtaposition of the colors."

Luke sighs.

"Okay. I'll buzz when I've found some sliced watermelon."

Before I arrived in New York, one of my Cambridge tutors told me that one of the many bonuses of living here was that you could buy turnips at three in the morning. This wasn't a draw for me, but the tutor was East Anglian born and bred, and so had a particular fondness for root vegetables. But the fact that I can pluck the idea of watermelon out of the blue, and a few minutes later there will be watermelon, is very pleasurable. Perhaps it is corrupting, too. We start to believe we can have whatever we want.

When Luke comes in, he has his guitar and half of an enormous watermelon.

"They had no sliced," he says. "Get back in bed. I'll cut some for you."

"Why have you got your guitar?" I ask him, when he comes in with a white plate and a huge red slice. "Are you going to play to me, like a minstrel?"

"No. I have a gig."

"Really?"

"Yeah—I play with a couple bands—we have a gig tonight."

"That's good. Where?"

Luke looks uncomfortable. He looks around the room and then says, "Brooklyn."

He lives somewhere in midtown. I am about to say how nice it is of him to come so far out of his way, when I realize that that's why he looks so uncomfortable. He is not the sort of person who wants a kind deed praised.

I eat some of the giant slice of watermelon. I don't want to spit out the seeds in front of Luke, so I hope that they are nutritious, and I swallow them. Why didn't I say apples?

"How you doing today, anyway?" he says. "Is it—better?"

"It is," I say. "It hasn't stopped completely, but I think it is better. I might call the doctor."

"Don't take it too fast. You want to be sure."

He looks nice again. He has a white linen shirt on with his jeans—it makes him look browner. I must remember about the hormones—they make me find almost everyone attractive. I had an interesting dream about Richard Nixon the other night, for instance, that is probably best forgotten.

"Luke—you never get hormones dancing around inside you, messing with your mind, do you?"

He shrugs. "How would I know?"

"When you're pregnant, they do all sorts of things to you. This morning, I got so upset about the soldiers in Afghanistan—you know, the British and American ones that die? It came out of nowhere. It must be hormones."

"Or empathy."

"It hit me, as well, about how scary it will be"—the gods force me to correct myself—"how scary it might be, to be a mother."

"That doesn't sound like hormones. It's gotta be real scary to be a mother."

"Yes. Yes."

I want him to stay, but—fairly unusually—I don't want to

talk at all. He doesn't seem to mind too much. We are there for quite a while, in silence. Then he says, "Maybe I should get going . . ."

I say, "If you've got time, would you play something? Like when you played 'You've Got a Friend'?"

He puts his head back, turns his face to the side a little, uncomfortable again.

"I would really like you to," I say, to persuade him out of what looks like shyness.

"Esme, something happened. We didn't know whether to tell you."

I wait, frightened, because he is so grave.

"It's Dennis." He stops. I put my hands to my mouth.

"He's dead, honey. They found him in a basement on Amsterdam."

"Who did?"

"I don't know—other street guys. Tee told DeeMo. He was taken to the morgue early this morning."

"What was it?" I ask. "When do they think he died? What did he die of?"

None of the questions I am asking matters, but we have to ask them. I want Luke not to know the answers, or I want to be able to say, *Aha! You're wrong, that's the wrong answer to that tiny question. Therefore he can't possibly be dead.*

He says, "The medical examiner figured it was an overdose, but he didn't know for sure on the spot. There was a needle near him."

"But that can't be right—he was an alcoholic."

"Yeah. I don't think you have to specialize."

I look down at the covers, thinking of Dennis, of his laughing at DeeMo's prison meadows, of how he ate his bagel.

"Could it have been something else? Hunger?"

Luke clasps his hands together and leans on them. "Hunger, exposure, drugs, drink—it could have been any of them, all of them. I'm sorry. We all liked him."

"Yes—yes—oh, Luke, have you known him a long time?"

"Yep. Years now. Strange but true."

"So it's hard for you. I'm sorry."

"I'm okay."

"I must be better in time for the funeral."

He looks startled. "Esme, there isn't likely to be one. He'll probably get buried in a potter's field—Hart Island, most likely. They don't have services."

I don't understand what he's talking about, with potter's fields and islands.

"How can they bury someone without a service?"

"That's what they do with the homeless, with unknowns, with people who don't have family. And nobody knows Dennis's last name."

"But he had a daughter. And why should the unknowns not have prayers?"

He looks surprised again. "I never knew that, about a daughter. He's never said anything about a daughter to me. He—you know, he might have made her up. He did tell lies all the damn time. Do you know her name?"

"It was Josie."

"Josie . . . ?"

"I—I don't remember her last name. How much is it to have a proper burial?" I ask.

He sighs. "Esme, I shouldn't have told you."

"Yes, you should. You should. How much is it?"

"Honey, we can't do it. It's, I dunno, it's got to be thousands. And don't ask George. He's really stretched, and he would try."

"I can ask Mitchell," I say. He doesn't reply.

"I will ask Mitchell," I say. I say it because it seemed wrong when I said it the first time. Luke is still silent.

"Aren't there Rights of Man?" I ask. "I mean, this is America, where all men were created equal; don't you get to at least have a funeral when you die, no matter where you lived, or how—?" Stupid tears are coming again.

"Don't cry," he says. "Honey, don't cry. Dennis as much as any of us wanted you to keep that baby safe."

"I'm not, I don't," I say, wiping them away.

"You cry a hell of a lot for someone who doesn't cry."

"I know. I liked Dennis, that's all."

"I liked him too."

We are both quiet. I say, "Luke, can you play something in memory of Dennis? That would be a way of doing it."

Luke looks extremely uncomfortable.

"I dunno. It seems—no, I can't."

"Oh, please. Please. Sing 'Danny Boy.'"

"I broke a string."

"Can't you play a tune that doesn't use that string?"

"It's a G," he says.

I nod as if I understand.

Luke says, "Listen, I didn't really break a string, but I can't do that, sing a song for Dennis. It doesn't feel right. It feels kind of cheesy. But how about I play a tune for your baby?"

He picks the guitar up.

"Your hands are like a bear's hands," I say.

"Bears don't have hands."

He plucks at the strings and plays a lovely, slow little tune.

I lie back on the pillows and listen, and send it outwards, wherever it wants to go. Inside the sadness, a peace blossoms.

When he has finished the music, I say, "That's beautiful. Is it Mozart?"

"No. It's *Lady and the Tramp*." He stands up, and then says, "Esme." He is looking out of the window. "It's snowing," he says.

Giant soft flakes are falling. I get out of bed and come to the window.

We watch as they fall, bigger and more rapid and more numerous than in England. At home, you watch so hopefully as they land, and then they dissolve into the wet ground; here they stay. In minutes we are in a white world. Bright, china-white light fills the room.

"It's so beautiful," says Luke. "Even Broadway."

"Especially Broadway," I say.

"Yeah, maybe you're right."

"I want to go out in it," I say.

"Too bad. Not until you're okay. I'm not helping you out here so that you can go running around in a snowstorm."

I turn to him to say thank you, and try to infuse into the two words how much I mean it. I put my hand on his arm as I say it. I never touch Luke. There is an expression in his eyes that I can't read. Then he glances down at his watch, but I know whatever time it is, he is going.

"I'd better get going," he says. "With the snow—this gig . . ."

He turns and gets his guitar, puts it in its bag. I stand still.

"Get back in bed," he says, nodding over at it.

"I will," I say. "Thanks, Luke."

"So long," he says.

The door closes behind him. I go back to the bed, and look out at the snow and wish I could untouch him. He didn't like it.

It is deeper than I have ever seen. Parked cars are covered in it. Every available horizontal space, however tiny, has a deep settlement of snow. Traffic is thinning and then slows and by evening there are only the buses, and then even they peter out; I wonder if there is some sort of severe-weather warning that is stopping them, but I still don't want to check online or switch the radio on. The intense quality of the silence is too precious. It is hard to imagine anything stopping New Yorkers, but here they are, stopped. The whole city is covered in white and none of the rules apply. I do not want to move, I do not want there to be time. I want to live in a world that has always just been covered with fresh snow.

I watch it all day. With Luke, I saw the first flakes fall and settle on the blue mailbox and the traffic lights and the green awning of the Koreans' market, and I carry on looking as they fall, deep and soft and silencing, until I am watching in the dark. I push open the window and feel the flakes as they melt on my outstretched hand. Then I lean out a little. Broadway. Broadway in the freshly fallen snow. There are times when you are more aware of being alive, aware that living is painful, not because it is terrible but because it is wonderful.

I think of how many different people it is falling on. How it is falling on the homeless guys on Riverside, who are hoping it won't slant into their tunnel, falling on the rich on Fifth Avenue, looking out of their high windows before they draw their high curtains, and on all the millions of others—the dog walkers and the doctors and the lawyers and the lovers. How it must be settling on the glinting silver of the Chrysler Building and on the chicken wire and rubbish bins of the Bowery, on the curves of the Guggenheim, and on the swooping lines of the George Washington Bridge, and on the noble heads of the library lions, and on Liberty's lamp, and into the Hudson River, white flakes into dark water. All of Manhattan, all of New York, must be transfigured by this snow that is falling, like a benediction, free and unearned, upon us. The slow swoon of it, but into life.

The peace that began when Luke was there settles like the fresh snow. I know this snow is really just snow; it is not a divine seal-setting on a petition and an answering gift. Yet if I lift up my face to accept the snow, might it not be wisdom to lift up my face and accept whatever else happens, whatever happens to the baby? Must there be grief if I lose it? Yes, there must, there will be, if I do. But this snow, this blessing—not for me, but for us all—makes me think that it is not what befalls us that we should be focused on, but how we react to the befalling.

It is easy to say it, especially on such a night. I know that this peace, or wisdom, is really because of a feeling that the danger is past; if there is fresh blood next time I check, there won't be any more pious reflections on benediction.

The phone rings and it is Mitchell, checking that I am all right. I say I am. He says he will brave all snow and rain and heat and gloom of night to reach me and check for himself.

CHAPTER TWENTY-TWO

In the morning, early, I wake up to the sound of shoveling. I lie and listen to it for a while, to the rhythmic scrape of spade on pavement. It is another sound that makes me think of England rather than Manhattan, but I am not sure why; do we shovel things more often in England? The Koreans are calling to each other, and I can hear Spanish too; there are Hispanic guys employed at the deli who slice the watermelon and pluck the brown petals off the roses, so that New York can live in a dream of perfection. They sound happy today, even though it must have been very hard to get to work, and it is only about six thirty now. I go to the window again, and I can see one of the Hispanic guys scraping some snow together to make a snowball. He aims it with fatal accuracy at the woolly hat of a coworker, who yells and bends to make his own revenge snowball. They have shoveled a channel through the snow so now there is a pathway through two steep banks. There is still no traffic.

When I check, there is no bleeding at all. I am sure the danger is over, with a curious certainty that I would be embarrassed to tell anyone about. But Dr. Sokolowski said two or three days, so I decide to stay inside again today, despite the temptation of the snow. Stella is in and out the whole time, reporting tweets and making me laugh and bringing me things to eat. Luke does not come. I knew that he wouldn't. George calls to check that I am all right.

After lunch, I call Dr. Sokolowski to tell him. He sounds pleased.

"It doesn't feel like I need to stay in bed . . ."

"I don't think so, I don't think so. If the bleeding has stopped, and there isn't any pain, I would say no longer is there any need. You can get up. And come and see me tomorrow. I will check everything is now good."

✦

I GO TO see him the next morning. Everything is now good. The one thing that is not good is that Dr. Sokolowski is retiring.

"I am going to go back to Estonia," he says. "America is better; there is not much to doubt about that, but I miss my country." He beams up at me suddenly, émigré to émigré. "That is love, no?" I say I am glad he is going back. He looks a lot more chipper than when I saw him last.

"I recommend to you therefore," he says, "a move—this is an opportunity for a move. It is not too late. I think it would be good to move to the midwives."

"The midwives?"

"The Manhattan Midwives. They are on 87th and West End. Go and see them. You will like them."

"Isn't there going to be a replacement for you?"

"Yes, but who knows what that means. These women are good. But Anya, she will make you drink so much raspberry-leaf tea, you will turn green."

"Not red?"

"Leaf tea. Leaves are green. The tea relaxes the cervix. The baby—it will slip out." He makes a slightly unpleasant slithery sound. "But not to drink yet! From five months. You are nearly there."

He gives me the card for the Manhattan Midwives. He stands up to open the door for me, and I give him a quick hug. I don't know if you're allowed to do that.

"Have a lovely time in Estonia," I say. "A lovely life."

"I will see you before that," he says, waving me away. We both know he won't.

Outside, I call Mitchell to tell him that Dr. Sokolowski says it all looks good for the baby.

I also tell him about the midwives, which he sounds doubtful about.

"Even the word 'midwife' creeps me out," he says. "It sounds medieval. It sounds like someone will be boiling cauldrons and casting spells. Stop being so old-world. Find an obstetrician."

"'Obstetrician' is a different word for the same thing. You guys just decided you would use a nice Latinate term instead, and take the job away from the women," I say.

"And add a sanitary environment."

"And forceps."

"Oh, please."

"Dr. Sokolowski likes these women, Mitchell, and he's a *man*. Anyway, I am going to see them."

He sighs. "You're so willful. Why did I choose a willful one?"

"I have something else to tell you, something upsetting." I tell him about Dennis.

He says, "Really? In a basement? Did he OD?"

I say that they don't know, and decide it isn't quite the right moment to ask if he has any spare money for a funeral. But if he does, then at least we would have ashes to give to his daughter, if we ever found her.

I google potter's fields, and Hart Island, to find out what Luke was talking about, where they will put Dennis unless we can find a different way. It makes very grim reading indeed. The city buries the homeless there, but also prisoners—and also babies. They bury them in mass graves. If your baby dies in a New York hospital, you might, in the whirl of grief and pain, sign a paper that says "city burial" without knowing what you are signing. It means your baby, your child, will be taken up to that island, piled up with others in a trench. It sounds like a horror story, but it happens.

Torrents and torrents of rain came down in the night, so that New York is transformed once more—this time away from the white wonderland into a sliding slush of gray ice and water and mud, and it seems as if there is too much of it ever to go. But the day after that, when I step out onto Broadway in the fresh sunlight for my first morning back at Columbia, the gray slush has gone in its turn, and the city has a look of being washed through and sparkling again. The yellow cabs are zipping by; people are all hurrying in different directions muffled up in woolly hats and scarves; the blue sky is bluer than I remember, and the reds redder. The watermelon deliveryman is throwing his watermelons to the Hispanic guys at the deli, because they are too heavy to move any quicker way. There is a young guy walking past with about eight dogs that continually get tangled up in each other, and around the legs of another man, who swears and aims a kick at one of the dogs. A woman bends to them; "Oh, puppies, oh, my babies," she says, crooning, "I'm a doggy mommy too! I'm a doggy mommy too. Yes, I am, beautiful, yes I am." The dogs all step on each other to be scratched and patted, tangling the man up further.

"Take them to the fucking park," says the man to the dog walker, through his teeth, like Jack Nicholson. The woman looks up from the dogs and says, "The *fucking* park? What about some fucking courtesy, you asshole?" The guy looks murderously at her for a second, and then lifts his hands to the heavens and walks on downtown.

I have been lying with the blinds down for too long.

I have a meeting with my professor that was postponed because of the bed rest, but first I call The Owl to see if there is any word on Dennis and his last name. There isn't.

Professor Hamer likes my paper, but she recommends a trip to San Francisco to see the light, the better to understand the light in many of Thiebaud's landscapes. I have already decided, because of the bleeding and despite having no medical knowledge whatsoever, that I won't fly while I am pregnant, so this trip would be after the birth. I picture what little I know of San Francisco, and what that trip might be like. Me and my baby in a cab to LaGuardia, going through security, spending hours on the flight, the baby crying, everyone on the plane wishing I could shut it up, all so that I can stand at the bottom of a lot of hills, thinking, *Hmmm. Lovely light.* But it must be fairly close to Los Angeles, so perhaps Stella could come with us, and then it would be fun.

Mitchell comes up to meet me for lunch outside Columbia, and takes me to V & T's for pizza. I wouldn't have ever gone into V & T's, because the décor must have looked tired in 1960, but Mitchell says that if a place can survive in New York looking like this, the food must be good. I pretend we don't both know that he has the Zagat app on his phone.

As I start on my pizza, which is good, I say, "I was in bed for hardly any time at all, and yet everything feels new."

"Did anyone visit apart from Stella?" Mitchell asks.

I say, fatally, "What?"

He is instantly taut. "You heard me."

"Yes," I say, "Luke did once, from the bookstore. George sent him, to tell me about Dennis."

That is more or less a lie. No, it is straightforwardly a lie. Why am I lying to Mitchell?

"Did anything happen?"

"Of course not," I say.

"Esme. Something did."

"Yes, something did—but not the kind of something you mean," I say. "For God's sake, Mitchell."

"'For God's sake, Mitchell'? You have a man in your bedroom, and you don't tell me, and you're 'For God's sake, Mitchell'–ing me? Tell me what happened."

"All that happened," I say back, "was that he told me about Dennis and that it was likely he would be buried in what they call a potter's field, where they bury homeless people. They bury them in batches. Isn't that awful to think of?"

"Yeah, it sucks. Did he hold you?"

"Who? Luke? No!"

"Where was he when he was in the room?"

"Sitting on the chair."

"Did you cry?

"I don't know—no, I don't think so."

"He didn't comfort you in any way?"

I push my plate away.

"If he comforted me, he's allowed to. I liked Dennis, and he liked Dennis, and we were both sad, and I was scared about the baby. Luke is my friend, he came to check that I was all right, and George wanted him to, and he brought me some watermelon, and I love you, Mitchell, I love you. But that doesn't mean I can't talk to any other man in the world. You've got to understand that. You've got to understand that you are everything to me, the east, the west, that nothing matters to me except you. You've got to believe me, and you've got to trust me, or we're nothing at all."

I have never said it all before, like that, straight out. Probably it is a bad idea, but surely there is a value in honesty? Mitchell leans back in his little wooden chair. The triumphant smile that he tries so hard to keep in check is back.

He glances around the restaurant, and turns up the volume a notch before he says, in a voice that is full of laughter, "I've got to understand you, and I've got to believe you, and I've got to trust you?"

"Yes," I say. "Yes."

He has some more of his pizza. Then he says, much more quietly, "You know, I play this game very, very well. And you play it very badly."

"I am not playing a game."

"Then you'll lose."

I shrug my shoulders at him. I think he is absolutely wrong. His face softens into wistful gentleness. He reaches for my hand.

"So listen. We should get married soon."

A voice behind me calls out, "If she's got other guys in her bedroom, buddy, I would hold off on the whole marrying thing."

"I can't help it," he calls back, grinning. "I fell in love with her."

"Oh. Then you're fucked," says the voice. I do not turn around.

"Please can we go?" I ask Mitchell. He looks down at his unfinished pizza but assents. I catch the waiter's eye and ask for the check. He says it is under the pepper flakes, and we can pay when we're ready. I pay the bill, and tell Mitchell I will wait for him outside.

He comes out, smiling from some final interchange with the other man.

"That guy said that if you are willing to pick up the tab then you're a keeper."

"I am pretty sure," I say, "that I'm supposed to stay on an even keel, and this isn't helping. Why do we have to be a spectacle?"

"You're the one who declared your undying love in a pizza parlor."

I tell him I've got to go to work.

"To the bookstore?"

"To the library."

"I mean it, about getting married soon," he says. He turns his footsteps in the same direction as mine, then stops dead.

"I've just had a great idea," he says. "Do you have any time now? When do you have to be at The Owl?"

"We're going to get married now?"

"No, no, Jesus, I'm not crazy, Esme, I'm just charmingly impulsive. I'm also making sure things are as they should be. I just had an idea about the venue. When do you have to be at work?"

"I have to go to the library before work. I have to put a lot of time into this paper; it's got to be good, it's in front of the whole department."

"This will be really quick. I'll just check." He gets his phone out and calls someone. I ask him what he's doing, but he cuts me off to speak enthusiastically to somebody called James.

When he's finished, he says, "We're in luck, he's there."

"Who is there? And where is there?"

He is striding towards the traffic, his arm in the air. A cab comes; he holds open the door.

"Where are we going?"

"I'll have you at your library in an hour," he says. And then, to the driver, "St. Thomas's Church on Fifth, please. The cross street is 53rd."

Mitchell leans back in the cab and grins at me. "I think you'll like James. He's right up your alley. And I was baptized at St. Thomas's; my parents still go there when they are in town. I think my mother even listens to some of their audio feeds in Paris."

The cab zips down Central Park West and across the park.

"Mitchell, I think it is terrible that Dennis will be buried in a grave for the homeless," I say.

"Yeah, it sucks. But if they can't find his family, then there's no one to pay for a funeral."

"You could pay for it," I say.

He looks incredulous. I suppose he well might. He reaches for my hand and brings it to his lips.

"My precious girl," he says. "My innocent Esme. I can't pay for it. For one thing, I'm not Bill Gates, for another, people can't go paying thousands of dollars for the funerals of people they don't know, and for another, I am not going to. Are you serious?"

"No," I say. He looks at me. He knows I was.

"I love that you asked me," he says.

I am quiet. He says, "Stop worrying about it. You were friendly to him when he was alive; that's what counts. Okay?"

I nod. But then I say, "But what are we, if we don't give people a decent burial if they have no money?"

Mitchell looks patient. "You see, I thought this was the case. This is really about self-perception, about you rather than Dennis. Isn't it a kind of selfishness, dressed up as kindness?"

I feel a shock all through me from that remark. Is he right?

"I hadn't thought of it like that," I say. "I was just so sad that he just gets—I don't know—sort of thrown away."

"Well, never mind about it. We're here."

The cab draws up outside what is surely a cathedral on Fifth Avenue. I have never noticed it before, but then this area isn't really a haunt of mine. And you're always going to notice the shops before the churches on Fifth Avenue. There is a great flight of steps and huge Gothic arches. I stand still. It is inconceivable that I could get married here. It is the ecclesiastical equivalent of the stores that are around it—Salvatore Ferragamo and Cartier and Fendi and Henri Bendel.

He smiles down at me. "Don't panic. It's just a church. It's not so spectacular inside—you'll feel better. Come on."

"I'm not panicking," I say, although I am. "Look, it's next to a Baby Gap. The guests could pop in there first and get us something useful."

We go up the steps and through the great Gothic arch. It is as spectacular inside as you might expect. I do not feel better.

"It's very English, don't you think?" he says, looking at a Catholic reredos that could have been pinched straight from Rome. "It always reminds me of England."

The inside of St. Thomas's has that look of rightness that makes you sigh with pleasure, the kind of pleasure that might be invoked by a Titian or a Bellini. The massy quality of the stone columns, the mellow glowing warmth of the wood—it is the Gothic softened by New England, as if the Gothic had retired to the new world and relaxed.

"It's lovely," I say, staring around me. "But, Mitchell—"

"Mitchell!" says a man who materializes out of the shadows. He is in his priestly dog collar, and his black hair is cut in a way that suggests a tonsure. He is around Mitchell's age, but is unlike Mitchell in almost every way. He looks rosy with faith. He comes forward to shake hands. "Great to see you. I don't think I've seen you since the game. Hello." This last word is for me. I say hello back.

"Great to see you, too, James," Mitchell is saying. "I'd like to introduce my fiancée to you—Esme Garland."

He shakes hands with me too. "Mitchell's fiancée? Congratulations! This is excellent news—Mitchell, I thought you were past praying for. I'm very pleased to meet you, Esme—I'm James Curtis."

"James and I go back a long way," says Mitchell. "We were even at Yale at the same time."

"Although I was a graduate and you were a mere whippersnapper," says James. "And I did a fair amount of teaching, but you were never in any of my classes. How did you weasel your way out of that?"

"Economics clashed with theology, I think."

James says, "Ah, it was ever thus. Why did you want to be an economist, Mitchell? It never seemed to me that it interested you."

"To annoy my mother, of course," replies Mitchell, with a look that suggests this should be evident to anyone who knows him. James smiles in a priestly way.

"And what do you do, Esme?"

"I'm studying for a PhD in art history at Columbia," I say.

"Ah—art history. So your interest in St. Thomas's will probably be architectural rather than theological? Not that the one is not an expression of the other. Would you like a tour?"

I say yes, because I am polite, and because I want to carry on looking at that soaring vault.

"The current structure was built in the French Gothic style, and to a large extent with the French Gothic construction methods also—there is no steel reinforcement, it is all stone."

Mitchell looks towards the altar. "Are you booked up here for years in advance, James? If we wanted something quite small?"

"Oh—for a wedding? For your wedding? It would be wonderful if you got married here, Mitchell. Your mother would be thrilled. But I don't know—there is always a great deal going on," replies James as I make furious gestures to stop Mitchell in his tracks, "but we could have a look at the calendar. Would you like to come with me to my office?"

Mitchell nods, and intimates that I should follow behind James to the office. I look back again at that nave. Does he really and truly think that I can walk down that aisle pregnant? It would be farcical. People would be laughing up their Balenciaga sleeves.

Mitchell puts a determined hand on the small of my back and guides me in James's wake. He says, "This is very much a casual inquiry—we haven't even decided on whether it is to be Sag Harbor or New York yet."

"Or England," I say quickly. "I mean—Mitchell—we should discuss this together before we take up James's time."

Mitchell makes a face at me, and propels me forward.

We go through to a paneled office that smells of lavender polish. James fetches a carved seat for me with a flat silk cushion, and a little pew-chair for Mitchell.

"We call this the bishop's chair, Miss Garland," he says, "although the bishop doesn't use it very often." He sits down before a state-of-the-art Mac, clicks open a file, and opens an enormous desk calendar.

"What month were you thinking of? And does it have to be a Saturday?"

"Any day, don't you think, Esme?" says Mitchell.

"I . . . I can't . . . ," I say, sitting down a little too heavily on the ornate chair that has probably housed bishops' bottoms for a couple of hundred years. "Mitchell, I can't—surely you can see—the situation? People will *notice*."

"I don't see why you can't. Don't be overwhelmed. It is just a parish church. And it's my family's church," says Mitchell.

"I can't. I can't. Father—I am sorry we have wasted your time—"

"Reverend," says Mitchell. "Not father."

"Oh, neither, just James, please. Is there any particular problem?" he asks. He asks it with a benign mildness they must practice when they are in the seminary. His eyes stay courteously on my face, though I must have just given him a big clue. I can feel the flush rise up.

I stare meaningfully at Mitchell, but he doesn't see what I mean. I turn back to the priest and shrug and say, "I'm pregnant. I can't go up the aisle in this church pregnant."

James smiles. "At the risk of sounding indelicate, I don't think you would be the first."

"Well, maybe they didn't mind. But I would mind; I couldn't get married here anyway—whether I was pregnant or not. I was thinking of a registry office, or city hall, or a church at home in England after the baby is born. This is—I don't know—like West-minster Abbey. The idea that my father would have to walk up the aisle with me here—just think what the dress would have to be like, and all the rest of the hoopla that would go with it."

"Esme—" says Mitchell, but Reverend James holds up a hand.

"No, no, Mitchell, this is very much my field. Let me see if I can help here, Miss Garland. You seem to be laboring under the misapprehension that this is an elitist institution. It isn't; it is just a church, the house of God, where everyone is welcome. In the end, despite appearances, there is no difference between St. Thomas's and the very simplest structure built for Christian worship."

I nod, mute. If I threw, oh, I don't know, a diamond ring from the steps of this place, it would probably hit Harry Winston's.

Reverend James is looking with disturbingly insightful eyes into my own.

"Congratulations, on your pregnancy," he says gently.

"Thank you," I whisper. "I'm—we're very happy."

"This is all a little impromptu, I know," he says, glancing at Mitchell, "but would you both like to talk about this? I understand if you don't . . ."

"It isn't some old-fashioned notion of doing the right thing, if that's what you're thinking, James," says Mitchell. "I—well, Esme and I were in a relationship, and then we found out she was preg-nant. And I'm afraid I was a little—surprised, and didn't handle the news all that well at first. We split up, for a time."

He stands up, and goes over to the mullioned window. That isn't the way I remember the story.

He turns back to me. His chin is lifted, as if he is filled with a fine sense of his own nobility. "It was then that I realized I had to be with you."

Both of them look at me with a certain degree of eagerness, ready for me to smile through sparkling tears and say something *Brief Encounter*–ish, like *Oh my daahling, do you relly think we could be heppy?* But I don't want to play a part any more than I want to play a game.

My eyes, therefore, are not misty with affection; I am not moved by his moving words. I can feel tears prick, but it is because I am feeling turbulent—that word must come because of the proximity of the priest—and because James is again inspecting the big calendar. One minute we are eating pizza, the next a priest at a Fifth Avenue church is writing down our wedding day. Mitchell and his family work in this way, so you get swept along. It would be wonderful, were it not for the dry-throated dread that, for Mitchell, marriage is one more performance. I want to believe him.

"There is a Saturday afternoon in June—the seventeenth," James says, tracing a finger down a page in the calendar. He looks up. "We could always put it in there in pencil."

"In pencil?" says Mitchell. "I'm an ink kind of guy."

"But, Mitchell—getting married—having to get married—we don't really have to. You don't have to rescue me—we're not living in Victorian England, or the Dark Ages—look around you, you're in New York—gay men adopt babies and lesbian couples adopt babies and—and turkey basters are regularly involved, and nobody bats an eyelid. I want the baby to have both its parents, Mitchell, I do, and I want to be with you. But let's see how we are without this; we shouldn't feel that we have to do this. It is horrible to make it all legalistic and public—it isn't really a romantic thing at all, is it?"

Can he hear what I am saying beneath this tumble of words? I want to say, *Love me, love me, love me, love me in sickness and in health, love me whether I've said the right thing or the wrong thing, love me when other men bring me watermelon, love me when they*

*don't, love me no matter what anyone else thinks or believes about it,
and I will love you, I will love you no matter how often you lay about
my soul with knives, no matter how hurt you feel inside, because you
are a man unendingly worth loving, and because it is that, the submission to one another, not to a God or a law, that is what matters, and
unless you have that, it is pointless to talk of standing before God and
promising it.*

Mitchell does not speak. Reverend James picks up a phone and
dials one number. "Meredith," he says, "could you call Mrs. St.
John-Parker with my apologies and tell her I've been unavoidably
detained? I won't be there until after four o'clock. Thank you."
He replaces the receiver and turns to us.

I am sitting bolt-upright in the bishop's uncomfortable chair. I
look once at Mitchell's face. He is pale.

James goes over to a cabinet and comes back with three glasses.
I think for a second that he's going to pour us some communion
wine, but he pours out some dry sherry. I accept my glass and take
a sip without thinking, before I remember the baby that is the root
cause of all of this. One sip won't hurt it, but for two pins I could
down the rest.

He says, "Oh, I am sorry—the sherry—I wasn't thinking."

"It's all right," I say. "Strictly speaking I am not allowed anything at all that is enjoyable. I still drink tea in the speakeasies for
pregnant women that are dotted around Manhattan."

"Esme," says Mitchell.

As he hands a glass to Mitchell, James says to him, "This nervousness about marriage is a very common thing. Believe me, it is
better for it to come now than later. I have seen it minutes before
the vows. It is normal, natural—and very human."

Mitchell's answering smile is thin.

The priest takes a sip of his drink and considers me. "Will you
listen to an Anglican defense of marriage?"

I say that I will.

"I don't think our intimate relationships are at their best if they
are merely private," he says. "Marriage is not a private contract

between two individuals, it is a public declaration of an intent to be a social unit. If you have a child within the institution of marriage, it is better for society as a whole, because society is held together by such units. It is also better for the individuals who undertake it, because it frees them from the tyranny of their own wishes and whims. You smile at that, and I understand why, but I would like you to think about it. How much of your life is dictated by a belief that you must submit to your own desire?

"Your unease about marriage is a basic fear of commitment. Why do we think, in our romantic way, that mutual affection without a legal framework is purer, fresher, more spontaneous? Why do we sneer at the idea of the bit of paper? Do you have any idea?"

I shake my head.

"It's because we're all emotion junkies," he says. He does not look like an emotion junkie. "We're high on the adrenaline of feeling, even though we know it is fleeting and evanescent. And we're getting worse—checking texts and e-mails and Facebook every five minutes, always searching for that next hit of feeling, that next morsel of approval. Esme, if you don't marry Mitchell, if you have the baby and stay in a relationship with him, you might never be free of the constant demand of your own psyche to evaluate how much you love him. Do I love him more than I loved him at breakfast, will I love him less by supper? Do I owe it to myself to look for someone else, do I owe it to myself to stay with him . . . you see? There is that tyranny too. But marriage obviates a lot of that. Marriage allows the individuals involved to free themselves of those anxieties, because they are held together by something greater than their own emotions—by society's recognition and approval. In marrying the father of your child, Esme, you are freeing yourself. Your freely given submission to that social framework would be the finest expression of your freedom." He stops.

"You're good," I say.

"I know," he says.

"You didn't mention God."

"God suffuses the whole." He pushes himself back from the desk and says, "I'm just going to have a word with Meredith in the other office. I'll only be a moment."

Once he has left, Mitchell moves his eyes in my direction without moving his head. "Well?"

"It was a very impressive speech."

"Yes."

I pause. "But I didn't need convincing that the institution is a good idea. It isn't about any of that, or about this church; it is more that I think you might be doing something against your nature, that you won't be happy, that it won't suit you."

Mitchell is staring at me with an arrested look. "Oh," he says softly, "why didn't I see before? What you need is for me to go down on bended knee and declare my undying love."

"No," I say quickly, "no, you're not listening."

"I am listening, and I was listening. I'm the east and the west, the sun and the moon. And I was supposed to say it back, when you told me you loved me. Wasn't I?"

"I only love you north-northwest."

His eyes crinkle, he relaxes. "Is that so? Then I am going to make you love me at every compass point there is."

When James comes back in, Mitchell says, "Write us in your book, my man, write us in."

"Really?"

"Really. Esme? Can he write us in?"

"If my parents can—"

"If your parents can. Of course. And mine, for that matter. Let's call them today, and in the meantime, James, keep our booking."

CHAPTER TWENTY-THREE

The next day I have my first shift at the bookshop since the bed rest. When I get there, the sun is shining. There is a homeless person whom I've never seen before, stacking up books for George to inspect. The multicolored roses that were tight buds the last time I was here have now exploded into flower, crammed cheek to cheek in the pot. There is a customer up a ladder and another one plowing deep into the fiction section.

George is peeling a couple of dollars from a big roll.

"Hi," he says.

"Hi."

"You're all better?"

"All better. Ready to work."

"Glad to hear it. We've missed you around here. Although your flowers seem to be thriving. I'm glad also—you know—" He waves a slightly embarrassed hand in the direction of my belly.

I wait for the street guy to leave before I say, "It's a shame about Dennis."

George nods slowly. "Mostly you don't hear what happens to them. They just suddenly go off your radar, so you figure they're either dead or in Philadelphia."

"There's no progress on finding his daughter?"

"No. Not so far as I know."

"And Luke said it was an overdose?"

"That's apparently what they said. They pretty much always do say that, of course, and it might be true, or it might be because most of the other possibilities don't look too good on the stats. And government forms need one cause. Bureaucracy needs simplicity, and the call for simplicity sometimes means you can't tell the truth.

"There have been some good guys over the years—Winston, Jerry, Michael—a lot of people. Some of those guys used to bring in some great books, and other things as well—maps and paintings and all sorts of things—and all of them are gone now. They weren't all homeless, but the rents, the changing face of the West Side—they've all been forced out. Winston—he was an old guy, he used to live in a tiny apartment that was near that Irish bar on 79th, the Dublin. Never mind being able to swing a cat in there—you couldn't *fit* a cat in that place. It was a pitiful place. I saw it when he was leaving—I bought a bookcase from him. It was a piece of crap—I had to throw it away once he'd left. The landlord put up his rent by seven and a half percent."

"That's not all that much . . . ," I say. I am thinking that if you can afford a dollar you can afford seven and a half cents more.

George looks at me, unimpressed. "It depends on how much you've got." He shakes his head and then says, "Listen. I hope I won't become the victim of a feminist tirade if I say I would rather you didn't pick up heavy piles of books, or go on the ladders, or do anything too strenuous, for the time being."

"You are all immovable in your silly idea of what feminism is. Thank you. And thank you for sending Luke. He really helped me."

George is setting up the books that he has just bought on the counter, and doesn't reply.

"What's missing?" he says. "There is at least one missing, I am sure."

I look. He has green hardcover copies of *Adam Bede, The Mill on the Floss, Silas Marner,* and a two-volume set of *Middlemarch.*

"There's no *Daniel Deronda,*" I say, "but you've got all the good ones."

"On the Upper West Side, that statement amounts to anti-Semitism," says George.

He gets a big reference book from under the counter and starts to leaf through it. "There's no *Felix Holt,* either. Or *Romola*. Jeez. I am losing my touch."

"No, these are fine. They are a subset—you can sell these all together."

"Yeah, maybe," he says. "Price them, and then find them a happy home, will you? Hi, Luke."

Luke is just coming in, maneuvering his guitar through the piles of books.

"Hey," he says. Then another hey to me, and a look of doubt. "You're sure you're well enough?"

"Yes."

"Okay. Lift more than three books at once and I'll wring your neck."

"Oh, and Luke," says George, "thanks *so* much for doing what I—er—asked, and checking in on Esme. That was very thoughtful."

"No problem," says Luke, and takes his guitar upstairs.

"Let's put all the George Eliots in the window," I say. "With a nice bright sign for their price as a sort of set."

George is grinning into his reference book for some reason, and isn't listening, so I have to say it again.

"Sure," he says, and raises his head to look for Luke, who is still upstairs. He calls out, "Do as the lady says, would you?"

"It's okay, I can do it, I'm fine," I say. I take out some of the books that are in the window, to make room, and decide that I am going to tell them about the wedding date. I didn't tell them about the proposal, and that all went badly wrong.

I say, "By the way, I have a date for my wedding, providing my parents can come, and they are looking for flights today. It's the seventeenth of June, so quite soon, and it is going to be at St. Thomas's Church, which is on—"

"Fifth Avenue," says George.

"Yes. Mitchell and I will send out invitations, I expect, but it is going to be a very small wedding. You are all invited; I really hope you can come."

Neither of them says a word.

"What's wrong?" I say.

Luke says, "I thought you were going to wait, going to be married in England, once the baby was born. Didn't you say something about that one time?"

"Yes," I say. "I did. And that was what I thought. That way my friends from home would come, and from Cambridge, and I imagined it like that, but Mitchell—he has a friend who is a priest at St. Thomas's, and he said he wants to marry me before the baby—and they have a space."

"Is legitimacy an issue?" asks George.

"I don't think so," I say. George is waving a torch towards caves best left dark. It is a motive that hadn't even occurred to me, and now I feel miserable again, unsure of Mitchell again. "I didn't think of that. It might be that."

"I don't think it's that," says Luke. "I think he knows a good thing when he sees it."

I smile at Luke. "Will you come, if you can?" I ask him, and glance at George to encompass him. Luke looks back at me.

"Sure, if we can, we will," George says. "Won't we, Luke?"

❧ CHAPTER TWENTY-FOUR ❧

Today is Saturday. I get up to streaming sunshine, as ever. I am six months pregnant. I stand naked in front of the mirror—the bump curves very pleasingly, from the front, but once I am dressed, and I turn to the side, I look like a wobbly man who won't fall over. How very irritating, that our haywire hormones mean that we can feel so erotically charged while we look like Weebles.

Yesterday I paid my first visit to the midwives recommended by Dr. Sokolowski. They made me feel as if I were back in England. They talked about home birth, about water birth, about natural birth, about all the birth that is far away from a tubular metal bed, far away from all those green hospital garments. I spoke to two of them, and I will meet all seven in due course, so that I will already know whichever one I get on the day. I also have to go to some childbirth classes. They were shocked that I haven't been already. They let me sign up for them, and I formally signed away my connection with Dr. Sokolowski. They also recommended someone on the Upper West Side for the childbirth classes, who has a practice quite near The Owl. I asked them, as they were all European, if I could ever have a drink, just a small one. They all said no. They told me to drink lots of raspberry-leaf tea.

I am meeting Mitchell for an early coffee at Sarabeth's. I would like him to stay over more often than he does, but he says he wants there to be a significant difference between being engaged and being married, so last night he went home at midnight. I am supposed to move into Sutton Place once we're married, and then about six weeks after that, the baby will be born. None of it seems real.

It is quite warm outside—the women walking down Broadway are not wearing coats. They all look pleased to be walking down Broadway in the sun. I look in my cupboard and wonder if I have any clothes at all that can transform me into a desirable woman. The short answer is no. People say pregnant women can look sexy, but I can't see it.

Mitchell is walking up to Sarabeth's as I am walking down to it; I feel that stab of happy surprise when I see him.

"You look good," he says.

As we sit down with our coffees, we pass a girl at a table in the window, with a low-cut blouse on; her breasts look perfect, like two big scoops of vanilla. Even to me, they look beautiful. Mitchell looks, and then looks at me, raising his eyebrows, the naughty schoolboy.

"I know exactly what they'll be like. Exactly. Round and creamy and firm, with big nipples—nipples, I think, of the palest pink. Coral. Delectable."

"Stop it."

"I don't want to stop it. I want you and me to discuss those perfect breasts. Did you like them?"

"They were very nice."

"I am going back for more napkins."

He does. I sigh.

He comes back. He asks me how my work is going. I begin to tell him that I have nearly finished the PowerPoint to go with the paper. His face takes on a dreamy aspect.

"Mitchell."

He looks a question.

"Did you ask me about my work so that I would talk, and you could think about that girl's breasts?"

"Yes. Yes. Esme? I love how you get me. I love it."

"That's nice. But there is a better way. If you want to think about the breasts, sit here and think about them all by yourself. You don't need me for this."

I stand up, sling my bag on my shoulder, raise my hand in farewell. He leans back in his seat, grins.

"You're so wrong. You're the point of the whole exercise."

A CHAT MESSAGE comes through around ten P.M., as I am studying in my apartment. It is from Mitchell. It says,

—I got her number

—Whose number?

—The girl

—In the coffee shop?

—Yes, ma'am.

—Good for you

—I want her

I am suddenly aware of all my veins, of the fact that they are a network all over and through me, so if my blood goes cold, all of me goes cold. It is always on the periphery of my relationship with Mitchell, that there will be another girl, that I will not be enough for him. My heart is pounding. I must not be long, must not let him think that I have gone cold, or that my heart is pounding.

—Then have her.

—I want her with you.

I gasp now, which just goes to show that gasps, which before this moment I always believed had an element of performance in them, can be real and unforced expressions of shock.

—Are you there?

—Yes.

—Do you understand? That I would like to have sex with you and Elise together?

I think, *Elise? Esme and Elise?*

—Do you know her?

—I know her now. I went up to her after you left, and explained.

—Explained?

—Yes. I told her that we are engaged. I told her that you are pregnant, and that is making you very, very horny. And that we both found her very attractive.

—You didn't say that. I didn't find her attractive, Mitchell.

—Yes, you did—I saw it in your eyes. You were turned on by her breasts too.

—I wasn't.

I pause. I sound so *dowdy*. And they were so round, so creamy white, so flawless. Like a Titian.

I write:

—I just have a very highly developed aesthetic sense.

—As do I. I also have a very highly developed erotic sense. In fact, I have buckets of eroticism. Buckets of it.

—Buckets and eroticism don't go together.

Mitchell is typing. Mitchell has entered text. I wait.

—I want to watch you touch her. I want you both to be completely naked in front of me. I want her to kiss your beautiful belly. You will caress her perfect breasts.

He then lists all the things I am to do to her, and she to me, with a precision that is impressive, although I think he overdoes the adverbs. Greedily, for example.

—Say yes, Esme, say yes. Stretch yourself towards this; embrace it. Don't shy away, don't say you can't possibly, because you're English. Sexuality is a sliding scale. Just type three letters. Type yes. Say it. Yes, yes, I will. Yes.

My fingers are on the keyboard. I am turned on by what he is writing. The shock and the eroticism merge and mingle. The shock is the eroticism. The transgression is the point.

I type Y-e-s to see what it looks like on the screen, but I do not send it. I look at it, there, the "Yes," quivering in the comment bar, between being and nonbeing. I backspace it into nothingness and type "no" without a capital, and send it.

There is a silence. The italics do not say that Mitchell is typing.

—I'm sorry, Mitchell, I just could not do it.

Mitchell van Leuven is no longer online.

He can make me feel desolate in seconds. I think of calling him, but it is too abject; I will not. I think instead of going to bed with my toothbrush, but that's too depressing considering the realms of sexual experimentation I've just refused. When the chat message appeared, I was in the middle of reading an interview with Patrick Procktor before he became old and serious (prior to which he was young and serious). I'll just carry on with that.

The next day, I text Mitchell to say I would like to see him, and a reply comes back after what I imagine is a carefully timed delay, saying that he is planning to spend a quiet night marking papers. I wish he was in front of me so I could slap him.

However right I am, however wrong he is, I spend far too much of the day wondering if I could do it, and why I said no. Am I just backing away from experience? Am I too conservative, am I bourgeois rather than aristocratic? Was I dishonest as well as unadventurous to say no?

I call up the chat and read it again. Over and over, I imagine saying yes, giving myself to the sensuality of it, slipping into it as easily as slipping between cool white sheets. But then I imagine watching as Mitchell caresses that girl's body, and I can't. And what happens afterwards? *Well, Elise, that was awfully nice, thanks very much, see you round.*

But does that leave me saying no to life? The everlasting no?

For my dinner, in a momentous departure from my normal ordered world, I eat a pint of Stonyfield French vanilla yogurt with cream on the top, followed by most of a packet of those thin ginger cookies that are shaped like flowers. While I eat them, I read *W* magazine. After that, I have a caffeinated coffee, the first in months. It tastes wonderful.

I have a shower after dinner. At about eight thirty, I open my lovely American closet and get out my mackintosh. It is knee-length, pale blue, with a Peter Pan collar and enormous pale blue buttons. I bought it because I thought it had a Jackie Kennedy flavor.

I take off all of my clothes, all of them, and then I put on the mackintosh. The lining is cool and slick against my skin. I button it up to the top and put on a pair of high-heeled shoes.

I walk to the subway.

I didn't bring a book, I left them all behind. I wait for the local at 116th Street, it comes, I get on it, sit down next to a woman. The man opposite is looking at me. Ordinarily I would look away; now I force myself to look back at him. I say to him with my mind, *Underneath this coat, I am stark naked. Yes. Really. It's just the coat and the shoes.*

He's the one who looks away. I feel a little rejected.

At Times Square I have to go up and down lots of steps. I hope I don't trip. I take the Q train, and this time there are no seats. I am jostled, I stand with everyone else, holding the pole.

The secret of it is thrilling. I feel deliciously wicked, subversive, powerful. Everyone else is definitely wearing all their clothes. How boring.

When I get to Sutton Place, I press the button for Mitchell's apartment, and it is only then, once I have pressed and I wait in the silence, that it flashes into my mind that he is there, and that he is there with Elise, in some sort of balletic and performative erotic congress. I feel every cell that was keyed up to the bursting point suddenly droop. I am not the epitome of sexual daring; I am jealous and ordinary, just a girl in a blue mac.

The buzzer buzzes. Mitchell's voice, offhandedly questioning. It does not sound as if it was interrupted from astonishing sex. I get buzzed in. In the lift, the keying up begins again. There is a mirror. I look quite pretty.

I stand in the tiny lobby of his apartment for a second to collect myself. There are two huge pottery elephants, a palm. I raise my hand to knock on the inner door as he opens it. He is standing there, looking pleased to see me, looking very handsome.

I step forward, and kiss him full on the mouth. Then I whisper into his ear.

"Underneath this coat, I am absolutely and completely naked." I did mean to just stand and unbutton, but I changed my mind in favor of the whisper.

Mitchell takes a step back from me, looks me up and down, locks my gaze with his.

Then he says, loudly, without turning his head away, "Mother, Esme's here. Would you pour her a drink?"

Olivia appears from the sitting room.

"Esme, how charming to see you," she says. I am given her cool kiss.

"You look a little overheated," says Mitchell, wickedly. "Is it warm out?"

"Yes," says Olivia, "Yes, Esme, do take off your coat and come through. I think there is some tonic water in the fridge; would you like some? Or perhaps just water? Have you eaten?"

"Just water, please," I say, "I—I am not stopping. I was just passing."

Nobody just passes Sutton Place.

"I came," I say, "to borrow some *New Yorker*s. Because they will make the finishing touches to my paper—I was thinking that having a look through your old *New Yorker*s would help me with what I am trying to say."

"And what are you trying to say?" Mitchell asks. He lifts his eyebrows.

"That—it is about Lacan, in fact, and the privacy options on Facebook—the idea of feeling yourself under the possible gaze of someone you can't see, about the possibility of there being someone looking at you that you don't see, nor even know—that we are aware of how we have access to power only through male power— how that is constituted on Facebook . . ."

Olivia comes back with the glass of water.

"Cornelius is on Facebook," she says.

"And how do the *New Yorker*s contribute to your paper?" asks Mitchell.

"The cartoons," I say, though that is just nonsense. "But more the adverts."

"Interesting. But surely fashion magazines, or even pornography, would be better targets for your attention? And I am afraid I am all out of those."

"Mitchell, if you are going to ask her these questions, at least let her take off her coat."

"Yes. Esme. Take off your coat."

"Thank you, but I—I am on a very tight deadline. Mrs. van Leuven—Olivia—it is nice to see you . . ."

"Yes; I hope we will see you both in Sag Harbor again shortly? Beeky is going to be there in a couple of weeks, I think."

Mitchell walks away towards the bathroom and comes back with a sizable pile of *New Yorker*s. I clasp them to my chest, and nod a good-bye to them both.

The lift comes. I expect Mitchell to engineer himself into coming down with me, but he doesn't move.

"Good luck with the paper," he says. His face is alight with unholy laughter.

I am in the lift again, and this time I am leaning against the mirror, not looking into it.

CHAPTER TWENTY-FIVE

I give the paper. For the few days before it I am wholly focused on it. When I finally stand up before the other art history graduates, as well as Mitchell, who is dutifully sitting at the front, I realize that I have written something that is too close to me, that is too raw, too felt—I am sending out each word laden with myself. Here I am. This is all of me. All they want is a competent academic paper—they are getting a self-absorbed essence that is both gift and obligation. It is too late to change it and give them something that doesn't reveal anything. They'll notice if I read Robert Hughes out and pretend it is me. The thing I have to remember is that I am the only person who will care that I am giving myself instead of a paper. Nobody else will pay any attention.

When it is happening, I manage to forget myself, and then, miraculously, it is finished. I have somehow got to the end of it, though I hardly remember saying any of it. If Bradley Brinkman comes to say he found it charming I'll flay his wolfish visage.

It does not happen. The people who come over to me, including my two professors, including Bradley, are gracious, engaged, and inquisitive. I answer more questions, some that are asked provoke more questions, and more. I sink into the remembered and revived fascination of it as into plumped silk cushions—as soon as you look hard at almost anything, it becomes interesting. It is only when we skim along on the surface that things seem boring, in the same way that a train journey across farmlands can be dull, compared to the minute noticing we can do if we walk. We can do better, at any rate, than worry eternally about our personal relationships.

I go over to Mitchell. "Did you like it?"

"Of course I did, it was very good," Mitchell says.

"Thank you. You don't think it was too simplistic?"

"No, no, I said—it was very good. Do you think we'll be much longer here? I thought we could go downtown to this new bar that's opened on 1st and First. Red velvet and candles. Your sort of thing. Well, let me rephrase that. My sort of thing."

Heady with success, heady with praise and good wishes, I want to stay in the midst of all the talk and energy. Praise has even come from Bradley Brinkman. But Mitchell doesn't look comfortable. "All right," I say, "let's go."

The bar—it's called the Silk Route—is down some steps into a crepuscular cellar. The décor is dark red and the general mood uterine. Billowing silk is pinned to the ceiling and there are heavy velvet curtains everywhere. We choose a little booth and a waitress comes over. Mitchell orders a bottle of rioja. I wonder if they deliver it by placenta. I am still feeling irrepressibly sunny. I am allowing myself to contemplate the scarcely articulated desire that I could, in sober fact, become a respected scholar, giving papers at international conferences, chairing symposia, sauntering through galleries while being filmed by the BBC, arguing all day with eager students, dining every evening at high table. *I say, pass the port, J.W., there's a good chap.* Dying in my nineties, slumping over my books in the small hours as the lamplight glows on.

"Mitchell. Do you think I could do it? Be a real academic?" I say it, and even speaking such a dream is to offer it up for taint. As long as it is secret, closed, full of blood, it is inviolable. Now I've presented it for piercing.

Mitchell shrugs. "It's a tough field, very competitive. In part because it is so subjective, right? Nobody can be wrong in your field, which must be nice."

I do not answer. He does not notice.

"And believe me, it's not as glamorous as it looks from the outside. I don't know what your definition of a real academic is, but if it has anything to do with Oxbridge, then, really? You'd be better off forgetting it."

"I don't think academia and Oxbridge are the same. I could make do with Harvard," I say. He doesn't smile. "Professor Hamer said I should send my paper to *n.paradoxa* and to one of the editors of *Aesthetics in America,* who would definitely like it. She says she knows her. That would be a start, wouldn't it? I'd be so proud I think I'd die. Even that she thinks I should send it makes me feel that there's a *chance*."

"I'm low today, Esme."

He leans back. I feel rebuked that I have been so self-involved. "What is it?"

"I don't know. I feel—as if I am waiting for something *perfect*. But I am waiting for it in the abyss."

He closes his eyes. Then he opens them.

"You're getting the real me, for once. You might get some intimate revelations."

"I don't want intimate revelations. They will all be about the disgusting sex you've enjoyed in the past."

He shakes his head, reaches for my hand, strokes it. "Sometimes, I think it would be good to die. Do you ever feel like that?"

"No," I say. "Or only like Othello, when he thinks he should die now because he is so happy. I always think that part—"

"Because I do," continues Mitchell. "I do sometimes feel that it would be good to give up the heart's beating in exchange for a relinquishment of pain."

"Is 'relinquishment' a word?" I say.

"Esme. You don't know what it is like to feel so deeply, to care so deeply about things. You're so bucked up by the reaction to your paper—it's great, it's really great to see. But you live your life on the surface, in large part. Some of us have subterranean caverns we don't want to visit, that we are fearful of."

"Is the isle full of noises?"

"No. It's full of pain. Or no, it's full of silence. That's the problem, Esme."

"But, Mitchell, I didn't know you felt like this. Has something happened to you?"

"Nothing has ever happened to me," he says simply. "It's exactly that—nothing. A feeling that nothing matters. About the dying. You really don't ever think of suicide? Interesting."

He is implying a sort of lack. I am not deep enough to see the drear nature of existence. I can't pretend that I dream of razors or rivers or acids or gas, but I think of something to palliate matters.

"I sometimes do when I see one of those films where the secret agent is given a cyanide pill for use in emergencies. I think, *What if I were a secret agent, and they were going to torture me*—would I ever be able to reach a point where I would think, *Okay, now would be a good time to take my pill*. I'm sure I would let the moment pass and be tortured to death."

Mitchell doesn't respond. He sits in despondent silence.

I say, "Do you think of it? I would never have imagined you to think like that."

He laughs a hollow laugh. "I told you—today you are getting the real me. I think of it because it is a comfort. There's comfort in the sharp blade waiting in the drawer, the white pills in the cupboard, the belt from my bathrobe."

"But, Mitchell—that's *awful*."

"I know," he says sadly. "The only real pain I have is—is in loving you."

"Pain in loving me!" I say, too surprised to do more than echo him.

"Yes. You're wonderful, captivating, an elixir. But this won't last. Nothing lasts. You will leave. This might even be the beginning." He smiles wistfully at me. "Your paper did go down very well."

My heart constricts. I say, "I won't leave, Mitchell. I am in it. I am—completely in it."

He releases my hand. It is an abrupt release. "Great," he says.

✦

GEORGE IS ABSORBED in a book. He is sitting at the front, at the counter, and so should have one eye, or one ear, out for customers. I am upstairs, and I have watched two or three people come in and look at him, expecting a greeting, to be rewarded with nothing at all. The book must be very good.

A boy comes in, a preppy boy, about seventeen or eighteen, in a blue shirt and beige chinos. He is clearly glad to be here, part of it even for a short while. He might soon volunteer the information that he loves books.

He looks over eagerly at George, who is buried even deeper in the thick old book. George is dressed perfectly for the part, with his creased and slightly woebegone clothes, his glasses perched on his nose, his whole being focused on the printed word, clearly oblivious to the lure of making a dime.

"This is an amazing place," says the boy. There is no response at all from George.

"I bet you guys have been here, like, forever," he says, gazing appreciatively at the books that touch the ceiling, the books that are overflowing into the aisles, wobbling on piles, jammed into gaps. He takes in the pictures and oddments too: the changeless owl, a map, a Lichtenstein print, and very high up, a tin hunting horn with a graceful sweep to it. Next to that is the great, huge photograph of the old Penn Station.

"That's Penn Station!" says the boy. George must have a filter for potentially interesting conversations, because this penetrates. Without looking up he says, "Yes it is."

"That's a beautiful picture," the boy says feelingly. "Robert Moses, huh?" He stares at George, who turns with assiduous attention to the last words on his page and then lifts his chin to begin at the top lines on the verso. "Do you have any other things like it?" he asks.

"Oh, yes, sir, we do," answers George.

"Can I see them? Where are they?"

"Tucked away, tucked away," says George, almost drowsily. The boy looks quite desperately at George now, who hasn't ever raised his head to look at him. He pushes the door open, and leaves the shop.

I think of running after him, but the moment has passed, and the moment, which could have been a bright gem in his memory, and not from want of trying, will now be like a bit of grit in his shoe. I come down the stairs.

"What are you reading, George?" I ask him. The minatory tone pierces his cocoon. He turns obediently to the title page, and says, "*A Complete Collection of State Trials and Proceedings for High Treason and Other Crimes and Misdemeanors from the Earliest Period to the Year 1783: With Notes and Other Illustrations, volume four: Charles 1st to Charles 2nd, 1640–1649.* It's a little on the gripping side. You don't know if they are going to get their heads stuck on pikes until the end of each trial, and nobody else does either. There isn't any authorial power behind these things, no willed teleology. You're not following another's mind, but what actually unfurled. Fascinating."

"That boy wanted to talk to you. He liked the shop. He went away unhappy."

"What boy?" says George, puzzled. "Oh, the customer. I didn't think he was serious. But I didn't really notice."

"No, you didn't."

"Well, you did. Why didn't you talk to him?"

"I think he wanted to talk to you, you were sitting there all scholarly and avuncular—there was romance in it for him. I'm too perky for it to have worked. He wanted some bond with you. He even mentioned Robert Moses, because of the Penn Station photograph."

"Robert Moses? He did?"

"Yes. He was the man who had it knocked down?"

"Ah, yeah, he was, but you know, in the end, as the famous *Times* editorial had it, we got what we deserved. If we couldn't manage to keep it, we didn't deserve to have it."

I stare at him. He looks back at me, questioning. "What?"

"But that's what you are doing! You are going to blame Robert Moses when your bookshop closes, and really it will have been you, and me, and all of us."

"I'm going to blame Robert Moses when the bookstore closes? Esme, do you need a little rest? And—*when* the bookstore closes?"

"Kindle, then, or Apple. It makes no difference, it won't really be their fault. That's a different need—that boy *needed* this shop to be here, lots of people need it to be here. There have to be old things as well as new things. There has to be—there has to be old stone to new building, old timber to new fires, old books to new minds."

George looks stricken. "You're right. Was that you, the timber to the fires and such?"

"No. T. S. Eliot. But he's right—T. S. Eliot and I, we're both right. And it only takes the tiniest discouragement—"

He holds his hands up. "I know, I know. I said, you're right. I was wrong." He peers out into the street. "I wish we could get him back."

"I don't think he will come back."

George says, "You know, a woman came in the other day with two outside books, and she said, 'Hey, this one is thin, and this one is fat, and they are both a dollar.' Luke was at the desk. He took them both, and he weighed them on the scales. And he said, 'Oh, yes, ma'am, you're right. This thin one should only be seventy-five cents.'"

"'And this one has no adjectives, so that's another quarter off . . . ,'" I say.

"My point is, that this is your point. We are getting it wrong. We mustn't become bitter, or forget our purpose." He closes the lovely old book and puts it, with his usual reverence, on the countertop. "Do you think we have to change things?"

"We could have poetry readings upstairs."

George grins. "And a coffee machine? And loyalty cards?"

"I mean it. Poetry readings, prose readings—why is it that only new bookshops do that stuff? We show people what a good place it is to be, and they will buy, and it will flourish, whatever the future brings."

"It might flourish with this kind of enthusiasm. But, Esme, you're going to be wrapped up in motherhood soon."

"It isn't about just one person."

"I guess." George sits, pensive, for a long time. In the end he looks up at me. "No. I don't think I agree with you after all. That boy wanted to talk to me because he saw that I was reading a book, precisely *because* I wasn't at the door offering him a latte and an invitation to a poetry reading. He wanted to *win* my attention, by trying. Bookshops have got to survive because people want them, Esme. You've got to *trust* people to want them, not try to trick people into wanting them."

"I think we should try to connect to people," I say. "Not in a commercial way, but in a real way. You ignored him."

"Yes, I did. I should have paid attention, but he at least tried to get it. This time he failed. Next time he won't. We're not going to serve lattes. We're going to sell books."

❋

I AM REWRITING my male-gaze essay for a feminist art journal when I get a text from Mitchell, asking me if I have time to meet him at Señor Swanky's for a coffee. Coffee is now code for "hot drink that won't contain anything interesting for Esme."

"I wouldn't have had you down as a Señor Swanky's fan," I say, as I sit down on the yellow chair at the yellow table outside the yellow restaurant. "I suppose I still don't get you . . ."

Mitchell takes my hand, sandwiches it between both of his. The gesture is tender.

"That's where you make your mistake," he says, in a voice to match the gesture, as soft as rainfall. "Don't you understand yet, my poor Esme, that there is no me to get?"

This demeanor does not match the choice of restaurant. Mitchell is meticulous about this sort of thing—as he showed when he picked the Modern for his proposal. So if it seems like it doesn't match, I am just not getting it. Again.

"There is a you to get," I say. "You notice people, when there is something wrong, when there is something sad about them—you have a sort of quick sympathy. Unless it's fake."

He shrugs, laughs. "It's mostly fake."

"Why?"

"Because I know how to behave. Because I know that's what you do."

"I don't believe you. I see you do it. I see that you mean it."

He looks weary. "That's part of it."

I sit without speaking, and so does he. Mitchell has switched off whatever it was that always glowed at me before. When I was walking here from Columbia, I thought I was coming to an ordinary lunch date.

This is something he has to get through, this uncomfortable scene. He has to get through it in order to get to the clear blue air beyond me. That's how he feels. I am sure.

He leans forward, his face in his hands. He is curled up, resistant. There is a flush of speckled red under his cheekbone; I can't tell what it means. Is he upset or angry? It might be a shaving rash. I have never seen him shave, or thought of him shaving. It would be an intimate thing to be there for; more intimate than sex, since it is a thing he keeps entirely private, the door always firmly shut. Imagining him with the soap on his face, the razor poised, brings a sudden rush of fondness. Mitchell always has the door shut.

Still shielding his eyes from me with his hands, he says, "I used to be very good friends with a couple of guys from Yale, Tam and

Greg. We went everywhere together; we went to Rome together, Paris. In the summers when we all started working in New York, we always went to Long Island together. I thought the world of them.

"One day when we were all staying at someone's house in Cape Cod, I woke up and I thought, *This relationship with these guys is hollow, there is nothing to it. They don't matter at all to me.* And I got up and I drove back to New York, and I never saw them again."

He emerges from his hands, and stares down Columbus Avenue. "And that's how I feel about you now," he says.

I do not move or speak.

Can you love someone *because* you see through all the barbed defenses to the center of a person, to his wounded heart? But what if it is a mistake? What if you peel back all those layers of cruelty to find a kernel, not of kindness that can't risk itself, but of more cruelty?

"It was—enchanting—wasn't it? For a while?"

"Yes," I say.

"I was enchanted. But I woke up. From the spell."

"Oh."

"So that's the end, I'm afraid."

"Just like that."

"Yes. Just like that."

"No wedding."

"No wedding."

"You should tell James—"

Compunction flickers briefly across his face.

"I have."

He does not make a move to go. I know, when he does, that we will never be together again, and I can't bear it. When he gets up to go, I won't be able to breathe.

"Is it because—is it because I said no to that thing—with the girl, in the coffee shop?"

"No."

"Because if it is, I can . . . I can do that . . . ," I say.

"Don't. Don't say it. Don't embarrass yourself."

"It *is* because of that. I can do it. I wanted to . . ."

He closes his eyes. "For God's sake."

"You think I don't grab hold of life, that I am too scared to live life to the full, but I'm not, Mitchell, I can live life . . ."

This time he covers his ears. See no evil, hear no evil. But he doesn't do the last one.

I say, slowly, "You're frightened of getting hurt, so you are pushing me away. You push everyone away so that you won't get hurt. If that's what it is, you will do it again and again, and you'll always think it is because it's the wrong girl."

He rears back from his fetal position and glares at me. There is no sea for these eyes; they're like ice-blue fire.

"Can we just stop this? I am telling you that I don't love you, Esme, that I don't love you at all, and you are trying to—to *help* me. It's like trying to piss off Florence Nightingale."

"I don't believe you. I think you love me." I do think it. I am absolutely sure of it. It is a thing you are not supposed to say, but it feels too late to be holding back.

"You think I love you? What monumental confidence you have. And all of it misplaced, I'm afraid. Sorry about that, toots."

"I love you," I say.

He shrugs. "What can I do with that?"

I think that all the words he hurls at me are poisoned arrows and boiling oil and sharpened stones to protect the forlorn man inside. So that I won't see he is there at all. There is a kind of blank agony in me, because I am losing him, and because I think he is in despair.

"I don't even particularly like you," he says now.

I say nothing.

"And if I had it to do over, I wouldn't dream of going to that gallery opening."

"Whereas I would," I snap back, "because all of my time since meeting you has been such a treat."

"I told you once before, being a bitch doesn't suit you."

"You said that I was your redemption, you said that I filled up all your gaps—"

"The past doesn't interest me. I don't feel like that now."

"You asked me to *marry* you, you took me to the *church* . . ." I know it is pointless, but I have to say the words. I have to say them out loud, I have to say them to him. The wild sadness of it; I won't get another chance.

"I told you, it was an enchantment. I've woken up."

"The baby. You—what about the baby?"

"I will have children when I choose to have children. And I will choose who to have them with."

"But there's a child already, you care about that, don't you—it will be your baby—"

"I know that. We'll get lawyers. That's what they're for."

"But I think you are rejecting me because—"

"Esme. For once in your life stop talking."

"What have I done? What is different?"

"Nothing. I am different."

"You're pushing me away on purpose."

"Finally, a breakthrough."

"It is because you are so sad—what you said about being depressed, about there being no point to anything—I can help you, Mitchell, I can save—"

"No, you can't," he says, angry. "You can't. Do you know how many women before you have tried?"

"No," I say. "I don't know. How many? You're thirty-three years old. There can't be that many."

He smiles a wide parody of a smile at me. "Do you want to know? I can start counting . . ."

"No."

"Sure? I can tell you how many I've fucked, or how many thought they could help me. It isn't the same figure, because some of the women didn't give a shit about me either. I preferred those, in fact. Less fuss."

I do not react to this. He puts his face close to mine. "This is where you storm off in tears."

"I am not going to storm off in tears. You have to walk away from me."

"I have to walk away from you?" He laughs. "What, for the symbolism to work? Man walks away from his beloved and his baby?"

"If you like."

He gets up.

"Fine by me," he says. "Good-bye, Esme."

"Good-bye, Mitchell," I say. I look up at him. He turns uptown, and he walks away.

I leave Señor Swanky's. I walk across to Amsterdam, and then to the park.

CHAPTER TWENTY-SIX

I thought that love was flowing through the cosmic strands of right and virtue in the universe, falling on us, making all things well. As if it were outside of us, that we just opened ourselves to it. But it can't be like that, it must be that we made it, and now we are unmaking it.

I try to think of what I have done. Is it that the wedding is closer, is it that I hesitated about marrying him that day at St. Thomas's? That was the day I told him I loved him. Is it that? The plain declaration that voided the game?

I don't think he was playing a game. He was as serious as I was. If it was a game, it was Mitchell, afraid of losing, who tipped the board up, sent the pieces flying.

I have to try to pin that curtain back up, that is needfully drawn between all of us. I ripped it down, thinking there was no use for it, thinking we could discard all convention, all withholding, and say what we thought, say what was real, speak out the truth.

All the wild words in the universe, spoken or written or sent, that the speakers ought to wish sucked back in and obliterated forever in the minds of everyone, the ones that cause wars, the ones that cause death and hatred and the suffering of thousands, all those; should we repent of "I love you" as well? Is it just a weakness, to love? I can't see it, I can't see how there is any point to life without it. Isn't relationship all in all?

All the errant "I love you"s don't have such an effect, they don't spark bonfires, either of tragic or magnificent dimensions. The spark they send out into the world whistles on a brick and dies.

I go home, and look in the mirror. In the same way that a person might draw a sharp blade across their flesh in order to have a physical pain to meet the pain in the mind, so I take my clothes off and stand naked there; naked, big bellied, alone, and sad. I smile at myself, because the haunted face does not improve the general impression. I look like a sad girl smiling.

The next morning, I wake up and remember, and the feeling is instantly there—the emptiness, the sense that there is no point doing anything, that all joy has drained out of the world.

I try to study to push it all away, but I can't. I decide to clean.

The apartment does not need to be cleaned, but I clean it anyway. I sweep the floor with my floral-handled broom (bought from University Student Supply), and I vacuum my little rugs. The vacuum has the suction power of a giant limpet, and my rugs are like postage stamps. I stand on both sides of the rug and try to push the vacuum over it, but it still chews it up like some sort of deranged Muppet.

I take a damp cloth and put a dab of Ecover cleaning fluid on it, and wipe all the light switches and the doorways and skirting boards. I clean the entire bathroom, although I cleaned it a couple of days ago. I get an old toothbrush and scrub the grout between the tiles around the bath. In the kitchen, the iron things that surround the gas hobs so that your pan isn't balancing on the hob itself—who knows what they are called—they actually do need cleaning. With great thankfulness I seize upon them and plunge them into hot soapy water. I get a pan scrub and set to work. I concentrate on the black bits that are cooked on. I work on them until they are gleaming.

This time, it really is an ending. This time, he has decided to cut me out of his life with surgical precision.

I used to be bemused by the heroines in Shakespeare's comedies, who suffer any amount of injustice from their silly suitors and are still happy to accept them at the end. *Why would you?* I thought. *Shakespeare got that wrong.* He didn't, of course. I am not sure he got anything wrong.

I look ahead down all the days that will not have Mitchell in them, and I think that in time, I will get over him. And part of me doesn't want to, because that's just another way of saying I will forget what delight feels like. *Let darkness keep her raven gloss.*

Despite the grayness and pointlessness that has covered me like a blanket, I carry on doing all the things I am supposed to do. Depressed people don't get out of bed. I get out of bed. Depressed people can't make decisions. I make lots of decisions. I carry on writing, carry on studying, carry on attending childbirth classes, carry on working at The Owl. I do not mope about, I do not look glumly on as people laugh about something. I pretend I am as merry as the next person, and hope that they're not pretending too.

I tell George, and I tell Stella. George says he is sorry; he looks grave, but not sorry. Stella says that he is not worth five minutes of my time, five atoms of my tears, and that he never was. I don't agree. He is still radiant to me, and without him everything is dark.

I send him a text. I say that I hope it wasn't something that I did that I don't know about, I say that I am not ashamed of loving him. I ask him if he would like to know when the baby is born.

The act of communicating with him, even one-way, just knowing that he will read it, or at least see my name on his phone, is a bitter pleasure.

I wait for hours expecting a reply, and then days hoping for one. Then the hope fades altogether. There is nothing.

⁙

GEORGE HAS ASKED me to come in, on Sunday. I have been reserving Sunday morning for staying in bed, hugging myself close, letting myself cry where nobody can see or judge. George says, "If you can't manage it, Esme, just tell me. I can ask Mary. I don't want to pass you over just because of the pregnancy." I say yes, then, of course. I should have said yes immediately, for the money.

At The Owl, George is sitting at the front desk, leaning back in the chair, his arms behind his head. He is grinning because someone, a customer, is leaning on the Southeast Asia section, telling him a funny story. He looks relaxed and happy, with his spirulina shake and his packet of triple-milled flaxseed. He is wearing a T-shirt too, instead of his usual shirt and leather waistcoat. His demeanor suggests a holiday.

When he sees me, he greets me, still laughing, and introduces me to Bob, who he says is a book scout.

"I don't imagine your young friend here would know what a book scout is," says Bob.

"I guess that's true," says George. "You're like a black rhino, Bob. Esme, a book scout is someone who—"

"Scouts for books?" I ask.

"She was at Cambridge," George explains. Bob nods thoughtfully.

"What can I do for you, Esme?" asks George.

"You *asked* me to come in."

"I . . . did. Indeed I did. I asked you to come in because I have an important job for you. I hope you won't find it too onerous."

Half an hour later Luke and I are in a cab on our way to Manhattan Mini Storage on Riverside and 134th. We are surrounded by bags of books; there are more in the boot, and more piled onto the passenger seat in the front. I am under a paternal-care order from George not to do any lifting; my job is to take an inventory of the books as they get packed away.

"I don't quite see the urgency of this," I say.

"You have to make a record of the books when you are about to lock them away from sight. Otherwise you might as well throw them into the Hudson. We're here."

It is one of those parts of New York that is not on anyone's mental map, just bleak streets and warehouses and no trees. The place itself, apart from its perky blue styling, is depressing, because it is a square box with the ghost outlines of windows that are now bricked up. I help Luke put the bags of books onto a trolley.

"We're on the third floor," he says.

The lift is cavernous, big enough for a stash of grand pianos. When we get out, we stare down the corridor. It looks like a morgue—or what I imagine a morgue looks like. Doors, just doors, sealed, clinical, receding.

"This is creepy," I say, as Luke pushes the trolley along. "Don't you think? I mean, you could kill someone and stash them here, and if you put them in a Ziploc bag, perhaps nobody would ever know."

"You can't get Ziplocs that big," says Luke. "And it would burst. It would burst because the body would rot."

"All right, then—what if you got one of those bags that you use to store fur coats and special dresses, the kind that has a fitting so that you can vacuum the air out? You could put the body in one of those, and then suck the air out, and then it wouldn't rot, and then nobody would ever know. It could be that there are hundreds of dead bodies in here."

"People are not using Manhattan Mini Storage to store dead people. They are using it to house textbooks that nobody's ever gonna open again, and old computers with stuff on them that one day someone is going to figure out a way to extract, and clothes that people are paying to store for a lifetime, so the bargain sweatshirt ends up costing them five hundred bucks . . . this one is ours."

He opens up a door and switches on a light. There are lots of boxes of books, labeled by subject, on metal shelving. There is a chair right in the middle of the room. It looks like an art installation.

"Sit down," he says. "I'll make up a couple new boxes, and then we'll get going. I'll read out the author and title to you, and you write it down. Real quick, or we'll be here until dark."

I open my notebook and wait to begin. Why does nothing seem to have any savor? Luke is crouched on the floor, sorting the books into sizes.

"Hardcover, *Pools,* Kelly Klein—"

"Oh!" I say. "Let me see that! That's got photos by great people in it—Bruce Weber and Mapplethorpe and people like that . . ."

"First edition, one hundred seventy-five dollars. You can't look at it. We'll be here all day. Write it down."

"I've always wanted to see that book . . ."

"Then go to Barnes and Noble and take a look in the photography section. Helen Levitt, *Here and There.* Seventy dollars. What?"

"Nothing. Nothing. I just like Helen Levitt. She took photographs of street children in New York—she died not that long ago. Why are these books getting packed up? It's silly, they're great."

"I dunno. Maybe they'll get more valuable, maybe they're dupes. Just make the note. Next, hardcover, Josef Sudek, first edition, *The Window of My Studio.*"

"Oh!" I say. "Oh, Luke, I don't care about the pools one, but I love Sudek, I really do, and particularly the ones he took through his window in the rain, that kind, so please let me see it—please, just that one . . ."

He passes it to me, bemused. "The Owl must be like a candy store to you," he says.

I look through it. George has it marked at forty dollars.

"Forty dollars," I say, "that's not much. If I am here with you for four hours . . ."

"Give it back to me," says Luke. "You're going to need your money, Esme." His tone is gentle.

I pass it back, wordless. I had been keeping it all at bay.

"You know you'll be okay?" he says, keeping his eyes on the books. I watch him. He is rearranging them in the box, and they were already fine.

"No," I say. "I don't know that."

"You're interested in stuff. You're hurting, and you're still interested in stuff. That's the sign. The sign you'll be okay. Maybe"—he hesitates—"maybe you didn't even really love him."

I start to nod my head, not in agreement, but in politeness, to acknowledge his kindness. But even the shallowest acquiescence to that idea is such a monumental untruth that revolt sweeps through me. I have to bolt for my bag, wrench it open. In front of Luke, because there is no alternative, I am sick into it. I am vomiting and crying at the same time, all for loss, and all under the male gaze.

"Or maybe you did," says Luke.

This makes me laugh, to add to the sickness and the tears.

"You vomited into your purse. There's a concrete floor in here."

"I know. I thought it was better to be sick into a receptacle."

"Your purse. I'll go and get some water."

"No, I will go downstairs to the toilets."

In the little gray bathroom of Manhattan Mini Storage, I try to rinse my vomit-covered possessions. I stuck a copy of *All the Pretty Horses* that I borrowed from The Owl into my bag before I left; I keep dutifully starting to read it. I wash it a little but then give up and drop it into the waste bin. My phone is not happy, either, but I have to clean that up. My phone. It used to connect me to Mitchell. Since Señor Swanky's, it has felt like a dead thing.

I do not believe that I will be okay. I believe that I can look at a photograph by Ansel Adams or Josef Sudek and think it is good without my heart being mended. I will not say so to Luke.

I go back up and help him finish the rest of the books. When we get back outside, Luke says, "In a few minutes I'll be back down in the basement at The Owl."

"Let's walk for a bit then," I say. "We can get a cab when we get tired."

"The subway," says Luke. "It was a cab here because of the books. But sure, we can walk for a little while."

We walk down the unprepossessing bit of Riverside.

"I wish we could do something about Dennis," I say. "I am sure if we tried harder we could."

"But this isn't the movies. We've got to let it go. You tried, we tried. And it will be too late now."

"I hate the thought of that cemetery."

"I know. But then, don't just keep focusing on Dennis. It's over for him. Join a campaign; if there isn't one, start one. Make something happen."

"I'm one person."

Luke says, "Everyone is one person. Look at the history books. Rosa Parks was one person. The other people moved."

"What other people?"

"On the bus, the other people moved. She didn't. I'm just saying."

I say, "I don't know if I can. I would hear so many awful stories, it would be so sad—and, Luke, it's too near—it's too close."

He nods. "I know, sweetheart. But nobody ever wants to go near those things. That's how nothing happens."

I decide that I will go home and see if the Wikipedia assertions about the babies and the city hospitals is true, and if it is, I will see if there is a campaign, and I will help. I don't say this out loud, because you can sometimes think you've done a thing when all you've done is declare it.

"All the same," I say, "I do believe that there ought to have been some sort of send-off for Dennis."

Luke looks down the street. I look in the same direction, and see a big New York church. He says, "You can go in there and say a prayer for him."

"I don't think I believe in God."

"No, neither do I. Maybe God doesn't care whether we believe in him or not." He looks wryly at me. "Go on, go in. Say a prayer for Dennis from the both of us. Who knows what works and what doesn't work? I'll wait for you."

Luke hails a cab when I come out again, and we get in. I do not say anything about the subway.

We are nearly back at The Owl when Luke says, "I've got a lot of rehearsals coming up, and they've got to be on Fridays. That was the only way we could work it. Bruce is doing my Friday shifts for me. And after that, I've going to the New York Folk Festival."

"Are you playing at the festival?"

Luke shrugs. "Yeah, sure. I'll take my guitar. It's one of the few places left where you can just jam. It's cool."

"I mean, are you playing? Performing?"

"You mean on the main stage at nine P.M., looking out at ten thousand eager faces in Battery Park? No." Luke shakes his head. "Oh, Esme," he says.

"Don't you want to?" I ask.

"No, I really don't."

"I don't believe you. You have something to say. So surely— you would want to say it?"

"I don't have anything to say, Esme. I have something to be. I am being it. I thought I should mention it," Luke says.

"Yes," I say. "Yes."

I want to say that I will miss him, because it will be true. But it is not as true as if I were saying it to Mitchell, for whom I am made of yearning. I have learned, in chastened-heroine style, that words are more important that I could possibly have imagined. You can't flip them into the air like ping-pong balls, rain them down on someone like confetti, just throw them about so happily. Saying what is true is difficult. So I don't say anything.

"You're quiet these days, sometimes, you know. Since—you know, I guess since Mitchell."

I smile at him. "Fridays won't be so good with Bruce instead of you," I say. "What are you practicing for?"

"We're going on tour after the festival. I will most likely miss the—the birth."

"You'll see us when you get back."

"Yep," says Luke. We pull up at The Owl.

CHAPTER TWENTY-SEVEN

It is my first Friday with Bruce instead of Luke. According to Bruce, Luke has exchanged the next *eight* Fridays with him. As he breaks this news, a customer comes in, and as I am in the main chair, he says, "Oh, hello, miss. Do you happen to have a biography of Lorenzo da Ponte?"

I have not even had a chance to look mystified when Bruce surges forward.

"No, sir, we don't, but interestingly enough, we just sold a biography of Emanuel Schikaneder."

"Ah," says the customer, knowingly. "But no da Ponte."

Bruce shakes his head, and the customer departs.

"You don't know who Schikaneder is, do you?" Bruce says.

"No," I say.

"I'm disappointed, but—honestly?—I am not surprised. Groucho Marx often used Schikaneder as an example of a man who was lost in history. He was the librettist on *The Magic Flute*."

I nod.

"I bet," says Bruce suddenly, "that he is forgotten because he was Jewish. Hold on."

He stomps up the stairs and goes to the computer.

"Oh, he wasn't Jewish. He was just German."

"Right. Bruce? The next *eight* Fridays?"

"Yeah," he says. "But don't worry—I don't mind—Luke would do the same for me. In fact he did, when I was helping to make the set for *I'm Not Rappaport*. We had to cover every leaf with fire-resistant spray, did I tell you?"

"Yes," I say, listlessly and dishonestly.

I am sorry about the Fridays. Fridays are my favorite night at The Owl; there is so often a lock-in. Even George sometimes comes, and Barney is a regular. I think of those lamp-lit nights, with the bottles of beer and the quiet friendliness, and my breath catches. I didn't know they were going to be part of the past so soon. I thought the first couple of times that Luke would play his guitar, but he never does. We talk, or we're quiet. It feels when we do this as if we are in a different era. But that won't be happening if it is Bruce and not Luke who is in charge: Bruce locks up and goes home.

"Oh." Bruce frowns. "I didn't know I'd told you about *I'm Not Rappaport*. The set got a special mention. We were trying to re-create Central Park in the autumn, so we had quite a job with the leaves. And we got the lamppost from the 1975 Broadway production of *The Third Man*. We needed to change the style, because postwar Vienna lampposts and Central Park lampposts are not quite the same."

"No. I don't suppose they would be."

"Although they are not as different as you might expect."

"Both black poles with lights on top?"

"The man who designed the 1930s poles in Vienna was a Swede, Gustav Benriksson, who had died in 1890. The poles were still there because of course, lampposts can far outlive the person who invented them."

"Yes." This is what life will always be like now.

"But anyway, Olmsted had seen the poles in Vienna and wanted similar ones for Central Park. Of course, a lot of the ones that are in the park wouldn't do at all for *I'm Not Rappaport*—we needed the bishop's-crook-style ones, not the French cherub ones. Some have been saved, you know, by the special effort of the Friends of Cast-Iron Architecture in New York."

"Bruce," says George, appearing from the back. "It is, as ever, a treat to have you here, but you've been working all day. Isn't Luke taking over?"

"Oh, no. Luke's got a rehearsal, so he's working here tomorrow on the day shift, but I am pulling a double shift tonight. It's fine. I have Esme to keep me company."

George looks expressionlessly at me. "That's good," he says. "But, Bruce, make sure Esme gets all her book entries done. She has a tendency to hang around and listen to anecdotes instead of working."

✦

I HAVE TO go to the midwives to see how I am doing. I have drunk several pints of raspberry-leaf tea since they recommended it for ease of delivery, so I am hoping I am doing fine. Misery can't make any difference now to the baby; it is nearly ready.

I go into the waiting room, and smile plastically at a pregnant woman who already has a child she has to occupy and entertain. How do you do that when you're feeling selfish and sad? I won't be able to do it.

The child is of course chocolatey and sticky, and comes over to lay a grubby hand on my pristine dove-gray trousers. The woman's faux-apologetic smile means *I know you now have a dirty mark on your trousers but my child is the cutest ever and toddlers will be toddlers and in a way this physical contact with him is putting you in touch with your motherly side, so soon to manifest itself, and in fact by my total lack of discipline, because I will start that when I find him doing cocaine in his room when he's fourteen, I have enhanced your day.*

I pick up a magazine. It is a baby magazine, naturally, because what else would you care about if you're in the midwifery center? Famine? The economy? It has more pictures of loving fathers in it. The big beehived air-bound candyfloss lie.

I am not in a good place.

The midwife this time is a comforting woman named Melanie who combines competence with warmth. I haven't met her before.

"Okay. You're two centimeters," she says as she examines me.

"I'm what?"

"You're two centimeters. Your cervix is dilated two centimeters."

"What does that mean?"

"It means you're in labor."

I take a breath. And another one.

She smiles. "It doesn't mean it's going to happen right away. You can be a couple of centimeters for a day or so, longer, before labor starts for real."

"But soon."

"Yeah. Soon."

Melanie is taking off her gloves, moving around the little room. I do not move. She looks back and says I can get dressed, so I do.

"You don't feel any pain? Around your pelvis or belly or back?"

I shake my head.

"Maybe you're gonna have an easy delivery," she says. "It might be this weekend. I'm on call Friday, and then it's Anouska."

Anouska is the one who looks like a supermodel. I hope I get Melanie.

✦

I ARRIVE AT Lamaze class a few minutes early the next day. It is likely to be my last if I am in labor. I should have a partner, because you need one for the breathing and the smiling, but I haven't got one this week.

The instructor, even older and cooler than she was the last time, asks me how I am. I decide to tell her, since she is a person who has involved herself in such things all her life, what the midwife has just said. She is nice enough to look excited for me.

"And now I am just waiting for the pain," I say.

When the others come, we get the chairs and sit in a circle as we have done the other times. I am hoping that she will get out the knitted breast I have heard tell of, because I have fairly vague notions of what breastfeeding is all about.

"Everyone, Esme has some very exciting news," the instructor says as her opening gambit. She turns to me. "Esme, please share your news with the class."

"Er ... yes ... er ..." Doesn't she understand that I am English, and we don't do this sort of thing? I feel a deep flush rise up.

"Go on," she says, gently prompting.

Ten faces look expectantly at me. Five men, five women.

"Apparently I am in labor," I say. "My clitoris is two centimeters engorged."

One of the men puts his face in his hands. His shoulders are shaking. His wife looks incredulously at me. I wonder if I misjudged my American audience, and that they are more squeamish or more easily amused than I thought. The instructor is a study in barely repressed mirth.

"I think you mean," she says, "that your cervix is two centimeters dilated." Alan hiccups into his hands.

"Yes," I say, as evenly as I can. "That's what I mean."

I wonder if I have everything for the baby. I have nappies. I have wipes. I have a Moses basket and bedding and a pretty blanket, a car seat but no car. I have little baby outfits that are called onesies, with snaps under the crotch. I have baby socks from the Gap. They are heartbreakingly small. I have a little hat made of turquoise and yellow stripes in stretchy material. I have cardigans, and two pairs of little trousers and two T-shirts. I have black and white and red toys, because babies can't see colors when they are born, except for red. How does anyone know that? Stella has bought a "flowing rhythm" mobile for it from the Guggenheim, in the prescribed black and red. I have a cheap stroller that is not the pale gray one of my Madison Avenue dreams. Have I missed anything? I do not know. What if something is wrong? What if it all gets messed up and something happens to my baby? What if I can't bear the pain? What if I die in childbirth? People still do. Does my mother get the baby? Will she be allowed to take an American baby home? I should write a letter saying what I want. A death coda for my birth plan. If I die, perhaps Mitchell will want it, as long as I am not there to be despised. And then Olivia would look after it a lot. What cool attendance that would be.

✦

MY NEXT SHIFT at The Owl is with Bruce and George again. Luke has already left on his tour. He won't see the baby for weeks, if it comes on time. The world is even grayer without Luke.

George still seems to be deep in sorrow at the unappreciative nature of his customers.

"Were you here for the Anatole France guy? Luke thinks I was an idiot. He wanted leather spines . . . I don't know. And I had a girl in here before you came in. She wanted some mystery books. 'What sort of mystery books?' Any mystery books. Did she have any favorites? No, but she was decorating her apartment, and she thought that mystery books might look cooler than regular novels. I thought of our new directive, and I wasn't rude to her—I took her to the mystery section. She said she didn't have time to look for herself—could I just pick some out for her while she went to get her nails done?"

"And so you said no."

"Oh, no," says George, glimmering a smile. "I picked out all the B's and all the S's."

Bruce and I start to laugh, and after a minute, so does George. And then the pain comes.

I lean over onto the counter. It is all over me. I thought it would be focused on my pelvis. Nope. After a couple of minutes, the pain flows away completely, like waves rolling back on a beach.

George says, "These are contractions? You're in labor?"

"I think so."

Bruce is standing glued to the spot, his face in a rictus of a smile, his attitude that of a man about to offer to find boiled towels.

"Have you someone you call?"

"Stella."

"Yes. Give me your phone, I'll call her."

"She's in the Hamptons for the weekend. I just remembered."

"So?"

"So, I'm not going to make her come back. She was so happy to be going—"

"She made a commitment—"

"Which she will keep if I call her. I am not going to. I'll be all right."

"You don't have a backup?"

I pause.

"Stella was my backup. Mitchell was—"

"Okay. Who else?"

"I am fine."

The pain comes back, another high wave, and again peaks and flows away.

Another one is going to come, so instead of performing it in the middle of The Owl, I go to the back again, to endure it in private amid the first editions.

I want to get an awful lot nearer to the hospital than I am now.

George anticipates me. "Was that another one? Shouldn't they be more spaced out than this? I think we should get you to the hospital right away. I will come with you."

"You said you were allergic to hospitals," I say.

"I get a reaction to industrial cleaning agents. I can take it."

George stands to hail a cab. I am next to him, my hands on my belly. The cabs fly by.

"Hide," he says. I do, stepping back and blending in with the surge of people. The next cab swerves in to pick him up. George opens the door and I get in first. George gives the address to him instead of naming the hospital. The driver is wise to it, though, and casts a sharp eye on me from his mirror. "Miss, ma'am—are you—?"

"No, no," I say, beaming manically at him, "I have weeks and weeks to go. I am going to have triplets. It's a checkup."

We pull back into the traffic and I lie back and have another contraction. I duck below the mirror.

When there is no contraction, there is no pain. When there is no pain, I feel quite chatty.

"I've got a book called *Painless Childbirth*. I found it in The Owl," I say to George.

"Maybe you should've read it."

"I did. It's by Grantly Dick-Read. Isn't that a great name? It sounds like an adverb. 'The old man was very courteous and grantly.'"

"You nevertheless seem to be experiencing some pain."

"It says painless childbirth is all about relaxing, about not believing there's any pain involved. Oh . . ." The new wave of pain is much worse. The wave is like one of those impossible breakers you see in films, and I feel like the tiny dinghy out there by mistake. When it goes, there is scarcely any relief before the next one. I start to believe I am going to have the baby in the cab.

I have learned how to breathe, I have learned how to concentrate. I should be able to do this.

We pull up at the hospital, and George helps me, and in what seems like two seconds I am in a birthing room that looks like a hotel suite. I have refused to let George come in with me, to his intense and evident relief.

The midwife comes in. She is wearing high leopard-skin-print boots and a short skirt. She looks exactly like Michelle Pfeiffer.

"Hi, Esme, we met, didn't we? I'm Anouska. I will just go to change and then we will deliver your baby. This is Hilda. She will stay with you."

"I want the drugs," I say. "I want the drugs."

But she has gone, and Hilda does not react.

Anouska comes back in. She's changed the slinky clothes and leopard-print boots for a green gown and white rubber clogs. She still looks gorgeous.

The pain comes back. This is the worst so far. Each one is. This one makes me inseparable from pain. Pain and I are the same thing.

"The contractions are every thirty seconds or so," says Hilda. "She's doing fine."

"I am not," I say. "The next one is coming."

"Good. I will examine you," says Anouska.

Pain engulfs me again. *This* is the worst; each one is the worst. This time the room is pain, the air is pain, I am pain.

"I—want—the—drugs," I say, when I can speak again.

Anouska smiles. "You are ten centimeters. The pain does not get worse than this. It is too late for drugs. I remember how this feels, you are doing well."

"I'm not," I repeat. It is all I can manage.

"It is time to push, Esme. Are you ready?"

In all the books, all the lying damn books I have read, it says that the urge to push will be uncontrollable. It says that that is why babies are born, because it is impossible not to push. That many women want to push before full dilation, and have to be stopped. That French nurses yell, "*Ne poussez pas,*" that German ones probably yell, "*Nicht puschen,*" that the world over, midwives are putting their hearts and souls into preventing women from pushing too soon.

There is no urge at all.

A new contraction comes. I cry out.

"Push into the next one," says Anouska.

"I can't," I sob. "I can't. It hurts."

I try to push with the next one, and I hear an unearthly, prolonged, agonized cry, from someone's very soul. And then I get a brisk tap on the cheek. Anouska is glaring down at me.

"No. No, no, no. Your energy is not for screaming. You need all of it. Look at me, look at me. Good. Do you understand me? You need all your energy for this. You are not to waste it. Now push."

I stare at her. During the scream, I remembered the name of

Dennis's daughter. Dennis himself told me, and it had gone out of my head. Josie Jones.

"Push. You must push."

I try again. She makes me hold my legs, but I can barely do that. My arms feel like boiled spaghetti. I look helplessly at her.

"I can't," I say.

"You *can*. Esme, if you do not push, your baby will not be born," says Anouska. "Now *do* it."

I do it. I push. I do not cry. I push, and when the pain comes, I push some more.

"Your water broke," she says.

My water broke? Doesn't that happen right at the start?

I push again.

"It's crowning," says Anouska to Hilda. "Esme! Esme!" She is shouting as if I am far away. "Esme, I can see the top of your baby's head. Do you want to see? Do you want a mirror? It will help you."

Do I want to see? Do I want to see my own vagina, distended beyond all imagining?

"No," I say, with as much firmness as I can summon. "No. I *don't*."

"Get her a mirror," says Anouska.

Hilda magics a mirror from somewhere.

"Look!" commands Anouska. "Look at your baby's hair."

I peep reluctantly into the mirror. Astonishingly, I can see it. My baby's hair.

"Your baby is nearly born. Now *push*!"

I close my eyes and push, one big, agony-ridden push.

"The head is out," cries Hilda.

"The head is out," cries Anouska.

I close my eyes and push again. This time there is a curious slippery feeling, and something wet and not so very painful slides out of me. And something else, not painful at all. It is the strangest experience I have ever had by a long, long way. Then I hear a loud, indignant cry from a tiny thing.

"Your baby is born, Esme," cries out Anouska.

I am laughing and crying. She is holding up the baby.

"What is it?" I ask. It is scrunched up and bawling with outrage at being born.

"It's a girl," she says. Anouska is laughing and crying too. It must be a pretty full-on job, midwifery.

She gives me my daughter, who stops crying.

It is a minute in a net of gold. She is perfect. All mothers say that. All babies are.

"Hello," I say to her. I kiss the top of her head. I want to be the first person to kiss her in the world. Her mouth is nubbing at my chest, the instinct, like a foal, like a lamb.

"Eleven twenty-two P.M.," says Hilda.

"She's looking for milk," says Anouska. "Let me help you."

She shows me how to get the baby to take the nipple. It hurts, but now I have a new yardstick to measure pain with, and this is only inches. She begins to suck, and is quiet. Her eyelashes are very long. She is a girl.

"That was a fast birth," says Anouska. "Only three hours or so. Normally they take a lot longer, are more painful."

I have nothing to say to the "more painful."

They take her to the table at the side of the bed. It is like a James Bond room—the table converts at the push of a button into some scales. They clean her up, too, and put a nappy on her. When they give her back to me, they have given her one of these little onesies that fastens underneath, and she is wearing a blue hat.

"Where did she get her hat?" I ask.

Hilda says, "The paperwork isn't here. I'll just be a second."

When she comes back in she says, "There are two people waiting in the waiting room."

For a second, my soul skips. Mitchell.

"Who are they?"

"The man who brought you, and a girl in a black leather jacket."

"Stella is here already? And George waited?"

"Yeah, they can come in soon."

Hilda looks at her watch for the date.

"She was born at eleven twenty-two on the eighteenth," says Hilda, and writes it down.

"What is her name?" she asks.

"I don't know," I say. "Her eyes are changing color. They were blue when I saw them first. They're changing to mushroom . . . Is that normal?"

Anouska says it is.

"You don't know her name?" says Hilda.

"No, I don't know yet."

"Honey, she has to have a name, for the birth certificate."

"Straightaway?"

"Yeah," says Hilda, her eyes wide.

That explains so much about American names.

I had thought already about naming her after a female artist. Sofonisba, Mary, Elizabeth, Tracy.

"Georgie, then," I say. "Georgie Garland."

Stella and George come in together; they seem to have bonded in the waiting room. They almost tiptoe, and they regard Georgie, fast asleep next to me in the big bed, in silence. Stella has tears in her eyes. She bends to kiss me.

"How did you know?" I say.

"I gave George and Luke my number. I knew you wouldn't call if I wasn't in the city. But this little girl came out too fast for me to be a doula! Next time . . . Can I?" She holds her camera up.

I nod. "Of course."

I tell George that I remembered Josie Jones while I was in labor.

"So now we can at least tell her," I say. I suddenly feel exhausted. "About her father."

"Yeah," he says. "We'll find her." He looks again at Georgie. "Congratulations, my dear. You are very blessed."

"I am," I whisper. "I am."

✦

STELLA COMES BACK again in the morning to help me get Georgie back home. We hire a Lincoln Town Car and take a long time fixing the car seat. The man says we have done it so right that we could be on the instruction video. Stella looks for the fifth time at the leaflet to make sure.

Now she, the baby, is lying here, in the Moses basket next to the bed, and Stella has gone, and we have been left to stillness and each other. The room is full of clear light, and Georgie is in her white sleep suit and a stripy hat. I wonder if her head is too warm. There is a white duvet cover on my bed, a little blue blanket on Georgie's. There are white pillows on my bed. Everything is still and clear and blue. Love is pouring out of me like milk.

❧ CHAPTER TWENTY-EIGHT ❧

These first days are like being underwater, as if the world has changed. Even the light seems different. It is very female. It is Stella, and my mother, who comes as fast as she can, and me, and Georgie. It is milk, and nappies, and macaroni and cheese for most meals. Much of the time, when she cries, a tiny, desperate cry, a breast of milk will quiet her.

We are in an enclosed world, a world of privilege and stillness, a charmed circle.

I decide that I will not abandon courtesy just because Mitchell has, and that I will tell him and his family that she is born. My mother sits on the sofa, with the baby in her arms, and I go outside. I stand near the flowers, near one of the Hispanic guys with his thousand-yard stare, and I call Mitchell's number. It goes, of course, to voice mail. He will, of course, be ignoring it. I leave him a message to tell him that Georgie is born. I say her birthday, and I say her weight, and her name. I do not cry. I say nothing else.

My eyes are resting on the Hispanic man. He springs to life for a second when an old lady asks him to gather some flowers up for her, and smiles in answer to her thanks. When she has gone, he resumes his quiet waiting. Like Dennis, he has the air of a person who is never looked at.

I call Olivia and Cornelius. Again, there is no reply. Again, I leave a message. Nothing happens at all. There is a part of me that expects an extravagant gift from Bloomingdale's, or at least a phone call, at least Olivia asking for a photograph of her granddaughter. But the time passes, and there is nothing.

After two weeks, my mother goes home. I emerge from the charmed circle the moment she is gone. Suddenly, it is just me and Georgie. *I and you now, alone.*

Did they tell me it would be boring? My friends, my mother? I don't think they did, but perhaps I wasn't ready to listen to a promise of tedium.

The feeding becomes more rhythmic. We wake up at the same time, I grab her, we stay in bed. The nights are not so bad. And I have American Movie Classics if she needs changing, along with their restful introductions. "This is when Carole Lombard was at the top of her game. And if you look very closely, you'll see a very young Cary Grant."

It is the daytime that is hard. We are underwater still, but now it is like being underwater with a film of ice on top. I am trapped underneath. I can't break through. We go for a careful walk and I am suddenly dreading that we will see DeeMo, or Tee, or one of the others, even though I like DeeMo and Tee and most of the others. They will touch my baby's cheek with a dirty hand, breathe disease on her. I am newly and fully neurotic.

When she is six weeks old, I go to Herald Square with her on the subway, to buy us both some new clothes. She cries. She is hungry, so I hug her and play with her and give her my finger to suck, but it is no good. She wants feeding. If I breast-feed in public, there will be people who don't like it; this isn't England. They blur out people's bottoms on TV here.

I go into a Starbucks and ask for a caramel macchiato, and then stick her under my shirt, to her relief and mine. I do not look at anyone. It makes no difference whether you look at people or not in New York; if you are a woman with a baby, in or out of utero, you are everyone's business. A woman stops, touches my shoulder, says congratulations. Another woman says, "Is that caffeinated?" nodding at my drink. "No," I say, pleasantly. "It's decaf." And I think that will be all, but it isn't. Two men are getting up to go, and one of them says, "I admire you, I admire what you're doing." I immediately want to confess to him that the drink is caffeinated, and he shouldn't admire me all that much. Not one of them would have spoken to me if I had been with Mitchell, or even if I had been with Stella. Another person closes you off from the world, but without anyone else there you are like a grain of pollen, vulnerable to or open to all these fleeting relationships.

After Starbucks, I walk. If we walk, she sleeps, and I can stride and stride, as if to walk right out of this reality and into another one.

Georgie is fast asleep, and I am walking along 63rd Street, wondering where the Argosy Book Store is, when I see Mitchell. He is sitting outside at a restaurant, and opposite him is Uncle Beeky. I think of turning around, going away, but I do not, I keep putting one foot in front of the other. Georgie is here. His baby, whom he has never seen. I never come this way. It must be fate.

My blood is not blood but something electric, hurting in my veins. My veins are singing, too high-pitched, the wrong key, like pylon wires. I am getting closer.

He is looking out into the street but has not seen me. His face is in repose, not smiling in anticipation, not sharp as it was when I saw him last. But "repose" is the wrong word. If you drew his expression, then unless you were Rembrandt you wouldn't be able to capture it, it would look merely blank. Rembrandt isn't right. A self-portrait, a late one, by van Gogh. No, because even then, van Gogh is still in love enough with the world to squeeze out the chrome yellow and the vermilion, to be restored and comforted by the particularity of things. Mitchell looks as if there is nothing good, as if there was never anything good, in the world. He makes me think of black shapes falling.

I lean my hands lightly on the little fence constructed round the café. I nod at Uncle Beeky, in whose eyes I see amiable recognition dawn.

I say, "Hello, Mitchell." He hates surprises, even nice ones, so this surprise makes for instant anger. He turns his face away from me.

"Mitchell?" I say, more disbelieving than imploring. He is keeping his jaw turned from me, as if he is a child, refusing to see, refusing to acknowledge. I feel a constriction around my heart; not a metaphorical one, a real one, as if it will just stop beating for sorrow and shock. And because I am in it now, I jut my own chin outward and I say, "This is Georgie."

"Esme, please," he says then. He flicks his hand at us to go away and keeps it there, frozen in air.

I feel, or imagine, dismay emanating from Beeky, but my own humiliation is too great to lift my eyes now.

"A beautiful child," I hear Beeky say. "Isn't that so, Mitchell?"

Mitchell's hand is still there. It is quivering. I meet Beeky's troubled eyes.

"Mitchell," says Beeky, in a tone that is both gentle and full of consternation. "Mitchell—the baby."

Mitchell returns his look with icy vacancy, and then turns his head. The beam of his gaze arcs like a searchlight, over the street, upon the crosstown traffic, sweeping for a fraction of a second over the sleeping baby before moving on to complete the curve.

"Oh yes, I see," he says to Beeky, with furious, brittle celerity.

I put my hands back on the pushchair, and push Georgie away from him.

When I get home I have her on my knee, and we gaze into each other's eyes. I say to her, "That was your father."

I change her, and lay her in her cot and flick her octopus with his checkered chef-trouser legs at her. She bats him with one accidental flailing arm, and sees that he moves, and bats him again. Evolution in front of my eyes, I suppose. I smile at her. I walk away, back to the window. It is beautiful, the blue of the river glimpsed through the green leaves, and yet there is no real solace. I turn away from the window; the baby is all right, there is not even that to do. I should study. I should clean. I do not want to. There is no remedy.

I don't want to be like this. I have done the right thing, in having her, my beloved baby, but I have ended up good, not happy. If you are good but not happy, are you any kind of role model for your child? I want mine to see me, blue skirts a-twirling, joyful at being alive. I want mine to see me laughing.

Mitchell will not come back, he will not think better of it, he will not give me a thought. There will be another girl, and perhaps another, or perhaps there will be one he stops at, perhaps a happy ever after. But he will not look back. Simply the thing he is shall make him live. He will eat and drink and sleep as soft as he always has, and each second he lives, each step he takes, will be another one away from me or any memory of me. There will be no stumble, no fall, no farthings to be paid in reckoning, no nothing. And I will see him every day in my baby, in expressions that race over her face as she sleeps, that are as fleeting as English sunlight, and are Mitchell, and are Mitchell, and are Mitchell.

Loving him will never make any difference. Like those mothers who love their dead sons, my love will flow towards him, unwanted, unregarded, as useless to him as if he were dead.

I want to cry out to him that he won't be loved like this again, but he doesn't want to be loved. Love is a binding.

IN THE NIGHT, after seeing Mitchell and Beeky, I awaken sharply and I don't know why. Something feels wrong. I lie still for a second, and then realize that someone is knocking on the door. It is three forty in the morning.

I leap up and into the other room, crossing to the door as stealthily as I can. I didn't draw the bolt before I went to sleep. The knock happens again, louder, imperative. I try to slide the bolt across the door but it needs a slight push to make it true, and I am scared that whoever it is will notice, and feed on my fear.

When my phone rings out into the darkness I nearly scream. I use the noise of the ring to push the door and slide the bolt home. Mitchell is on the phone, and, apparently, outside my door.

"Esme. Let me in."

"What do you want?"

"Just let me in. I come in peace."

I stop still. It is the very middle of the night, the deepest watches. Before Georgie, I would have opened the door, given him a reproachful look, let him walk in. Is there any possible way he would want to hurt Georgie? He is not a psychopath. But might even hearing us now hurt her somehow, hard-wire a pattern of dissonance and distress into her new mind?

I want Mitchell all the time. Most of my body, most of myself, is spent in a mute wanting of him. Even when I am not thinking about it, it is still there, as if I am composed of iron filings and he is the magnet that they all point to. But here he is, and I have not opened the door.

"Let me in, Esme."

I draw back the bolt, turn the latch, open the door. Absurdly, we are looking at each other now with our phones to our ears. The corridor is all light, in here is all dark.

He is fully and formally dressed, and he looks impeccable. I'm in a nightshirt. We stand in silence, facing each other, the muted glow from the street our only light.

"Are you drunk?" I ask him.

He stretches his mouth in his smile that is not one. "What do you think?" he asks. I have never seen him even close to being drunk. I think he can't loosen that cold grip on reality, on himself.

"How did you know I was at that restaurant?" he asks.

I don't know what he means, for a second, and he adds, impatiently, "With Beeky. *Today,* Esme. How did you know I was there?"

"I didn't."

"Yeah, right. Sixty-third and Lexington is naturally where you would be."

"I was just walking with the baby, so that she would sleep. Blame fate."

His smile becomes even more wry. "I do."

The seconds go by. I notice the multifarious dots of color in the blackness, the grain of the dark. I can't read his silence. Is it regret, need, pain, love? To think of his walking forward, catching me in his arms, feeling his kiss, is almost to swoon with want. I think of moving to him instead, holding his face in my hands, trying to make him believe that it doesn't constitute failure to admit need. But then he will despise my own. So I don't move. We neither of us move.

After many minutes, I fold my arms, and look out to the lit windows on the opposite side of Broadway, and say, "Do you want to see Georgie? It must have been a shock, before."

"No," he says. "No, I don't think so."

"Okay," I say, and although I know that nobody gets to be the tiniest bit cruel to Mitchell without an instant reprisal, I add, with a tiny spurt of venom, "Well, if that's all, I really need to be getting back to bed."

When he goes, when he is gone, I will be desolate. And here I am, pushing him to go. But there is only another kind of desolation in wait for me if he stays. With either choice, the high places will still come down to smoke and ash.

"Sure," he says instantly. "Yes, you should go back to bed. Are you eating properly?"

"I think so," I say.

"It's just that I've never seen you look so—I don't know. Swallowed up. That's how you look. Swallowed up. Consumed."

"Why did you come?" I ask him.

"I have no idea," he says. "I'm going to go, I made a mistake."

He opens the door and looks back at me quietly. "I guess I just followed my heart."

"Your what?" I say.

He nods. "Nice, Esme. Very nice," he says, and then he is gone.

＊

THE NEXT DAY, I go into a card shop to buy a card for my mother's birthday. A middle-aged woman is in there, chatting to the owner. Georgie starts to cry, that plaintive lamb-bleat of the baby animal for milk.

"That's a newborn," she says. "I can always tell."

I smile a thin, tired smile. She comes over to me and grips my arm, her face all benevolence.

"It goes so fast," she says, "and the first year with your new baby goes fastest of all. Everyone knows that. Blink and you miss it."

There is the sound of a tiny snap in the universe. I am the only one to hear it. "Blink and I miss it?" I say. "Really? No. Blink and I open my eyes and I am half a second further on than I was half a second ago. Blink and I still have nobody to talk to, nobody to help me, nobody to take her for twenty seconds so that—"

The women are staring at me; I have broken the covenant. I rush out of the store and head home.

Now, it is just me and Georgie.

All the books say she will sleep a lot, but she hasn't read any of them. She sleeps twenty minutes in the mornings, if I am lucky. If I tiptoe away her eyes flick open as if she's a dozing jailer, and she cries for me to come back. I lie on the bed with my back to her, reading *Shackleton's Boat Journey*. Shackleton's men are cold and lost, and so am I. The book has nothing at all to do with babies. Reading it is a snub to Georgie that obscurely pleases me, and makes me feel obscurely guilty.

Often we play. I feel like someone in a picture book of good motherhood, acting a part. Peekaboo! How big is Georgie? So-o-o-o big! Round and round the garden. Round and round the apartment.

Then, on the news, on New York One, they say that a girl has thrown her baby out of a tenth-story window of an apartment on 112th Street. She is sixteen, Hispanic, Catholic, two hundred yards away from me. I weep for her baby, but I weep more for the mother, for all the years in front of her that will be saturated with regret. The weeping helps nobody.

The local priest is on television, saying that the girl and her family live in an apartment right next to the church. "She could have left it on the steps," he is saying, his face lined with other people's pain. The cameras still roll as he says it over and over again, softly, racked by the girl's wild despair. "She could have left the child on the steps."

I can help neither the girl nor her baby. All I can do is get out of this, stop being the person still in a dressing gown at three in the afternoon, drowning in self-pity.

I choose a better journey out with Georgie. This one is to go down to Battery Park. I will hold Georgie up and show her the Statue of Liberty, the symbol of her nation.

I put Georgie in the pushchair, and take two Ezra Jack Keats board books with me, because nobody has a word to say against him, and as little as she is, she can see the colors or the shapes, and they seem to tire her out. Apparently being a newborn baby in New York City is as nothing compared to the exhausting qualities of Ezra Jack Keats. We get to Battery Park, and look out past the Victorian railings and the lamppost that Bruce would probably know the history of, to the sparkling Atlantic, and to Liberty herself, her arm holding her lamp aloft, to guide safely into harbor the huddled masses yearning to breathe free. Or that was the idea.

Georgie has fallen asleep. I am almost alone now, for a few minutes.

Spaced out along the promenade are patient fishermen, their long poles at low angles out towards the sea. Behind them corporate America looms high in steel and glass, and they are turning their backs on it, looking out to the sea instead, knowing that the dreams that are built of sand and glass are not their dreams. They are quiet; some nod as I go by, and they seem—not radiant, not excited, but contented.

One old man, an old black man in a pale gray Gap sweatshirt and jeans, is working at a table, filleting a fish. I stop a moment with the stroller, so that I can watch and be near the contentment.

He notices me after a while.

"Ever eaten mackerel?" he asks.

I nod.

"Ever seen one fresh caught?"

I shake my head. He stoops down to a white plastic bin, and takes out another fish. He holds it out to me. I don't really want to touch it, but I take it from him. It is shining in the morning sun, light rainbows over it. Its weight suits it; it is heavy with a sorrowful, peculiar beauty.

The man shows me the gills and the fins and the black pool of an eye.

"Ever seen one gutted?" He is taking it away from me, placing it with a kind of eager reverence on the plastic table.

The knife pierces the taut skin, into the flesh. He slices quickly, superbly. Two mackerel fillets are now lying on the table, and the carcass is folded in three, like a letter, then wrapped in newspaper. He offers me the knife.

"Want to try?"

Yes. Holding the knife, and the beautiful fish cold under my warm, sunlit hand. The old man shows me just where to cut, how to cut. "Just above the backbone, in and further . . . slice, don't saw . . . you can feel the way the knife feels when you do it properly, so that you know it is right."

When it is done, raggedly, he takes back the knife and slices some off the fillet. He holds out the bit of raw fish to me.

"I couldn't—it's not cooked."

"It's fresh, it's fine," he says, and I take it and eat it. I look down at Georgie sleeping, at the perfect curve of her perfect cheek.

There must be a million, a trillion actions like this every hour, these little tiny acts of kindness that we don't notice, that prove our altruism, the generosity that is in us all. We fetch our being from love, giving or receiving it. All else is beggarly.

After that, it feels different. When we get home after the visit to the fishermen, I lie down on the bed with her, and this time I turn my body to her and feed her until she is asleep. I sleep too.

I find over the next few days that acceptance is the way to go. You have to bend your mind around from the path it has always taken to a path where your own direction does not matter. You are there for someone else. It is easier if you don't struggle against that, if you simply bow your head down to it, acquiesce, comply, love.

IT IS A warm afternoon in late August, so warm that I think of a summer afternoon in England, and wish I were in a garden, with glasses of wine and tinkling voices and flowers. Here there are rules about drinking alcohol outside, so even in the little green squares, even in Central Park, nobody drinks, unless they drink beer in paper bags, and that's not the kind of party I am missing.

I decide to walk with Georgie down to the bookshop. Whoever is on the shift, the reception for us both is assured; even Bruce has tentatively taken it upon himself to hold Georgie in his arms.

George's initial conviction that I could work at the store while Ideal Baby slept on a blanket behind the transport section has been busted by the arrival of Real Baby, who proves resistant to sleeping bouts of longer than eight minutes when she is out anywhere, and whom I could not possibly leave in a public place, despite the fact that there are tumbleweeds blowing through The Owl's transport section.

I put Georgie in her stroller and walk all the way. The sun is still warm; it feels wonderful out here. And I don't move like an old bag lady anymore. I fairly spring along.

When we get there Mary is on a shift, which means Bridget the German shepherd is here, which means it is even less likely that Georgie will sleep. George is on the computer upstairs entering books into the system. He comes down to say hello to his name-sake.

I put her in Mary's arms. I want to go and get some tea. I get a sense of weightlessness from giving her up, and a sense of both freedom and immediate yearning.

George looks down at her.

"I've never held a baby," he remarks.

"If you sit down, you can hold one now," says Mary. He sits down and Mary teaches him how to hold her, how to support her head. George holds her awkwardly and reverently, like an offering to the gods.

I slip outside to buy the tea. It is the first time I have not been the person solely responsible for her since my mother left, an eternity ago. I have about five minutes. It is five minutes of freedom.

When I come back, after three minutes instead of five, because the freedom is shot through with anxiety, Luke is standing outside the store. He is looking through the window at George holding my daughter.

He looks for a long time. He senses that I am there after a while, and turns around.

"Hey." He looks back through the window. "That's her?"

"Yes. Georgie."

He nods. Then he steps forward and opens the door for me. She is placid in George's arms. Luke comes in too and sits on the counter. He bends down to her.

"Hi, Georgie," he says. She stares at him for a long moment with her big round eyes, and suddenly answers his smile with her own. I think her smile is like the sun coming out, but then I would. Luke laughs.

"The birth was okay?" he says to me.

"Yes. Do you want the details?"

"Nope." He waves an airy hand. "I can see it all worked out fine."

"Yes. It was easy peasy."

"Oh, yeah," says George, "it was easy peasy all right. I was down the hall, and she was in a soundproofed room, and I could still hear the screams."

"You poor thing," I say. "That you had to endure my pain."

"It was extremely difficult," says George. "Mary, would you like to go with me to Big Nick's for a vegetarian pizza?"

Mary says yes, on the condition that Bridget gets to go too.

"That means we will have to sit outside," he says.

"It's a nice evening," says Mary.

"It's going to rain," says George.

"It's not going to rain," Mary and I say in unison.

Once they have gone, we have a run of customers. Some of the customers are regulars and so want to see Georgie. She behaves with great equanimity to all of them, including Barney, who seems delighted with her, and asks if he can hold her.

"She's a beautiful child," he says, when she is in his arms. "Like her mother. Seriously, you look great. You won't be without a guy for long. She's radiant, right, Luke?"

He looks down at Georgie.

"So, has this guy seen his daughter?"

Luke shakes his head at him, less in reply than to make him stop.

"He is missing out on the pinnacle of life, Luke, that's all I mean. That's all. I'm not about to go after him for child support."

"Let it go, Barney."

"It's okay," I say. "He hasn't really seen her, Barney. I did bump into him, but he barely glanced at her."

"Poor guy," says Barney. "Poor guy. Daddy is fucked up, isn't he, baby?"

Luke puts his face in his hands, laughing.

"What is it now?" says Barney.

When I feel the milk come in, I scoop her up and take her upstairs to the old, taut leather chair. I feed her up there, where once upon a time I listened to Luke's *Negro Folk Music of Alabama* volume 5, where once I rang up the doctor because I thought I was losing her, where a few weeks ago she was still inside me.

I don't know if it is possible to feed your baby with your own milk and not find out something new about love. Love is a giving, an outpouring—an outpouring that refills itself by the fact of its own emptying.

Barney sprints up the stairs to say good-bye. When he has gone, Luke calls up to ask if I want a beer.

I bring Georgie to the top of the stairs, and say that I can't.

"Esme. You've had the baby."

"I know—it's the breast-feeding. But I'd have a ginger beer with you."

"Yeah. Can you come down and look after the front? I will go over and get something."

I come downstairs with Georgie as he leaves. It is dark now outside, and it is raining.

DeeMo bursts in. "Fuck that weather, man," he says, to whoever is here. "It's like, the sun's shining, sky's blue, then it's dark and there's a fucking thunderstorm. Fucking August." He rubs his hair to dry it.

"Hi, DeeMo."

He stops dead. A customer comes up from the back with a pile of plays, and I try to look in the flyleaf of each one with one hand. DeeMo sits down in the second chair, wipes his hands on his T-shirt.

"Give that little one to me," he says.

I do. While I finish serving the customer, he gives her a finger to hold, and she clutches it. Her fingers are tiny, an apricot blush against his dark brown skin.

"You need moisturizer," I say. "Your skin is cracking."

"That's not all I need, sugar."

I tell DeeMo her name. He nods.

"Yeah. You call her after George because of what he did for Dennis?"

"Yes, after George, and after Georgia O'Keeffe, the painter," I say. Then I say, "What he did for Dennis? What do you mean?"

"He paid for his funeral. I mean, cremation. The basic kind. So that there are ashes."

Luke comes back in in a hurry, all wet as well.

"It's raining like crazy out there," he says. "I hope Mary and George abandoned Bridget."

"George paid for a funeral for Dennis?"

Luke looks completely blank. "News to me."

"He did," DeeMo says. "Well, he *said* Dennis paid for it hisself. Said Dennis brought in a book, a first edition, that was worth like eight hundred bucks, and so that paid for a cremation. George has the ashes. He told me."

Luke says, "Dennis did bring in a first of *A Moveable Feast*. It hasn't sold, though, it's still upstairs."

"George gave him a hundred dollars for that book," I say. Luke shrugs.

"George is a good man," says DeeMo.

We are all quiet. Georgie is struggling against sleep in DeeMo's arms. She is milk-drunk. A milk-drunk baby is a sight to see. We all watch her as she struggles to stay awake, and her eyelids fall, flutter open, fall again. I wonder if she can tell it is not me, that the arms around her are not my arms.

"I'll have her back, if you're not comfortable?"

DeeMo looks back at me. He must be remembering the hand sanitizer, my anxiety.

"I'm comfortable," he says. "You okay?"

I am. I look out again at the street. The rain is falling. This is the way to go, through the good people, through George, and Luke, Stella, Barney, the mackerel man, DeeMo.

I watch Luke as he shifts a little in his chair to get more comfortable, until it fits his back. I've seen him do it a thousand times, now, settling down into a space and getting comfortable in it. He catches me looking as he does it, and gives me a funny little frown at my recognition. This moment feels like an abiding one; the past and the future are contained inside it, and it feels like a homecoming. As if all comes to this and the future unfurls from this.

Georgie is asleep, and we sit without speaking. We did this in the winter, Luke and I, drinking beers at night when it was raining. Before Georgie, before anything. We are listening to the music, as we did then, and looking out again from our glowing little jewel of a shop to the drenching summer rain, which washes all things new.

ACKNOWLEDGMENTS

I wish first to thank Phil Meyler, who gave to this book countless days of kind scrutiny, and next to thank Isobel, Katie and Hero Meyler, who have graciously put up with many an hour of benevolent neglect. I am very grateful to Linda Yeatman, for her discerning rigor and warm encouragement. Many thanks to Siobhan Garrigan, whose good offices helped me to an agent, and to those who have read this book and/or helped to make writing a less lonely occupation: Anna King, Allen Michie, Dan Pool, Sinead Garrigan-Mattar, Angela Tilby, Charlie Mattar, Chris Scanlan, Ian Patterson, Anne Malcolm, Martin Bond, Harry Percival, Ray Franks, Debbie Ford, Phillip Mallett, Christine McCrum, Meg Tait, Dorian Thornley, Simone Brenneis, Mary Steel, Tara O'Connor, Miranda Landgraf, David Theaker, Bruce Eder, Jo Wroe, Graham Pechey, Charlotte Tarrant, Leila Vignal, Alexis Tadié and Anthony Mellors. Thanks too to Dorian and Bryan of Westsider Books, whose bookshop on Broadway and 80th Street bears absolutely no resemblance whatsoever to The Owl, living or dead. . . .

I am grateful to Father Joel Daniels at St. Thomas Church, Fifth Avenue; to David Ford for facilitating the visit; to the librarians at the Avery Library, Columbia; to the Arts Council for a grant to work with Jill Dawson at Gold Dust. Thanks to Dorian for giving up his bedroom when I come to New York, and to Henry Holman for his booklore and friendship.

Special thanks are due to Nick Barraclough and Tony Goryn for all the Wednesdays, and to those people whose generous encouragement, sometimes just given in passing, nevertheless made an enormous difference to me, including John Shuttleworth, the late Jeremy Maule, Veronica Horwell, Geraldine Higgins, Dino Valaoritis and Robert Warner.

I want to express my gratitude also to my warm and wise agent Eleanor Jackson, and to Julia Kenny, for all their hard work and impressive results, and thanks to Jonathan Sissons for letting me write in his attic and bringing tea and biscuits to me at regular intervals. Warm thanks to Emilia Pisani, my editor at Simon & Schuster, who is not only insightful and incisive but whose exclamation marks at the funny bits have cheered me up any number of times.

Finally my deep thanks to Andrew Zurcher, whose close reading of all texts continues to be of inestimable value; thanks and love always to my mother, Jean McLauchlan, my sister, Fiona McLauchlan-Hyde, and some more love to those daughters again.

The Bookstore

DEBORAH MEYLER

A CONVERSATION WITH DEBORAH MEYLER

According to your author biography, you worked in a bookstore in New York City for six years. How did that experience inform *The Bookstore*?

The whole book is infused with that experience, especially with the sense of place, with New York. Unfortunately, I have a terrible memory, so I have to make things up—or, as some people phrase it, write fiction.

I think so many of us let events and funny moments slip through our memories into oblivion, like jewels into the dirt. I always mean to keep a journal and never do. My solace is that perhaps the memories really do merge over time to make something else, something new.

I worked in two independent bookstores in New York, one on Broadway and one on 57th Street, but it was really the shop on Broadway that captured my heart, as you can perhaps see from the book. I can remember only two phone numbers without difficulty: my own from childhood, and the number of that store.

As an Englishwoman living in New York, readers might assume that you experienced some of Esme's sense of being the stranger in a strange land. Is this accurate? Does Esme share any other characteristics with you?

I think when people first come to New York they often experience a very strong sense of recognition, because we've all seen the movies and the TV shows and the photographs. We look for the landmarks and the clichés that we expect, and there they all are. There is the Chrysler Building, glinting, and there are all the yellow cabs surfing the green lights. We all feel as if it is *our* city. But that recognition proves—not untrustworthy, exactly, but to some extent a mistake. It is a different culture, and there are rules that you have to learn; you are, at first, a stranger. It takes time to adjust to the reality rather than the image.

For my own part, I was homesick and uneasy at the beginning. My Englishness didn't seem to work in New York. I found it hard at first; perhaps I was obscurely annoyed with myself for choosing somewhere so obvious, so iconic, so much of a cliché if a person were thinking of reinventing herself. I resisted it. But it is hard to imagine, now, like looking at someone you love and trying to remember how you felt about them before the love came.

Perhaps one of my favorite quotations, from Robert MacNeil, sums up what happens very well. He says: "There is a moment when all that is manifestly ugly, noisy and expensive can suddenly appear beautiful, civilized and desirable. The moment New York plays that trick of vision on you, it's impossible to go back through the looking-glass again. The city has made you a New Yorker."

As for shared characteristics: I have to admit that I gave Esme some characteristics that I wanted myself. For example, I made her tidy. If I can't be tidy, I can at least invent someone who is. I enjoyed making her want to clean things in moments of stress. And I think fundamentally I share a sense of gratitude with Esme, or she shares it with me. I wanted to imbue her with that. You can't be truly miserable if you're grateful for something.

Now that you have returned to your native country, do you miss anything about New York? Do you ever return or plan to return?

I miss the beauty of it. It is unbelievably beautiful, exciting, full of great abstract fields of color. I miss the surging energy of it, which you can mistake for your own energy. I miss the cheese danishes. I miss how ridiculously intense the seasons are in New York, where it rains harder and snows more and the sun shines more brightly. The light really does feel different from English light—it *is* sharper, more lucid. Esme and I feel much the same on that point. I love walking in New York, and I hate walking anywhere else. I miss the intimacy of New York, the huddle of it, the expansiveness of it—how long have you got?

I do try to come back once a year, and I would love to be able to afford to live here part of the year. And retiring here seems like a good idea to me. Retiring to New York—you know, to get away from it all.

In today's economy, many small, independent bookstores are closing their doors, yet some endure, as The Owl does in the story. How do you see the bookstore format evolving in the future?

I take heart from the fact that radios are still around, decades after the internet juggernauted into our lives. I think bookshops will last in some form or other, too. There might even be a resurgence of them. I know this is largely wishful thinking. However, my children, who like other children spend a lot of time on the computer, still like to switch off from all of that and find a corner, and read a real book. And so do I. I read some things electronically, but the feeling of being unassailable by the outside world when we are reading real books is a powerful one. The sentimental or fashionable nostalgia for "vintage" things and experiences is one thing, but there is also a new push, an appetite, to carve out spaces free from digital, electronic, radio-fuelled connectivity. Sometimes people need to be quiet. I think that the best way for that might still be to read a real old-fashioned book, but that we are only just beginning to realize that, too late for some bookshops. But others will pop up.

You include candid sex scenes in the story. Were there any particular challenges to writing these?

I am not sure they are tremendously candid compared to some things that are out there. The bar is pretty high, in a low sort of way, these days. But I did read the first couple of chapters aloud to my mother when I was writing it. She sat quietly on the sofa when I had finished reading it, and she said, "Do you *have* an electric toothbrush?" I said that I didn't. She said, "Well, I think if it gets published, you'd better get one."

I suppose there is some residual timidity that I bring to writing sex scenes. I try to overcome it. It would be easy if it were anonymous, of course, but if you attach your name to your writing you also attach your being, in some sense or other—or at least, I have. That might be a rookie's mistake, although I think it is something we can hardly help.

In your book the van Leuven family members treat Esme rudely and with remarkable disdain. Did you base any of these characters on real people? Are the van Leuvens symbolic of American privilege in particular or are they more universal?

They are most definitely more universal than that. If anything, I feel that they see themselves as having a slightly European aura—as if there is a little-known bloodline connecting them to old-world princes.

The van Leuvens are based on a jumble of observations I've made over the years, beginning with university, I suppose. I met one of the main sources for Olivia in Cambridge recently, where I live, and I was so pleased; it's like being an ornithologist and finding a golden eagle in your back garden.

You have a relatively new presence on online forums such as Facebook and Twitter. How do you hope these vehicles will influence contact and communication with fans of your book?

The thing about The Owl is that it is a place where people come to talk and get to know one another, and when Twitter and Facebook work well that's what is really happening there as well. And the wonder of the internet, of course, is that it can happen between people who are thousands of miles apart, who don't have the privilege of sauntering down to a local bookstore or coffee shop. These forums are an escape or a pleasure for so many people, including me. We were often more lonely before.

I wish, though, there was a way within online communities to be more accountable to one another. It is often shocking, what people believe is acceptable to say to someone else on the internet. In a real life meeting, we mingle and have to look at each other face to face, so it is very unlikely that we would say the kind of irate and unmeasured and insensitive things that often get said online.

One of the things Esme really learns at The Owl is how other people should respect her and she them. All of the conflicts in this book arise in situations where people haven't listened to each other yet, haven't encountered one another thoughtfully or decently. In some ways this book is a narrative about growing up to an ethical and emotional maturity, coming to peace with others because you're at peace with yourself. The book isn't that different from Facebook; it's a fantasy place where people present images of themselves and encounter versions of others, and yet behind the versions we have of ourselves and each other, we are all real. We have to look beyond the cover.

What inspires you to write?

The inability to sing. Really.

It is so easy to read great books; we can never exhaust the supply of them. And it is such a blessing to know that they are there, waiting for you on the shelf, but I think in the end, after years of happiness with these books, you don't want forever to be the recipient of someone else's gift. You just want to have a go yourself.

You left the ending of *The Bookstore* somewhat open. Do you have plans to include any of the characters or setting in new projects?

I did leave *The Bookstore* somewhat open, but that was more to do with the fact that it seemed absurd to me to put any kind of full stop on Esme's life at that point. It's funny, though—after finishing it I felt glum for weeks, as if my friends had gone on holiday without me. I really missed my characters. So, who knows?

This is your debut novel. How did the actual writing experience compare with your expectations?

I didn't have any expectations, particularly. I felt before I started to write that I hadn't lived up to my promise, or at least to the promise that other people had seen in me. I was tremendously fortunate to go to Oxford—it was the usual thing of being the first in my family to go to university—and that education was paid for by the state, the tax-payer. I hadn't done much with it. I was standing back and hoping that my daughters would have rich and fulfilling careers, as my mother had stood back, as her mother had stood back. So when there was a new government scheme to fund some nursery time for children, I put the children in nursery for three hours a day and wrote for two of those hours, each day, every day. While I was writing, I was entirely absorbed and happy. I meant to write something learned and deep, and instead I kept writing things that made me laugh. So I suppose I began writing because I felt I had to, and I kept writing because I loved to.

I resist sitting down to write. I have to sneak up on it unexpectedly. I think that is because I am always worried that the pleasure or the ability will not be there next time. But when I do, I wonder why I delayed—I feel so happy and absorbed when I am doing it. It's like carving a sculpture—the idea is there before you pick up your tools, as the angel is in the marble, but the idea has no real being until you form it with words, and then shape it, planing it here, polishing it there. There are few greater pleasures than this one, I think. It is crafting the sentence that I particularly like, making something out of nothing. Also, it's in the rigorous formulation of words on paper that you can find out about yourself. As E. M. Forster says, "How can I know what I think till I see what I write?"